Praise for **This Is Not Chick Lit**

"This isn't chick lit, but maybe chick lit should aspire to be this good."
— *The Miami Herald*

"These tales ask us to take a break from the cream-puff narratives we may have been splurging on and to remember how good it feels to read something nourishing and substantive, to once again engage in stories that feed the soul."
— *Los Angeles Times*

"Far from breezy chick lit, these stories are for anyone who enjoys fine fiction."
— *Rocky Mountain News*

"Readers who've been Fendi'd and Choo'd to distraction would do well to pick this up."
— *Publishers Weekly*

"Narrative-fracturing works by Carolyn Ferrell and Lynne Tillman are jarring, beguiling and wholly original."
— *Time Out New York*

"Funny and inventive."
— *The Village Voice*

"This, as it turns out, is discourse—and as long as it's showcasing some good, smart, accomplished women writers, then I think it takes us that much closer to turning the chick lit frog into a prince."
— *The Huffington Post*

"Merrick's feminist project has women talking about books and reading across genres, which, all told, has got to be good."
— *Small Spiral Notebook*

THIS IS
NOT
CHICK LIT

Original Stories by America's
Best Women Writers

Edited by Elizabeth Merrick

RANDOM HOUSE TRADE PAPERBACKS

NEW YORK

Introduction copyright © 2006 by Elizabeth Merrick
Compilation copyright © 2006 by Random House, Inc.

Published in the United States by Random House Trade Paperbacks,
an imprint of The Random House Publishing Group,
a division of Random House, Inc., New York.

RANDOM HOUSE and colophon are registered
trademarks of Random House, Inc.

Copyright information for the individual stories in this collection
can be found on page 322.

LIBRARY OF CONGRESS CATALOGING-IN-PUBLICATION DATA

This is not chick lit: original stories by America's best women writers.
p.   cm.
Edited by Elizabeth Merrick.
ISBN 0-8129-7567-7
1. Short stories, American—Women authors   2. Women—United States—Fiction.
3. American fiction—21st century.   I. Merrick, Elizabeth.

PS647.W6T5 2006
813'.01089287090511—dc22   2006045206

www.atrandom.com

89

Book design by Dana Leigh Blanchette

Contents

Introduction

Why Chick Lit Matters

I don't love literary labels, nor do I usually find them helpful. But since you have just picked up a book called *This Is Not Chick Lit*, I will start with a definition (though if you've been in a bookstore in the past five years, you probably don't need one). Quite simply: Chick lit is a genre, like the thriller, the sci-fi novel, or the fantasy epic. Its form and content are, more or less, formulaic: white girl in the big city searches for Prince Charming, all the while shopping, alternately cheating on or adhering to her diet, dodging her boss, and enjoying the occasional teary-eyed lunch with her token Sassy Gay Friend. Chick lit is the daughter of the romance novel and the stepsister to the fashion magazine. Details about race and class are almost always absent except, of course, for the protagonist's relentless pursuit of Money, a Makeover, and Mr. Right.

Chick lit essentially began in 1996 with the iconic *Bridget Jones's Diary*, a novel culled from Helen Fielding's newspaper columns. It's no surprise that many chick lit authors are former fashion or entertainment journalists—the genre's interest in glamour and goods is perfectly suited to consumer-based media. Sure, Bridget was frothy, and, no, I wasn't interested in reading her daily calorie count, but back in 1996 I was happy to see any story about a young woman negotiating her place in the world get so much attention. Here was a novel about the nooks and crannies of a woman's professional and personal life, twenty-five years into feminism's transformation of the Western world, a novel that investigated what was then surprisingly fresh, uncharted territory. With its accessible, bubbly style, it's no surprise that *Bridget Jones's Diary* was a runaway bestseller.

Yet after *Bridget Jones*, and the well-crafted and successful *Good in Bed* by Jennifer Weiner, a deluge began, and the consumerist aspect of chick lit swung into high gear, with blockbusters such as *The Devil Wears Prada*, *Confessions of a Shopaholic*, and *Jemima J*. Soon after the millennium, it became nearly impossible to enter a bookstore without tripping over a pile of pink books covered with truncated legs, shoes, or handbags. The genre had exploded.

So, what's the big deal? What's wrong with a little fluffy reading? As Choire Sicha wrote in his *New York Times* review of Plum Sykes's *Bergdorf Blondes*, "Look: we all have our own taste in beach trash." (He also wrote—lest you assume I am the only one with a complaint—that Sykes's ode to a clichéd vision of aristocratic social-X-rays-in-training "should inspire readers everywhere to rise up and rip one another limbless.")

And Sicha is right. We all need occasional cotton-candy entertainment to transport us from our increasingly overworked and overstimulated lives. I will happily admit to my own sporadic pleasure in celebrity rags like *Us Weekly* when I want to pass the time on the treadmill: give me the actual red carpet and stylist-controlled wardrobe over the fawning imitator any day. The problem isn't that this descendant of the Harlequin romance is a commercial hit. In fact, I believe it's essential to celebrate the success of women writers of any genre. And I certainly do not want to attack the whole of genre fiction (some of my favorite books are detective novels and superhero comics). The problem is, rather, that the chick lit deluge has helped to obscure the literary fiction being written by some of our country's most gifted women—many of whom you've never even heard of.

I'm going to let you in on a big secret: women writers of literary fiction are having a golden moment, *right now*. For every stock protagonist with an Hermès Birkin bag and a bead on an investment banker, there is a woman writer pushing the envelope of serious fiction with depth and humor. It's sad to say, but some of the most dazzling novels and story collections enter the world with little more than the blink of an eye. Readers who want thought-provoking, imaginative books often simply don't have them at their fingertips—an unfortunate irony, because the writers of these works of fiction want to find their audience as much as readers want to find the books. For this reason it gives me great pleasure to bring you *This Is Not Chick Lit: Original Stories by America's Best Women Writers*.

Chick lit's formula numbs our senses. Literature, by contrast, grants us access to countless new cultures, places, and inner lives. Where chick lit reduces the complexity of the human experience, literature increases our awareness of other perspectives and paths. Literature employs carefully crafted language to expand our reality, instead of beating us over the head with clichés that promote a narrow worldview. Chick lit shuts down our consciousness. Literature expands our imaginations.

The artist's job is to expose us to what is hidden, what is "imperfect," what popular culture might not be ready to hear. The stories collected here reveal the power of a kind of storytelling that doesn't always make it to the front of the bookstore. In "Joan, Jeanne, La Pucelle, Maid of Orléans," Judy Budnitz engages no smaller a story than that of Joan of Arc as seen by a reality television crew. Jennifer Egan imagines one woman's dilemma on the world stage as a newly hired PR guru for a South American dictator. In Carolyn Ferrell's "Documents of Passion Love," we gain access to the world of a photograph from 1914 portraying the first African American couple married in a tiny county courthouse in North Carolina; Ferrell's potent examination of history and race shows us that sometimes the desire for romantic love takes a backseat to survival. Likewise, Jennifer Davis reveals how race and class *do* impact on her characters' lives in the New Orleans of "Ava Bean." In Mary Gordon's "The Epiphany Branch," the pleasure of reading in a local library provides sustenance to a woman who is by no means an intellectual. We are confronted with the threat of nuclear detonation in Samantha Hunt's "Love Machine," which also features a girl robot and a lonely guy named Ted who bears more than a passing resemblance to the Unabomber. Even further expanding the range of stories collected here, Francine Prose and Cristina Henríquez choose to narrate in a man's voice, demonstrating the concept of "getting the guy" in an entirely different manner.

Of course, many of the writers turn their gaze to love in its varied forms—turf certainly covered in chick lit, but addressed more expansively here. In Curtis Sittenfeld's "Volunteers Are Shining Stars," single twenty-something Frances pines for a nonexistent boyfriend but finds connection and engagement spending time with the children at a homeless shelter. We see how the loneliness she sometimes wrestles with, sometimes denies, sometimes reflexively fantasizes a perfect guy will alleviate, is also a state she desires, one in which the possibility exists "to sit on your couch and balance your checkbook and not

hear another person breathing." Chimamanda Ngozi Adichie investi-
gates the nexus of family, culture, and change surrounding a young
Nigerian narrator and the wealthy white student she begins dating
after uprooting herself and moving to New England. Aimee Bender
shows us the hope of a first date in "Two Days," where the protagonist's concerns as to whether her date is THE ONE fade as her curiosity leads her to focus on the beauty of the world around her. In
Holiday Reinhorn's "Gabe," our narrator isn't panicked about finding
Prince Charming either—she's got a husband. The man she's worried
about is her husband's lost cousin, who falls in love with all the wrong
women—how will he ever survive *his* loneliness? In Roxana Robinson's "Embrace," we see the compromises two people make over the
span of a lifetime and the range of their experience: passion, dissatis-
faction, contentment, and, ultimately, the shock of a previously
unimaginable destiny. Binnie Kirshenbaum and Caitlin Macy pull
back the curtain on domestic bliss to reveal the disarming malaise
that can creep into a comfortable life. Martha Witt and Lynne Tillman examine the limits of language and connection. And if you've
never considered a western Canadian meat-eating contest as an effec-
tive spiritual tonic, then sidle on up to a new take on the pain of divorce in Dika Lam's "The Seventy-two-Ounce Steak Challenge."

Chick lit as a genre presents one very narrow representation of
women's lives, one that is "the literary equivalent of a tract-house development," as novelist Whitney Otto recently wrote in *The New York
Times.* I hope you'll turn the page and explore, with delight and curiosity, stories that are *not* chick lit—stories that investigate what else is valuable, what else is beautiful, what else is scary, what else holds power,
what else can capture our hearts, our imaginations, and our minds.

—*Elizabeth Merrick*

THIS IS NOT CHICK LIT

The Thing Around Your Neck

Chimamanda Ngozi Adichie

You thought everybody in America had a car and a gun, your uncles and aunts thought so, too. Right after you won the American visa lottery, your uncles and aunts and cousins told you, "In a month, you will have a big car. Soon, a big house. But don't buy a gun like those Americans."

They trooped into the shantytown house in Lagos, standing beside the nail-studded zinc walls because chairs did not go round, to say good-bye in loud voices and tell you with lowered voices what they wanted you to send them. In comparison to the big car and house (and possibly gun), the things they wanted were minor— handbags and shoes and perfumes and clothes. You said okay, no problem.

Your uncle in America said you could live with him until you got on your feet. He picked you up at the airport and bought you a big hot dog with yellow mustard that nauseated you. Introduction to America, he said with a laugh. He lived in a small white town in Maine, in a thirty-year-old house by a lake. He told you that the company he worked for had offered him a few thousand more plus stocks because they were desperately trying to look diverse. They included him in every brochure, even those that had nothing to do with engineering. He laughed and said the job was good, was worth living in an all-white town even though his wife had to drive an hour to find a hair salon that did black hair. The trick was to understand America, to know that America was give-and-take. You gave up a lot but you gained a lot too.

He showed you how to apply for a cashier job in the gas station on Main Street and he enrolled you in a community college, where the girls gawked at your hair. Does it stand up or fall down when you take the braids out? All of it stands up? How? Why? Do you use a comb?

You smiled tightly when they asked those questions. Your uncle told you to expect it—a mixture of ignorance and arrogance, he called it. Then he told you how the neighbors said, a few months after he moved into his house, that the squirrels had started to disappear. They had heard Africans ate all kinds of wild animals.

You laughed with your uncle and you felt at home in his house, his wife called you *nwanne*, sister, and his two school-age children called you Aunty. They spoke Igbo and ate *garri* for lunch and it was like home. Until your uncle came into the cramped basement where you slept with old boxes and trunks and books and pulled your breasts, as though he were plucking mangoes from a tree, moaning. He wasn't really your uncle; he was actually a distant cousin of your aunt's husband, not related by blood.

As you packed your bags that night, he sat on your bed—it was his house after all—and smiled and said you had nowhere to go. If you let him, he would do many things for you. Smart women did it all the time. How did you think those women back home in Lagos with well-paying jobs made it? Even women in New York City?

You locked yourself in the bathroom, and the next morning, you left, walking the long windy road, smelling the baby fish in the lake. You saw him drive past—he had always dropped you off at Main Street—and he didn't honk. You wondered what he would tell his wife, why you had left. And you remembered what he said, that America was give-and-take.

You ended up in Connecticut, in another little town, because it was the last stop of the Bonanza bus you got on; Bonanza was the cheapest bus. You walked into the restaurant nearby and said you would work for two dollars less than the other waitresses. The owner, Juan, had inky black hair and smiled to show a bright yellowish tooth. He said he had never had a Nigerian employee but all immigrants worked hard. He knew, he'd been there. He'd pay you a dollar less, but under the table; he didn't like all the taxes they were making him pay.

You could not afford to go to school, because now you paid rent for the tiny room with the stained carpet. Besides, the small Connecticut town didn't have a community college and a credit at the state university cost too much. So you went to the public library, you looked up course syllabi on school websites and read some of the books. Sometimes you sat on the lumpy mattress of your twin bed and thought about home, your parents, your uncles and aunts, your cousins, your friends. The people who never broke a profit from the mangoes and *akara* they hawked, whose houses—zinc sheets precariously held by nails—fell apart in the rainy season. The people who came out to say good-bye, to rejoice because you won the American

visa lottery, to confess their envy. The people who sent their children
to the secondary school where teachers gave an A when someone
slipped them brown envelopes.

You had never needed to pay for an A, never slipped a brown envelope to a teacher in secondary school. Still, you chose long brown
envelopes to send half your month's earnings to your parents; you
always used the bills that Juan gave you because those were crisp, unlike the tips. Every month. You didn't write a letter. There was nothing to write about.

The first weeks you wanted to write though, because you had
stories to tell. You wanted to write about the surprising openness of
people in America, how eagerly they told you about their mother
fighting cancer, about their sister-in-law's preemie—things people
should hide, should reveal only to the family members who wished
them well. You wanted to write about the way people left so much
food on their plates and crumpled a few dollar bills down, as though
it were an offering, expiation for the wasted food. You wanted to write
about the child who started to cry and pull at her blond hair and instead of the parents making her shut up, they pleaded with her and
then they all got up and left.

You wanted to write about the rich Americans who wore shabby
clothes and tattered sneakers, who looked like the night watchmen
in front of the large compounds in Lagos. You wanted to write about
the poor people who were fat and the rich people who were thin.
And you wanted to write that everybody in America did not have a
big house and car; you still were not sure about the guns, though, because they might have them inside their bags and pockets.

It wasn't just your parents you wanted to write, it was your friends,
and cousins and aunts and uncles. But you could never afford
enough perfumes and clothes and handbags and shoes to go around
and still pay your rent on the waitressing job so you wrote nobody.

Nobody knew where you were because you told no one. Sometimes you felt invisible and tried to walk through your room wall into the hallway and when you bumped into the wall, it left bruises on your arms. Once, Juan asked if you had a man who hit you because he would take care of him, and you laughed a mysterious laugh.

At nights, something wrapped itself around your neck, something that very nearly always choked you before you woke up.

Some people thought you were from Jamaica because they thought that every black person with an accent was Jamaican. Or some who guessed that you were African asked if you knew so and so from Kenya or so and so from Zimbabwe because they thought Africa was a country where everyone knew everyone else.

So when he asked you, in the dimness of the restaurant after you recited the daily specials, what African country you were from, you said Nigeria and expected him to ask if you knew a friend he had made in Senegal or Botswana. But he asked if you were Yoruba or Igbo, because you didn't have a Fulani face. You were surprised—you thought he must be a professor of anthropology, a little young but who was to say? Igbo, you said. He asked your name and said Akunna was pretty. He did not ask what it meant, fortunately, because you were sick of how people said, Father's Wealth? You mean, like, your father will actually sell you to a husband?

He had been to Ghana and Kenya and Tanzania, he had read about all the other African countries, their histories, their complexities. You wanted to feel disdain, to show it as you brought his order, because white people who liked Africa too much and who liked Africa too little were the same—condescending. But he didn't act like he knew too much, didn't shake his head in the superior way a professor back at the Maine community college once did as he talked about Angola, didn't show any condescension. He came in the next day and sat at the same table, and when you asked if the chicken was okay, he asked you something about Lagos. He came in the second day and talked for so long—asking you often if you didn't think Mobutu and Idi Amin were similar—you had to tell him it was against restaurant policy. He brushed your hand when you placed the coffee down. The third day, you told Juan you didn't want that table anymore.

After your shift that day, he was waiting outside, leaning on a pole, asking you to go out with him because your name rhymed with *hakuna matata* and *The Lion King* was the only maudlin movie he'd ever liked. You didn't know what *The Lion King* was. You looked at him in the bright light and realized that his eyes were the color of extra-virgin olive oil, a greenish gold. Extra-virgin olive oil was the only thing you loved, truly loved, in America.

He was a senior at the state university. He told you how old he was and you asked why he had not graduated yet. This was America, after all, it was not like back home where universities closed so often that people added three years to their normal course of study and lecturers went on strike after strike and were still not paid. He said he had taken time off, a couple of years after high school, to discover himself and travel, mostly to Africa and Asia. You asked him where he ended up finding himself and he laughed. You did not laugh. You did not know that people could simply choose not to go to school, that people could dictate to life. You were used to accepting what life gave, writing down what life dictated.

You said no the following three days, to going out with him, because you didn't think it was right, because you were uncomfortable with the way he looked in your eyes, the way you laughed so easily at what he said. And then the fourth night, you panicked when he was not standing at the door, after your shift. You prayed for the first time in a long time, and when he came up behind you and said hey, you said yes you would go out with him even before he asked. You were scared he would not ask again.

The next day, he took you to Chang's and your fortune cookie had two strips of paper. Both of them were blank.

You knew you had become comfortable when you told him the real reason you asked Juan for a different table—*Jeopardy!* When you watched *Jeopardy!* on the restaurant TV, you rooted for the following, in this order—women of color, black men, white women, before finally, white men, which meant you never rooted for white men. He laughed and told you he was used to not being rooted for, his mother taught women's studies.

And you knew you had become close when you told him that your father was really not a schoolteacher in Lagos, that he was a taxi driver. And you told him about that day in Lagos traffic in your father's car, it was raining and your seat was wet because of the rust-eaten hole in the roof. The traffic was heavy, the traffic was always heavy in Lagos, and when it rained it was chaos. The roads were so badly drained some cars would get stuck in muddy potholes and some of your cousins got paid to push the cars out. The rain and the swampy road—you thought—made your father step on the brakes too late that day. You heard the bump before you felt it. The car your father rammed into was wide, foreign, and dark green, with yellow headlights like the eyes of a cat. Your father started to cry and beg even before he got out of the car and laid himself flat on the road, stopping the traffic. Sorry sir, sorry sir, if you sell me and my family you cannot even buy one tire in your car, he chanted. Sorry sir.

The Big Man seated at the back did not come out, his driver did, examining the damage, looking at your father's sprawled form from the corner of his eye as though the pleading was a song he was ashamed to admit he liked. Finally, he let your father go. Waved him away. The other cars honked and drivers cursed. When your father came back into the car you refused to look at him because he was just like the pigs that waddled in the marshes around the market. Your father looked like *nsi*. Shit.

After you told him this, he pursed his lips and held your hand and said he understood. You shook your hand free, annoyed, because he thought the world was, or ought to be, full of people like him. You told him there was nothing to understand, it was just the way it was.

He didn't eat meat, because he thought it was wrong the way they killed animals, he said they released fear toxins into the animals and the fear toxins made people paranoid. Back home, the meat pieces you ate, when there was meat, were the size of half your finger. But you did not tell him that. You did not tell him either that the *dawadawa* cubes your mother cooked everything with, because curry and thyme were too expensive, had MSG, *was* MSG. He said MSG caused cancer, it was the reason he liked Chang's; Chang didn't cook with MSG.

Once, at Chang's, he told the waiter he lived in Shanghai for a year, that he spoke some Mandarin. The waiter warmed up and told him what soup was best and then asked him, "You have girlfriend in Shanghai?" And he smiled and said nothing.

You lost your appetite, the region beneath your breasts felt clogged, inside. That night, you didn't moan when he was inside you, you bit your lips and pretended that you didn't come because you knew he would worry. Finally you told him why you were upset, that the Chinese man assumed you could not possibly be his girlfriend, and that he smiled and said nothing. Before he apologized, he gazed at you blankly and you knew that he did not understand.

He bought you presents and when you objected about the cost, he said he had a trust fund, it was okay. His presents mystified you. A fist-sized ball that you shook to watch snow fall on a tiny house, or watch a plastic ballerina in pink spin around. A shiny rock. An expensive scarf hand-painted in Mexico that you could never wear because of the color. Finally you told him, your voice stretched in irony, that Third World presents were always useful. The rock, for instance, would work if you could grind things with it, or wear it. He laughed long and hard, but you did not laugh. You realized that in his life, he could buy presents that were just presents and nothing else, nothing useful. When he started to buy you shoes and clothes and books, you asked him not to, you didn't want any presents at all.

Still, you did not fight. Not really. You argued and then you made up and made love and ran your hands through each other's hair, his soft and yellow like the swinging tassels of growing corncobs, yours dark and bouncy like the filling of a pillow. You felt safe in his arms, the same safeness you felt back home, in the shantytown house of zinc, the same safeness you felt when he got too much sun and his skin turned the color of a ripe watermelon and you kissed portions of his back before you rubbed lotion on it. He found the African store in the Hartford Yellow Pages and drove you there. The store owner, a Ghanaian, asked him if he was African, like the white Kenyans or South Africans, and he laughed and said yes, but he'd been in America for a long time, had missed the food of his childhood. He didn't tell the store owner that he was just joking. You cooked for him; he liked *jollof* rice, but after he ate *garri* and *onugbu* soup, he threw up in your sink. You didn't mind, though, because now you could cook *onugbu* soup with meat.

The thing that wrapped itself around your neck, that nearly always choked you before you fell asleep, started to loosen, to let go.

You knew by people's reactions that you were abnormal—the way the nasty ones were too nasty and the nice ones too nice. The old white women who muttered and glared at him, the black men who shook their heads at you, the black women whose pitiful eyes bemoaned your lack of self-esteem, your self-loathing. Or the black women who smiled swift secret solidarity smiles, the black men who tried too hard to forgive you, saying a too-obvious hi to him, the white women who said, "What a good-looking pair," too brightly, too loudly, as though to prove their own tolerance to themselves.

But his parents were different; they almost made you think it was all normal. His mother told you that he had never brought a girl to meet them, except for his high school prom date, and he smiled stiffly and held your hand. The tablecloth shielded your clasped hands. He squeezed your hand and you squeezed back and wondered why he was so stiff, why his extra-virgin olive-colored eyes darkened as he spoke to his parents. His mother asked if those were real cowries strung through your dreadlocks and if you'd read Simone de Beauvoir and Nawal El Saadawi. His father asked how similar Indian food was to Nigerian food and teased you about paying when the check came. You looked at them and felt grateful that they did not examine you like an exotic trophy, an ivory tusk.

He told you about his issues with his parents later, how they portioned out love like a birthday cake, how they would give him a bigger slice if only he'd go to law school. You wanted to sympathize. But instead you were angry.

You were angrier when he told you he had refused to go up to Canada with them for a week or two, to their summer cottage in the Quebec countryside. They had even asked him to bring you. He showed you pictures of the cottage, and you wondered why it was

called a cottage because the buildings that big around your neighborhood back home were banks and churches. You dropped a glass
and it shattered on the hardwood of his apartment floor and he asked
what was wrong and you said nothing, although you thought a lot
was wrong. Your worlds were wrong.

Later, in the shower, you started to cry, you watched the water di-
lute your tears and you didn't know why you were crying.

You wrote home finally, when the thing around your neck had almost completely let go. Almost. A short letter to your parents and
brothers and sisters, slipped in between the crisp dollar bills, and you
included your address. You got a reply only days later, by courier.
Your mother wrote the letter herself—you knew from the spidery
penmanship, from the misspelled words.

Your father was dead; he had slumped over the steering wheel of
his taxi. Five months now, she wrote. They had used some of the
money you sent to give him a nice funeral. They killed a goat for the
guests and buried him in a real coffin, not just planks of wood.

You curled up in bed, pressed your knees tight to your chest, and
cried. He held you while you cried, smoothed your hair, and offered
to go with you, back home to Nigeria. You said no, you needed to
go alone. He asked if you would come back and you reminded him
that you had a green card and you would lose it if you did not come
back in one year. He said you knew what he meant, would you
come back, come back?

You turned away and said nothing, and when he drove you to the
airport, you hugged him tight, clutching at the muscles of his back,
until your ribs hurt. And you said thank you.

Two Days

Aimee Bender

I met Adam at the bookstore. He was in the section marked Biography/History, and he was looking, extensively, at a book about some historical event no one's ever heard of. The only way I knew it was a historical event was because the cover was in black and white and had a photo on it of a tank. But it wasn't a World War II book; World War II has its own section, two tall bookshelves over.

I myself was aiming for the art books, because my friend Terrie had just had a life-changing experience from looking at a photograph of a clown. She'd spent her childhood terrified of clowns, but when she saw this photo, in a friend's coffee-table book, she experienced a 180-degree shift—one of those rare moments when the other side becomes clear as anything and we can no longer understand why it was so hard to get before.

"Clowns are *desperate*," she'd told me, with wonder in her voice. "That's why they're so scary."

It hadn't occurred to me either, and I wanted to see if she was right. I too had had the experience of a childhood clown doll that one day had transformed from delightful toy-friend into the diabolical engineer of my nightmares. It had to be sold at the neighbor's garage sale, because I refused to sell it at my own. Someone bought it for seventy-five cents—some kid too young to feel the fear yet—and I threw the cursed coins into the outdoor trash, observing as the other neighborhood kids spotted and retrieved them. Let them spend it, I thought, from the safety of my bedroom. It will only bring them grief.

They used the quarters to buy ice cream.

Story of my life.

. I found the art book Terrie had been talking about and flipped toward the photo of the clown, which, according to the table of contents, was on page 32. As I skipped through those shiny pages, pages that smelled like a hair salon, Adam turned and held up the war book. "Do you know this photo?" he asked me, tapping the cover.

"Oh," I said. "Is that World War I?"

He shook his head, and his hair was very light brown, almost colorless, and as it shifted, it caught no light.

"Korean War," he said. "A photo from then."

"Mmm."

He shelved the book. "They told me it was a good read, but I just read a page and it was so dull," he said, and then he stepped closer. Aside from that colorless hair, he had a wide open face, sort of big-featured, with a big nose and big eyes and teeth. Likeable. The kind of face you could immediately trust, even against better judgment.

I held my finger before page 32. I didn't want to look at the clown first off. It seemed too intimate, even if I was just looking with myself. So I was looking, then, instead, at a washed-up movie star wearing sequins in some kind of aquarium tank emptied of water. I guess they were trying to work with the phrase "washed up," but the star didn't seem aware of that because she was grinning in the tank like it was all funny and fun. Maybe the whole book should've been titled *Desperation*.

"What are you looking at?" he asked, peering over my shoulder.

"Art photos," I said.

"Wait, wasn't she in that cop movie?"

We stared at her together, in that tank. "Was she?" I asked. She had giant breasts, ornamented by magenta sequins. I found her painful, so I turned the page to have something to do, and there was the clown, with its big nose and scary mouth makeup and scary eyes and red costume. And I could see what she meant, Terrie. Right off, I got what she was saying. It was trying so hard. That was part of what was so menacing, was its enormous effort to amuse. You kind of wanted to hurt the clown, before it smothered you into total suffocation.

"Do you think it looks desperate?" I asked him.

He squinted and stared at the photo for at least a minute. "Why do they do the eyes like that?" he said at last. "I mean, the star-shaped thing? Is that clown protocol?"

We ended up at the Greek coffee place next door, and he bought no biography and before we left the store, I flipped through the rest of the photo book to see if the others were desperate too, but they weren't, not in the same way. They were just pictures of other shiny figures that looked good in bright colors, like Vegas acrobatic performers at Rite Aid, or a tomato farmer in his garden reading *Newsweek*. Only pages 30–32 were terrifying.

Adam got up to get the coffees while I looked out at the cars driving by on Sunset. It was raining a little, and watching the wind-shield wipers made me feel more settled. The air smelled like city, like damp city.

"They told me that was the definitive book on Korea," he said, returning with the coffees. "I'm disappointed."

I felt attractive, talking to him. Next to those big features of his, I could feel myself as delicate. When the conversation waned, I sipped from my bitter little Greek coffee and told him that my friend Terrie was having surgery the following day. That she was young, still, but they'd found problematic shapes in her bronchitis X-ray. "Lumpy shapes," I said, "inside her lungs."

He stirred his coffee and nodded with appropriate solemnity. He seemed more measured, now that he was caffeinated.

The cars whisked by.

"You know," I said, "I just lied. That's not true."

"About Debby?"

I reached out and touched his arm. "I didn't know what to say," I said, and his arm was warm, "so I made up Terrie's lumps. That's awful of me."

He leaned in then, and he didn't kiss me but it was too close for regular. We spent a few minutes there, blinking together, breathing the coffee-scented air. Who knew what would happen? He had that trust-worthy face, a face I didn't trust, simply because I'd trusted it so swiftly.

We agreed to meet the following afternoon at the beach in Santa Monica, and the directions we gave each other were complicated enough, were distinct enough, so neither could possibly get lost. Of course I was early because I'm always early, and I didn't head over to the water just yet, instead wandering past the snack bar, reading the names of foods listed in black plastic stick-on letters: Chili dog. Onion rings. Popsicle. Words I love to see in black plastic stick-on, words that conveyed summer to me, on this cloudy November afternoon. I hadn't called Terrie the night before, because I'd sold her out for flirting; it seemed I'd cursed her, and although I was fairly certain I had no cursing abilities, it was not in the spirit of good friendship— and this I knew. But I had not been flirted with in many months, and this man had not rejected the reeking desperation of either the clown or the old star, and asking for sympathy about a dying friend was the first tool that appeared from my own personal flirting toolbox. Sometimes my capacity for smallness is surprising, even to myself.

Adam was already at the beach when I walked over, and he had a picnic basket in his hands. He'd set up a blowzy checkered blanket, whose corners picked up with the wind, and when I walked across the sand, bumpy and difficult to traverse, he smiled at me with those wide-open eyes. For a few minutes we chitchatted, and at one point he threw his hands into the air and exclaimed some things, about nothing, really, just showing a sense of spirit. I felt the love, spreading roots in my chest, making it so easy to smile; the way the promise of love loosens and eases the muscles of the face, and how the onset of pain had tightened them before, into tense lines and grit. How good it felt, to let go of grit for a second! We settled onto the blanket and he opened a small bottle of champagne and we toasted and the water waves crashed, and other than a homeless man way to the left and two teenagers trying to get tan on the right, we were alone. I reached out a hand and touched his colorless hair, and he turned his face to my palm. Then he reached into the picnic basket and pulled out two plates, two checkered napkins, and two forks.

"Wow," I said. "You go all out."

As he removed the plastic food containers, he told me he used to be a chef, that he used to own his own restaurant. He told me the name of it, and how he'd gotten a great review last year in the *LA Weekly*, saying he had a knack for unusual flavor combinations.

"Really?" I said, impressed, and then, after a pause, he said no.

"I mean, I've always liked to cook. Never got paid for it. Sorry." We looked out at the water. It was the second lie, and it was clear, from the tone of his takeback, that he had surprised himself with it. For whatever reason, it seemed we couldn't help but lie to each other. It didn't even feel like a big deal to me at first, but like an unexpected shift in weather, as the food came out of the basket his mood collapsed. When he removed pieces of a roasted chicken from the container, and handfuls of green grapes, they were almost like apologies, for something he had committed long ago and I would never understand. Certainly he had no reason to apologize to me, me who was so ready to love him. He handed me a charred chicken leg, and a bunch of grapes, and refilled my champagne. "It's lovely," I said, about five times, but he wriggled under the compliment, and the way he sealed the remaining food back into its containers, with careful palm and thumb, made me feel badly, as if I'd done something wrong, or as if we both knew, in the future, that we would wrong each other irreparably. The seagulls approached. I ate the chicken and grapes, peeling stripes of chicken from the leg, but everything tasted a little off. Not like poison, but just not fulfilling, and Adam was striking me now as very difficult to know.

"Why'd you want that book?" I asked, as I peeled the skin off a grape in slippery little triangles, and I understood then that I would be undressing every item of food I could because my clothes would be staying on.

"I like war books," he said, out to the ocean. "Of wars people don't read. I like to remember the forgotten wars."

For dessert, he brought out oatmeal macadamia cookies that he had baked himself, but I could hardly eat them, my mouth felt so dry, and without thinking, I threw a few sprinkles to the seagulls, who stepped closer on their webbed feet. Adam and I walked to the water and held hands and touched our bare cold toes to the foam. I felt like crying, then, with those seagulls invading our perfect picnic behind us, eating the cookies and the chicken, stepping all over the napkins, cackling, shoving each other out of the way.

I touched his arm again, and my eyes filled with tears.

"I know," he said. "It isn't right."

When we finally kissed, it was clear that it was our last. His lips pressed gently against mine. I felt that kind of wrenching in my heart, and as I turned and walked the other way, I could hear him packing the picnic back into his basket. It took some effort to shoo away the seagulls, but finally they squawked and flew over us. A flock of seagulls. As a child, I'd found them so wonderful, seabirds, with their curving yellow-orange beaks and funny strut. They lived at the ocean, and anything that lived at the ocean I felt I could love forever. But they turned, in my mind. Sometime around adolescence, after hitting the critical mass of beach picnics, after seeing them come over again and again, pushing each other out of the way, squawking so loud, eating chicken and turkey sandwiches without pause, I found them repulsive.

At the snack bar I ordered a basket of onion rings and sat on the green-painted ocean bench, watching the water. The clouds were thick, and the water took on a metallic gray sheen that settled my mind. When Adam passed by, with his picnic basket all packed up, I nodded, and he nodded. The look he gave my onion rings was that of a betrayed lover. But I have always liked onion rings. They were the thickly cut kind, each ring the width of a wide plastic bracelet, dipped in golden brown crumbs. I ate almost the whole basket, licking the bits off my fingers, and when I was done, I threw the remaining few to the trio of waiting seagulls, who, after all, were only hungry. Opinions change.

An Open Letter to Doctor X

Francine Prose

Dear Doctor X, if I may call you that:

Perhaps I should introduce myself. I am an attorney, currently employed by the Manhattan District Attorney's Office. Relax, Doctor. Let me assure you. This is not that kind of letter. I mention my work only preemptively, anticipating what you might say: For just as it is your business to diagnose the physical and psychic pain of your patients, so my job requires me to be a bit of a student of human nature. To be good at what I do, I have had to learn to read the minds of criminals and innocent men, witnesses and jurors.

So, at times, my work requires me to leave my own skin and enter the skins of others. Yours, for example, Doctor. I should be able to take one look at a man like yourself and know what you are thinking and feeling, perhaps even begin to figure out *why* you do what you do. That is how we win cases, Doctor.

Which is why I am writing this. Sometimes we hit a wall. We cannot imagine what is going through someone else's mind. Which is what happened with us, Doctor X—that is, you and me—just before noon this past Wednesday on the Fifth Avenue bus. And so I am writing this open letter in the hope that you will recognize yourself and come forward and give me a hint.

I notice that I have written: *take one look at a man like yourself.* Maybe that is my problem. I never saw your face. I only overheard you talking on your cell phone, from which I gathered that you are a highly respected family doctor with a subspeciality in adolescent eating disorders and that you have many friends who are also doctors, to one of whom you were speaking. I realize that men like myself— middle-class, married, reasonably healthy specimens with all the ex- pectable anxieties but, believe me, nothing abnormal—are probably not what get you out of bed in the morning, raring to get to the office.

So excuse me if you feel that I am sounding like one of your pa- tients: that is to say, confessing. Like most people, I'm a little scared of doctors. Especially shrinks. Maybe I am worried they will recog- nize some symptom, unsuspected by me, that means I am crazy, or fatally ill. So, when I'm around a doctor, say, at a dinner party, or even my own internist, Dr. Mike Mulvaney, an exemplary human being, I often find myself saying things that I might not normally say, preemptively confessing before they find out on their own.

So I confess. I'd been having a difficult morning, before you got on the bus.

I'd like to think it began in the museum. But it must have started earlier, with the fact that I *was* in the museum, instead of at work. I've been calling in sick lately, taking mornings off. Playing hooky. Depression, you're thinking, Doctor. But it was hardly as if I were shuffling around in my pajamas. I was doing interesting things. I'd spent the morning at a museum show of masterpieces of photojournalism.

The museum was nearly empty. I glided across the polished floor from one disaster to another. Hiroshima, the Spanish Civil War. Ethiopia. Sarajevo. I moved from image to image. The diamond mines, Iraq. The Sudan. I was distracted, wondering, How am I supposed to feel? I was glad that someone was doing something, that people were taking those pictures. Then I thought: that's how bad things are, if those photos are cheering me up.

If I had seen you, Doctor, perhaps I could picture you leaning across your desk and telling me that's how adults live: with disturbing thoughts, confusions, with an uncertain future. I can hear your voice, saying, "Bill, that *defines* an adult." I know that, Doctor, trust me. A man in my profession understands that the world we have is not the world we would like.

But lately it has occurred to me that every human being, even the ones who seem to have no trouble putting one foot after another, many of these people are actually gyroscopes, Doctor, spinning on nothing, on air. And one little push, one breath, can knock them off course forever. I don't mean *gyroscope* literally. You understand that, I hope. Does this sound crazy, Doctor? I don't think so, really.

I'm not saying it was the museum's fault. But something sent me into a tailspin. I felt as if I were watching myself on a security camera, stuck there, like a tethered ox, in the middle of the last gallery. I was actually standing in place, taking little steps forward, then back, like a very sick caribou I'd seen once when I made the mistake of looking behind a partition at the Central Park Zoo. Thank God there was no one there to see me and call one of your colleagues.

I recovered, eventually. I don't know how much time passed. Peo-

ple use the expression *snap out of it*, and it was actually a *snap* that
rubber-banded me onto the street, where I made it as far as a bench
along the edge of the park.

I sat on the bench with my head in my hands awaiting another
snap. I know it must try your patience, Doctor, to hear your patients
talk about their symptoms in the unscientific, maddening language
ordinary people use. All I can tell you, Doctor, is that every cell in my
body felt soggy, as if my soul had been used as a paper towel to mop
everything up. Mop *what* up, Bill? you must be asking. But if I knew
that, Doctor X, clearly I wouldn't have been there.

Possibly, you're thinking, I'd had a series of small strokes. You
might order the appropriate tests, whipping pages off your prescrip-
tion pad, one for each procedure.

But wouldn't a stroke have dulled me? It wasn't like that, Dr. X.
It was more like diving. An underwater descent and then the bob into
the brilliant light. I was very clear by the time the Limited came, and
I stood and got on the bus. The bus seemed like a great idea. Instead
of taking the subway, I would take the bus down to Forty-second
Street and get off and have a delicious steamy roast-pork wonton-
noodle soup at the noodle shop off Madison, and then take the train
the rest of the way to the office. By then I'd be feeling fine.

I dipped my MetroCard the right way, on the first try, and found
my favorite spot, a single seat, halfway back. Better yet, on the park
side. It was a sunny day in late April, the yellow-green grass glowed
beneath the pastel flowering trees, an Impressionist painting or a
landscape from a picture book I used to read my daughter. Perhaps
you know it, Doctor. It's a story about a little-girl pig who outfoxes
a wolf.

I concentrated on the landscape, ignoring the passengers who
filed past me. That was when you must have gotten on. Or perhaps
you were already seated in back when I got on the bus, and I didn't

notice you until I heard your voice. By then, we were still on upper Fifth Avenue, sailing down the channel between the luxury buildings, the museums, the limestone mansions, the park.

Even then, when the whole bus could hear, it took me a while to focus. I've lived in Manhattan all of my life, during which time I have learned to screen out anything short of a taxi speeding in my direction. As loud as your conversation was, there was nothing in it for me, since as far as I could tell it concerned some fine points of medical billing seen from the physician's point of view. Complaints about the insurance companies, the hoops they made you jump. Matters of that sort. Many people on the bus could have told the same story, at least from the patient's side, and we were the lucky ones, the insured, though perhaps not as lucky as you. So we listened with part of our brains, just enough to find out which side you were on: the patient's, or Big Money's. And Doctor X, you sounded fine. Your heart was in the right place, though that may be another expression that you find annoying. In any case, the whole bus was on your side. We were right there with you. Though maybe I am imagining this, maybe no one else was listening. But how could they not have heard you? Your voice carried through the quarter-full bus: the perfect audience size.

I think it was the word *menses* that finally caught my attention.

You said, "With the girls, it's easier. Three menses, and you're in. Bingo. Check the box. Let the bastards *go* through your charts."

Doctor X, I hope you're not thinking that I have taken the long way round to one of those anti-cell-phone rants. The rudeness, the banality! Oh, the quiet cars on Amtrak! Everyone on the bus probably had his own cell-phone story. One evening, at a Japanese restaurant, Doctor, my wife and daughter and I sat beside a young couple, obviously on their first date. When the girl went to the bathroom, the boy called whoever had set them up and said, "I'd rate her six, maybe seven on a scale of ten." I found it especially painful to have him say this within earshot of our daughter. A young attorney I work with claims to have heard a mafioso ordering a hit, loud, from the next table in a restaurant. I know my colleague exaggerates, but the reason I think it could be true is how often the rest of the world disappears for the cell-phone user.

Doctor, you were one of those. There is no way not to say it. If any one us had been real to you, could you have announced, so loud, over the noise of the traffic and the occasional siren: "With the boys it's trickier. The kid was five-eight, Jerry. He weighed a hundred and ten. This was serious borderline shit. And he had a *girls'* disease! Jerry, you can't imagine what a tightrope I was walking. But I handled it, I handled it. I don't mean to boast, but Jerry, dude . . ."

The fact that you called your colleague *dude* was not lost on us, Doctor. But we couldn't linger on that, because of the speed with which you went on to tell Dr. Jerry, or dude, about the consummate sensitivity and expertise with which you had faced this professional challenge.

You said, "Two minutes, I knew I had to break up their little trio and talk to the kid separately from the parents. Together they were so strangling, no one knew how to begin, except that there was this skinny kid, slumped, not looking at any of us. Alienated affect, Jerry, does not begin to describe it. It was clear I had to isolate them, I had to start with the kid."

It's a funny thing, Doctor, that I have often observed. You might think that overhearing the inappropriate cell-phone conversation would cause the overhearers to roll their eyes, exchange glances, looks, whatever. But you know, that rarely happens, perhaps because each listener is trying so hard not to be there. We were models of politeness. A perfectly orderly, well-behaved bus. We didn't turn to look, or glare at you, we didn't look at each other, so I have no way of knowing how many of my fellow passengers were leaning forward, as I was, to hear what happened when you got the skinny kid alone.

"I got nowhere with him, either. I couldn't get him to make even minimal eye contact. We could have been in different rooms! The only thing he said was that his parents had no sense of humor. Which was true, so we could have bonded on that, it could have made me like him. Another kid, I would have laughed. It would have been a risk I'd have taken. But I'll tell you something, Jerry. It's not supposed to happen, but you and I know, it happens, sometimes you meet a kid, and who knows what it is, something chemical, something physical, who knows what, maybe he reminds you of some kid you knew at school, but you want to haul off and smack the little creep, you can see why the parents have a problem. It doesn't happen often, thank God, but there it was. It wasn't the kid's fault, it was me, but it was better for both of us if I admitted it to myself. Everything got a lot harder. I just wanted to be out of there. I asked the kid if he would mind if I talked to his parents without him."

If everyone on the bus had a different cell-phone horror story, perhaps they all would have featured that moment when the listener cannot believe what he is hearing. That was it for us, Doctor, or anyway for me. Maybe everyone else had music streaming into their earplugs. My daughter is never without her iPod from the minute she gets up till the time she goes to bed. My wife says it is her fault, because when Nina was a baby, she'd put one of those early baby monitors in her cradle. My wife says Nina fixed on that like a baby duckling. I think, but don't say, that whatever problems Nina has have more to do with my wife's worry, the *reason* for the monitor, than with the little plastic box transmitting the baby's even breaths.

So, Doctor, let me speak for myself. I was amazed that you would say this so loud to an audience, and a captive one, at that. Weren't you worried that one of us—me, for example, Doctor—might sensibly wonder how much you had charged this family whose little creep you would have hauled off and smacked, if not for your professional training? It was hardly the sort of remark guaranteed to revive our declining confidence in the medical profession. Did you know that we were there? But that is the question underneath every cell-phone horror story.

So let me add another element to the question I am asking. To sum up: you were having a conversation about a troubled teenager. And my daughter, Nina, has had some problems. Not an eating disorder, as it happens. But to employ the shorthand you would probably use, she has been, at times, "a cutter." It disturbs me to use the word. Just saying it seems complicitous in some trendy diagnosis for the oily slick that surfaced out of nowhere into our golden family life.

What had we not noticed? The long sleeves? There was that. But it was a point of pride with us to let Nina wear what she wanted, dye her hair in spikes. They grew out. Mostly she looked like any scruffy jeans-wearing New York kid who did reasonably well in school and who had friends whose parents we knew. We were relaxed, Nina liked us, she felt she could talk to us, and we mostly let her be.

That was why, we flattered ourselves, Nina never got pierced or tattooed, so when the long sleeves started, it *did* cross my mind that she maybe had a tattoo and was hiding it. On that morning, when my wife found the blood all over the bathroom, I had been trying to come up with some joke that would make it clear to Nina that her mother and father were cool, we would forgive that little rosebud or dragonfly on her arm. What I wouldn't have given, Doctor, for it to have been a tattoo.

After something like that happens, you see things differently. Or perhaps you realize how little you see. Which is why it may make no difference, Doctor, that I never actually saw you as you asked, "How many years have we been in practice? Right." I assume that you and

Jerry went to medical school together. How attentive we were, how attuned to the mystery of you, which is why I am writing this letter. In that way, Doctor, the bus trip was like a love affair, and you were the beloved, or like a prayer meeting, with you as the distant God whose nature we speculated about. But you never thought about us as you said:

"Over fifteen years and I'll never get used to the kinds of things people think are normal. The kid had totally fetishized food. He went on these crazy diets. Nothing but radishes and butter for two weeks, then hazelnuts and papaya. The hazelnuts had to be unshelled. Wait. It got worse. He did these . . . science experiments. Grew mold on stuff and ate it. Natural penicillin, he said. He ate it and threw up. And that was the stuff they *knew* about. I got this all from the mother. The father didn't say a word. From time to time, he snorted. Every time he snorted, the mother cried. Of course they despised each other. Of course she was in love with the kid. The father hated her for it. The usual family romance, Jerry. You've seen it a million times."

Some months ago, Doctor, I argued a case against a public defender who claimed that my office's accusations were based not on facts, as indeed they were, but on a series of coincidences. *Coincidence*, I'd repeated, as if it were another name for Santa Claus or the Tooth Fairy. But I myself have often noticed how often coincidence plays a role in our daily interactions, rolling the dice in ways we could not have predicted. For a while I kept a notebook just to see for myself if such things happen as often as I thought, and they did.

So maybe I am coincidence-prone. Or maybe it was simple statistics. Maybe half the people on that bus had children with serious emotional problems. Maybe that is modern life, and no one will say it, no more than I would come up to you or anyone else on the bus and say that my daughter is now a freshman at college and seems to be doing well. She has a therapist she likes and trusts. Dr. Janet Finch. Perhaps you knew her, Doctor. She's very much like her name.

But even with Dr. Finch's help, my wife and I will never in our lives enjoy another moment when we aren't holding our breaths. Which maybe was the point of it all. If you aren't holding your breath, you should be. Certainly, in my daily work, I meet a lot of people who were never expecting to have something terrible happen. Who weren't watching out. Who were not waiting, as they say, for the other shoe to drop. Perhaps you too have wondered about that expression, Doctor. Isn't the logic inexorable? The other shoe *will* drop. How common is it for people to go to bed wearing one shoe?

Doctor, that hardly gives me hope, which merely compounds the gloomy residue layered on us by the hours that my wife and daughter and I spent in the offices of Gloomy Gus professionals not unlike yourself. How distractedly all the doctors said, "There's always a chance." They meant to reassure us by invoking the very slim chance that things would turn out to be all right.

Forgive me, Doctor, for second-guessing you. How you must hate when that happens. The layman, with a few fuzzy ideas he's picked up from TV, presuming to understand how the medical mind works. Even so, Doctor, I guess you're thinking you understand the reason why I am writing this letter. You think it's about my daughter, that I associate you with her problems, or with the doctors who failed to help us. But you, as a doctor, should know—just as I do, in my profession—that there is never just *one* thing, one reason, one motive.

Of course, it was just at this moment that the midtown traffic slowed and stopped and sealed us in that belching tin can ringing with your voice. Like my fellow passengers, though I can only assume this, I staved off panic by telling myself it couldn't last. Sooner or later, the traffic would move. Your conversation would end. Perhaps I was the only one who wondered about your battery life, your calling plan. Dr. Janet Finch advised us to make certain boundaries clear. Our daughter can't be on our cell-phone plan, though we pay her bill and sharing a plan would save money.

And of course we passengers were right. Traffic started moving again. But if it had ended there, if you had gotten off the bus in midtown, or if I had stepped down and stopped for that wonton-noodle soup, I would have missed the end of the story. I would have left the bus with a very different impression of you than the one I eventually took away, and I would have no reason to be writing you this letter.

I must have had some instinct, Doctor. For some reason I stayed on the bus. You said, "Normally, I'd just hand them a referral. Not even charge for the consultation." You laughed, Doctor. Presumably Jerry had made some joke about money. "But what made the difference, and I'm not kidding you about this, Jerry, was that weekend retreat I spent in Sedona with the Tibetan lama. I know you guys got a good laugh about it, but the guy was *something*. And I think it changed me, Jerry. It's affected my practice. You want to know an example? I'll give you an example."

I was listening hard, Doctor, and trying not to be distracted by yet another coincidence, which is that my wife spends occasional weekends at a Zen Buddhist monastery up near Woodstock. We don't talk much about it. I don't ask, she doesn't volunteer. She goes with a friend of hers, another teacher at her school. One night, we went out for dinner with the friend and the friend's husband, and the husband kept mentioning the Zen stuff and rolling his eyes, much the way I imagined my fellow passengers rolling their eyes about your conversation, Doctor. But I couldn't participate in the eye rolling, if you know what I mean. Because the truth is that on the Sunday nights when my wife comes home from the monastery, I feel a special tenderness for her, even more than normal, and it seems to me that she is more placid, or in any case less afraid.

"Okay," you said, "here's an example, Jerry. The lama said, 'Always look harder. There is something you are missing.' So I called the kid back in, and the three of us, I mean the four of us, we just sat there and looked. I mean, I looked. I kept looking. The kid was looking at the carpet. And then I saw it. The flecks of color, of paint, on the kid's hand.

"'You like art?' I said. He nodded.

"'How do you know?' he said.

"'I can read minds,' I said. And you know, I think he believed me. People have that thing about doctors. The poor little fucker thought I was a magician. So I decided to run with it. I said, 'I want you to paint for me. I want you to paint *food*. But the only way you get to paint it is to eat it afterward. Then you bring me the paintings. I buy them. They'd better be cheap.'

"'How do you know I can paint?' said the kid.

"'I can see it,' I said. 'Trust me.'"

And now, Doctor, more than ever before, I positively longed to look around to actually see how many fellow listeners I had, and of those how many were as surprised as I was, to hear your story take this turn toward Buddhism and art.

"So here's why I'm calling you, Jerry," you said. "This morning the kid's mother phones. And she says the kid has gained a few pounds, and he's got this painting for me. A picture of a steak. A fucking *steak*, Jerry, can you believe that? He ate the steak. Right, right. I know it's too good to be true, I don't believe in quick fixes, either. You think I'm confusing a painting of some meat with a *cure*? But you can't help admitting it's interesting. The kid's stopped losing weight.

He's bringing the painting in next week. You need any art for your office? Okay, here's my stop. I'll call you later. Gotta run."

And that was it, Doctor. The bus stopped. I assume you left. I didn't turn to see you go. Some delicacy prevented me from looking, I don't know. But instantly, I wished I *had* looked, and I scanned the street for some sign of you. But you had already disappeared beneath the scaffolding at the base of the Empire State Building, and into the crowds swarming west on Thirty-fourth Street. I regretted not having seen your face, as if that might have provided some clue to the mystery of why you did what you did. Why you betrayed a professional confidence, why you told a bus full of strangers about the intimate life of a troubled boy, and your feelings about him. Was it so we could admire you, Doctor, so we could praise you, along with Jerry, even after we had been held prisoner by your voice, by your story?

And how should we weigh all that against the fact that you may have saved the life of this boy, that you saw something in him, and helped him? If you saved him, it would be worth it, whatever discomfort we felt listening to a story that we should not have been hearing, together with the more particular pains suffered by me and any other of the passengers who happened to have something in common with the characters in the story you were telling.

Was it worth it, Doctor? And how would we have chosen if we'd had a choice between your saving the boy and our having to listen to it, or your having failed with the kid—and our being spared? Because it seems less likely that you would have been telling your friend and, by extension, the whole bus the story of how you'd fucked up. Life is full of choices, Doctor, and part of my job as a lawyer involves thinking those choices through. And forming some opinion about innocence or guilt. I realize that we may have strayed here into some philosophical region, somewhere in the vicinity of that tired old question about saving the Rembrandt or the old woman. But what am I in that equation, the Rembrandt or the old woman? And what about the poor kid eating radishes and painting pictures of steaks, and eating?

Ever since that morning, I have been weighing it in my mind. And I find that the scale keeps tipping, first one way, then the other. Which is why I am writing this letter to you, as one professional to another, in the hope that you will come forward and tell me what you were doing that morning, and that a word of explanation from you will tip the balance this way or that, and let me put this matter to rest, and go back to my normal life.

Gabe

Holiday Reinhorn

Tommy's cousin Gabe. Tommy's distant cousin Gabe from Still-water, Minnesota. Tommy's cousin Gabe, related to my husband through divorce and remarriage, in lieu of actual blood, who arrives on my front porch at dinnertime with a duffel bag and fanny pack. Industrial-sized.

Gabe. Two hungry blue eyes, trapped in a giant body. Infinite, knowing eyes of an orca whale. This is Gabe.

Sea monster son of Vickie, the housewife, and Gary, the unemployed architect. Grandson of Lillith, the secretary, and Chester, the inventor of the lightning rod.

Gabe, clinically depressed, he announces at the table after Tommy gets up to go check his e-mail, and not taking his Paxil.

Tommy's cousin Gabe, who admits to falling in love with married women only, who has flown out to Los Angeles this time to deliver a hardbound copy of *The Celestine Prophecy* to a married woman he knows in Calabasas.

Strawberry blond, 275-pound Gabe, whose job it is to run employee vacation and incentive programs for Buy Rite International Corporation. Gabe, who can, on any given weekend, fly down to Fort Worth in order to tell several people (always women and usually married) that they have just won a free weekend trip to Cabo San Lucas.

Gabe, who tells me (and my husband's currently empty dining room chair) that he gives all the women he loves a copy of *The Celestine Prophecy*. Laurie, Molly, Susan.

GABE EDWARD ARTHUR KAKE. Twenty-four years of age. Recent graduate of a Lutheran university, which he attended over the dead, severely diabetic body of his Catholic father, Gary, the unemployed architect. With undergrad friends from around the globe who were all deported last year, leaving him with absolutely "zero" people.

Gabe, who will be the first to admit he has a problem with Pop-Tarts sometimes, and who asks me, did I know, was I aware, that after he gives out trips to Puerto Vallarta and Acapulco to these married women he knows are married (that he has read about in the personnel files), after they scream and laugh and he gets, quote, "a free hug," after he asks these selfsame women out for a celebratory drink or dinner and they say no, they are engaged, betrothed, previously committed, whatever! After that did I know that then, stranded in these very foreign American places, did I know that he, Gabe, always goes back to his second-class hotel with no toaster in sight and eats raw Pop-Tarts and turns on the water of the sink full-blast so nobody can hear him crying? Did I know that? Could I guess?

"No, Gabe," I say. "I couldn't have guessed."

Gabe: moving from topic to topic without changing tone, taking a breath, or blinking, who has had more than just one psychic dream come true in his life, and who, more than anything, wants an Irish setter, because they were described in the Dog Fancier's book he got free from a friend at work as being full of abounding love, even if there is no one there to receive it.

Gabe, who tells me all of the above while Tommy is still conveniently in his office, MIA. And who tells me, in addition to all of this, that every single untouchable married woman in his life, the Lauries Mollys Susans, he has just now, this very second, realized, remind him of me.

Gabe tells me he is aware that I am married and that I am also thirty-six. "The age difference would be a problem, wouldn't it?" he asks, and I answer him in all seriousness over the sound of Tommy washing his hands in the bathroom.

"Yes."

Gabe, who follows me through the house after dinner while I sweep. Who trails out into the driveway after me when I take out the recycling. Who puts his pistachio shells down the garbage disposal even though I tell him, "Gabe, please don't put your pistachio shells down the garbage disposal."

Gabe, who would climb into a woman and live there forever like a castaway if she'd let him. Gabe, who has scurvy, practically, from his desire for these pirate-fantasy women he cannot touch.

"I guess I'll take this as a compliment, Gabe," I say, when I turn around and find him four inches from me as I finish the dishes.

"Do so," he says quietly. And then winks.

Porous, soft, almost albino Gabe. Who leaves his advice books about women on the coffee table for me to find after he unpacks. Like *Maxim's Pocket Book of Women*, and WOMEN: *The Unautho-*

rized Guide, which when I do find them, and of course, open them once Tommy and I are in the bedroom, advise men to speak in a lower register to women because it reminds them of their father's authority, and to speak in rhythmic tones to women because it lulls them into feeling comforted and protected, and quote, "ready for anything."

"There's someone I want to show you to, okay?" Tommy whispers after we hear the squish of Gabe in the living room, lowering himself onto the blow-up mattress, and as he points the webcam toward my side of the bed, I roll my eyes at him before I pull off my shirt.

"You better do it fast."

Gabe: in the house for eight days so far. Who eats entire bags of sesame sticks covered with Italian dressing and calls this dinner. Who says even though we've met him only once before, that Tommy and me, we feel like his only family.

"We should introduce him to Summer," Tommy says. "Remember? That girl with the e-tutorial for virgins?"

But God knows he'd fall in love with her. He'd fall in love with a woman in a Crisco commercial. He'd send her fan letter after fan letter: "*When you picked up the corncob that way, I found you beautiful.*"

Gabe, reviled by his own body. Gabe, who looks unlived, whose skin is pale, fetal-looking. Whose skin has the milky quality of having been torn from the womb too soon. Gabe, who barely has palm lines, whose eyes trace my silhouette at the sink as he picks gum off the lining of his ski jacket with a butter knife. Gum that got stuck there when he went alone to see *Unleashed* at the 22-plex because we had to go to one of Tommy's parties and couldn't take him.

And finally, Gabe. Who is sitting in the living room with all the lights off when I come home from work on the afternoon of Day 9, cradling my sixty-pound pit bull in his lap.

"How's it going, Gabe," I ask, and when he hears my voice, he looks up and smiles beatifically.

"Not good."

And this is when Gabe tells me about "recently," when he was just sitting at his desk inside Buy Rite corporate headquarters. How he was just sitting there, in his cubby, when he, quote, "hit a wall." Literally. And his hand popped straight through the particleboard in a geometric circle. Perfectly round.

And at that precise moment, he had to get away from Laurie, typing away in the cubby right next to him. Married Laurie. Wife of somebody else. Laurie, who owns one shepherd mix and one full-bred shepherd, and who, if he's honest with himself, is actually the one who gave Gabe the idea about the Irish setter and the Dog Fancier's book too, in fact, when she and the husband invited him over that one great year on Super Bowl Sunday.

Laurie, who was diagnosed recently with both breast and ovarian malignancies. Laurie, who is getting radiation here in Calabasas, by the way, where she is currently staying with her cousin Molly, and her cousin Susan. Cousins and next-door neighbors, he adds. Both already married.

"Calabasas?" I say, before it occurs to me. "Oh."

"But it wasn't stalking her to come here," Gabe assures me. "Not by a long shot." They worked together at the Buy Rite. She was sick and it was obvious. Before he punched a hole in it, their cubbies used to share a common wall.

"Used to?"

Gabe sighs and nuzzles the dog, who lathers him with her tongue from chin to forehead. "If you hear someone throwing up in the women's bathroom," he says, "and you can recognize from the sound of the retching who it is, shouldn't you go in? Following someone you love to the bathroom isn't inappropriate. In a perfect, evolving world like the one in *The Celestine Prophecy*, this kind of service would be called 'friendship slash concern.'"

"People don't get fired because they walk into the women's room, though."

Gabe pushes the dog from his lap and his shoulders droop. "It was just an e-mail to a few people on the sales floor," he says. "If someone cares whether or not you die, I don't see the problem with letting several key individuals know about it, do you?"

"Wow, Gabe," I say, staring across the coffee table at him without blinking. "A group e-mail."

"I know," Gabe sighs, bowing his head. "Do you think I could get a free hug?"

Gabe, in my living room with a swirl of black dog hair on the pocket of his button-down.

Gabe, who promises, as our arms jerk uncomfortably around each other, that on his next visit he will definitely give me a copy of *The Celestine Prophecy*, or have one of Laurie's cousins from Calabasas drop it by. Either one.

Gabe, who leaves on Day 10 while Tommy is doing errands, requesting a ride to LAX five and a half hours before the departure of his plane. Who we will not hear from again until we receive his family's Christmas letter two months later. "Gabe got fired from Buy Rite for some reason," it says, "and Gary has to get his leg amputated in April from the diabetes. His attitude is positive and he wants to start playing golf."

Gabe, who tells me at curbside check-in that he may try for an accounting position at Fingerhut, a company that sells women's clothing patterns throughout the Midwest. Gabe, who I wish I could tell, before he departs this less than clean Nissan, that Tommy, he never leaves the house to do errands without his laptop, not anymore. Gabe, who makes me think:

Why are we put here if not to live in torment?

Who makes me wonder: How can our gods bear to watch us do it?

God, up there in the Sunroom, the Universe Room. God, up there on the Bridge. God, just a kid in wayfarer sandals who likes it dirty. A horny kid in front of a blurry screen, aiming His viewfinder down at us ants.

Gabe, who makes me want to cry out to whoever's in charge, like Isaiah did or something, with a voice lifted up to every mountain rough place, across every fertile valley and desert highway, every scarred, uneven plain, to the east and to the west, to starboard, port and aft, up and down this barren concourse of strangers.

And consider: every ticketed passenger dragging a secret suitcase, each daughter of Egypt and son of Israel traveling first-class, business, or otherwise. Calling all of them by name: every lifestyle enthusiast and compulsive masturbator.

I am Begging. Please.

Mon dieu. Dios mío.

To the Chief of Operations. The One who has measured the waters and marked off the heavens, supposedly, with the hollow of His fucking hand.

Won't somebody, somewhere. Someone human, anywhere?

Won't some person who is not already married or dying ever love this naked Gabe?

Documents of Passion Love

Carolyn Ferrell

From Wanda Farrelly-Johnson. *Are We God's Children of Ham? And Other Dilemmas of Black Historical Research* (Pilot, N.C.: Lizard Ladies Press, 1983):

ACKNOWLEDGMENTS

I would like to thank my professors, Dr. Diana Aminata-Peterson and Dr. Buford Bhagdatis, both of the Amistad Center for Race Relations at Tulane University, for their unwavering, unflagging, and unmitigated support of my dissertation-turned-memoir, *Are We God's Children of Ham? And Other Dilemmas of Black Historical Research*, the book currently enfolded in your hands. I am

deeply indebted to Dr. Burton Foss of the University of North
Carolina for answering my queries in a timely and polite fashion.
I am also most grateful to the children of Mrs. Evelyn Sweetbriar
Hill, who gave me complete access to her papers. Miss Greenie
Washington of Lizard Lick, North Carolina, was a guiding light at
the edge of night. Thanks on High to my best friend, Ms. Lenore
Chaney Williams, granddaughter of Marion Chaney.

Support for this book also came from the National Endowment for African American Scholarship, the Elizabeth City Coun-
cil on Negro Adoptions, AIR CANADA, Simon Fraser University,
and the North Carolina Union of Firefighters and Community
Outreach, Raleigh.

A NOTE TO MY TREASURED READER

We Black People need to preserve ourselves, we need to preserve
our own history. As it stands now, We Black People are in such
demise—of the mind, of the spirit, of our legacy to future generations. We are fading from memory like dust in the wind. If the
Black Race doesn't save itself from obliteration, who will?

I, as your researcher and trusted scribe, am here to make a
change.

I AM HERE TO SET THE RECORDS STRAIGHT.

Photograph 1, UNC-Chapel Hill, Special Collections;
Catalogue Listing 336A-48K,
Rural Wedding, North Carolina, ca. 1914.

Here he sits on the curb outside the Zebulon County Courthouse,
his face a delirium of joy. Her face is a puzzle. She stands behind her

future groom and in front of the white deputy who looks as stiff as a playing-card king. The sun overhead is a stark white ball; even in this worn print, you can almost feel the egg-white heat rising from the paper.

Grover Devine, last of Elizabeth City, North Carolina. You never knew him. Before today you'd never even heard his name. He waited on this curb outside the Zebulon County Courthouse for two whole hours while Dolly Mae Washington, weeping in the anteroom, wondered if she'd made a grave error. At ten forty-five in the morning, as the sun ascended through the clouds, she came out with her face creased, her hips wider than a panhandle. She was his.

From girlhood on, Dolly Mae had been saving herself for the footsteps of happiness to come treading toward earth, for that loud slap-tapping to make its way straight to her bedroom, where she would be waiting beneath the quilt. She was well into her thirty-fifth year. The married women in Lizard Lick no longer invited her to dinner for fear their husbands might admire her threadbare longing.

Now she and Grover were man and wife. Legal, in the Zebulon County Courthouse, July of 1914. Now you know.

Neither Grover nor Dolly Mae moved from their spot on the curb for quite some time; look deeply into the photograph and you'll see that the white deputy's face is palpable rage. He'd waited, hoping she would change her mind. The world was changing despite the white deputy's prayers. He was a devout Witness, prepared for the end of the world to tromp down (any moment now, according to the Elders), and yet he couldn't stand the despicable freedoms and desires between whites and Negroes that seemed to have slipped in behind everyone's back. The white deputy despised the judge, whom he considered little more than a fool for abiding animals in his courthouse. Why, the deputy wondered, had God closed his eyes to the world? At his feet, discarded sheets of the *Zebulon Intelligencer* shuffled along the curb in the faint wind. All these freedoms and desires. The white deputy tried to will Dolly Mae and Grover into oblivion but could not help glancing at the stark headline: IS THIS WAR?

After their honeymoon Grover Devine planned on carrying his bride to the coast, where she would find work alongside him at the fisheries near Kitty Hawk. He'd wanted a clean break from home, where for years he'd done women's work alongside his foster mother in the Elizabeth City Negro Orphanage, of which she was chief matron. Hands raw as dirt: until now his life had been composed of laundering, starching, bluing, wringing, boiling, chopping, threading, fastening. Cooking stews in cauldrons as large as the moon. Singing lullabies that left his voice as hoarse as a bullfrog's. Grover Devine had recently turned eighteen and desired a clean break. He was needing to love with his hands.

Grover sometimes walked the streets of Elizabeth City at night and watched the women lingering by the edge of the Pasquotank River. Laundresses, cooks, lovers, dreamers. All he did was watch, nightly; and then he watched in the daylight; and then, there she was: Dolly Mae, arm in arm with a certain Mrs. Marion Chaney, a heartily married family friend who had been entrusted to watch Dolly Mae during her week there. The pair were hurrying toward Lena's, a fabric shop on the edge of the river, laughing like sisters. It was then that Grover knew.

He knew. Dolly Mae was visibly older, yet her curves were still new and untangled, waiting for his hands. He followed them into Lena's.

You know how this will end. Exactly nine days later Grover came to Lizard Lick to get Dolly Mae. He climbed through the window of her daddy's house, then stole a large machete to cut their way out of the tangle that led to the pasture gate. When they reached this gate (the Washington land stretched for acres), Grover realized he was so happy it actually hurt him to move his feet. His hands were fine, though, and he used them to cup water from a cow pond and serve it to Dolly Mae. He used them to tell her stories about his life as they walked along the dawning road. With his hands he fed her the petals of goatweed, which staved off hunger, and the shavings of a golden-seal root, which had the power to clean out memory.

He had learned such things from the days when he and his foster mother were on the run from the law, forced to spend whole nights in the ruinate. They once lived for three months in a cave along the Virginia coast. To his mind, they'd behaved like animals, him and her, all in the name of freedom.

Grover and Dolly Mae arrived in Zebulon to be married as the birds of morning creaked into song. The streets were already bustling. Folks looked at them but neither looked up from their feet. The court-house was, as usual in this kind of hamlet, dead in the center of town, so you didn't have to really look to see where you were going.

At the first intersection in the main road (slaughterhouse, school-house, deputy's, tailor) Dolly Mae tugged at Grover's sleeve and begged him to be more specific: why did he never want to see his fos-ter mother again? What crime of the heart had she committed, what offense so great that her son would turn his back on her forever?

— Dolly Mae. Never mind her. You the only one now.

— But to leave her forever. Won't she want to see our children?

— Won't be none.

— No children?

— Not a one.

— How we going to live without family? Who will care for us?

— The moon will care for us. It'll be our cheese. The stars our milk. The black night will cover us like babies.

These riddles were among the first of many hints that this man was not all she'd dreamed him to be. They stood in front of the court-house and again studied their feet.

—But ain't your mama waiting for us in Elizabeth City?

—She my foster mama. And no. You the only one.

—Grover. Grover.

Her eyes sat perfectly still on her face, oval and brown-black, like little bird's eggs.

You might find this interesting. Two hours before this photo was taken, the white deputy had told them they could not be legally mar-ried in the Zebulon County Courthouse. Grover prepared to strike—he was not against the idea of licking this white man—when all of a sudden the old judge trudged out from the building, declaring he would perform the ceremony. The white deputy then had some more words, to which the old judge replied,—Why you acting like you the boss round here, Hill? Ain't nobody died and made you boss.

It was just past eight-thirty in the morning. Dolly Mae wore a flowered crape made from the material she'd purchased at Lena's Fabric Shop with Mrs. Marion Chaney. The dress looked as if it were about to fly away in the wind-still air.

The old judge asked,—You still want to do this? It's against the law. You all could just say you married, like you always done from the beginning.

—We ain't like that no more, Grover replied, wiping the tears from Dolly Mae's face.

—They animals, every last one of them, the white deputy mut-tered.

—We ain't that way no more, Grover said, turning to face him. —We left that way behind.

The white deputy looked at his feet.—What any of them know of starting new? They all go at it like cats.

—Now, Hill.

—Always humping. The world gone to hell in a handbasket from them animals.

—Now, Hill.

The white deputy murmured,—That make you a nigger-lover, Judge.

—Let us go, said the judge, leading the pair indoors.—I'll deal with you later, Hill.

To be exact, this took place on July 5, start of the driest summer season Zebulon County had known in over half a century. Grover Devine and Dolly Mae Washington exchanged vows in whispered rushes—the first colored couple to become man and wife in this courthouse. The groom then waited on the curb while the bride retreated to the anteroom to weep. His childish promises from late the night before rang in her ears as she watched the cockroaches climb the wall:

—*We look up and see clouds like feather beds.*

—*Sky like a bowl of grits.*

—*Moon like a great big old piece of cheese.*

She emerged, and when Grover finally rose from that curb to take Dolly Mae by the arm, he carried her back through the woods, this time to Cow River, to the cabin where they would begin their love. Once more he became talkative, letting out more details about his life, sometimes in wild, unwieldy gulps. Fires and bare escapes. Life from weeds, food from dirt and stones. Ghosts trailing in broad daylight.

Dolly Mae listened. And every now and then her eyes began to crack. But still she kept on at his side.

As you know, terror was brewing in Europe at this time, so much so that the residents of every minuscule Carolinian corner found ways to buy, read, and interpret newspapers. They knew that the assassination in Sarajevo wasn't a colored man's affair, and yet. Things could get worse. Things always got worse for colored folks when they were just busy minding their own business, trying to catch up to yesterday.

On her wedding night, as her husband fell into dreams, Dolly Mae slipped out the cabin door. No shoes, not even her flowered crape. She threw on Grover's trousers and overcoat. In another age she could have been a romantic heroine scantily clad, fleeing a walled castle. But now she was simply Dolly Mae Washington Devine. Moonlight was her guide as she retraced her steps back to Zebulon.

You never knew her. Now you do.

By dawn she'd arrived—burnt feet, toes screwed by nails, face sharpened by lust. Dolly Mae gripped her sides as if she could already feel life taking root on her stomach's floor. *Oh why in heavens,* she was thinking, *why did he have to tell me all that?*

From the jailhouse window, the white deputy saw her leaping onto a boxcar of the Norfolk Southern but—as you can surmise—didn't move a muscle to stop her.

From Farrelly-Johnson, *Are We God's Children of Ham?*:

CHAPTER ONE
"Mama, Were There Really Slaves in This World?"

[. . .] all the photographs saved from the incinerator in the Vancouver nursing home were in good to poor condition. They had originally been stored in a woodshed in North Carolina, which explains the insect and water damage.

The woodshed sat on the property of a Mr. Major Dean Washington on Route 1 in Lizard Lick. Major Dean lived there with his wife, Essie, and five children: Greenie, Mary, Bess, Furletta, and Dolly Mae. According to folk documentation (Dunbar, 1938), Major Dean had toiled for years gathering pictures, taking notes, and listening to endless talk stories but feared that the "university people" would come and abscond with the whole collection, every last daguerreotype, every bill of sale and fugitive slave notice, every birth certificate and marriage license, including those artifacts leading up to the First World War (Wallace and Marcus, 1971). He had in his possession, among the greatest treasures, many photographs belonging to Miss Jerlean Fanfaria Devine and her foster son, Grover (Buxom, 1942). In 1981 a posthumous citation for honorable citizenry was bestowed upon Major Dean Washington by the Zebulon County Sheriff's Office.

Just before the Great War ended (on Armistice Day in 1918) Major Dean Washington died of a drug overdose. Shortly thereafter Essie Washington demanded a thousand dollars for herself in restitution from the University at Chapel Hill—she claimed they brought on his sorrows—before she accidentally caught herself in a wringer and met her untimely end.

January 1919, the Chapel Hill students came and took nearly everything.

But *not* everything. Some pieces were rescued from the woodshed just minutes before those university people came. They were taken by Miss Dolly Mae Washington—who'd returned to Lizard Lick after a long absence—and then carried back with her to Elizabeth City. In her lifetime she carried those photographs across the country, to Richmond, Cleveland, the Bronx, Boise, Charleston, Tuskegee, Seattle, and finally Vancouver, British Columbia, where she was remanded into a nursing home (Wallace and Marcus, 1971). The photographs were later placed in the hands of an acquaintance of Dolly Mae's, a Mrs. Marion Chaney of Zebulon, North Carolina.

In 1977 Mrs. Marion gave them to her granddaughter, Ms. Lenore Chaney Williams, who in turn contacted the author of this book, and thereby saved a corner of the Black World for posterity.

From *Look Who's Talking*
A Publication of the Vancouver Plains Rest Home
CHRISTMAS, 1977

"As told to," recorded by Mrs. W. Wilford Milkman, resident secretary and piano player, aged 102

And Grover pulling me over the threshold to Marvella's cabin on the Cow River.

Day was so inland hot, but nothing we ain't suffered before. Flies and wasps stirring the little bit of air, floor aching hot. Could any two people on the planet be less prepared to care for each other? Hell.

There he is, watching me. Maybe sorry for all the things he told me.

He touch my shoulder. He touch it with his hand. Water, he said. Please make me water to wash, Dolly Mae.

Night we eat us a dinner of corn bread hard as stone. I'm a goddamn bride, why I'm eating this crap? Should be in Elizabeth City, eating crown roast. Marvella Dunbar—gossip as long as the day—had brang us the corn bread—homemade, oh Lord!—on account of us being nudie-weds.

The tallow candles on the table burnt to a pool. I know this man will soon be wanting me.

The bed under the cobwebs—mattress filled with straw. On the way to getting married in Zebulon *he had told me things* and I was afraid.

Now I know he'll be wanting me. Now I real afraid.

So I say, I could throw together a pie. Don't think about how or where I'm a get the ingredients.

He say, Ain't no need. He reach for my elbow.

And then.

Then and then.

Hours we laying together, fits and starts, blood bursting. Grover say he gone butter my skin to cool the burn. The burn of love. But first I got to stop crying, even if they are tears of joy.

And then. More.

And then.

Middle of the night I hear Grover talking. I open my eyes and see a lady there, plain as day. A specter.

Get on out I ain't marry you, is what my husband answering even though his eyes are closed in sleep.

Specter say, *You'll never leave.*

Long slave dress, buttons so high up the neck you wonder how they breathed. Sort of like the kind my good friend Marion used to wear, God rest her soul she died not two weeks ago. Back then she wore a bustle looking like a camel's hump. Why the hell we need so much ass in those days?

Specter say to Grover, *You got blood on your hands.*

Grover sleep say, *Now GET! I ain't passioned you. NOW GET!*

Specter say, *We ain't never truly leaving. You ain't never truly leaving.*

Grover commence to snore. But *I* do run away, treading in that pitch night, feeling with Grover's walking stick for any water moccasin in the footpath.

All that I learnt from my mama and my daddy and my best friend Marion from Elizabeth City—gone. My head's on fire. A damn right shame, but Grover Devine not the man for me.

That's how I be thinking in those days.

From Evelyn Sweetbriar Hill, *The War Bride* (novel) (Boston: Houghton Mifflin, 1936):

—I love you with my heart and soul, the suitor told her as he slunk into her bedroom. The night vines shivered with animal love. The pair was impassioned with the fever of passion, though all around them, the world was in a tailspin. It was the End of Days, as the Bible stated. But did these two lovers think of that?

From Farrelly-Johnson, *Are We God's Children of Ham?*:

CHAPTER THREE
Poe's Mammy, and Other Tales of Superstition

Dear Readers: This bit of research was Guaranteed Overheard at the "Weddin House," an establishment on the Cow River which was once run by a certain Miss Marvella Dunbar as a sort of honeymoon hotel for local newlyweds (Dunbar, 1938). One night in early July, shortly after the War of the Nations had begun, Miss Marvella heard strange noises coming from her rental cabin (she lived in a small shed out back). Around daybreak she put her ear to the door and heard (to her everlasting dismay) a group of dead babies tromping on the floor. They mashed up all her good corn bread with their soft baby heels.

This is her claim. Naturally she was too frightened to look in.

Miss Marvella couldn't make out the words, though to her ear it sounded like a mixture of Latin and Swahili (Buxom, 1942). From her last residence (Social Plains Rest Home, where she was gently committed in 1915 at the tender age of forty) she did claim that their racket stopped the birds from truly bringing in the day (Dunbar, 1938).

That very day, Miss Marvella Dunbar escaped from her own property, making for the tracks of the Norfolk Southern Railway, where she hid out until one of the slow trains happened by.

Weddin House was demolished in 1936.

Photograph 2, UNC-Chapel Hill, Special Collections;

Catalogue Listing 336A-45N,

Negro Man at Stricklands Crossroads, North Carolina, undated.

The morning after he got married, when he was a single man again, Grover Devine packed his few belongings (Dolly Mae's father's machete blade and the marriage certificate and a sliver of goldenseal root) and dashed out the front door. Some say he headed back to his foster mother to beg her forgiveness. Some say he buried himself in a little silver box and stayed in the ground for a hundred years. You know how our kind will wag their tongues. His exact destination has never been accurately ascertained.

In this photograph he stands alone in the dust road. The clouds hang like draperies. Not a drop of rain for three whole seasons, as you can tell from the skeletal trees in the back.

Grover Devine was not heard from again. Over the years, a few roped-up bodies were dragged from the bottom of the Cow River, but none belonged to him.

From *Look Who's Talking*
A Publication of the Vancouver Plains Rest Home
ST. VALENTINE'S DAY, 1978

"As told to," recorded by the former Mrs. W. Wilford Milkman, now Widow Geneva Milkman, chief cook and bottle washer

What I dreamed him to be? Anything, really. I was old, poor, love-less. He was young enough to be my child, but when he put his hands on me, there was nothing child about him. I had me my dreams, you know. I was expecting to be put somewhere on a farm. Cows, pigs, that sort of thing. I could do it all. Milk, cheese, butter. Pork, lard, candles, soap. I could do it all.

What done surprised me, though. Fire and frozen at once. Being with Grover Devine for one night was like being born again.

Licked my toes with his tongue. Told me we was heading out to the coast. Was I up to man's work? I said I was.

Smothered my titties in love. Said he would passion me for-ever. Was I up to that? Lord help me, was my reply.

Traveled my body like it was Route 1 in the nighttime. Stopped his passion to ask me would I be interested in flying back home? You mean Lizard Lick, I ask? He frown, a veritable Devine frown. I can tell he fed up with my lack of brains.

No, silly girl. Flying BACK HOME.

You so full of surprises, I say, and he know I don't mean it goodly of him.

Then he start mumbling, pushing me away from him. Said he was done killing. Did I still think I could love him with all this blood on his hands? Mainly it was Miss Jerlean—just look at any photograph. Just look and see her eyes.

He say he wasn't anything like his foster mama.

Lord, I wanted to run. But then he was back to kissing me in this way that prevented my immediate running. Fire and frozen at once. But I wanted to run.

How can a murderer passion anyone this good?

Back then there was no words. Still ain't no accurate ones. I just have to say it agin: fire and frozen. Do you understand?

Photograph 3, UNC-Chapel Hill, Special Collections;
Catalogue Listing 336A-43J,
Negro Couple, Elizabeth City, June 1914.

Before their marriage at the Zebulon County Courthouse. Before they slipped away in the night from her father's property. Before she looked out the window and admired stars made from goat's milk.

They'd locked eyes over bolts of calico, muslin, and flower crape: love at first sight. He whispered that he was going to wander the promenade in Elizabeth City that evening, and would she care to join him? At night no one never did bother colored folk much.

Maybe they could just walk.

Photograph 4, UNC-Chapel Hill, Special Collections;
Catalogue Listing 336A-72R,
Colored Matron, 1909.

The photographer's date in the corner is clearly marked 1903 though the Chapel Hill students claimed that date was a forgery. Here she wears a dress made of stiff black fabric, perhaps a cheap velvet. Miss Jerlean wears a long key chain around her crimped waist with a monocle in the one eye; her other eye, a glass marble, had been lost in one of the fires. Her head is done up in an old-fashioned turban, the towering kind you associate with pinprick slave portraits. You never knew her either.

In the photograph, Miss Jerlean drapes her arms around a line of brown-skinned boys and girls, all glassy-faced and composed in front of the institution. The Chapel Hill students (all completing assignments for the seminar "Origins of Recent Blaxploitation Films") have identified the orphanage, smack in the center of Elizabeth City, as being on West Main, in one of those postbellum structures whose architecture had been designed to give distinction to the city. In fact, Miss Jerlean has been credited with saving it from the wrecking ball. It and the children; her hands rest doggedly on their shoulders.

Miss Jerlean Fanfaria Devine ran the Elizabeth City Negro Orphanage from 1905 until 1914. But did you know that before that, in 1903, she ran the Baltimore Home for Colored Foundlings, for about six months? And that earlier, about 1896, when she was fresh out of Morris Park Normal, she had worked as a matron's helper at the Colored Orphan Asylum in Riverdale, New York? In those days, the Riverdale asylum was still reeling from the famous torching of the colored orphanage on Fifth Avenue some decades before. Miss Jerlean Devine stayed at Riverdale until its demise in 1902.

How old was this woman? Impossible to pin down. Rumor was she'd saved all the children from the angry mob during the Civil War draft riots. Rumor was she'd taken on the angry crowd with a shotgun, that she went about New York City torching places where white children slept peacefully. But rumors are not facts.

While working at Riverdale as a matron's helper, Miss Jerlean met her favorite charge, a baby she christened Grover. Nothing is known about his blood kin.

Things went smoothly at the Colored Orphan Asylum — Miss Jerlean was heralded by all as a true "natural" — when, in December

1902, a blaze broke out killing nearly all the inmates. Forty-five dead out of forty-seven. There was an inquest, a sleepy investigation. Hardly anyone noticed when Miss Jerlean pulled up roots, leaving Riverdale at first for Ossining and later for points south. Rumor was she carried little Grover in the palm of her hand, on pain of death.

You never knew her. In the photograph, there is no river breeze to be felt, though Miss Jerlean's turban seems ready to topple from her head from some sort of hidden gravity.

From *Civil War Legacy: Oral Histories of the Southeast,* recorded and edited by Burton Foss, Ph.D. (Chapel Hill: University of North Carolina Press, 1980):

MARION CHANEY, ELIZABETH CITY, NORTH CAROLINA, 1977

She was my best friend even when I watched her like a hawk for her mama when she came to buy her cloth. Dolly Mae Devine never thanked me.

[. . .] years, and then she finds me in a newspaper advert, we write. 1935 I come down to Elizabeth City to visit—I'd been living with my second husband's people in Richmond. Dolly Mae's face as big as a moon. Looked like she had some sort of disease. No, she says. Just years of tending children. Collecting papers and photographs. Writing my manuals. I'm lonely, Marion. Missed you something awful.

I want to stay longer but she bring me to the wagon the next day. Then between me and her, years of nothing.

[. . .] the next time I see her was up there at the Vancouver
Plains Rest Home. That was 1976. I had got word that she was
ailing—and me, near a hundred years old but never fitter—and
then I travel up to Canada with my granddaughter Lenore.

Dolly Mae looked the spit and image of her mama, bless her
soul, who had entrusted Dolly Mae to me years before, but the
girl done run off with that boy. She being a grown woman so
what did she have to find in a boy?

Please don't ask me anything else. Please ask me in five minutes.

She lost four babies in her life. Poison, she claimed. Goldenseal root
given to her by her mother-in-law. In the nursing home she told
me about how she had wrote the Irishman in Baltimore and said,
Come to Elizabeth City, I got the old bitch ready for you to arrest.

[. . .] I come sit with her every day in the home.

She kept her oxygen mask on high-speed air, mainly to keep
the girl students from Simon Fraser from getting too close. Whenever they come by, they ask me would she be up for a day of
cameras and makeup, everything paid for, by the Rainbow Student Coalition of Simon Fraser University.

—She ain't up for that sort of thing, I say.

The one girl in cornrows says,—From all our research, we believe this lady was an early black feminist. We think she invented
the term "passion love" that everyone throws about so carelessly
nowadays.

—Lord have mercy!

—We want to know for sure.

—Foolishness! I'm her best friend and I should know!

I want to tell them that she actually saved all those orphans in Elizabeth City from dying at the hands of Miss Jerlean. I want to tell them Dolly Mae took care of those orphans till they was all grown and in Elizabeth City she was a bona-fide hero even though forty years she never saw my friendship as anything significant. But those girl students already working another angle.

The one in cornrows say,—You mind if *we* return those photographs and things to Chapel Hill? We promise on a stack of Bibles.

This girl I know she come from the South, passing herself now as pure Canada.

—I can't, I tell them.

—Please, Miss Chaney. For your best friend's sake—for history's sake. Let us have those documents. It's a matter of life and death.

—What is?

—We believe Dolly Mae Devine was the author of a book entitled *A Black Lady's Manual to Passion Love.* The first of its kind, probably from around the late 1920s. You know anything about that?

—Never, I answer.

The cornrow student say to me,—Dolly Mae Devine was the first to talk honestly about the sexual desires of black women. What can you tell us about that?

—Nothing, I say again. They know I am lying. And in the Bible the Lord says, Take not my name in vain three times, and here I done did it.

Laughing at the olden ways. I tell them,—You know, there used to be this lady in Elizabeth City had a shop. Sold fabric to us when no one else would. Lena was her name—now over 120 years old, God's truth!

—You mean when no one else would . . . what?

—Sell bolts of cloth. To darkies. Lena was only shop in Elizabeth City.

—Lady, no one says "darkies" anymore.

—I'm sorry, girls. I have to send these pictures back to Chapel Hill tomorrow, special delivery.

—*You're not being fair to the black feminist community!* This comes from the other girl student, a white one. French accent.

—Please, I say.—The past belongs in the past.

—*Traitor,* Frenchie say right back in my face.

From Hill, *The War Bride:*

He told her he was full of desires. Desires that needed to be unfolded in the warmth of her sable body. He asked her if she knew what it meant to be totally gratified. Not a human being with feet on the ground, but an angel dangling by the chains of heaven.

I can cook, clean, nurse, and lie, she answered in the pale moonlight.

There is ever so much more, he answered, preparing his musket.

From *Look Who's Talking*
A Publication of the Vancouver Plains Rest Home
EASTER, 1978

"As told to," recorded by Geneva Duncan Milkman, resident secretary

I left from my wedding night. What manner of girl leaves on her wedding night? But I believed he was not the man for me.

I traveled on the Norfolk Southern for a bit, summer 1914. Raleigh, Asheville, Charlotte, Wilmington, Plymouth. Elizabeth City by August. Stop and asked my friend Marion would she help me but she too upset. Say I'm no way for a married lady to be acting. Call me fast, a heifer. That was the end of my friendship for then.

So I went over to my mother-in-law that lived in Elizabeth City and I say to her I seen a bunch of dead babies in the room on my wedding night and what did you have to do with it? Just like that, I didn't make no introduction, all I say was, Why did you put those babies in my wedding cabin and like to scare me to death?

And she say back to me, Girl, you best be watching that mouth.

I asked her if it was true, did she set fire to all those orphanage homes and kill all those babies?

She say, Some of them wasn't babies.

Riverdale? Baltimore? I call her a FIEND.

My dear, I'm no FIEND. I'm simply preventing these babes from being killed by future mobs that are all too happy to do such things.

Why not save them? Why kill them? Why burn them to the ground?

Honeychild, I was saving them! I would rather it be me that leads them to greener pastures than some stinking filthy white mob. White men. White women. White children. My stomach is turning. I wanted to spare those babes a tragic death at the hands of such creatures.

You are stone crazy.

Watchtower has been predicting Armageddon for this year October. You know what that means?

Crazy behind Witnesses! Don't blame them for what you did!

I'll tell you: it means more white folks coming to do harm.

Stone cold crazy bitch!

Watchtower predicts the end of all things, and I know that means for the first time in history: COLORED IN FRONT PLEASE! YOUR TURN TO BURN IN HELL FIRST.

Stone cold fiend!

I'm sending those little ones to a place where no earthly Armageddon will do them harm.

Well, you know. If I'd a had the strength, I'd a killed her on the spot. Honeychild my ass. But then she give me a tea, put me in a sleep for four days. When I wake, she tell me it's the four babies I'm carrying in me that got me sleeping so.

She tell me I should make my way back to Grover, but I can't. I can't find any energy but to lie back down and pray to Lord Jesus I won't burn in hell for possessing this knowledge.

From Farrelly-Johnson, *Are We God's Children of Ham?:*

CHAPTER FOUR

Love in the Time of Ringworm:
The Mulattress and the Irishman

In 1863, it was a certain Mr. Cyrus Farrelly—the lone white voice waving the flag of peace before the angry draft riot mob on Fifth Avenue, begging them to halt their violence and not burn the orphanage. All those poor colored children!

His voice, however, was in vain, though the children were saved and eventually moved up to Bronx County.

Years later he stood at the scene of the Riverdale fire. He was working as a detective for the county police, and had taken it upon himself to interview a number of employees. He recorded his findings in a small diary (Lewis, 1966). Then he sat up many nights, trying to solve the mystery.

Once during that spring—four months after the fire—he went back to the site of the blaze and unearthed a small silver box, no larger than a chocolate tin. How could this have escaped trained eyes? He broke its lock and studied its contents till he knew them by heart. He did not share his findings (Wallace and Marcus, 1971).

Sickness and other personal misfortune kept Mr. Farrelly from truly pursuing the mystery of the Riverdale blaze. Time passed (Nod, 1972).

Then one autumn day he received an anonymous missive begging him to "come and arrest the greatest fiend known to mankind." In September 1914, Detective Farrelly arrived in Elizabeth City, where he found Miss Jerlean at 420 West Main (a real beauty of an edifice, but craggy and old) serving tea and crown roast to her daughter-in-law, a Miss Dolly Mae Washington Devine, who had on her a mouth as foul as any sailor's (Nod, 1972).

Photograph 5, UNC-Chapel Hill, 45467 STEREO;

Catalogue Listing 336A-55M,

Negress and Police Officer, ca. September 1914.

This double image is of Miss Jerlean Fanfaria Devine, head matron of the Elizabeth City Negro Orphanage, and Cyrus Farrelly, formerly of Bronx County, New York. Look at it through the stereoscope and you see her as she always was, proud and tall. You also notice that he got her by the wrists, silver handcuffs.

It is clear as day to me, though, that they in love.

From Foss, *Civil War Legacy:*

MARION CHANEY, ELIZABETH CITY, 1977

Won't no orphans ever died in the Elizabeth City 'cause won't ever a fire set. Dolly Mae took over the orphanage until 1966. I believe she seen her husband in dreams.

Photograph 6, UNC-Chapel Hill, Special Collections;
Catalogue Listing 336A-999-UPS,
Negro Home, Cow River, North Carolina, 1915.

They could not live out their lives in Elizabeth City because they were complete outcasts. You never knew this. Jerlean and Cyrus moved to Lizard Lick and bathed, ate, and drank from the Cow River. Here they stand side by side with that close-up faraway glance you see in all these photograph faces. The weeping willows behind them are still there to this day.

It was said that in 1916 the white deputy came out to Cow River to make things bad for them. Before he knew it, the white deputy fell under a spell and was thereafter made to chop the wood, milk the cow, launder the clothes, clear the land. Folks said he carved a cradle from birch at the birth of their baby girl, Juanita, who came into this world when her mother was nearing her sixties.

Eventually the white deputy went away and married a woman in Shoeheel. She birthed him a daughter named Evelyn Sweetbriar, and a year later stabbed him in the heart.

Cyrus Farrelly died in 1924. Miss Jerlean was moved to a nursing home in Social Plains but escaped a few months later. She has not been seen since.

Of course you know this is all pure myth. The white deputy would surely have killed Miss Jerlean and Cyrus Farrelly had he found them together.

Folks claim so many things. But you know that all they ever want is the truth.

From Foss, *Civil War Legacy:*

MARION CHANEY, ELIZABETH CITY, 1977

She was holding that very photograph, and the next thing she say to me was,—Them Chapel Hill folks was wrong! Think they know everything! How you going to have a *Negro* wedding with an Irishman at your side?

She laughed. I took her hand in mines. 1976. A lifetime. Why didn't I try to love her the way I should have?

[. . .] she whispers,—Kill these things later, will you? Kill them. They don't mean nothing to nobody.

So I take the photographs, the regular ones, the daguerreo-types, tintypes, stereoscopic, and fragments. I take them to my hotel, the Vancouver Sheraton, real down pillows, where my granddaughter Lenore's waiting on me.

I can't kill those photographs. Lord forgive me.

A few days go by, and Dolly Mae asking me did I do what I was supposed to do?

No.

Do it.

So I take the pictures back to the nursing home but I keep them in the trunk of the rental car. My granddaughter

Lenore weary of my crying—she regret she agreed to come along.

Then Dolly Mae ask me again. Did I get rid of them pictures?

Three times, the Lord says. My dear Dolly Mae. I never did appreciate you running with that boy. I never did appreciate your talk of the woman's body in the pages of a book. But I am tired of lying. I ask my granddaughter Lenore what should I do.

She says,—Let me make a call.

But I can't wait no longer, and after another day, I take those pictures and get ready to toss them into the nursing home incinerator, just like Dolly Mae tell me to.

I stand before the fire. Janitor off somewhere drunk.

I stand before the fire.

Who needs to live in the past, I ask myself, my voice an echo of hers. Life is all about waiting for those footsteps of happiness to get to you in the first place.

Suddenly this lady comes running up to me. Right down there at the nursing home incinerator. Hair all whichaways, an afro. She ask me,—Are you Miss Marion?

When I say yes, she take the pictures out my hand, commences crying and laughing at the same time.

She say, —Forgive me. My name is Wanda Johnson.

Photograph 7, UNC-Chapel Hill, Special Collections;

Catalogue Listing 336A-99J,

Male Attendant with Baby at Elizabeth City

Negro Orphanage, ca. 1914.

Here he's holding me close to his heart, tucked away from the sun in his arm. His jacket is tattered, his toes are bursting at the seams of his boots. There are other children about, smiling, trying to hold his hand; but it is as if they all know that this day will be his last in Elizabeth City. You can make out a face in one of the upper windows. She is staring at him, waiting, planning. They later told me I was his favorite charge.

I survived Miss Jerlean as a baby. I survived Miss Dolly Mae as a young girl. Years of hate and love in the confines of the Elizabeth City Negro Orphanage. When I had you, I felt I was an orphan no more.

My child, have you ever felt the same about me?

From Hill, *The War Bride:*

He came around looking for her in the river towns. He was no longer human—grizzled hair, misshapen limbs, dirt covering his hide from head to toe. People believed they were looking at a Half-Man-Half-Beast. They didn't realize they were looking at a suitor who had been so much in love it hurt his feet to walk.

He found her in Elizabeth City. He begged her to follow him to Kitty Hawk. They had not laid eyes upon each other in over fifty years. She would only go but so far, despite the love she felt bursting her seams.

At Kitty Hawk he climbed a tree as large as a mountain. In the darkness she heard his voice for the last time.

The moon is our cheese!

The stars is our milk!

Do you love me, Dolly Mae?

A huge wind swept down and took him out of the tree, and the poor man sailed into the blackness, on his way to the Promised Land.

One could almost hear the stars tinkling in the branches. The Negress crossed herself. Her husband was going back home, and she had stupidly stayed behind. She asked her beating heart: Why was forgiveness always a necessity? Why did we always have to be good?

Wasn't love in heaven the same beautiful squalor it was on earth?

From Farrelly-Johnson, *Are We God's Children of Ham?:*

CHAPTER EIGHT

Heard It Through the Grapevine, or:
Is There Hope for the Black Race as a Whole?

This would have to have been around 1979 or so. One of the Chapel Hill students knocked on the rusted screen door of Greenie Washington, the last of the Washington family in Lizard Lick. The student had discovered that Greenie's sister, a Miss Dolly Mae Devine, had actually been the first to open a women's health clinic in North Carolina in 1946. In addition, Dolly Mae Devine had been honored in 1950 by *Architectural Digest* for having saved one of Elizabeth City's finest old edifices—the old Negro Orphanage on West Main—from the wrecking ball.

It was something of a story. The student—herself from Lizard Lick, where nothing interesting ever seemed to happen—felt like writing her thesis on it. Would Miss Greenie please help?

Greenie Washington rubbed her balding head and told the student, —Save your breath, girl. Tall tales and local yarns. Ain't none of us yet lived a real life on paper.

Volunteers Are Shining Stars

Curtis Sittenfeld

When I started out volunteering on Monday nights at New Day House, it was just me, Karen, and a rotating cast of eight or ten kids who, with their sticky marker-covered hands and mysteriously damp clothes, would greet us by lunging into our arms and leading us into the basement playroom. Karen was a tall, thin black woman in her late thirties who had a loud laugh and worked as a lobbyist on Capitol Hill. She once told me that she was the oldest of five sisters raised on a farm outside Columbia, South Carolina, and I think this upbringing contributed to her laid-back attitude as a volunteer. Karen and I had basically the same philosophy toward the kids, which was, *We'll try to entertain you, but we're not going to give in to your every whim, and if you're annoying us, we'll say so, and if you're the type to sit by yourself, chewing on a plastic frog in the corner, we'll let you hang out and chew as long as it doesn't look like you're about to cause yourself bodily harm.* For over ten months, before I did the thing I shouldn't have done, Karen and the kids and I existed in a kind of raucous harmony. It was the beginning of June when the third volunteer showed up.

As I punched in the code that unlocked the front door, I could see a white woman sitting on the bench in the entry hall, and I knew immediately she was the new volunteer. Because of how she was dressed, she clearly wasn't one of the mothers, and because of how uncomfortable and out of place she looked, she clearly wasn't a shelter employee. Once inside, I saw that she had bad skin, which she'd covered in a pale concealer so it was uniform in tone but still bumpy and greasy, and shoulder-length wavy brown hair that was rough in that way that means you're too old to wear it long. She was probably about Karen's age.

When we made eye contact, she smiled in an eager, nervous, closed-lipped way, and I offered a closed-lipped smile in return. I sat on the other end of the bench, as far from her as possible. From the dining room, I could hear the clink and clatter of silverware and dishes, and a baby wailing. The families ate dinner at five-thirty, and we came at six, to give the mothers a break. That was the point of volunteers.

At five before six, Na'Shell and Tasaundra sprinted into the hall and hurled themselves onto my lap. Just behind them was Tasaundra's younger brother, Dewey, who was two and walked in a staggering way. Behind him was another boy who had been there for the first time the week before, whose name I couldn't remember—he looked about four and had tiny gold studs in either ear. He stood by the pay phone near the doorway between the dining room and the entry hall, watching us, and I waved and said, "Hey there."

"I'm braiding your hair," Tasaundra announced. She had already wedged herself behind me and was easing the rubber band out of my ponytail, and Na'Shell said, "Can I braid your hair, too? Miss Volunteer, I want to do your hair." Both of them were five. Once, early on, Tasaundra had asked me, "Can you do this?" and jumped three times. I had jumped just as she had, at which point she'd grinned, pointed at me with her index finger, and said, "Your boobies is *bouncin'*." Then she and Na'Shell had shrieked with laughter.

The woman on the other side of the bench said, "Oh!"

I turned.

"I heard them call you—you must be—I'm just starting—" She giggled a little.

"I'm Frances," I said.

"Elsa." She stuck out her hand, but I motioned with my chin down to my own right hand, which Na'Shell was gripping. The truth is that if my hand hadn't been occupied, I still wouldn't have wanted to shake Elsa's. I had a thing then about touching certain people, about dirtiness, and I didn't like Elsa's hair and skin. Strangely, being groped by the kids didn't bother me because there was a purity to their dirtiness; they were so young. But if, say, I was on a crowded elevator and a woman in a tank top was standing next to me and the top of her arm was pressed to the top of mine—if, especially, it was skin on skin instead of skin on clothes—I would feel so trapped and accosted that I'd want to cry.

"They sure like you, don't they?" Elsa said, and she giggled again.

"Did you guys hear that?" I said. "You sure like me, right?"

Na'Shell squealed noncommittally. Elsa would figure out soon enough how generous the children were with their affection and also how quickly they'd turn on you, deciding you had let them down or hurt their feelings. None of it really meant that much. You tried to show them a good time for two hours once a week and not to become attached because they left without warning. One Monday, a kid was there, and the next, he wasn't—his mom had found a place for them to live, with her sister or her mother or her ex-boyfriend or as part of some new program where her own place was subsidized. The longest the families ever stayed at the shelter was six months, but most of them were gone far sooner.

Mikhail and Orlean walked through the doorway from the dining room. At nine and ten, they were the oldest; boys older than twelve weren't allowed in the shelter because in the past, they'd gotten involved with some of the younger mothers. "Can we go downstairs now?" Mikhail asked. His two front teeth pointed in opposite directions, so that two sides of a triangle formed in the space where they weren't. In idle moments, he had a habit of twisting his tongue sideways and poking it through the triangle.

I looked at my watch. "It's not quite six."

"But there's two of yous."

If we had been in the basement, I'd have said, "Two of you." But I never corrected their grammar upstairs, where the mothers might overhear. I turned to Elsa. "The rule is that two volunteers have to be present before we go downstairs. You've been through the training, right?"

"I'm ready to dive in headfirst." She actually extended her arms in front of her head.

I walked to the threshold of the dining room, where the air smelled like steamed vegetables and fish. Scattered around the tables were a few mothers and a few babies—the babies weren't allowed down in the playroom—and about five more children I recognized. "We're going downstairs," I called. "So if you guys want to come—"

"Miss Volunteer!" cried out Derek, and he stood as if to run toward me before his mother pulled him back by one strap of his overalls.

"Boy, you need to finish your dinner," she snapped, and Derek burst into tears. Derek was my favorite; he was three years old and had beautiful long eyelashes and glittering alert eyes and pale brown skin—his mother was white, so I assumed his father was black—and when Derek laughed, his smile was enormous and his laughter was noisy and hoarse. He was the only one I had ever fantasized about taking home with me, setting up a cot for him and feeding him milk and animal crackers and buying him hardcover books with bright illustrations of mountaintop castles or sailboats on the ocean at night. Never mind that I had student loans to pay off and was living with a roommate, and never mind that Derek already had a mother and that, in fact, she was one of the more intimidating figures at the shelter. She probably weighed three hundred pounds and often wore sweatpants through which you could see the cellulite on her buttocks and the back of her thighs; she pulled her hair back in a ponytail that looked painfully tight; her teeth were yellowing; her expression was unvaryingly sour. It seemed to me nothing short of miraculous that she had been the one to give birth to Derek.

Seeing him cry, I wanted simultaneously to apologize to his mother and to pull him away from her and up into my arms, to feel his little calves clamped around my waist, his head pressed between my shoulder and jaw. But I merely ducked back into the entry hall.

Downstairs, I asked loudly, "Who wants to draw?"

Several of the kids shouted, "Me!"

"And who wants to play farm animals?" I asked.

Several of the same ones shouted, "Me!"

"I suppose I can be a cow," Elsa said. "Moo!"

She looked at me expectantly, and I understood that I was supposed to laugh. "It's not acting like farm animals," I said. "It's playing with them." I gestured toward the shelf where the bin of plastic figures was stored. "Either you could do the farm animals with them, and I could do the drawing, or the other way around."

She walked to the shelf and lifted the bin. "Look at all these fabulous creatures!" she exclaimed. "Oh my goodness! There's a horse, and a chicken, and a pig. Will anyone help me play with these, or do I have to play all alone?"

Tasaundra and Na'Shell hurried over. "I'm the baby sheep," Tasaundra said. "Miss Volunteer, do I get to be the baby sheep?"

"You was the baby sheep before," Na'Shell said.

"But I called it."

"But you already was the baby sheep."

"Na'Shell, be the baby chicks," I said while I pulled the markers from the drawer beneath the sink. "There are *two* baby chicks."

"Then I want to be the baby chicks!" Tasaundra yelled.

I passed paper to Mikhail and Orlean and Dewey and to the boy whose name I hadn't been able to remember upstairs but remembered now: it was Meshaun. The paper came from the shelter's administrative office, with graphs on the back, or letters requesting funding, or information about welfare studies from 1994. Everything the kids played with was somehow second-rate—the markers were dried out, the coloring books were already colored in, the wooden puzzles were gnawed on and had pieces missing. When the boys made paper airplanes, you could see the graphs or the typed words where the wings folded up.

"And what have we here?" I heard Elsa say. "If this is a panda bear, we're living on a very unusual farm indeed. And an alligator? My heavens—perhaps the farm has a little bayou in the back."

I didn't look at her, because if I did, I feared she'd make some conspiratorial gesture at me, like winking. I wanted to say to her, "Shut up and play with the kids."

This was when Karen arrived, holding Derek's hand. "Sorry I'm late." Seeing Elsa, she added, "I'm Karen."

Elsa stood and extended her arm, and unlike me, Karen shook her hand. "I'm Elsa, and I'm finding that this is *quite* the exotic farm here at New Day House."

"Hey, Derek," I said. "Want to come make a picture?"

As I lifted him onto my lap, he reached for the black marker and said, "I'm a draw me a sword." I loved Derek's husky voice, how surprising it was in a child.

The drawing and farm animals lasted for about ten minutes. Then they built a walled town out of blocks, then Orlean knocked it over and Na'Shell began crying, then we played "Mother, may I?" until they all started cheating, and then they started chasing each other around the playroom shouting and Mikhail flicked the lights on and off, which he or someone else always did whenever things became unbearably exciting. Just before eight, during cleanup, Karen and I decided that Na'Shell had behaved the best and therefore could turn off the lights for the night. Karen and Elsa headed into the hall with the other kids, and I washed my hands while Na'Shell stood by the sink, watching me. She motioned to the inside of her elbow. "Why you do it all the way up here?"

"To be extra clean," I said. When I'd dried my hands and forearms with a paper towel, I picked her up and she flicked the light switch. Upstairs, the kids had dispersed. Na'Shell's mom, who had a skinny body and skinny eyebrows and pink eye shadow and enormous gold hoop earrings and who looked no older than fifteen, was waiting in the entry hall. I didn't know her name, or the names of any of the mothers. "Come here, baby," she said to Na'Shell. "What you got there?" Our last activity of the night had been making paper jewelry, and Na'Shell passed her mother a purple bracelet.

"Good news," Karen said. "Elsa offered to give us a ride." Karen and I always walked home together. The shelter was a few blocks east of Dupont Circle—weirdly, the building it occupied was probably worth a fortune—and Karen and I both lived about a mile away in Cleveland Park.

"I'm fine walking," I said. The thought of being inside Elsa's car was distinctly unappealing. There were probably long, dry hairs on the seats, and old coffee cups with the imprint of her lipstick.

"Don't be a silly goose," Elsa said. "I live in Bethesda, so you're on my way."

I didn't know how to refuse a second time. Her car was a two-door, and I sat in back. As Elsa pulled out of the parking lot behind the shelter, Karen said, "They're hell-raisers, huh? Have any kids yourself?"

"As a matter of fact, I just went through a divorce," Elsa said. "But we didn't have children, which was probably a blessing in disguise."

I had noticed earlier that Elsa wasn't wearing a wedding ring; it surprised me that she'd ever been married.

"I'm sorry," Karen said.

"I'm taking it day by day—that old cliché. What about you?"

"Card-carrying spinster," Karen said, and laughed.

This was a slightly shocking comment. At the volunteer training almost a year earlier, it had seemed that the majority of people there were unmarried women who probably wanted children and who were nearing the age when they'd be too old to have them. This fact was so obvious that it seemed unnecessary to ever discuss it. Plus, it made me nervous, because what I wondered was, was this the time in my own life before I found someone to love and had a family and looked back longingly on my youthful freedom? Or was it the beginning of what my life would be like forever? We were driving north on

Connecticut Avenue, and out the window it was just starting to get dark. Elsa's and Karen's voices were like a discussion between guests on a radio program playing in the background.

"And how about you?" Elsa asked.

The car was silent for several seconds before I realized she was talking to me. "I don't have any kids," I said.

"Are you married?"

In the rearview mirror, we made eye contact.

"No," I said.

"Frances is a baby," Karen said. "Guess how old she is."

Elsa furrowed her eyebrows, as if thinking very hard. "Twenty-four?"

"Close," I said. "Twenty-three."

Karen turned around. "You're twenty-three? I thought you were twenty-two."

"I was," I said. "But then I had a birthday."

I hadn't been making a joke, but they both laughed.

"Are you, like, getting school credit for being a volunteer?" Elsa asked.

"No, I've graduated."

"Where do you work?"

Normally, I felt flattered when people asked me questions. With Elsa, I was wary of revealing information. I hesitated, then said, "A graphic-design firm."

"That sounds glamorous."

"It's not."

"What's it called?"

"Artisan Design."

"Okay." Elsa nodded. "I think I've heard of them."

I doubted she had. The firm was three years old and had only six full-time staff members. Before she could ask me another question, I said, "Where do you work?"

"Right now, I'm freelancing from home. I've cut back on my hours lately, but what I do is I help nonprofits and NGOs with fundraising."

Right, I thought. *You're unemployed.*

"Like a consultant?" Karen said.

"Yep." Elsa grinned. "Answering to no one."

You're so unemployed, I thought.

After Elsa had dropped Karen off and I'd climbed into the front seat, I could not help thinking—I was now alone in an enclosed space with Elsa—that perhaps she was genuinely unbalanced. But if she were violent, I thought, she'd be violent in an insane rather than a criminal way. She wouldn't want to rob me; she'd just want to do something bizarre and pointless, like cutting off my thumb. Neither of us spoke, and in the silence, I imagined her making some creepy, telling remark: *Do you ever feel like your eyes are really, really itchy and you just want to scrape at them with a fork?*

But when she spoke, what she said was, "It's great that you're volunteering at your age. That's really admirable."

I was almost disappointed. "The kids are fun," I said.

"Oh, I just want to gobble them up. You know who's especially sweet is, who's the little boy with the long eyelashes?"

The question made my ears seize up like when you hear an unexpected noise. "I'm not sure who you're thinking of," I said. "But you can just stop here. At the next corner, by that supermarket." It suddenly seemed imperative that Elsa not know where I live.

"I'll wait if you're picking up stuff. I remember what it's like to carry groceries on foot."

"My apartment isn't far," I said. She hadn't yet come to a complete stop, but I'd opened the door and had one leg hanging out. "Thanks for the ride," I added, and slammed the door.

Without turning around, I could tell that she had not driven off.

Go, I thought. *Get out of here.* What was she waiting for? The supermarket door opened automatically, and just before it shut behind me, I finally heard her pull away. For a few minutes, I peered out the door at the street, making sure she didn't pass by again. Then I walked back out empty-handed.

At this time in my life, I spent the weekends running errands; during the week, I was often so exhausted after work that I'd go to bed at eight-thirty or quarter to nine. Then on Saturdays and Sundays, I'd hurry up and down Connecticut, to the Laundromat and the supermarket and CVS.

   Sometimes I'd pass couples eating brunch at the outdoor cafés or inside restaurants with doors that opened onto the sidewalk, and when I looked at them (I tried not to stare, but rarely did any of them look back anyway) I felt a confusion bordering on hostility. Flirting with a guy in a dark bar, at night, when you'd both been drinking—I understood the appeal. But to sit across the table from each other in the daylight, to watch each other's jaws working over pancakes and scrambled eggs, seemed embarrassing and impossible. The compromises you'd made would be so apparent, I thought; this other person before you with their patches of dry skin and protruding nose hairs and the drop of syrup on their chin and the way they spit when they talked and the boring cheerful complaints you'd make to each other about traffic or current events while the horrible sun hung over you. I could see how during the night people preferred the reassurance of another body in their bed, but in the day wouldn't you just rather be alone, both of you, so you could go back to your apartment and sit on the toilet for a while, or take a nap without someone's sweaty arm around you? Or maybe you'd just want to sit on your couch and balance your checkbook and not hear another person breathing while they read the newspaper five feet away and looked over every ten or fifteen minutes so that you had to smile back—about nothing!—and periodically utter a term of endearment.

As I ran errands, I'd wear soccer shorts from high school and T-shirts that I'd have perspired through in the back; passing by the cafés, I'd feel hulking and monstrous, and sometimes, to calm down, I would count. I always started with my right hand, one number for each finger except my pinky: thumb, *one*; index finger, *two*; middle finger, *three*; third finger, *four*. Then I'd go to the left hand, then back to the right. I knew this wasn't the most normal thing in the world, but I thought the fact that I didn't count high was a good sign. Triple digits, double digits even—then I might have worried for myself, but staying under five felt manageable. Anyway, it was like hiccups; after a few blocks, I'd realize that while I'd been thinking of something else, the impulse to count had gone away.

The following week, as soon as I entered the shelter, Elsa jumped up from the hall bench holding a grocery bag and, proffering each item for my inspection, withdrew a box of markers, a packet of construction paper, two vials of glitter, a tube of glue, and finally, a carton of tiny American flags whose poles were made of toothpicks. "The kids can make Uncle Sam hats," she said. "For the Fourth of July."

In the last week, I had decided that my initial reaction to Elsa had been unfair; she hadn't done anything that was truly all that strange or offensive. But being in her presence again, I was immediately reminded of a hyper, panting dog with bad breath.

"Then we'll have a parade," she continued. "You know, get in the spirit."

"We're not allowed to take the kids outside." Not only were we not allowed to take them outside, but if our paths should cross theirs in the normal world—if, say, I saw Tasaundra and her mother at the Judiciary Square Metro stop one day—I was not even supposed to speak to them. I also was not supposed to learn their last names.

"Inside then," Elsa said. "We'll have the first annual super-duper New Day House indoor parade. And I have an idea for next week, too. I was thinking we could do a dress-up kind of thing with old clothes and whatnot. I've been cleaning out my basement, and I found some bridesmaid dresses that I'm sure Tasaundra and Na'Shell would think are to die for. So when you go home, look in your closet and see what you have—graduation gowns, Halloween costumes. I'll swing by the Salvation Army this weekend."

I thought of my own half-empty closet. Unlike Elsa, apparently, I actually wore all my clothes.

"Now that you're here, I'll go get the kids," she said, and I watched as she walked into the dining room and said in a loud, fake-forlorn voice, "I can't find anyone to play with. Are there any fun boys or girls in here who'll be my friends?"

I imagined the mothers scowling at her, though what I heard was the screams of the kids, followed by the squeaks and thuds of their feet as they hurried across the linoleum floor to fling themselves at Elsa. I wondered if she thought that winning them over so quickly was an achievement.

In the basement—Karen arrived shortly after we'd gone down—the hat making occurred with a few glitches, most notably when Na'Shell spilled the red glitter on the floor, then wept, but it didn't go as badly as I'd hoped. "Great idea, Elsa," Karen said.

Elsa stood. "Okay, everyone," she said. "Now we're going on a parade."

"I ain't going on no stupid parade," Orlean said.

"I ain't going on no stupid parade," Tasaundra echoed.

"You guys," I said. "It's, 'I'm *not* going on *any* stupid parade.'"

"But that's why you made the hats," Elsa said. She set a cylinder of blue construction paper on top of her head—of course she had made one for herself—but it didn't fit, and she had to hold it in place. "Do I look *exactly* like Lady Liberty?"

The kids regarded her blankly.

"We need a leader for the parade, right?" Karen said.

"Oh!" Derek's eyes widened. "Miss Volunteer! Pick me!"

Pretty soon, they all had assigned positions, even Orlean and Tasaundra. They lined up in front of the door in their hats, their chins raised high in the air. As we exited the playroom—I was in the middle, holding Derek's hand—I heard singing. It was Elsa, I realized, and the song was "America the Beautiful." And she was really belting it out. Had I only imagined her twittering, inhibited persona from the week before?

We cut through the dining room, where the only person present was Svetlana, the shelter employee on duty Monday nights, who was either flaky or not fluent in English; if you asked her anything about anything, she would simply shrug. She was sitting at a table doing a crossword puzzle, and she blinked slowly at us as we walked around the periphery of the room. By then, Elsa was singing "The Star-Spangled Banner," and Mikhail was blowing a kazoo whose origins I was unsure of. From behind her, I looked at Elsa's awful hair, her cotton sleeveless sweater, which was cream-colored and cabled, and her dry and undefined upper arms.

Back in the stairwell, I saw that Elsa was not going downstairs; she was going up.

"Hey," I said.

She didn't stop.

"*Hey.*"

She looked at me over one shoulder.

"Those are the bedrooms," I said.

"So?"

"I think we should respect their privacy."

"But look how cute the kids are." Elsa leaned over and cupped Derek's chin with one hand. "What a handsome boy you are, Derek," she crooned. She straightened up and said to me, "I'm sure it's fine."

I looked at her face, and I could see that this wasn't about challenging me, that in fact, I had nothing to do with it. This really was about the parade; something in the situation had made her giddy in a way I myself had never, ever been—utterly unself-conscious and eager. Her chest rose and fell as if she'd been exercising, she was panting a little, and as she smiled, I could see her big front teeth and gums, I could see her mustache of pale hairs above her lips, her uneven skin, her bright and happy eyes. She was experiencing a moment of profound personal triumph, though nothing was occurring that was remotely profound or triumphant. It was a Monday evening; these were children; and really, underneath it all, weren't we just killing time, didn't none of it matter?

"Karen, don't you feel like we shouldn't go upstairs?" I asked.

"Ehh—I don't think anyone would mind."

I stared between them. I had felt certain that Karen would agree with me.

"Don't worry so much." Elsa punched my shoulder. "It'll give you wrinkles."

The second floor was a corridor with two rooms on either side, like a dorm, but none of the rooms had any doors. Inside the rooms were bunk beds, as many as four in a row; I knew they made the families double up. The first room on the right was empty. I glanced through the doorway on the left and saw Mikhail's mother slouched on a bottom bunk, leaning against the wall, nursing her daughter. The baby was turning her head so her mouth was not actually clamped around the nipple, and as I glanced away from the huge, pale, veiny breast, my eyes met Mikhail's mother's. Her mouth was pursed contemptuously, and her eyebrows were raised, as if to say, *So you enjoy looking at my tit?* I kept walking.

In the second room on the left, two mothers were sleeping. As I passed that doorway, continuing to follow Elsa, who was still singing, and Mikhail, who was still playing the kazoo, one of the mothers rolled over, and I hurried by—let her see someone else when she looked out to see who'd awakened her. In the last room on the right, Elsa found the audience she'd been searching for. She knocked ceremoniously on the doorframe.

"Excuse me, ladies," she said. "I have with me a group of patriots eager to show you their artistic creations. Will you permit us to enter?"

A pause followed, and then one woman said, "You want to, you can come in."

We filed into the room—there were so many of us that Karen had to remain in the hall—and I saw that Derek's mother and Orlean's mother were sitting on the floor with a basket of laundry between them and piles of folded clothes set in stacks on a lower bunk.

Derek yelled, "Mama!" and tumbled into her lap.

"Would someone like to say the Pledge of Allegiance?" Elsa looked around at the children. "Who knows the Pledge of Allegiance? 'I pledge allegiance to the flag . . .' "

" '. . . of the United States of America,' " Orlean said, but then he didn't continue; only Elsa did.

It was excruciating. When she got to the end, the room was silent, and I couldn't look at the mothers. How loud and earnest we must have seemed to them, how moronically bourgeois, clutching at their children. I started clapping, because I didn't know what else to do, and then the kids clapped, too.

It wasn't just that the mothers intimidated me; it was also that, in a strange way, they inspired my envy. I'd once heard Na'Shell and Dewey's mother having an argument on the pay phone about buying diapers, and as she yelled and cursed, I couldn't help but be impressed by her sheer forcefulness. The mothers' lives were complicated and unwieldy. They had debts and addictions, and most of all, they had children, who had come from having sex, and if sex didn't always coexist with love, well, at least it did some of the time. Even when they lived in New Day, a place where men were prohibited from entering, love found these women: romantic entanglements, problems you thought about hard while sitting on the front steps smoking. Other people were so unsuccessful in fending off love! Congressmen or senators who had adulterous affairs with their aides, or students I'd known slightly in college, girls who as freshmen declared themselves lesbians and then graduated with boyfriends—to give in to love represented, for them, a capitulation or a betrayal, yet apparently the pull was so strong that they couldn't resist. That's what I didn't understand, how people made the leap from not mattering in each other's lives to mattering.

Another thing that impressed me about the mothers was their sexiness. The really big ones like Derek's mom wore sweatpants and T-shirts, but some of the others who were twenty or thirty pounds overweight dressed in tight, revealing clothes, and they looked good: tank tops and short skirts and no stockings and high-heeled mules, gold necklaces and bracelets and rings.

Back in the playroom, Elsa beamed and giggled, and I could tell that she considered the parade an unqualified success. "Frances, are you always such a stickler for the rules?" she asked in a teasing voice.

"I guess I am." I forced a laugh. Though what happened later might make this seem like a dubious claim, I'm pretty sure I already knew then that it's not worth it to have conflict with people you aren't invested in.

"No hard feelings, right?" Elsa said. "It seemed like the moms were totally psyched to have us come through."

I said nothing, and turned away from her.

At the end of the night, when we chose Derek to turn off the lights, Elsa said, "I'll stay behind with him. You can go up."

"That's okay," I said. "I'm usually the one to stay behind."

"All the more reason for you to go up." Her tone was friendly, like she was doing me a favor.

"Actually," I said, "I prefer to stay." I was standing by the sink, and I turned on the water.

"You're doing a very thorough job," Elsa said, and I flinched. I'd thought she had left with Karen and the kids, but she was standing next to me.

"Gotta watch out for cooties," I said. "Ready, Derek?" He raised his arms, and I lifted him.

"I've noticed that you wash your hands a lot," Elsa said.

I turned and looked at her, and I could feel how my mouth was a hard line. "You're very observant," I said.

She took a step back.

I carried Derek to the light switch, and he turned it off. On the other side of the door, I set him down. He took my hand, and though my entire body was tense from the exchange with Elsa, I felt some of Derek's placidity, his sweetness, seep into me. Elsa reached for his other hand.

"Oh my," she said. "What have we here?"

"No!" Derek said. "It's mine."

I glanced down and saw that Elsa was extracting from his grip one of the piglets from the farm-animal box.

"That's not yours," Elsa said. "That belongs to all the children at New Day. Look." She held the piglet toward me. It had peach skin and pink hooves and a little curly tail, and it was arching up, its snout pointed skyward. "This pig doesn't belong to Derek, does it, Frances? If he took it, I bet the other kids would feel really sad."

I said through clenched teeth, "Let him have it."

"What?" Her voice was confused, no longer intended for Derek.

"It's not a big deal," I said.

"Don't you think that sends a confusing message?"

"It's a plastic pig," I said. "He's three." I thought of the objects I had coveted as a child: an eraser in the shape of a strawberry, which belonged to Deanna Miller, the girl who sat next to me in first grade; a miniature perfume bottle of my mother's with a round top of frosted glass. My mother had promised that she would give the bottle to me when she was finished with the perfume, but year after year, a little of the amber liquid always remained. There were not that many times in your life when you believed a possession would bring you happiness and you were actually right.

"You know what I'll do, Derek?" Elsa said. "I'll put the pig back, but I'll put it in your cubby. That way, when you come down here tomorrow, you'll know just where it is. Okay?"

I knew she would think we'd compromised, but she could compromise by herself. While she was in the playroom, I lifted Derek and carried him upstairs.

I kept waiting that week to get a call from Abigail, the New Day director, saying she'd received complaints from the mothers about our excursion to the second floor. I would apologize and take responsibility for my participation in the parade, but I'd also explain that Elsa was the one who had initiated it and that, in general, I had some concerns about her behavior as a volunteer; while eating dinner at night,

I rehearsed the way I'd phrase this. But the days kept passing without a call. By the end of the week, I still hadn't heard from Abigail, and then I knew I wasn't going to.

The next Monday was quiet. Orlean had, to the envy of everyone, gone out for pizza with his father, and Dewey didn't come downstairs because he had a cold, and Tasaundra and her mom had moved out of the shelter and gone to stay with a cousin in Prince George's County. A new girl named Marcella was there, a chubby, dreamy eight-year-old with long black hair.

Elsa's dress-up clothes went over well enough, except that the entire process, from the kids' choosing what to wear to putting on the outfits to taking the clothes back off again, took less than fifteen minutes. Elsa encouraged the kids to draw pictures of themselves in the clothes, but all anybody wanted to play was "Mother, may I?" I wondered if Elsa would keep hatching schemes week after week or if she would soon realize that from kids, you didn't get points just for trying.

While I was putting together a wooden puzzle of the United States with Marcella and Meshaun, Derek came over to the table. He said, "Miss Volunteer," and when I said, "Yes, Derek?" he giggled and ran behind my chair.

"Where's Derek?" I said. "Where did he go?"

"He behind you," Meshaun said.

I whirled around, and Derek shrieked. He tossed something into the air, and when it landed on the floor, I saw that it was the pig from the week before. He picked it up and made it walk up my arm.

Elsa squatted by Derek. "Do you like your pig?" she asked.

I couldn't help myself. "*His* pig?"

But I noticed that Elsa had that fighting-a-smile expression people get when they've received a compliment and want you to think they don't believe it. "It is his," she said. "I gave it to him."

Then I saw that the pig wasn't identical to the one from the week before—this pig's snout was pointed straight in front of it, and its skin was more pink than peach.

"I felt like such a witch taking the other one away," she said.

I stared at her. "When did you give it to him?"

"I dropped it off last week."

Knowing she had come to the shelter at a time other than Monday evening, I wondered what Abigail had made of that, or whether Elsa had met other volunteers. And had Elsa summoned Derek in order to give him the pig in private, or had she handed it over in front of other children? She should be fired, I thought, if it was possible to fire a volunteer.

That night as we left the shelter, Elsa said, "Anyone up for a beer?"

"Sounds good to me," Karen said.

"I need to be at work early tomorrow," I said. Karen and I had never socialized outside the shelter.

"Come on, gal," Karen said, and at the same time, Elsa said, "You know, Frances, I looked up your company on the Web the other day, and it seems pretty cool. My clients sometimes need graphic work, letterheads and the like, so I'm always on the lookout for people doing innovative work."

"I mostly do administrative stuff," I said.

Elsa elbowed me. "No low self-esteem, you hear? You're just starting out. Listen, I'm impressed that you even landed a job at such a great place."

I offered her my closed-lipped smile.

Elsa turned away from me. "Karen," she said, "do we have to forcibly drag this girl out for one lousy Budweiser?"

"At her age, she should be dragging us," Karen said.

"I really can't," I said. "Sorry."

As I walked away, Elsa called, "Hey, Frances," and when I turned back, she said, "Bye, Miss Volunteer." Her voice contained a singsongy, excessively pleased note that made me suspect she'd thought up the farewell earlier and saved it, for just this moment, to say aloud.

When I got back to my apartment, I again washed my hands and forearms and then I changed out of my street clothes. I knew that I washed my hands a lot—I wasn't an idiot—but it was always for a reason: because I'd come in from outside, because I'd been on the subway or used the toilet or touched money. It wasn't as if, sitting at my desk at the office, I simply jumped up, hurried to the bathroom, and began to scrub.

Usually when I got home at night, my roommate, whom I hardly knew, wasn't there. She had a boyfriend, a Romanian grad student, and she spent a lot of time at his place. It was mostly on the weekends that I saw them. Sometimes on Saturday mornings when I left to run errands, they'd be entwined on the living room couch, watching television, and when I returned hours later, they'd be in the same position. Once I saw him prepare breakfast in bed for her by toasting frozen waffles, then coating them with spray-on olive oil, and I wondered if this was an error due to the language barrier or if he was just a gross person. I was glad on the nights they weren't around. After I was finished washing my hands and changing my clothes, it was like I'd completed everything in the day that was required of me and I could just give in to being tired.

The next week, when Elsa let Karen off, I leapt from the car as well. "I'll walk from here," I said. "I need some air."

"Are you kidding me? It's ninety-five degrees." Elsa patted the seat. "Get back in."

"It's cooled down a lot since this afternoon," I said. By the time I turned toward Karen, she'd climbed the steps to her building and was reaching for the door handle. Her building was on the corner of Connecticut and Cathedral, and though I'd passed it many times — my own apartment was just a few blocks north, on Porter — I was struck as I never had been before this moment that it was just the kind of place where a moderately successful single woman in her late thirties would live: on a heavily trafficked street, with a brightly lit and tastefully appointed lobby visible through the glass door. From behind her, I said, "Karen, can I talk to you for a sec?"

She turned around. "What's cooking?"

"Has it ever occurred to you that Elsa might be a little — I don't know — unhinged?"

Karen laughed. "She marches to the beat of a different drummer, that's for sure."

"I think it goes beyond that. She seems to have really bad judgment, like with the parade. She didn't even realize how the mothers reacted."

"I thought the parade was kind of cute."

I tried not to show my surprise. Maybe the parade hadn't been the best example. "She doesn't talk to the kids on their level," I said.

I waited for Karen to react, but she was chewing on the inside corner of her lip. Even to my own ears, my assessment of Elsa sounded less like concern than gossip.

"I can picture something bad happening to one of the kids because of her," I said.

"Granted, she's eccentric," Karen said. "I take it her divorce was pretty rough and now she's putting the pieces back together." I wondered if Elsa had confided in Karen — perhaps when they'd gone out for beer. "But I'm not real concerned," Karen added. "She'll calm down in a few weeks."

So for Karen, life was unmenacing until hard evidence proved otherwise; despite her laid-back demeanor, I'd pegged her for being, at her core, a preemptive worrier like me. After all, given that she was unmarried, hadn't the world failed her already? There were many less appealing women who found husbands, so why hadn't she? Didn't she see that life could be unfair and unpredictable and that you needed to exercise some vigilance?

"You don't think I should say anything to Abigail?" I finally asked.

Karen shrugged. "I just don't know what there is to say."

It was storming the next Monday: not just rain but big rolling gray clouds split by lightning, followed by cracks of thunder that faded into softer rumbles. Abigail was peering out the front door when I arrived. She was often leaving as I was arriving, and I said, "Don't get too wet."

She shook her head. "Svetlana called in sick. I'm staying over."

"Lucky you," I said, and she grinned. Abigail was in her fifties, a woman with short silver hair who wore jumpers or long cotton skirts and had a master's degree from Harvard; I knew this because the diploma hung framed in her office, where I'd sat for an interview.

I was, apparently, the first volunteer there. When the kids came out from the dining room, Meshaun was clutching a red rubber ball, and Orlean was trying to take it away, which made Meshaun howl. "Whose ball is it?" I asked.

"Me!" Meshaun shouted.

I turned to Orlean. "Is that true?"

"Yeah, but he ain't playin' with it. He just holdin' it."

"If it belongs to him, he gets to decide what happens to it."

"Geez, woman." Orlean sighed loudly. He crossed the hall, passing Derek's mother as she emerged from the stairwell. Orlean leaned his back against the wall, folded his arms across his chest, and glared, and I tried, out of respect for his disappointment in me, not to smile.

"You know where D's at?" Derek's mother said.

"Are you talking to me?" I said. "Sorry, but I just got here."

"Monique told me she was gonna watch him while I was at the CVS, and now she says she don't know where he is."

"Derek's lost?" I stood, my heart beating faster. "If he's lost, you should tell Abigail."

As Derek's mother walked toward Abigail's office, I hurried downstairs, but the playroom was silent, and all the lights were off. "Derek?" I called. "Are you here, Derek?" I flicked the lights on and looked under the tables, behind the shelves. But I would have been able to hear him breathe, and the only sound was the drip of the sink.

When I returned upstairs, the hall was crowded with Abigail, Derek's mother, Na'Shell's mother, Na'Shell, Meshaun, and Orlean, plus Elsa and Karen had both arrived; Elsa was holding a collapsed, dripping umbrella as Abigail talked. I was glad I hadn't been present when Abigail told them Derek was missing—Elsa probably had opened her mouth, covered it with her palm, and gasped. Abigail gestured at me and Derek's mother. "I want the two of you to look outside. Elsa, you go upstairs, and Karen, you go downstairs. I know we've already checked the building, but we've got to be thorough."

I still had on a raincoat, and Elsa offered me her umbrella, which I didn't take. Despite the seriousness of the moment, it felt awkward to walk outside with Derek's mother—I wasn't sure if we were supposed to split up or stay together. I glanced at her, and her face was scrunched with anxiety.

"He couldn't have gone far, right?" I said.

"I'm gonna beat his ass when I find that boy," she said, but she sounded more frightened than mean.

We did split up—I walked toward one end of the block, turning my head from side to side and calling his name (a passerby might have thought I was calling for a puppy), then I walked to the other end of the block. The rain was falling solidly. Out on the street, the cars made swishing noises as they passed, and my stomach tightened with each one. The roads had to be slick, and the rain on the windshields would make everything blurry. It was hard to know if it was worse to imagine him alone or with someone—if he were alone, surely the thunder and lightning were terrifying him.

I walked around the side of the shelter, expecting and not expecting to see him everywhere I looked. In my mind, he was wearing what he'd been wearing the day Elsa had taken the pig away from him—a red-and-blue striped T-shirt and black sweatpants. I found his mother standing on tiptoe, peering into the Dumpster in the back parking lot and shoving aside pieces of cardboard. "You think he could have gotten in there?" I said. She didn't reply, and I said, "You know the volunteer who has kind of light brown hair and hasn't been coming here for very long?"

Without looking at me, Derek's mother said, "You mean Elsa?" If a bird had flown out of her open mouth, I would not have been more astonished.

"I think she came here a few weeks ago some night besides Monday," I said. "Right? She brought Derek a little pig?"

"I don't know nothing about that."

"I'm wondering if you've seen her here other times. Has she ever invited Derek to do stuff during the day?"

For the first time, Derek's mother looked at me, and I saw that she was on the verge of crying. "Monique's a fool," she said. "I knew I shouldn't of left her with D."

"It's not your fault," I said. "It's really not. Kids wander off."

Then her face collapsed—big, fat, scary Derek's mother—and as she brought her hands up to shield it, her shoulders shook. What I was supposed to do, what the situation unmistakably called for, was to hug her, or at the very least to set an arm around her back. I couldn't do it. She was wearing an old-looking, off-white T-shirt that said LUCK O' THE IRISH across the chest in puffy green letters and had multiple stains on it, and I just couldn't. If I did, after I got home, even if I changed out of my clothes and showered, her hug would still be on me.

"I'm sorry," I said. "I'm so sorry—I'm—by the way, I don't think we've ever been introduced. I'm Frances."

She lifted her head and looked at me, appearing bewildered. In that moment, from inside the dining room window, Karen joyously called, "We found him! Come inside, y'all! We found Derek!"

The entry hall was so thick with mothers and children that I couldn't even locate him at first, and then I saw him, before she passed him off to his mother, in Elsa's arms. On his left cheek was the imprint of a pillow or a wrinkled sheet, and he was yawning without covering his mouth. I heard Elsa say, "And then I just thought, could that little lump on the top bunk be Derek? I was on my way out, but something made me check one more time . . ."

The combination of the accumulated people, the relieved energy, and the storm outside made it seem almost like we were having a party; at any moment, a cake would appear. "You gotta watch your babies like a hawk," someone beside me said, and when I glanced over, I saw that it was Meshaun's mother. Her voice was not disapproving, but happy. "Like. A. Hawk," she repeated, nodding once for each word.

When we finally took the children down to the playroom, I couldn't shake a feeling of agitation. While Elsa was holding hands in a circle with Na'Shell and Marcella and, in an English accent, singing the *My Fair Lady* song "I Could Have Danced All Night," I said I needed to go make a phone call. Upstairs, I knocked on the frame of Abigail's open door. "Are you busy?"

"Come on in," she said.

"I have this weird feeling," I said. "Like maybe Elsa had something to do with Derek's disappearance. She's kind of obsessed with him."

"Frances, Elsa *found* Derek."

"Yeah, supposedly," I said.

"I'm not certain what you're getting at."

"She came here once in the middle of the week just to give him a present. And she showed up late tonight, which she never does." I took a breath. "I wouldn't put it past Elsa to have hidden Derek in some closet so she could be the one to find him," I said. "I just don't trust her."

For several seconds, Abigail looked at me. All she said was, "Let me think on this."

We were leaving the shelter when Abigail stuck her head out and said, "Frances and Elsa, come into my office for a minute."

She sat at her desk, and we sat in side-by-side chairs, facing her. "I understand there's some tension between the two of you," she said. "As far as I can see, you're both doing a terrific job, but I'd like to take a minute and clear the air."

I felt Elsa looking at me, and then she said, "Is this because I asked Frances about her OCD?"

I jerked toward her. "Excuse me?"

"I know that conversation we had was sort of awkward," Elsa said. "But I have a cousin who has it, and it can be treated. My cousin's on medication and now she's doing real well. It doesn't have to be this debilitating thing."

I felt that if I did not grip the arms of my chair, I might spring from it. "I'm not obsessive-compulsive," I said. "And it's none of your business."

"Frances, it's okay. It's not—"

"It's okay?" I said. "You're telling me it's okay?" I could hear my voice growing louder.

"Frances, relax," Abigail said.

"When you're the one who has no grip on reality?" I said to Elsa. "It's pretty obvious that you live in this imaginary world where you believe—you believe—" I paused. Our faces were only a few feet apart, and I saw a tiny dot of my spit land on Elsa's jaw. She didn't rub it away; she seemed paralyzed, staring at me with curiosity and confusion. "You believe that people are watching you go through your life," I said. "That if you use a big vocabulary word, someone will be impressed, or if you make a joke, someone will laugh, or that you're scoring points by buying glitter for underprivileged children because someone sees you pay for it and makes a note of how generous you are. But no one cares. Do you understand that? No one gives a shit what you do. And everyone can see how desperate and messed up you are, so you might as well just stop pretending that you—"

"This is unacceptable," Abigail said. "You're way out of line."

"Next time she'll probably kidnap Derek for good," I said. "Then tell me I'm out of line."

"Frances, an accusation like that—" Abigail began, but I cut her off. I had always respected Abigail. She had struck me as both smart and down-to-earth, and I'd admired the fact that she was devoting her career to a cause for which I spared only two hours a week. But in this moment she seemed dismissive of me because I was young, and fundamentally indifferent to what was happening. What was it to her if two of the volunteers didn't get along? I stood up.

"Forget it," I said.

I was almost out the door when Elsa said, "We just want to help you, Frances."

I whirled around. Though this was when I placed my hands on

either side of her throat, though I pressed them inward and I could feel the delicate bones of Elsa's neck beneath her warm and grotesque skin, I really didn't mean to hurt her; it's not that I was trying to *strangle* her. Her eyes had widened and she was blinking a lot, her eyelids flapping as she brought her own hands up to my wrists to pry my hands away. But that gave me something to resist. I squeezed more tightly, and she made a retching noise.

"Let go of Elsa *immediately*," Abigail said. "I'm calling the police."

It actually wasn't the threat so much as the interruption—an outside voice, a third party—that made me release my grip. Elsa coughed and panted in a way that struck me even then as theatrical. On my way out, I stopped and looked back at her once. "You're sickening," I said.

I never went back to the shelter, and I never spoke to any of them again. I received five messages at work from Abigail—I was purposely not answering my phone—and in the second one, she said they wouldn't press charges if I sent a letter from a therapist proving that I'd sought counseling. When you work for a graphic-design firm, or even, I imagine, when you don't, this is not a particularly difficult thing to fake.

Three months had passed and it was a Sunday morning when I saw Karen. Actually, what I noticed first was a couple who emerged from the bagel place near my apartment holding hands, the guy carrying a brown bag, and I watched them for a moment before I realized the woman was Karen—tall, cheerful Karen, the self-declared spinster. Was this a new development? They were talking and then he turned and kissed her on the nose; he was also black, and slightly shorter than she was. Before she could spot me, I crossed the street.

Around Christmas, I received a donation request from New Day, which, given the circumstances under which I'd stopped volunteering, was probably an oversight. New Day was affiliated with two shelters on Capitol Hill, and the request came with a calendar that said on the front *Volunteers Are Shining Stars!* For each month, the picture was of kids and adults at the various shelters playing, and Elsa was featured for the month of March. Had she been posing with Derek, the calendar would have felt karmic and punitive; in fact, she was doing a puzzle with a boy I'd never seen.

I couldn't help wondering if any of the children noticed my absence or asked where I'd gone, or if I was just another in a long line of adults who slipped without explanation from their lives. For a while, I contemplated what I'd do if I saw one of them on the street. Because of the shelter rules, it would have to be a subtle gesture, less than a wave, something a mother wouldn't notice—a wiggle of the eyebrows, a flare of the nostrils, a flickering pinky finger. In the end, it didn't matter, because I moved away from Washington without running into any of them.

As for the adults, I can't say that I cared much what Abigail or Elsa thought of me after the incident in Abigail's office, though I did regret that they must have told Karen about it. In Karen's eyes, I probably became a person she once knew who turned out to be crazy.

Selling the General

Jennifer Egan

Dolly's first big idea was the hat. She picked teal blue, fuzzy, with flaps that came down over the general's large, dried-apricot ears. The ears were unsightly, she thought, and best covered up.

When she saw the general's picture in the *Times* a few days later, she almost choked on her poached egg: he looked like a baby, a big sick baby with a giant mustache and a double chin. The headline couldn't have been worse: GENERAL B's ODD HEADGEAR SPURS CANCER RUMORS/LOCAL UNREST GROWS.

Dolly bolted to her feet in her dingy kitchen and turned in a frantic circle, spilling tea on her bathrobe. She looked wildly at the general's picture. And then she realized: the ties. They hadn't cut off the ties under the hat as she'd instructed, and a big fuzzy bow under the general's double chin was disastrous. Dolly ran barefoot into her office/bedroom and began plowing through fax pages, trying to unearth the most recent sequence of numbers she was supposed to call to reach Arc, the general's Human Relations Captain. The general moved a lot to avoid assassination, but Arc was meticulous about faxing Dolly their updated contact information. These faxes usually came at around 3:00 A.M., waking Dolly and sometimes her daughter, Lulu. Dolly never mentioned the disruption; the general and his team were under the impression that she was the top publicist in New York, a woman whose fax machine would be in an office with a panoramic view of New York City, not ten inches from the foldout sofa where she slept. Dolly could only attribute this misapprehension to some dated article that had drifted their way on Google. Or maybe the general had known four years ago that he would want a publicist eventually, and had saved old newspapers or copies of *Vanity Fair* or *In Style* or *People*, where Dolly had been written about and profiled by her then-nickname: La Doll.

The first call from the general's camp had come just in time; Dolly had hocked her last piece of jewelry. She was copyediting textbooks until 2:00 A.M., sleeping until 5:00, and then providing polite phone chitchat to aspiring English-speakers in Tokyo until it was time to wake Lulu and fix her breakfast. And all of that wasn't nearly enough to keep Lulu at Miss Rutgers's School for Girls. Often Dolly's three allotted hours of sleep were spent in spasms of worry at the thought of the next monstrous tuition bill.

And then Arc had called. The general wanted an exclusive retainer. He wanted rehabilitation, American sympathy, an end to the CIA's assassination attempts. If Qaddafi could do it, why not he? Dolly wondered seriously if overwork and lack of sleep were making her hallucinate, but she named a price. Arc began taking down her banking information. "The general presumed your fee would be higher," he said, and if Dolly had been able to speak at that moment, she would have said, *That's my weekly retainer,* hombre, *not my monthly,* or *Hey, I haven't given you the formula that lets you calculate the actual price,* or *That's just for the two-week trial period when I decide whether I want to work with you.* But Dolly couldn't speak. She was crying.

When the first installment appeared in her bank account, Dolly's relief was so immense that it almost obliterated the tiny anxious muttering voice inside her: *Your client is a genocidal dictator.* Dolly had worked for shitheads before, God knew; if she didn't take this job, someone else would snap it up; being a publicist is about not judging your clients — these excuses were lined up in formation, ready for deployment should that small dissident voice pluck up its courage to speak with any volume. But lately, Dolly couldn't even hear it.

Now, as she scuttled over her frayed Persian rug looking for the general's most recent numbers, the phone rang. It was six A.M. Dolly lunged, praying Lulu's sleep hadn't been disturbed.

"Hello?" But she knew who it was.

"We are not happy," said Arc.

"Me either," Dolly said. "You didn't cut off the—"

"The general is not happy."

"Arc, listen to me. You need to cut off the—"

"The general is not happy, Miss Peale."

"Listen to me, Arc."

"He is not happy."

"That's because—Look, take a scissors—"

"He is not happy, Miss Peale."

Dolly went quiet. There were times, listening to Arc's silken monotone, when she'd been sure she'd heard a curl of irony around the words he'd been ordered to say, like he was speaking to her in code. Now there was a long, long pause. Then Dolly spoke very softly.

"Arc, take a scissors and cut the ties off the hat. There shouldn't be a goddamned bow under the general's chin."

"He will no longer wear this hat."

"He *has* to wear the hat."

"He will not wear it. He refuses."

"Cut off the ties, Arc."

"Rumors have reached us, Miss Peale."

Her stomach lurched. "Rumors?"

"That you are not 'on top' as you once were. And now the hat is unsuccessful."

Dolly felt the negative forces pulling in around her. Standing there with the traffic of Eighth Avenue grinding past beneath her window, fingering the frizzy hair that she'd stopped coloring and allowed to grow in long and gray, she felt a kick of some deep urgency.

"I have enemies, Arc," she said. "Just like the general."

He was silent.

"If you listen to my enemies, I can't do my job. Now take out that nice silver pen I can see in your pocket every time you get your picture in the paper and write this down: '*Cut the strings off the hat. Lose the bow. Push the hat farther back on the general's head so some of his hair fluffs out in front.*' Do that, Arc, and let's see what happens."

Lulu had come into the room and was rubbing her eyes in her pink pajamas. Dolly looked at her watch, saw that her daughter had lost a half hour of sleep, and experienced a terrible inner collapse at the thought of Lulu feeling tired at school. She rushed over and put her arms around her daughter's shoulders. Lulu received this embrace with the regal bearing that was her trademark.

Dolly had forgotten Arc, but now he spoke from the phone at her neck: "I will do it, Miss Peale."

It was several weeks before the general's picture appeared in the paper again. Now the hat was pushed back and the ties were gone. The headline read, EXTENT OF B'S WAR CRIMES MAY BE EXAGGERATED, NEW EVIDENCE SHOWS.

It was the hat. He looked sweet in the hat. How could a man in a fuzzy blue hat have used human bones to pave his roads?

La Doll met with ruin on New Year's Eve three years ago, at a wildly anticipated party that was projected, by the pundits she'd considered worth inviting, to rival Truman Capote's Black and White Ball. The Party, it was called, or just the List. As in: *Is he on the list?* There were nominal hosts, all famous, but the real host, as everyone knew, was La Doll, who had more connections and access and juju than all of these people combined. And La Doll had made a very human mistake—or so she tried to soothe herself at night when memories of her demise plowed through her like a hot poker, skewering her in her sofa bed so she writhed in agony and drank brandy from the bottle— she'd thought that because she could do something very, very well (namely, get the best people in the world into one room at one time), she could do other things well, too. Like design. And La Doll had had a vision: broad, translucent trays of oil and water suspended beneath small brightly colored spotlights whose heat would make the opposing liquids twist and bubble and swirl over everyone's heads. She'd imagined people craning their necks, spellbound by the shifting liquid shapes. And they did look up. They marveled at the lighted trays; La Doll saw them do it from a small booth she'd had built high and to one side so she could view the panorama of her achievement. From there, she was the first to notice, as midnight approached, that something was going wrong with the translucent trays holding the water and oil: they were sagging a little—were they? They were slumping like sacks from their chains and *melting*, in other words.

And then the trays began to collapse, flop and drape and fall away, sending hot oil onto the heads of every glamorous person in the country and some other countries, too. They were burned, scarred, maimed in the sense that a fall of tear-shaped droplets of scar tissue on the forehead of a movie star or small bald patches on the head of an art dealer or model or generally fabulous person constitute maiming. But something shut down in La Doll as she stood there, at a safe distance from the burning oil: she didn't call 911. She watched in frozen disbelief as her guests shrieked and staggered and covered their heads, tore hot, soaked garments from their flesh, and crawled over the floor like people in medieval altar paintings whose earthly luxuries have consigned them to hell.

The accusations later: that she'd done it on purpose, that she was a sadist who stood there delighting as people suffered—were actually more terrible, for La Doll, than watching the oil pour mercilessly onto the heads of her five hundred guests. Then she'd been protected by a cocoon of shock. But what followed she had to watch in a lucid state: they hated her. They were dying to get rid of her. It was as if she weren't human, but a rat or a bug. And they succeeded. Even before she'd served her six months for criminal negligence, before the class-action suit that resulted in her entire net worth (never as large as it had seemed) being distributed in small parcels to her victims, La Doll was gone. Wiped out. She emerged from jail thirty pounds heavier and fifty years older, with wild gray hair. No one recognized her, and after a few gleeful headlines and photos of her new, ruined state, they forgot about her.

When the headlines relating to General B had definitively softened, when several witnesses against him were shown to have received money from the opposition, Arc called again. "The general pays you each month a sum," he said. "That is not for one idea only."

"It was a good idea, Arc. You have to admit."

"The general is impatient, Miss Peale," he said, and Dolly imagined him smiling. "The hat is no longer new."

That night, the general came to Dolly in a dream. The hat was gone, and he was meeting a pretty blonde outside a revolving door. The blonde took his arm and they walked inside. Then Dolly was aware of herself in the dream, sitting in a chair watching the general and his lover, thinking what a good job they were doing playing their roles. She jerked awake as if someone had shaken her. The dream nearly escaped, but Dolly caught it, pressed it to her chest. She understood: the general should be linked to a movie star.

Dolly scrambled off the sofa bed, waxy legs flashing in the street light that leaked in through a broken blind. A movie star. Someone recognizable, appealing—what better way to humanize a man who seemed inhuman? *If he's good enough for Her . . .* That was one line of thinking. And also: *The general and I have similar tastes: Her.* Or else: *She must find that triangular head of his sexy.* And even: *I wonder how the general dances?* And if Dolly could get people to ask that question, the general's image problems would be solved. Gone. It didn't matter how many thousands he'd slaughtered—if the collective vision of him could include a dance floor, all that would be behind him.

There were scores of washed-up female stars who might work, but Dolly had a particular one in mind: Pia Arten, who six or seven years ago had debuted as the nervy, stoic girlfriend of a professional football player stricken with leukemia and had stolen the movie out from under the famous male lead. She'd been nominated for Best Supporting Actress, and standing on the red carpet in a gold crushed-velvet dress, she'd been impossible to look away from. But Pia had turned out to be one of those unfortunate people who *couldn't take the bullshit*, a handicap that had resulted in perfectionism, bad be-

108   THIS IS NOT CHICK LIT

havior, and (it was rumored) occasional spectacular acts of self-
destruction: sending a bag of horse shit to an iconic male actor, yanking the baseball cap off a balding director's head and tossing it into an
airplane propeller. No one would hire Pia anymore, but the public
would remember her. That was what mattered to Dolly.

Pia wasn't hard to find; no one was putting much energy into pro-
tecting her. By noon, Dolly had reached her: weary-sounding, smoking audibly. Pia heard Dolly out, asked her to repeat the generous fee
she'd quoted, then paused. In that pause, Dolly detected a familiar mix
of desperation and squeamishness. She felt a queasy jab of pity for the
actress, whose choices had boiled down to this one. Then Pia said yes.

Singing to herself, wired on cappuccino made on her old Krups
machine, Dolly called Arc and laid out her plan.

"The general does not enjoy American movies," came Arc's re-
sponse.

"Who cares? *Americans* know who she is."

"The general has very particular tastes," Arc said. "He is not flexible."

"He doesn't have to touch her, Arc. He doesn't have to speak to
her. All he has to do is stand near her and get his picture taken. And
he has to smile."

"Smile?"

"He has to look happy."

"The general rarely smiles, Miss Peale."

"He wore the hat, didn't he?"

There was a long pause. Finally Arc said, "You must accompany
this actress. Then we will see."

"Accompany her where?"

"Here. To us."

"Oh, Arc."

"You must," he said.

Entering Lulu's bedroom, Dolly felt like Dorothy waking up in Oz: everything was in color. A pink shade encircled the overhead lamp. Pink gauzy fabric hung from the ceiling. Pink winged princesses were stenciled onto the walls: Dolly had learned how to make the stencils at a jailhouse art class and had spent days decorating the room while Lulu was at school. Long strings of pink beads hung from the ceiling. When she was home, Lulu emerged from her room only to eat.

She was part of an intricate weave of girls at Miss Rutgers's School, a mesh so fine and scarily intimate that even her mother's flameout and jail sentence (during which Lulu's grandmother had come from Minnesota to live with her) couldn't dissolve it. It wasn't thread holding these girls together, it was wire. And Lulu was the steel rod around which the wires were wrapped. Overhearing her daughter on the phone with her friends at night, Dolly was awed by her authority: stern when she needed to be, but also soft. Sweet. Lulu was nine.

She sat in a pink beanbag chair, doing homework on her laptop and IM-ing her friends (since the general, Dolly had been paying for wireless). "Hi, Dolly," she said, having stopped using *Mom* when Dolly got out of jail nine months ago. Lulu narrowed her eyes at her mother like it was hard to see her. And Dolly did feel like a black-and-white intrusion into this bower of color, a refugee from the dinginess surrounding it.

"I have to take a business trip," she said. "To visit a client. I thought you might want to stay with one of your friends so you won't miss school."

School was where Lulu's life took place. She'd been adamant about not allowing her mother, who once had been a fixture at Miss

Rutgers's, to jeopardize Lulu's status with her new disgrace. Nowa-days, Dolly dropped Lulu off around the corner, peering around dank Upper East Side stone to make sure she got safely in the door. At pickup time, Dolly waited in the same spot while Lulu dawdled with her friends outside school, toeing the perfectly manicured bushes and (in spring) flower beds, completing whatever transactions were required to affirm and sustain her power. When Lulu had a playdate, Dolly came no farther than the lobby to retrieve her. Lulu would emerge from an elevator flushed, smelling of perfume or freshly baked brownies, take her mother's hand, and walk with her past the doorman into the night. Not in apology—Lulu had nothing to apologize for—but in sympathy that things had to be so difficult for both of them.

Lulu cocked her head, curious. "A business trip. That's good, right?"

"It is good, absolutely," Dolly said a little nervously. Lulu knew nothing of the general.

"How long will you be gone?"

"A few days. Four, maybe."

There was a long pause. Finally Lulu said, "Can I come?"

"With me?" Dolly was startled. "Can you—but you'd have to miss school."

Another pause. Lulu was performing some mental calculation that might have involved measuring the peer impact of missing school versus being a guest in someone's home, or the question of whether you could manage an extended stay at someone's home without that someone's parents speaking with your mother. Dolly couldn't tell. Maybe Lulu didn't know herself.

"Where?" Lulu asked.

Dolly was flustered; she'd never been much good at saying no to Lulu. But the thought of her daughter and the general in one loca-tion made her throat clamp. "I—I can't tell you that."

Lulu didn't protest. "But Dolly?"

"Yes, darling?"

"Can your hair be blond again?"

They waited for Pia Arten in a lounge by a private runway at Kennedy Airport. When the actress finally arrived, dirty-haired, reeking of smoke, dressed in jeans and a faded yellow sweatshirt, Dolly was assailed with regrets—she should have met Pia first! The girl looked too far gone, too spent; people might not even recognize her! While Lulu used the bathroom, Dolly hastily laid things out for the actress: no mention of the general's name in front of Lulu; look as glamorous as possible (Dolly glanced at Pia's small, beaten suitcase); cozy up to the general with some serious PDA while Dolly took pictures with a hidden camera. She had a real camera, too, but that was a prop.

They boarded the general's plane at dusk. After takeoff, Pia ordered a double martini from the general's airline hostess, sucked it down, reclined her seat to a horizontal position, pulled a sleep mask (the only thing on her that looked new) over her eyes, and commenced to snore. Lulu leaned over her, studying the actress's worn, delicate face. "Is she sick?"

"No." Dolly sighed. "Maybe. I don't know."

"I think she needs a vacation," Lulu said.

Twenty checkpoints presaged their arrival at the general's compound. At each, two soldiers with submachine guns peered suspiciously into the black Mercedes with Dolly and Lulu and Pia in the backseat. Four times, they were forced outside into the scouring sunshine and patted down at gunpoint. Each time, Dolly cringed on Lulu's behalf, searching her daughter's studied calm for signs of trauma. In the car Lulu sat perfectly straight, pink Kate Spade book bag nestled in her lap. She met the eyes of the machine-gun holders with the same even look she must have used to stare down the many girls who had tried in vain, over the years, to unseat her.

High white walls enclosed the road. They were lined with hundreds of plump shiny black birds whose long purple beaks curved like scythes. Dolly had never seen birds like these. They looked like birds who would screech, but each time a car window slid down to accommodate another squinting gunslinger, Dolly was surprised by the silence.

Eventually a section of wall swung open, and the car veered off the road and pulled to a stop in front of a massive compound: lush green gardens, a sparkle of water, a white house whose end was nowhere in sight. The birds squatted along its roof, looking down.

Their driver opened the car doors, and Dolly and Lulu and Pia stepped out into the sun. Dolly felt it on her neck, newly exposed by a discount version of her trademark blond chin-length cut. The heat forced Pia out of her soiled sweatshirt, which mercifully revealed a clean white T-shirt underneath. Dolly noticed marks on Pia's bare arms: small pink scars. "Pia, are those . . ." She faltered. "On your arms, are they . . . ?"

"Burns," Pia said. And she gave Dolly a look that made her stomach twist until she remembered very dimly, like something that had happened in a fog or when she was a child, someone asking her — begging her, actually — to put Pia on the list, and telling them no. No way, it was out of the question — Pia's stock was too low.

"I did it myself," Pia said.

Dolly stared at her, uncomprehending. This made Pia grin, and for a second she looked mischievous and young. "Lots of people have, Dolly. You didn't know?"

Dolly wondered if this might be a joke. She didn't want to fall for it in front of Lulu.

"You can't find a person who wasn't at that party. And they've got proof. We've all got proof—who's gonna say we're lying?"

"I know who was there," Dolly said. "I've still got the list in my head."

"You?" Pia said, smiling at Dolly. "Who are you?"

Dolly was quiet. She felt Lulu's gray eyes on her.

Pia did something unexpected then: she reached through the sunlight and took Dolly's hand. Her grip was warm and firm, like a man's. Dolly was startled to feel a prickling in her eyes.

"It's bigger than all of us," Pia said tenderly. "That's the horror of it."

A trim, compact man in a beautifully cut suit emerged from the compound to greet them: Arc. The sight of him eased the tension that had been building in Dolly.

"Miss Peale. We meet at last," he said with a smile. "And Miss Arten"—he turned to Pia, who looked even scruffier beside the meticulous Arc—"it is a great honor as well as a pleasure." He kissed Pia's hand with a slightly teasing look, Dolly thought. "I have seen all of your movies," Arc said. "The general and I watched them together."

Dolly steeled herself for what Pia might say, but her answer came in a sweet voice that was like a child's, except for the slight curve of flirtation. "Oh, I'm sure you've seen better movies," she said.

"The general was impressed."

"Well, I'm honored. I'm honored that the general found them worth watching." Dolly glanced at the actress, expecting mockery. But Pia looked humble, absolutely sincere.

"Alas, I have unfortunate news," Arc said. "The general has had to make a sudden trip." They stared at him. "It is very regrettable," he went on. "The general sends his sincere apologies."

"But we . . . can we go to where he is?" Dolly asked.

"Perhaps," Arc said. "You will not mind some additional travels?"

"Well," Dolly said, glancing at Lulu. "It depends how—"

"Absolutely not," Pia interrupted. "We'll go wherever the general wants us to go. We'll do what it takes. Right, kiddo?"

Lulu was slow to connect the diminutive *kiddo* to herself. It was the first time Pia had spoken to her directly. Lulu glanced at the actress, then smiled. "Right," she said.

They would leave for a new location the next morning. Arc offered to drive them into the city that evening, but Pia wasn't interested. "Forgive my lack of curiosity," she said as they settled into their two-bedroom suite, which opened onto a private swimming pool. "But I'd rather enjoy these digs. They used to put me up in places like this." She gave a bitter laugh.

"Just don't overdo it," Dolly said as Pia headed for the wet bar.

Pia turned. "Hey. How was I out there, Mamacita? Any complaints so far?"

"You were excellent," Dolly said, then added softly, so Lulu wouldn't hear, "Just don't forget who we're dealing with."

"I want to forget," Pia said, pouring herself a drink. "I'm trying to forget, aren't you?" She raised her glass to Dolly and took a sip.

So Dolly and Lulu rode alone with Arc in his charcoal-gray Jaguar, a driver peeling downhill along tiny streets, sending pedestrians lunging against walls and darting into doorways to avoid being crushed. The city shimmered below: millions of white slanted buildings steeping in a smoky haze. Soon they were surrounded by it. The city's chief source of color seemed to be the laundry flapping on every balcony.

The driver pulled over beside an outdoor market: mounds of

sweating fruit and fragrant nuts and fake leather purses. Dolly eyed the produce critically as she and Lulu followed Arc among the stalls. The oranges and bananas were the largest she'd seen, but the meat looked dangerous. Dolly could see from the careful nonchalance of vendors and customers alike that they knew who Arc was.

"Is there anything you would like to buy?" Arc asked Lulu.

"Yes, please," Lulu said, "one of those." It was a starfruit. Dolly had seen them at Dean & DeLuca a few times. Here they lay in obscene heaps, studded with flies. Arc took one, nodding curtly at the vendor, an older man with a knobby chest and a kind, worried face. The man smiled, nodding eagerly at Dolly and Lulu, and Dolly was taken aback to see that he looked afraid. As if she could hurt him. As if she would ever do such a thing.

Lulu took the dusty, unwashed fruit, cleaned it carefully on her shirt, and sank her teeth into its bright green rind. Juice sprayed her collar. She laughed and wiped her mouth on her hand. "Mom, you have to try this," she said, and Dolly took a bite. She and Lulu shared the starfruit, licking their fingers under Arc's watchful eyes. Dolly felt oddly buoyant. Then she realized why: *Mom.* It was the first time Lulu had used the word in nearly a year.

Arc led the way inside a tea shop. A group of men hastened away from a corner table to give them a place to sit, and a forced approximation of the café's former happy bustle resumed. A waiter poured sweet mint tea into their cups with a shaking hand. Dolly tried to give him a reassuring look, but his eyes fled hers.

"Do you do this often?" she asked Arc. "Walk around the city?"

"The general makes a habit of moving among the people," Arc said. "He wants them to feel his humanity, to witness it. Of course, he must do this very carefully."

"Because of his enemies."

Arc nodded. "The general unfortunately has many enemies. Today, for example, there were threats to his home, and it was necessary to relocate. He does this often, as you know."

Dolly nodded. *Threats to his home?*

Arc smiled. "His enemies believe he is there, but he is far away."

Dolly glanced at Lulu. The starfruit had left a shiny ring around her mouth. "But . . . we're there," she said.

"Yes," Arc said. "Only us."

Dolly lay awake most of that night, listening to coos and rustles and squawks that sounded like assassins prowling the grounds in search of the general and his cohort: herself, in other words. She had become the helpmate and fellow target of General B, a source of fear to those he ruled.

How had it come to this? As usual, Dolly found herself revisiting the moment when the plastic trays first buckled and the life she had relished for so many years poured away. But tonight, unlike countless other nights when Dolly tipped down that memory chute, Lulu lay across from her in the king-sized bed, asleep in a frilly pink nightie, her doe's knees tucked under her. Dolly felt the warmth of her daughter's body, this child of her middle age, of an accidental pregnancy resulting from a fling with a movie-star client. Lulu believed her father was dead; Dolly had shown her pictures of an old boyfriend.

She slid across the bed and kissed the side of Lulu's face. It had made no sense at all to have a child—Dolly was pro-choice, riveted to her career. Her decision had been clear, yet she'd hesitated to make the appointment—hesitated through morning sickness, mood swings, exhaustion. Hesitated until she knew, with a shock of relief and terrified joy, that it was too late.

Lulu stirred and Dolly moved closer, enclosing her daughter in her arms. In contrast to when she was awake, Lulu relaxed into her mother's touch. Dolly felt a swell of irrational gratitude toward the general for providing this one bed—it was such a rare luxury to hold her daughter this way, to feel the faint tap of her heartbeat.

"You know I'll always protect you," Dolly whispered into Lulu's fragile ear. "Nothing bad will ever happen to us."

Lulu slept on.

The next day they piled into two black armored cars that resembled jeeps, only heavier. Arc and some soldiers went in the first car, Dolly and Lulu and Pia in the second. Sitting in the backseat, Dolly thought she could feel the weight of the car shoving them into the earth. She was exhausted, full of dread.

Pia had undergone a staggering transformation since the day before: she'd washed her hair, put on full makeup, and slipped into a gold crushed-velvet dress Dolly instantly recognized as the one she'd worn to the Academy Awards years ago, after her first movie. The gold fabric of the dress brought out flecks of gold in Pia's eyes. The effect was beyond anything Dolly could have hoped for. She found Pia oddly painful to look at.

They breezed through the checkpoints and soon were on the open road, circling the pale city from above. Dolly noticed vendors by the roadside. Often they were children, who held up handfuls of fruit or cardboard signs to the jeeps as they approached. When the vehicles flew past, the children fell back against the embankment, as if knocked down by the force of their speed. Dolly let out an involuntary cry the first time she saw this and leaned forward, wanting to say something to the driver. But what exactly? She hesitated, then sat back and tried not to look at the windows. Lulu watched the children, her math book open in her lap.

It was a relief when they left the city behind and began driving through empty land that looked like desert: antelopes and cows nibbling the stingy plant life. Without asking permission, Pia began to smoke, exhaling through a thin slit of open window before tossing out the butt. "So, kiddo," she said, turning to Lulu. "What big plans are you hatching?"

"You mean . . . for my life?" Lulu asked.

"Absolutely."

"I don't know," Lulu said, thoughtful. "I'm only nine."

"Well, that's sensible."

"Lulu is very sensible," Dolly said.

"But what do you *imagine* for yourself, that's what I'm asking," Pia said. She was restless, fidgeting her dry, manicured fingers as if she wanted another cigarette but was making herself wait. "Or do kids not do that anymore."

Lulu, in her wisdom, seemed to divine that what Pia really wanted was to talk. "What did you imagine for yourself," she asked, "when you were nine?"

Pia suddenly laughed. "I wanted to become a movie star."

"And then you did."

Pia lit a fresh cigarette. "I did," she said, closing her eyes as she exhaled. "I did."

Lulu turned to her gravely. "Was it not as fun as you thought?"

Pia opened her eyes. "The acting? God, I could do it every minute. Every second. But I hated the people."

"How come?"

"They were phony. They lied constantly. And when you got through all the phoniness and the lying, it turned out they were mean."

Lulu nodded as if this was something she knew all about. "Did you try lying too?"

Pia laughed. "I did, actually. I tried it a lot. But whenever I pulled it off, I had this urge to put a gun in my mouth. That's what's called a no-win situation, kiddo."

"I don't want to be an actress," Lulu said. "I don't like having to say the same thing again and again."

Pia glanced at Dolly. "Where did you get this kid?"

They drove and drove. Lulu did math. Then social studies. She wrote an essay on owls. After what felt like hundreds of miles of desert, punctuated by bathroom stops at outposts patrolled by soldiers, they tilted up into the hills. The foliage grew dense, filtering out the sunlight.

Without warning, the cars swung off the road and stopped. Dozens of solders in camouflage seemed to materialize from the trees. Dolly and Lulu and Pia stepped out of the car into a jungle crazed with birdcalls.

Arc appeared. "The general is waiting," he said. "He is eager to greet you."

Everyone moved as a group through the jungle. The earth under their feet was soft and red. Monkeys scuttled in the trees. Eventually they reached a set of crude concrete steps built into the side of a hill. More soldiers appeared, and there was a creak and grind of boots on concrete as all of them climbed. Dolly kept her hands on Lulu's shoulders. She heard Pia humming behind her: not a tune, just the same two notes repeated.

The hidden camera was ready in Dolly's purse. As they climbed the steps, she took out the activator and held it in her palm.

At the top of the stairs the jungle had been cleared away to accommodate a slab of concrete that might have been a landing pad. Sunlight poured down through the humid jungle air, making wisps of steam at their feet. The general stood in the middle of the concrete, flanked by soldiers. He looked short, but that was always true of famous people. He wasn't wearing the blue hat, or any hat, and his hair was thick and unruly around his grim triangular face. He wore his usual military regalia, but something about it all seemed slightly askew, or in need of cleaning. The general looked tired — there were pouches under his eyes. He looked grumpy. He looked like someone had just yanked him out of bed and said, "They're here," and he'd had to remind himself of who the hell they were talking about.

There was a strange, short pause when no one seemed to know what to do.

Then Pia reached the top of the stairs. Dolly heard the humming behind her, but she didn't turn to look; instead, she watched the general recognize Pia, watched the power of that recognition move across his face in a look of appetite and uncertainty. Pia came toward him slowly — poured toward him, really, that was how smoothly she moved in her gold dress, like the jerking awkwardness of walking was something she'd never experienced. She poured toward the general and took his hand as if to shake it, smiling, circling him a little, seeming embarrassed to the point of laughter, like they knew each other too well to shake hands. Dolly was so taken by the strangeness of it all that at first she didn't think to shoot; she missed the handshake completely. It was only when Pia pressed her narrow gold body to the general's uniformed chest and closed her eyes for a moment that Dolly came to — *click* — and the general seemed disconcerted, unsure what to do, patting Pia's back out of politeness — *click* — at which point Pia took both his hands (heavy and warped, the hands of a bigger man) into her own slender hands and leaned back, smiling into his face — *click* — laughing a little, shyly, her head back like it was all so silly, so self-conscious-making for them both. And then the general smiled. It happened without warning: his lips pulled open and away to reveal two rows of small yellow teeth — *click* — that made him appear vulnerable, eager to please. *Click, click, click* — Dolly was shooting as fast as she could without moving her hand, because that smile was *it*, the thing no one had seen, the hidden human side of the general that would stun the world.

All this happened in the span of a minute. Not a word had been spoken. Pia and the general stood hand in hand, both a little flushed, and it was all Dolly could do not to scream, because they were done! She had what she needed! She felt a mix of awe and love for Pia, this miracle, this genius who had not merely posed with the general but tamed him. That was how it felt to Dolly now—like there was a one-way door between the general's world and Pia's, and she'd eased him across it without his even noticing. He couldn't go back! And Dolly had made this happen—for once in her life, she had done a helpful thing. And Lulu had seen it.

Pia's face still held the winsome smile she'd been wearing for the general. Dolly watched her scan the crowd, taking in the dozens of soldiers with their automatic weapons, Arc and Lulu and Dolly with her ecstatic shining face, her brimming eyes. And Pia must have known then that she'd pulled it off, engineered her own salvation, clawed her way back from oblivion and cleared the way to resume the work she loved more than anything. All with a little help from the dictator to her left.

"So," Pia said, "is this where you bury the bodies?"

The general glanced at her, not understanding. Arc stepped quickly forward, as did Dolly. Lulu came too.

"Do you bury them here, in pits," Pia asked the general in the most friendly, conversational voice, "or do you burn them first?"

"Miss Arten," Arc said, with a tense, meaningful look, "the general cannot understand you."

The general wasn't smiling anymore. He was not a man who could tolerate not knowing what was going on. He'd let go of Pia's hand and was speaking sternly to Arc.

Lulu was yanking Dolly's hand. "Mom," she hissed, "make her stop!"

Her daughter's voice jerked Dolly out of a momentary paralysis. "Knock it off, Pia," she said.

"Do you eat them?" Pia asked the general, "or do you leave them out so the vultures can do it?"

"Shut up, Pia," Dolly said, more loudly. "Stop playing games."

The general spoke harshly to Arc, who turned to Dolly. His forehead was visibly moist. "The general is becoming angry, Miss Peale," he said. There was the code; Dolly read it clearly. She went to Pia and took hold of her bare arm. She leaned close to Pia's face.

"If you keep this up," Dolly said softly, "we will die."

But one glance into Pia's pained, broken eyes told her it was hopeless; Pia couldn't stop.

"Oops!" Pia said loudly, in mock surprise. "Was I not supposed to bring up the genocide?"

Here was a word the general knew. He flung himself away from Pia as if she were on fire, commanding his solders in a strangled voice. They shoved Dolly away, knocking her to the ground. When she looked back at Pia, the soldiers had contracted around her, and the actress was hidden in their midst.

Lulu was shouting, trying to drag Dolly onto her feet: "Mommy, do something, do something! Make it stop!"

"Arc," Dolly called, but Arc was lost to her now. He'd taken his place beside the general, who was screaming with rage. The soldiers were carrying Pia; Dolly had an impression of kicking from within their circle. She could still hear Pia's voice:

"Do you drink their blood, or just use it to mop up your floors?"

"Do you wear their teeth on a string?"

There was the sound of a blow, then a cry. Dolly jumped to her feet. But Pia went on, unbowed. "I hope they haunt you," she bellowed hoarsely. "I hope they visit you in your sleep."

And then she was gone; the soldiers took her through the door of some structure nestled in the trees beside the landing pad. The general and Arc followed them in. The jungle was eerily silent: just parrot calls, and Lulu's sobs.

It was because of Arc that Dolly and Lulu got out. While the general raged, Arc whispered orders to two soldiers, and when the general was out of sight they hustled Dolly and Lulu down the hill through the jungle and back to the cars. The drivers were waiting, smoking cigarettes. During the ride Lulu lay with her head in Dolly's lap, sobbing as they sped back through the jungle and then the desert. Dolly rubbed her daughter's soft hair, wondering in a numb, helpless way if they were being taken to prison. But eventually, as the sun leaked toward the horizon, they found themselves at the airport. The general's plane was waiting. By then, Lulu had sat up and moved across the seat.

Lulu slept hard during the flight, clutching her Kate Spade bag. But Dolly didn't sleep. She stared straight ahead at Pia's empty seat.

In the dark of early morning, they took a taxi from Kennedy to Hell's Kitchen. Neither of them spoke. Dolly was surprised to find their building intact, the apartment still at the top of the stairs, the keys in her pocket. It hardly seemed possible.

Lulu went straight to her room and shut the door. Dolly sat in her office, addled from lack of sleep, and tried to organize her thoughts. Should she start with the embassy? Congress? How long would it take to get someone on the phone who could actually help her? And what would she say?

Lulu emerged from her room in her school uniform, hair

brushed. Dolly hadn't even noticed it was light. Lulu looked askance at her mother, still in yesterday's clothes, and said, "It's time to go."

"You're going to school?"

"Of course I'm going to school. What else would I do?"

They took the subway. The silence between them had become inviolable; Dolly feared it would never end. Watching Lulu's wan, pinched face, she felt a cold wave of conviction: if Pia died, Lulu would be lost to her.

At their corner, Lulu turned without saying good-bye.

Shopkeepers were lifting their metal gates on Lexington Avenue. Dolly bought a cup of coffee and drank it on the corner. She wanted to be near Lulu. She decided to wait on that corner until her daughter's school day had ended: five and a half more hours. Meanwhile, she would make calls on her cell phone. But Dolly was distracted by thoughts of Pia in the gold dress, oil burns winking on her arms, then her own insane pride, thinking she'd made the world a better place. The memory made her sick.

The phone was idle in her hand. These were not the sorts of calls she knew how to make.

When the gate directly behind her shuddered up, she saw that it was a two-hour photo shop. The hidden camera with its roll of film was still in her purse. It was something to do; she opened the door and went in.

She was still standing outside the shop an hour later when the guy came out with her pictures. By then she'd made a few calls about Pia, but no one seemed to take her seriously. *Who could blame them?* Dolly thought.

"These, uh . . . did you use Photoshop or—or what?" the guy asked. "They look, like, totally real."

"They *are* real," she said. "I took them myself."

The guy laughed. "Come on," he said, and Dolly felt a shudder deep in her brain.

What else would I do?

She rushed back home and called her old contacts at the *Enquirer* and the *Star*, a few of whom were still there. Let the news trickle up. This had worked for Dolly before.

Soon a messenger arrived at her apartment to pick up the prints. Within a couple of hours, images of General B nuzzling Pia Arten were being posted and traded on the Web. By nightfall, reporters from the major papers around the world had started calling. They called the general, too, whose Human Relations Captain emphatically denied the rumors.

That night, while Lulu did homework in her room, Dolly ate cold sesame noodles and set out to reach Arc. It took fourteen tries.

"We can no longer speak, Miss Peale," he said.

"Arc."

"We cannot speak. The general is angry."

"Listen to me."

"The general is angry, Miss Peale."

"Is she alive, Arc? That's all that matters."

"She is alive."

"Thank God." Tears filled Dolly's eyes. "Is she—are they—treating her okay?"

"She is unharmed, Miss Peale," Arc said. "We will not speak again." They were silent, listening to the hum of the overseas connection. "It is a pity," Arc said, and hung up.

But Dolly and Arc did speak again. Months later—a year, almost—when the general visited Washington and then came to New York to speak at the UN about transitioning to democracy. Dolly and Lulu had moved away from the city by then, but they drove into Manhattan one night to meet Arc at a restaurant. He wore a black suit and a wine-colored tie. He seemed to savor retelling the story, as if he'd memorized its details especially for Dolly: how three or four days after she and Lulu had left the general's redoubt, the photographers began showing up, first one or two whom the soldiers ferreted out of the jungle and imprisoned, then more, too many to capture or even locate—they were superb hiders, crouching like monkeys in the trees, burying themselves in shallow pits, camouflaging themselves in leaves. Assassins had never managed to locate the general with any precision, but the photographers did: scores of them surging across the borders without visas, curled in baskets and wine casks, rolled up in rugs, juddering over unpaved roads in the backs of trucks and eventually surrounding the general's enclave, which he didn't dare leave.

It took ten days to persuade the general he had no choice but to face his inquisitors. He donned his military coat with the medals and epaulettes, pulled the blue hat over his head, took Pia's arm, and walked with her into the phalanx of cameras awaiting him. Dolly remembered how startled the general had looked in those pictures, newly born in his soft blue hat, unsure how to proceed. Beside him Pia was smiling, wearing a dress Dolly hadn't seen before, black and close-fitting. Her eyes were hard to read, but each time Dolly looked at them, rubbing her gaze obsessively over the newsprint, she heard Pia's laugh in her ears.

"Have you see Miss Arten's new movie?" Arc asked. "I thought it was her finest yet."

Dolly had seen it: a romantic comedy that showed Pia in an easy, footloose mode. She'd gone with Lulu to the local theater in the small upstate town where they'd moved shortly after the other generals began to call: first G, then A, then L and P and Y. Word had gotten out, and Dolly was deluged with offers of work from mass murderers eager for a fresh start. "I'm out of the game," she'd told them all, and directed them to her former competitors.

Lulu had opposed the move at first, but Dolly was firm. And Lulu had settled in quickly at the local public school, where she took up soccer and found a new coterie of girls who seemed to follow her everywhere. No one in town had ever heard of La Doll, which meant Lulu had nothing to hide.

Dolly had received a generous lump sum from the general shortly after his rendezvous with the photographers. "A gift to express our immense gratitude for your invaluable expertise, Miss Peale," Arc had said over the telephone, but Dolly had heard the smile and understood: hush money. She used it to open a small gourmet shop on Main Street, where she sold fine produce and unusual cheeses, artfully displayed and lit by a system of small spotlights Dolly had designed herself. "This feels like Paris," was a comment she often heard from New Yorkers who came on weekends to visit their country houses.

Now and then Dolly would get a shipment of starfruit, and she always made sure to put a few aside to eat with Lulu. She would bring them to the small house they shared at the end of a quiet street. After supper, the radio on, windows open to the night, she and Lulu would feast on the sweet, strange flesh.

The Seventy-two-Ounce
Steak Challenge

Dika Lam

Years before my sister Allie became the champion you know and
love—winner of the International Matzo-Ball-Eating Contest, title-
holder of the Conch Fritter Invitational, the girl who downed nine
sticks of butter in five minutes—she binged her way through a dinner
dare that became her finest hour (and my longest).

Allie had moved back to Toronto that May. She had dropped out
of her biology program at the University of British Columbia for the
usual reasons—boredom, problems with authority, and an unscrupu-
lous lab partner who stole her transfer pipette—but she had also discovered that she was not made for science, and to admit that she
missed the point of higher education was not very Chinese. By then,
the Toronto travel magazine that had hired me to pen captions and

reject unsolicited manuscripts had finally decided to send me some-
place that might actually give me jet lag; when our mother found out
I was going to Alberta to cover the annual rodeo extravaganza known
as the Calgary Stampede, she urged me to take Allie along.

"She likes cowboy boots," my mother said, as if this were a weakness to add to my sister's MedicAlert bracelet. "I'll pay for her ticket."
She pressed a check into my palm, wildly inflating the airfare by several hundred dollars. The amount looked even more absurd against
a background of soft-focus puppies, one of those sample designs at
the back of the book. I thought of all the checks she'd handed over
when I was little so I could pay the hydro bill or fix supper when
adult supervision remained several subway stops away.

As I sat downstairs in my parents' kitchen, pondering Ma's latest
bribe, the youngster with no future napped upstairs in our old bedroom. In the past three years, she had learned how to identify five
types of Pacific salmon, but she had never learned how to unpack.
Her suitcase lay wounded on the floor. Our bunk beds were long
gone, but I could see the gouges left in the moth-colored carpet.
Our mother had given up on the carpet, but not on her youngest
daughter.

"Cecilia," she said, "this might be a good time to talk some sense
into her. Find out what her plans are." She did not ask whether my
husband, Lewis, would be joining us.

"You know, this *is* a working trip," I said, irked at the lack of
praise. This was my first major assignment. I had already photo-
copied my driver's license, hidden my credit-card numbers in three
places, and laminated my permanent packing list, which was divided
into categories: beach, city, ski, and summer/rural. I was excited to go
west because I'd already resigned myself to the likelihood of spending my twenties in a cubicle, with glorious postcards tacked to the
walls to remind me of a world unilluminated by fluorescent light.

After I told Lewis my plans, he left the business card of an associate taped to the phone. The note read, *Since you've never been to Calgary, you've got to call this guy. He'll tell you where to go.*

I waited until I was jetbound, thirty thousand feet above Saskatchewan, before abandoning the card in the seat-back pocket.

I had been talking sense into Allie my entire life. Our parents clocked impossible hours at the family fabric store; whenever they shambled into the apartment and spotted us, they grunted with confusion. They acted as if my sister spoke the Shanghainese dialect and I was the only translator, particularly during Allie's bouts of severe asthma. When she was ten and I was thirteen, she caught pneumonia and ended up in an oxygen tent, refusing to take her medicine. Ma and Ba threatened force.

I said, "I'll bet the medicine tastes like shit. She needs a chaser." For once, they didn't scold me for saying "shit." They didn't ask how "chaser" came to live in my vocabulary. They were too busy peering through the plastic curtain that encircled the bed, checking to see if Allie was still there. Droplets of water clung to the inside of the tent, obscuring her round face; she reminded me of one of those collector's dolls that are never removed from the box. Her tiny hand cleared a window in the plastic; I thought I could see her waving.

I prescribed the Crispy Crunch bar in my backpack. "She also likes Coffee Crisp," I said. "And Popsicles."

Our father began to take notes. Our mother rolled her eyes.

Later, Allie scribbled *Thank you* on the chocolate wrapper (that she wasn't supposed to talk was the only aspect of her condition that resembled a blessing). To amuse ourselves, we compiled reviews of her various drugs: *If a rock could fart, it would taste like Ventolin,* she wrote.

Every day after school, I took the streetcar to the Hospital for Sick

Children, pulled up a chair, and listened to her breathe. I learned every note of this horrible music, what our father called the jungle of bad lungs—the birdcalls, the wheezy thunder—dreading the loneliness of the empty bunk above me.

At the Calgary airport, we fought over the rental car, but I came to appreciate Allie's insistence on a convertible. The wind kissed our bare arms as we cruised past the headquarters of oil companies and the Romanesque leftovers of downtown, the Rockies thumping out their ancient EKG in the distance.

But we hadn't trekked to the prairie for urban pleasures. The city we'd left behind had theater, museums, and one of Earth's tallest structures. It had fine dining and enough immigrants to make comparisons to New York only faintly ridiculous. Toronto even roosted on a Great Lake that people remembered to love in the summer, but it could not boast snowy peaks or a familiarity with livestock. In Allie's opinion, Calgary's status as the host of the 1988 Winter Olympics automatically made our hometown inferior.

"You have to respect a place that has a stadium shaped like a giant saddle," she said, as we approached Stampede Park along MacLeod Trail.

On our first date, Lewis told a great joke about King Kong, Hong Kong, and the Saddledome (both our mothers hailed from Hong Kong). He wasn't tall, but he had an outdoor voice and strong cheekbones, and I thought of him in terms of my preference for small hotels. They had more character. For once, I didn't have to make the dinner reservation; he picked me up in a car with leather seats and took me to see the Leafs versus the Flames, whispering the play-by-play as we gazed at center ice from our luxury box. Never had the comment "That guy was totally offside" sounded so alluring. I had dated men with money before, but they seemed distracted, as if listening to distant symphonies. Lewis was entirely present. I worshipped his relatives—two independent brothers, parents who literally *spent* their weekends stocking Saturday and Sunday with golf and brunch and a lake cottage in Muskoka. Their laughs jingled like the lift tickets that validated the zippers of their ski jackets.

The Calgary Stampede takes place every July, luring competitive cowboys to a celebration of the Wild West complete with parade floats and chuck-wagon races and sunstruck arenas where the dust rises in clouds. We wolf-whistled from the grandstand; in the saddle-bronc event, men in denim shirts and improbably white hats got points for coordinating their movements to their bucking horses. How did I know it wasn't enough just to stay on? My shameless sister immediately went native, coveting a Stetson and a pair of pointy boots. I slipped her the extra money from our mother's check and said, "I dare you to wear that getup back home."

Perhaps her hunger was stoked by the sight of all those bulls being roped by men in dented hats. Perhaps it was the heat, a kind of free-range headache seasoned with cotton candy, alfalfa, and victory. Allie loved winning. Her favorite films involved training scenes—apprentices beating on punching bags or flubbing triple axels on the road to perfection. Allie would get so excited, she'd bounce in her seat, her night-colored hair escaping its ponytail.

Bypassing the screaming roller-coasters and the Old Tyme Photo Parlor, my sister hunted prizes in the midway, stuffed animals ripening on the vine at every booth. I followed as she threw darts and aimed softballs. I loaded my arms with the spoils: a tiger, some fuzzy dice, and a defective teddy bear. "The secret to water-gun races," she assured me, expertly hosing the smile of a clown until the balloon atop its head exploded, "is to pick the most exhausted balloon." I was familiar with the philosophy. Before I met Lewis, it was usually how I had managed to secure dates.

At the Skee-Ball challenge, she held out her hands, motioning for her toys. "Your turn."

"Nah, you know, most of these games are rigged. I watched this whole documentary about it—" A rain of clapping mocked my words as a guy behind me socked a ball into the hundred-point ring. Allie grinned and tugged on the foot of her teddy bear; his eyes were glued on lopsided.

"You should exchange him for another one," I said.

"Why? He's perfect. You can keep him if you want."

I shook the bear, his eyes jiggling. "He looks like he has mad cow disease."

She snorted and bit her lip. Allie's mouth was always moving, a fact that might have explained her tendency for non sequiturs.

She took the animal off my hands and said, "Ceci, are you okay?" Although my sister's asthma was under control, we instinctively took care of her; whenever she tried to return the favor, she sounded like she was reading from a TelePrompTer.

"Yeah, yeah, I'm just tired," I said. But I wanted her to keep prying.

"You must be hungry," she said, poking me in the stomach. "I am so famished, I could eat this bear." As she walked away, I observed the parts of her shoulders where her sunscreen had let her down.

I stayed rooted to the spot, hoping she would turn around. She didn't. I kicked a plastic cup that lay on the pavement. It rolled in a lazy circle and bled Coke all over my running shoes.

"Why don't you just get a corn dog?" I yelled after her, but she was already beyond hearing.

To look at my baby sister, you would never guess at her insatiable capacity for food. When we were children, I used to warn Allie that she was skinny enough to choke on water, and I took great pleasure in informing her that in the hardscrabble fields of Old China, she would have been the first to expire in times of famine. Allie's metabolism was the fastest thing I had ever seen, shunting the fuel through her system before she even had time to rest her fork.

Just off the Trans-Canada Highway, we chose an eatery based on its barbed-wire sculpture, which graced the front porch of the road-house like hallucinations etched in stars: a rusty pig floated in the air; a cowgirl reached for her lasso. Inside, the dining room was paneled with old barnboard, saddles gleaming in display cases. Giant arm-chairs hewn from rough logs waited for the out-of-season fireplace to roar back to life.

"Lewis would get a kick out of this place," said Allie.

I noticed the antique rifles hanging above the bar. "Probably," I said.

"Work must be crazy. Is that why he didn't come?" My husband was the co-manager of a mutual fund on Bay Street. He rarely traveled for pleasure.

"There's a lot going on right now." The excuse made my throat ache.

At the hostess station, Allie requested a table for two. I couldn't even enter a restaurant these days without thinking of the hundreds of times Lewis and I had stared at each other over a meal. We had met at a similarly kitschy establishment a few years ago when I was still a history major at the University of Toronto. Lewis, six years my senior, had joined me at my table.

"The waitress told me you're collecting ghost stories for a book," he said. This was true. My favorite tales involved mundane spec-ters, eternal hostages who waited for the elevator or opened their mail, night after night.

"My aunt's basement is haunted," he said. "By a family of cats."

For once, I didn't mind being mocked. I said, "Everybody has a ghost story, even if it's someone else's."

As Allie and I were seated at a window table covered in gingham, she noted that the cracked-plastic tumblers reminded her of shower doors.

"Speaking of hygiene," she said, "can you stop taking all the shampoo from the hotel room?"

"What?"

"I'll bet your purse is full of little soaps."

"Yeah, well, whenever you need a Band-Aid or an aspirin, who gives it to you?" My voice jumped an octave.

I was afraid she was going to remind me of the time she found me washing umbrellas in the bathtub, but she took a long drink of water instead. My elbows avoided the greasy tablecloth; cartoon cows mooned out at me from the menu, which also happened to be the placemat. I tried not to sully my hands, but when I attempted to read the specialties, which were trapped in an illustrated corral, I was forced to wipe off a lick of barbecue sauce.

At the bottom of the menu, a dancing cactus issued a dare:

THE 72 OZ. STEAK CHALLENGE. EAT THIS BABY WITHIN
60 MINUTES AND THE MEAT'S ON US.

"Hey, check this out," I said. "One man's insanity is another man's supper."

Allie turned sideways, repeatedly smacking her flip-flop against her heel. "It's only insane if you don't finish it."

"No, it's fifty dollars if you don't finish it."

Shaking the ice in her glass, she said, "Ma told me I was insane when I decided to go to school in Vancouver."

"Yeah, and you dropped out anyway," I said. "So maybe she was right."

She picked a sugar cube out of the bowl and hurled it at me. Maybe this was not the best way to proceed.

The waitress came to our rescue. I said, "I'll have the burger, medium, with Swiss cheese." I scanned the desserts (I like to decide these things ahead of time), but my sister's silence compelled me to glance up. Allie's fist was pressed against her lips, her eyes glittering like fairy lights.

"No," I said. "You couldn't possibly."

Her hands rearranged the silverware in etiquette-unfriendly designations (I was the one who taught her how to set a table). Her clothes made her look even smaller than she was, her legs pushing through her red short-shorts like drinking straws. She hooked both thumbs in her waistband and tested for flexibility.

"Why not?" she said. "Dress for excess."

"Because nobody who wears spaghetti straps can finish a seventy-two-ounce steak. That's four and a half pounds of carnage."

Before I'd even finished voicing my objections, I knew I had essentially given her a gorge order.

Many before her had tried and failed. Grimy photos quilted the room, their Scotch tape curling in the heat from the grill. The walls were divided into losers and winners. Like wealthy landowners, the victors stood out against a meadow of blank wall, their feats reflected in their queasy smirks, empty plates brandished as trophies. In the losers' section, elderly ladies waved bleeding morsels on forks, drunken contenders holding the uneaten steaks against their eyes.

Allie turned to the waitress and said, "I'll take seventy-two ounces of your best Alberta beef. Rare."

I should have hauled her out of the place by her ponytail. It's what our mother would have done. It's what Lewis would have done. "Fine," I said. "It's your coronary." I shook my head until my eyes hurt. My sister ignored me as the waitress slapped a form on the table for her to fill out. As soon as the chit went up, an announcement sent the PA system into feedback, an amused voice directing diners to focus their attention on the madwoman at table five. The lights snapped off and a spotlight awoke, ricocheting off the walls before staining our table. Allie was ignited, all 110 pounds of her, wearing the hot halo of attention. Bringing her fingers to her lips, she blew kisses to the crowd as I pretended not to exist.

"Alexandra Wu has decided to take the Seventy-two-Ounce Steak Challenge. Will she succeed?"

"You gave them your full name?" I said.

Guffaws drifted from the other side of the room; in a rising tide of plaid shirts and dirty jeans, men stood up to get a better look at the lightweight. Bets were tabled.

No doubt you have heard of Takeru Kobayashi, who can consume almost as many hot dogs in one minute as there are syllables in his notorious name. (His record is fifty-three in twelve minutes.) The 144-pound reedling has earned top honors for five years running at Nathan's Famous Fourth of July International Hot Dog Eating Contest in Coney Island, splitting his hot dogs in a personal method dubbed the Solomon technique. When our mother heard that one of the *yat bun* people had distinguished himself by inhaling wieners, she said, "And to think we were scared of them during the war." Kobayashi is a celebrity in Japan and a freak of nature.

The freak opposite me pushed her water glass away. "Don't want to fill up on drinks," she said.

Snickering, the waitress dumped a breadbasket on the table as if to say, "You won't be needing this." I took a roll and watched my sister's eyes close—two dashes above her flushed cheeks. She took what my yoga teacher called a "deep cleansing breath" and, sensing my unease, said, "I'm meditating, Cecilia. Just give me a minute."

I looked at my watch. After the second hand finished its revolution, I said, "So what's with the Ladies' Barrel Racing? Why can't it be Women's Barrel Racing?" Conversationally, I was a lousy cowgirl, my lariat falling on all the wrong topics.

Allie sighed and opened her eyes. "Look at Wimbledon. The ladies win a plate, the guys get a trophy." Her hunger was making her flippant.

My burger arrived—a modest puck consorting with a gang of fries. I bit into the patty and waved a fry at her. "You'd better not yak in the car afterward," I said.

If Lewis had been there, he might have reminded me that the vehicle was a rental. He once said, "You care too much about things that aren't yours."

I whipped a legal pad out of my bag and reviewed my notes.

"Have you started the article yet?"

I winced. When I'd fired up my computer at the hotel, writing seemed trivial—I felt the same futility that overwhelms me at planetariums when the lights are extinguished and the fake skies light up with my own irrelevance. "I've typed a few paragraphs," I lied.

The steak restored the peace. When my sister's meal arrived, I heard it before I saw it: the platter thunked on the table like drawbridges slamming, like Bibles closing, the beef hanging over the edge. Opening before me was my sister's maw, and what she was intending to put in it was the long-lost eighth continent.

We were agog. It was the same size as my laptop. "Look," I said. "It's creating its own weather." Allie shut her eyes again.

There were rules, of course. At no point would she be allowed to leave the table—yet another good reason for limiting water intake. Her companion was not permitted to assist, not even to help cut her food, not that my sister would have wanted to be treated like a six-year-old. Furthermore, the steak dinner included a baked potato and coleslaw, fixings that Allie couldn't afford to underestimate.

A huge cheer buoyed the crowd when she fed herself the first bite. The waitress had delivered my sister's nemesis along with a ticking clock, and I caught Allie's eyes already flickering to the countdown. She expertly sawed the slab into manageable pieces, paring the gristle and mounding it on her bread dish. A flare of hope lit her face.

She ate steadily, smiling as grease painted her chin, as pink juice dribbled off her cutlery. I lost my appetite, shredding my stale bun as my sister went to work. A couple of times she punctuated the ordeal with offhand comments like "We need to buy gas," or "When we get back, I'd like to buy new sheets."

I decided to try again. "Do you ever think about all the things you might be good at, but you don't know because you've never given it a shot? Like, you might be really great at tennis. Or you might be the best ukelele player who ever lived."

She chewed and swallowed. "Ceci, if you want to wear a lab coat for the rest of your life, be my guest."

The room pared down to two adjectives, *hot* and *quiet*. Across the province, as the grain elevators continued to fade, the winds moved from town to town and the meat moved from tine to mouth and my sister's eyes blinked into another dimension, an aerobics of mind-over-belly. Another deep cleansing breath, this time from me. Although our table sat under a window overlooking the parking lot, I don't think Allie saw a thing. Outside, big sedans glided to rest, their engines ticking. It was still light out. Under a street lamp, an alley cat tasted the ground before sitting back on its haunches, one leg flung up by its ear. One of Lewis's ghost cats? I thought about wrapping it in a towel and taking it home with me.

I went back to observing the ritual meatification. After a while, I stopped watching her and watched the dish instead, the platter remembering itself as the steak retreated; underneath was a low tide of pretty flowers that matched my sister's halter top. Once in a while, the waitress would stop by, gawk, and refill my water glass. In the open kitchen, the staff that had begat the steak analyzed my sister's odds as if following a hockey game.

"Ten bucks says she puts the biscuit in the basket," said the cook.

"Nah, warm up the bus. She's going home," said the busboy.

As she hacked at her side dishes, murmuring to herself, part of me wanted to go home, to halt the contest by scooping her coleslaw, by stealing a career-ending chunk of spud. At one point, she paused, losing precious minutes, her knife drooping in her fingers, blood darkening her skin. I put a hand on her arm.

"Allie," I said, "it's okay to stop." She shook me off, soldiering on as if she (like the cow she was consuming) was gifted with multiple stomachs.

Plenty of contests feature the healthier levels of the food pyramid. Pies are in a special category. Hot chilies, yes. Seafood holds its own: in New Orleans, at the Acme Oyster House, the oyster-eating record is forty-six dozen in ten minutes. The International Federation of Competitive Eating lists baked beans and sweet-potato casseroles among its many trials. But there's something about the consumption of flesh that impresses people.

The meal was not the heart-to-heart I'd visualized. Beyond our mother's sphere of influence, I had another reason for taking my sister to Calgary. What I wanted to tell her was simple: I was getting a divorce.

"Allie," I said, polishing my spoon with the edge of my serviette.

"Um," she said.

"Lewis and I . . . we're not together. We're breaking up."

Blinking furiously, she shook potato crumbs onto the table. "What do you mean? What happened?"

"Nothing happened. It was a mutual decision, and—"

"Well, you must have done something."

I jumped up, pushing my chair back so violently that I knocked over my glass. Water flooded the tablecloth, making islands of her many plates. She kept eating.

Seething in the back hallway, I stared at the pay phone (such a charming relic, like my marriage), wondering whether to call my parents and inform them that the most selfish person on the planet was consuming a seventy-two-ounce steak, and that we might be coming home later than expected. I did not know when I would break the news about my husband. Anyone could see that Lewis was a fine man, but I recalled my mother's reaction when I introduced him, an appraisal that started with the shoes, detoured from his heart to his back pocket, and ended with her frowning. He was too old for me, she said. His parents were snobs. Astrologically, he was a dragon and I was a dog. We were doomed.

A man walked by and yanked a pack of Export A's out of the cigarette machine. I moved to let him pass, but instead he stopped in front of me, easing a cancer stick between his lips. His hair couldn't escape the fact that it would have looked better on a girl—miniature waves danced all over his head like a motel painting of the seashore. A bottle of beer sweated in his fist. When he raised his eyebrows, I knew what he was going to say.

"So, you folks from Japan?"

I gritted my teeth. I was about to chide him with a history lesson when I spotted my sister across the room. "Actually, *she* is. My job is to take tourists around and show them the local color." I chuckled at my own joke, my voice tinny and strange. Usually, Lewis was the wiseacre.

The man, who was hoping to qualify as local color, said, "Would you like some beer? I haven't touched it yet." I considered admitting I was from Ontario. Surely that would work. Albertans were still peeved about the federal government taking control of their oil. I thought about driving him away by oversharing: I could tell him that I'd married too young, that I'd chosen an administrator instead of a husband, that the very qualities I'd loved in Lewis had strangled our softer traits until we were nothing but a pair of competing Palm-Pilots.

Instead, I said, "Sure, I'll have a sip." The sip graduated into a swig, the liquid smooth and yeasty. "Thanks."

"Do you want to go dancing?" he said.

I showed him my wedding band.

He shrugged, and the shrug said, *Hey, what do I know?* Where I saw a dead promise, he saw a piece of jewelry, and who was I to be wielding a talisman that no longer worked?

I sat down again, clutching an empty doggie bag just in case Allie needed to toss her steer. My stomach churned with the unexpected alcohol. She wouldn't look me in the eye.

"I'm sorry," she mumbled, her apology smothered in beef. "It'll probably work itself out." I shook my head. Coming from her, "sorry" was a ball gown on display, formal and empty. It reminded me of the time my boss tried to ban the word *view* from all copy. This was the hardest catchall for a travel writer to avoid. You could use *panorama*, or *vista*, or *scene*, but sooner or later, you had to spell out what was in front of you.

More than forty minutes into the marathon, the esophageal wonder that was my sister was in the homestretch, quivering as she hunched over her plate. Ten more bites. Eight more bites. The baked potato was an upside-down helmet, hollowed out to the point where it might have collapsed had I prodded it with my finger. The coleslaw fueled her last heroic shovelings. Five more bites. Her fist anchored her to the table. Fat coated her smile like lip gloss. The platter was almost naked now, the burlesque of eating stripping it down to a garland of poppies around a happy calf. *Isn't that morbid,* I thought.

And then she was done.

They fell on her, whooping and hollering. A flashbulb anointed her gluttony. I abandoned the doggie bag. As for Allie and the state she was in, I can only say that when her Polaroid went up on the wall, she looked drunk. En route to the ladies' room, she was waylaid by admirers at the long wooden bar. The bartender glued his high-five to hers, an old waiter ruffled her hair; my beer friend was there, with his bottled affection.

Alone, I continued to the washroom, entering the sweet fallout of bubble gum, nicotine, and perfume samples, the calling card of teenagers just passing through. My teen years had been owned by the family business, an adolescence suffered among bolts of silk instead of other girls.

I guessed that the wallpaper and the menu had been designed by the same person; as I stepped in front of the mirror to check my hair, I was dismayed by a pattern of ranch hands in the never-ending motif of trying to catch a steer. It was unspeakably sad. Under the jaundice of the lightbulb, I tilted my "married hand" back and forth, waiting for the reassuring dazzle of diamonds throwing off light. I was busy trying on the words again—*divorcée, ex-husband*—wanting to make them sound as common as they were. I could predict my mother's reaction when I informed her of my twin failures—to brainwash Allie, to keep my ring finger in platinum. She wouldn't even pretend to be surprised, and her judgment would fall on me like winter.

I pivoted into a stall and vomited. The noise echoed off the tile. There was no one to hold back my hair. As I braced myself against the wall, I noticed a crayoned sign that said PLEASE DO NOT FLUSH PAPER TOWELS DOWN THE TOILET!

The door to the ladies' room opened, leaking sounds of celebration from the dining room. The waitress poked her head in, excited by the prospect of disqualification. When she found out that the regurgitator was merely the winner's sister, she said the same thing I'd said when Lewis broached the topic of separation. "Oh." The door swung shut. After rinsing away the taste of acid, I wiped my forehead and tossed the paper towel in the toilet.

When I materialized at the bar, I discovered that one of my sister's fans had taken care of our paltry bill. Allie continued to hold court like a sunflower at a garden party, her back to me, the bartender straining toward her with a lecherous familiarity that should have worried me. "I'm in a food coma," she giggled. My chest burned as I nudged past, desperate for air. Not comatose in the slightest, she glanced at me and mouthed the words *Five minutes.*

Out in the parking lot, I failed to replace the convertible top by myself, splitting a nail. I thought I might tune to a radio station and sing along to other people's misery. I thought I'd wait on the hood like the cool youth I'd never been, long enough for twilight to show its guts, for my sister to tire of the adulation. The deejay's voice was sheer puree. "Hey, it's dedication hour at the ELK, Calgary's place for your favorite oldies and the hits of today. Pick up the phone to give a shout-out to that special someone."

As caller after caller dialed in, I wondered what the deejay thought of their choices. But after five laughable dedications, including gems by Bachman Turner Overdrive and Rush, I was surprised to find myself humming—my body in the driver's seat, my fingers on the gearshift. I thought about turning the key and revving the engine, but after a while, I wasn't thinking, but motoring.

At 110 clicks per hour, the wind boxed me from all sides, my hands wrestling the steering wheel. The pink sky was like the virgin drift of newly opened ice cream, so gorgeous I had to remind myself that it wasn't the planetarium. The day after tomorrow I would hop on a plane and wing back to my problems, but for now, as I gunned toward the grand peaks of Banff, I lost my interest in ghosts, and in crises that could not be solved in mountain time, because mountains are for people who need to know they're destined for something beautiful.

Love Machine

Samantha Hunt

Once upon a time two men lived down at the bottom of a nuclear-missile silo. They were barely men, just out of their teens, and yet they were charged with the responsibility of pushing the button when it came time for nuclear apocalypse. Technically there were no buttons, but rather two keys to turn. They just used the word *button* as it made it easier for civilians to visualize what they were doing down in their missile silo. In actuality, each man would have to insert his own key and turn it. Together they would have to decide whether or not to destroy the world.

Wayne and Dwight paid attention in alternating shifts, each ready to wake the other if the signal to act ever came through. They were not allowed to leave the missile silo and so each night and each day—the sixteen-inch poured concrete walls made it hard to tell which—they slept locked underground, not too far away from the huge hole that cradled a massive warhead already pointed up at the sky.

When Wayne and Dwight were both awake they either played Nerf basketball on a small court they'd rigged in the control room or shot the bull. They'd discuss the moment they were both waiting for. They would try to imagine what would happen when it came down to it, if they'd be able to turn their keys and end the world. They had decided that they would do their duty. They would turn their keys and then they would forsake the canned provisions that had been supplied for them in order to survive the months after the apocalypse down there in the silo. They thought instead they would turn their keys, open the hatch, climb back up to the surface of the earth, and watch the fireworks as the world died.

While they waited, Dwight used to ask Wayne the big questions, like "Why do you think we're here?" or "Do you believe in God?" or "What are you most afraid of?" Wayne always tried his best to answer Dwight's questions, but sometimes he didn't know what to say and the two men would sit listening to the quiet clicks and whirls that the control console made inside their nuclear silo.

The call never came. The keys remained on chains around their necks, never getting to sink into the dark keyholes that Wayne had spent hours, days, and weeks studying. And then their time in the military was up, and then Dwight and Wayne drifted apart as people do.

But Wayne remembered.

On their last night in the silo they'd opened up a bottle of sparkling cider to celebrate the end of their term. Soon they would be seeing the sun again on a regular basis. They would see other people as well, and while it was a little frightening to leave their secured zone after two years together, they both tried to smile and concentrate on the good that would come from returning to the surface. Dwight and Wayne were close that night in a way Wayne's not been able to recall since, as if there were a small man in his brain who remembers exactly what happened that last night down in the silo but whenever Wayne tries to remember for himself the little man says, "Well, I could tell you, but then I'd have to kill you."

This all happened after ROTC, before the FBI, and now, from time to time, Wayne misses Dwight. He misses having someone to share the long hours with, the waiting. And so Wayne finds himself thinking about Dwight, about the cold war, while he twiddles his thumbs in a van, on an FBI stakeout in Montana.

Wayne's on assignment, Operation Bombshell, a pet project of his. Wayne has done well for himself the past five years at the Bureau, accessing higher and higher levels of security. He's racked up top-secret clearances like poker chips. Operation Bombshell is his brainchild, though sure, he'd have to credit the team of guys from Development and Fabrication who'd actually built her down to the very last detail of weaving human hair, mostly collected from wives and sisters, into a wig that they'd bleached and later on conditioned with a hot oil treatment for softness and scent. And there were the guys down in Robotics of course. They'd had a big hand in developing both her language and mobility functions. And of course there was Marc from Explosives. He'd been a big help. Still, everyone down at the Bureau generally agrees, she, Operation Bombshell, belongs to Wayne.

And so here they were in the Montana woods, she and Wayne, down the road a small stretch from a cabin that belongs to one of the most wanted criminals in all of America. Wayne has been on the trail of this scumbag for so many years now almost no one at the Bureau believes the guy will ever be caught. Well, that'll change when

Wayne brings this sucker's charred remains into the lab for dental and DNA analysis. He'll show the naysayers and all those hot-shot agents who'd make fun of Wayne behind closed doors, joking about his inability to make an arrest stick on this guy. He'd heard them. He's a surveillance expert for criminy's sake. He'd heard, "There goes Wayne, down the drain" and "Operation Bumshell," and, the worst, he heard his name, Wayne, followed by an explosion of giggles as if his career were the punch line.

A branch ticks and scrapes against the roof of the van. Wayne studies the dark speedometer. The vehicle has been made to resemble a pool cleaner's van, but outside of the surveillance equipment stashed in the back, there is little in the way of high-tech luxury. Wayne rests his feet up on the hard plastic console between the driver's and passenger's sides. He sticks his heel down into the cubbyhole made to hold hot beverages. Leaning back in the captain's seat, he rubs at a small swatch that he keeps in his pocket. It is a bit of her skin, a square silicone sample. He raises the skin up to his nose, tickling a number of his wiry nostril hairs. He inhales her faint plastic scent, recalling moments of bliss, some that transpired mere hours earlier in this van as he smiled and selected an outfit for her to wear, helped her test the charge in her battery pack, stuffed her body cavity full of explosives, and then saluted her as she signed off on her mission with a quick nod and the word "Sir." He'd taught her how to be a proper soldier. He'd sent her off to knock on the door of the cabin.

"We don't want any!" Ted screams through the bolted door. But Ted isn't a "we." He's just an I.

In the cabin there is one small window from which he often peers out across the valley, startled by how steadfast the mountains can be. Ted waits for the mountains to move or exhale or explode.

He's got all the time in the world. He could wait all day, but nothing ever happens besides the mountains changing colors with the sun at night. Ted tries to achieve such stillness himself and would be able to if not for an itch he always gets right where his hair parts and the grease of his scalp dredges up a dull ache so that he must scratch the itch or be driven insane.

Ted has been alone for a very long time.

Some nights, as the sky turns pink at sunset, he lies on his back staring out the window. The trees' limbs become a darker shade of black, outlines that resemble huge dendrites of nerve endings against the sky. Some nights he will lie there until there is no light left at all, until one shade of black swallows the subtleties and he is alone lying on his back staring at the square window of black as though it were a TV set.

Or other nights he'll spend his time building small bombs, some that are thin enough to slip into the open arms of an envelope.

The knocking hasn't stopped. "We don't want any!" Ted screams again to no effect. He cannot believe someone is knocking on his door. He is a million miles away from any civilization. But there it is, steady and rhythmic, the knocks fall like the footsteps of an approaching giant. There is a joke in this somewhere, Ted's sure. What dedication. The knocking continues at a regular pace for thirty, thirty-five minutes. He almost can't believe a passion so unparalleled. This knocker is no quitter, or else, he thinks, this knocker is a robot. Ha! He laughs, finding the joke. A robot in the wilderness of Montana. It's not a very funny joke, not really a joke at all, but he laughs anyway.

"Go away!" The knocking continues. Ted lies on his back smelling the pine from the floorboards. It is a plague of knocks, a Chinese water torture of a sort. He turns his cheek down to the rough boards. The corner of his lip touches the wood. He curls his body and counts the seconds between each pounding, waiting for the fol-

lowing thud to arrive so that the sliver of silence, the moments between each knock, grow swollen, become rooms where long, long
years of thought are stored, hallways filled with stalled breaths.

He tries to remember the last time he encountered a human
being. "Late last month? I believe so. I went to town for batteries and
Fruit Roll-Ups, and the woman behind the cash register said, 'Will
that be all?' and I nodded my head meaning yes."

Knock.

Ted doesn't really like people. He prefers the woods, the cabin,
and the long dirt road one has to take to get here. The road is over-
grown in part with berry bramble that scratches at any vehicle. In
some places dead branches fall across the road and he just leaves
them there rotting, blocking passage. Such a road is necessary to feel
the way he does, that society, if it has to exist, is best kept far, far away,
remaining to him like some sort of rare granite outcropping or
species of palm tree, hermit crab, or saltwater estuary—something
that is, but just isn't here, not in the Montana woods.

Ted opens his eyes. The last rays of the sun shine in through the
window. The knock comes again. Who is it? He can't imagine. It
isn't a postman because he doesn't receive any mail. He makes sure
of that by not having a mailbox at all. Why should the United States
government be allowed to come to his house, every day except Sunday, to deliver strychnine printed in four colors? They shouldn't be.

Knock.

No one even knows he is here except for his brother, and his
brother would not knock.

America moves so quickly it blurs itself into a coma. Ted moves
slowly and nothing gets past him. He lifts his spine from the wooden
floor like a cobra lifting its head, one vertebra at a time, alert.

Knock.

The curiosity's the killing part. Ted can't take it anymore. Slowly he hoists himself up off the floor of the cabin. He does a quick duck and roll over to the door and peering through a crack he sees something that surprises him. He slides back the bolt. He answers his door, something he's never done before.

"Finally," she says and grabs at her chest as though her breasts are pillows she is trying to fluff. "I thought you had died."

"What?" he asks, and nothing else.

"Well," she says, beginning to explain. "You're not going to believe this," she says as he starts to close the door on her, regretting having opened it. "Wait, please." The door continues to close. "WAIT!" The door stops.

"What?" he asks again.

"They're chasing me. Please."

"Who?"

She looks over her shoulders. "The bad guys."

"Why?" he asks.

"Because I've been a very naughty girl," she says flatly, sincerely, no innuendo.

Ted is puzzled. He is curious. "What'd you do?"

"I shot a man in Reno just to watch him die."

"Huh?"

"He was a U.S. marshal," she says and her words work. Something turns in Ted. He doesn't care for U.S. marshals either. Indeed he doesn't care for the entire U.S. government.

"Do I know you?" he asks her, still standing with his arm across the doorjamb, blocking her entrance.

"Don't you want to know me?' She cocks her elbow out to the side and places her hand on her hip, accentuating its curve. She winks and then stomps her foot, like she's a racehorse waiting to run from the starting gate. Her feet are shod in a small pair of steel-toed work boots that cut a strange angle to her skin-tight jeans. The boots look bulky, like a klutzy, possibly retarded cousin to her gorgeous hips. He stares. He's never seen a woman like this. Her message becomes vibrantly clear. Everybody needs somebody.

"So can I come in?" she asks.

He steps back. He lets her inside.

"Well," she says, dusting her hands off on her thighs, stepping through the door, and taking a look around the small room. "That's much better."

There's something weird about the way she speaks. It is both startling and attractive. "Are you from Florida?" Ted asks because something about her seems brand new.

"Florida?" she asks. "Nope!" The tips of her perfect lips curve into a smile.

Her lips *are* perfect, as is her skin or at least the skin Ted can see underneath her flannel top and jeans. The skin has a glow to it, like a waxwork he once saw of Joseph Smith and the early pioneers in a Utah rest area. Her skin is so smooth it looks as though it has once been melted, liquid, and then, when it found the place that was just right, it hardened up that way like a pond in winter that freezes before the first snow. Or maybe it has just been a while since Ted has seen a beautiful woman.

"Listen, I don't need any trouble. I've got enough," he says.

"I won't give you any. I just need a place to hide out for a few days."

Ted considers his cabin. No one would find her here, and he does like the way she speaks plainly. He thinks he can trust her maybe. Or maybe it has just been a while since he has seen a beautiful woman.

"And in the meantime," she says, "Vroom. Vrooom. Maybe I can get your engine started."

This comment makes Ted blush until, in a moment of confusion, he starts to wonder whether she means the broken-down generator he keeps just outside the door.

She makes herself comfortable, puts some water on the cookstove for coffee. He notices that she knows how to use a cookstove, and he likes that about her. He likes the way she sets right to work, fussing in the kitchen. Once she's got the kettle on, she looks at him again. "Vroom. Vrooom," she repeats, and walks toward him, slowly twisting each hip. She wraps her fingers around his forearm.

"Oh. Oh," he says. "My," Ted says, surprised at being touched. Normally the most suspicious man in Montana, he thinks that she is cute with her steel-toed boots. Still he ducks away from her because just at that moment he notices his box of fuses and wires plus an empty container of ammonium nitrate has been left out in the open on his work table. The kettle whistle blows. She turns her back for a moment to brew the coffee and Ted takes that brief window of opportunity to lift a grungy serape that had been draped across the back of an old bench. He throws the serape over the table where he often sits to think and sometimes sits to build mail bombs that he later addresses to the filthy technologists.

"Coffee?" she asks. She didn't notice a thing.

"Yes. I'd love a cup. Thank you." Ted hardly knows the words to say, it has been so long since he has had a conversation.

She winks at him again. "Why don't you and I get to know one another in the old-fashioned way," she proposes. "Over a cup of coffee."

"Good idea," he says.

"Let's just talk. You first," she says, sitting down on the old bench and patting the spot beside her.

"Me?" he asks, taking the cup of coffee from her outstretched hand. She nods. "Okay. Me." He has to sit and think before he starts.

"Well, there's not much to tell. I grew up in a house that wasn't too big or too small. It was just right. Son of a sausage maker. Perfectly plain."

"Go on," she says, and bats her eyes, which he notes have lashes nearly as long as the kicker on a stick of dynamite. "I'm enchanted," she says. "Enthralled."

"Well, in junior high I nearly won a Scrabble tournament, but my opponent at the last minute laid out *ozone* on a triple-word score. The Z alone was worth thirty points, and I was stuck holding the J, minus eight, you know."

"Fascinating," she says as she leans back, stretching her arm out along the top of the bench, creeping a hair closer to him.

"It's hard to remember much else," he says, and looks up to the window, surprised and a bit winded by really how few details it can take to make a life and how difficult it is for him, at this minute, to recall how he'd spent his years so far. They sped past.

"I do remember one thing that was sort of special. I was a kid. I was sitting on the curb outside our house and the macadam road was hot. I remember the heat rising off that blacktop felt like"—Ted stops and smiles at her, doing his best Kris Kristofferson—"felt like a religious experience. I sat there staring straight ahead, perfectly pleased with life on earth, wanting and needing nothing. I lay back." Ted sips his coffee and continues.

"Then two kids from across the street came out and started to lob tiny stones, tiny kernels of asphalt, at my stomach. But I didn't move a muscle. They giggled. I think they called me names but after a few minutes they walked on. I still didn't move. I stared straight up at the sun and I felt like if I concentrated hard enough, I could sink down into the street, become something solid and hard, like the blacktop road. I lay there like that all day, and when I finally sat up, I saw how

I'd gotten burned, a sunburn that left a perfect white silhouette of my hand and fingers right there on the skin of my thigh just below the fringe of my cut-off shorts. I'd been burned by the sun."

"You're a wonderful storyteller," she says, and blinks her eyes languidly, once, like an engine slowing down.

Ted considers her comment. He's never seen it that way before, primarily because he's never really had someone to tell stories to, but now that she mentions it he thinks about how the work he does—building bombs, rigging wires in a pattern, constructing a path that resembles the trail left behind by a moth eating its way across a woolen blanket—these wires and bombs make a narrative. The red wires lead to the blue wires lead to the trigger which leads to the black powder. His bombs are written like masterpieces. Sadly, no one ever gets to actually read these stories, except, perhaps, for the scientist who might catch one last glimpse before the story blows a hole right through his brain. Moth-eaten.

Back out in the van Wayne taps his fingernail against the plastic casing of his surveillance headphones. He could listen to her talk all day. Her awkward, unknowing way with language. Or how she accents the wrong syllable. It's adorable.

The Bureau had thought of everything. She has a nearly complete digestive and excretory system. She has beautiful baked white enamel teeth that can bite and chew. She even has a saliva simulator. Her anatomy is complete and flawless. Her ears curl like a baby's. She is beyond perfection, she is more than a woman. She's ageless. Her thighs will always stay tight, her cheeks will stay soft and moderately blushed even if her batteries still sometimes require catnaps to recharge.

Through the headphones Wayne listens to her conversation with Ted. He listens to her charm that scumbag. He looks through the camera that is in her eyes, as he remotely commands her to romance this criminal, to demurely cast her gaze down. Wayne looks through her eyes and there, beyond her bosom, he sees her hand laced within this public menace's thick, dark digits.

Once, down in the silo, Wayne and Dwight had been discussing their onerous, slightly nerdy names. Dwight was in honor of Eisenhower, and Wayne, Wayne Newton. They were giggling over how together they made Dwayne, but as their giggles subsided Dwight asked, "Wayne, have you ever been in love?" It was the sort of question they liked to lob at each other down in the hole.

"Not yet," Wayne answered. "How about you?"

Dwight had his boots up on the console. "Yes. Yes, I have," he replied.

"What does it feel like?" Wayne asked him and for once Dwight had no answer. Instead his gaze dashed around the silo. First his eyes rested on the steel-reinforced concrete wall that was poured sixteen inches thick, then on the bank of walkie-talkies, the haz-mat suits hanging empty, the cache of survival rations stacked neatly on an aluminum shelf and arranged by ingredient. Chicken à la King, Dried Tuna Noodle, Chipped Beef. Wayne waited for Dwight to answer. Dwight stared at the console and its blinking lights, its potential to start a nuclear war, and finally Dwight did answer. "It feels a lot like this, Wayne."

In the cabin Ted is still talking to her. "When I close my eyes," he says, "I see a revolution as mesmerizing as any rainbow. People will stop and stare as factories and research universities come tumbling down. People will die, that is for certain." He turns to her and blushes, as he doesn't usually speak in metaphors, and wonders what sunshine has come over him. "There is a poison in the blood and leeches aren't going to do the trick."

"Hey, what are you so angry about, big boy?"

"You could say I don't like technology."

"What, not even video games, TV?"

He doesn't answer her question. "Imagine that I am a machine."

There's silence in the cabin while she tries to obey his command. She blinks twice.

"Machines," he continues, "have one of only two choices. Either they are run by humans or else they run themselves. And the way I see it, either choice is no good for me. If machines are run by humans, the elite class takes over, kills the rest of us off because they don't need worker bees anymore—they have the machines. And if the machines are run by themselves, they take over and kill us all. I mean, of course they do. Who doesn't know that? Machines always beat the people who resist them. Take cars as your example. Say you resist the automobile. Say you walk everywhere. You still have to obey traffic signals. You can't cross the road wherever you'd like to because the machines have won. Try to walk *into* New York City. Try crossing Route 80. You can't. See, machines will become responsible for doing every job we humans were put on earth here to do, and what does that leave me with?"

"I don't know, sailor boy, what?"

"Not much. A handful of antidepressant pills to pop, pills that were made by the machines in the first place to keep us from revolting."

"I don't know, sailor boy, what?"

"Huh?"

"I don't know, sailor boy, what?"

"What the heck are you talking about?" Ted asks, and grabs her shoulder. They'd been getting along so well.

"Fascinating," she says, and then, rather suddenly, rather robotically, "I've become extremely tired. I must take a nap." And with that she closes her eyes, brings her chin to her chest, and begins to snore, her powerful exhales stirring the fringe of the serape that's covering Ted's bomb-building materials.

Poor thing, Ted thinks. She's been on the run. She's exhausted. I'm tired too, he thinks, because he has also killed people and injured many more. He tries not to think about it too much, but a person has urges. He'll tell her this when she wakes, natural urges to defend ourselves when under attack. He's being attacked by machines. He's being attacked by the government. He's only defending himself. And anyway, who is he to go against nature? Who is she? A person has urges. Yes, a person does, and as if to demonstrate this Ted cups her breast in the palm of his hand and squeezes once while she sleeps. He removes his hand. There is no tenderness left in him, and the experience is not as soft as Ted remembered it once was when he was young. He lets her be. He stares out the window for a while until quite suddenly, after five minutes or so, she flinches before sitting up quickly, stiffly.

"I've been thinking about what you said." She cocks her head toward him, fully awake. "And I have a question for you."

"What is it?" Ted asks.

"Where do you put beauty?"

"Beauty?"

"Yes," she says. "Beauty. Imagine a small green pond somewhere in the mountains of Montana. There, in the middle of this cool, clear water, floats a man, legs together, arms stretched out to the sides like a white bird lit from within. The man glows from the green of the water."

Ted pinches his lips in consideration.

"See, machines have made it possible for humans to concentrate on beauty," she continues.

"The man glows?" Ted asks.

"Yes, metaphorically."

"Is that man supposed to be me?" he asks.

She shrugs. "Well, I don't see how it could be if you're going to be so busy tending your crops or tilling your fields or walking for three days into Missoula."

"I hadn't thought of beauty," Ted says, and sinks his head down below the plane of his shoulders. He tucks his chin. He feels like a simpleton for forgetting beauty. "But there's no beauty in machines, and anyway all those people whose lives have been *simplified* by machines, they don't spend their days concentrating on beauty. They watch TV. Right? What do you think?"

She shrugs again because in truth she doesn't think. She can't think. She's not built to think. She's just a highly evolved robot, packed with explosives, ready to serve the USA on her final mission.

Wayne is listening in the van. He has a timetable, a plan for this criminal scumbag. He'll let Ted go all the way. Wayne wants Ted to know just how good a machine can feel inside. She feels good. Wayne can attest to just how good she feels. He'd volunteered to run Authenticity and Quality Control on her. R&D. Plus there'd been other times. Special moments. Yes, she feels good.

The sun has set and under the darkening sky Wayne dares to pull the van up closer to the cabin to get a better look. He watches through the windshield while inside they turn on a light. A golden glow creeps out through the one high window. Yellow light can make the coldest of homes look like a palace to someone waiting outside in a cold van, his Thermos of coffee having long ago expired. The sky slips from royal to navy blue. The black branches look like a secret army lying in wait, like bayonets raised up to the sky. Very quietly Wayne opens the door to the van and steps out into the dark.

Wayne remembers a Robert Frost poem he'd had to memorize in

grade school, two roads diverge in a yellow wood. Yellow wood? Maybe *yellow*'s not the right word. Yellow seems odd for a wood. He can't be sure now, but he'd liked the poem. He'd selected the poem to be his high school senior quote in the yearbook. And so he is surprised to find that here in Montana, years and years later, two roads are diverging. Not actual roads, but something more like poetic roads: one that says, "Turn the key, Wayne," and the other that asks, "Have you ever been in love?" Wayne squeezes at the swatch of skin he keeps in his pocket to answer yes.

Wayne creeps up to the cabin. He can hear movement inside, and voices, friendly voices, spots of giggling. He presses his ear directly up to the cold, rough siding as though he were a doctor listening through a stethoscope for traces of lung disease or heart irregularities. She'd enabled her debating software. Jealousy wells up in him. He holds his breath.

Ted looks up from his teepeed fingers at her while she speaks.

"So what do you expect us to do? Plant vegetable gardens when we can just go down to the grocery store, or do you want us to live off other people's trash? Dig through the garbage heap and that will make us happy?" she asks him. "I don't think that will make me happy."

"The garden might."

"Yes, it's true. The garden might."

She pauses for a moment before continuing. "Okay. So say we go ahead with your plan, build lots of bombs, kill all the machines. Say we get past the point of revolution, all the cities are gone, the interstates, all the strip malls, industrial complexes and health clubs are gone and we're all using our bodies to work really hard again, tilling the fields, killing bears with rocks, living off of honeysuckle, building wigwams and igloos, hiding in trees, digging in the dirt for grubs, it still wouldn't matter because somewhere there'll be a spark in some youngster's brain, someone who thinks, Hmm, if I build myself a gin I could sure pick a whole lot more cotton."

Her perfection is alarming.

"It'll just start all over again," she says.

And, in the cabin, Ted knows she is right. He hangs his head, defeated. He'd already thought of that youngster with the big ideas himself. He'd tried to ignore that youngster. In his head, in his plan, he only saw undulating fields of golden wheat and children playing hide-and-go-seek in the corn. He saw how the woods really are the poor man's overcoat, with mushrooms, hazelnuts, a soft pine-needle bed, sweet maple sap, and a fire to reduce the sap to syrup on. So much has already been given to us. He just couldn't believe people could want more.

"What do you want?" he asks her, and she makes an expression that looks like thinking while her computers search for anything lacking. "Detonation" is all her computers come up with, but that result lies beyond her top-secret firewall, along with all the other essential truths about herself that she isn't allowed to reveal, a glitch they'd had to fix after she said too much to that U.S. marshal in Reno. And so her computer instructs her to lie. She answers, "Nothing really. What do you want?"

Ted stops to consider. His mug of coffee has reached the bottom but he doesn't really want a refill. If he has too much caffeine he won't sleep well tonight. He looks around. What does he want?

"Do you want me?" she asks.

But Ted is staring out the window, his theories slipping away from him. He lets her words pile up on his stomach like tiny asphalt pebbles. Beauty, even her beauty, has become something to him like a stone, a solid pit in his chest. His answer would have broken her heart if she'd had one.

"Wayne, you were supposed to detonate me while I was there in his cabin."

"I know."

"You failed in your duty to serve the United States of America, Honor Code section four, paragraph nineteen."

"I know."

"There are consequences," she says.

"I know," Wayne answers, and reaches out to hold her cheek in his hand. She doesn't move away. She is programmed not to resist male advances. He pulls her down onto the floor of the van, beside the pool-cleaning apparatus. He nestles his face in her neck. He wraps his hand around her waist underneath her flannel shirt and pulls her closer, feeling the silicone lumps that are her breasts push into him. He smells the chalk of her scent while her arms remain limp by her sides. "Hold me," he commands her, though he feels immediately ashamed, desperate. Still, "Hold me," he repeats. She complies and wraps her mechanical arms around him while he speaks words of loving sweetness into her ear, the ones she's been waiting to hear, hot breath against plastic. Wayne whispers the magic words that send a repressed tremor through the quiet night, an explosion that could only be described as American.

Ava Bean

Jennifer S. Davis

On the way home from the hospital, Ava tells Charlotte that after her first husband was killed during a German air attack on Bari in 1943, she cried without pause for weeks, only to emerge from her stunning grief temporarily blind. She blames this temporary disability for the early demise of her screen career.

"No one wants a *real* blind person in a film," Ava says from the backseat of the Chevette. Charlotte watches in the rearview mirror as the old woman rummages through a Burger King bag propped on the cast that covers her leg from toe to hip. She tosses handfuls of salt and catsup on the floorboard, finally finds the French fries, shoves a handful in her mouth, then sighs.

"Fake blind, sure," Ava says with her mouth full. "But when

you're bopping off the set and knocking things over, well, let's just say you draw the wrong kind of attention to yourself."

"You'd think it'd make you look more authentic," Charlotte says, pulling into the narrow gravel strip that runs between Ava's house and the neighbor's to the right.

"Nobody wants authentic," Ava says. "We're all so brainwashed that fake usually seems realer than real. Like if your kids never call or visit or send Christmas cards, and you go about your business, feeding the dog and making dinner, because you have to, because no one else is going to do it for you—those same kids might think that you don't care, that you ain't dying inside." Ava points a limp French fry at her chest, mimicking a dagger slipping into her heart. "Now, if an actor in that situation on TV cried and threw things and called the children in the middle of the night begging for attention, something no one who thinks anything of herself would actually do, the people watching would say *Wow. That's real.*"

On the sidewalk, a toddler stumbles in circles. Braids poke out of the Tupperware bowl she wears on her head. Occasionally the girl whacks the bowl with a carrot she carries like a wand, and Charlotte thinks of Lucy, her long yellow pigtails, the way they glowed in the fading sunlight one afternoon at the beach, a long-ago memory that has fused into all the others.

Ava's neighbor, the toddler's great-grandmother, is sprawled across a foldout chair on her front lawn, her thick legs mottled by the sun. She shakes a flyswatter at Charlotte's Chevette, yells something in an indistinguishable European language.

"The neighborhood is going to hell in a handbasket," Ava says, rolling down her window. "I thought that was the whole point of the war, to take care of these heathens." Then, to the neighbor, "I've told you, this is my goddamn driveway."

"I can park on the street," Charlotte offers.

"I got my sight back in an A&P," Ava is saying to Charlotte as she struggles to reach over her cast-encased leg to open the back door. "That's the God's truth. I was groping along the produce bins when *boom*. I must've passed out, 'cause when I came to, I could see as clear as I'm seeing you, clearer even, since now I can't seem to see a damned thing, and there was a sign hanging over me, Jonathan Apples, ten cents a pound, which wasn't a bad price. Produce is outrageous these days."

"Hold on," Charlotte says, getting out of the car. When Charlotte opens the back door, Ava begins scooting off the seat, her cast missiled straight toward Charlotte's belly. By the time Ava is propped against the dented Chevette with her crutches under her arms, Charlotte's new shirt is covered in the old woman's makeup. Ava had refused to leave the hospital until Charlotte helped apply her "face," the pasty, exaggerated mask Ava has worn every day of her adult life.

The neighbor yells something garbled, something that sounds like *whore*.

"The food." Ava points into the car. Charlotte crawls into the backseat, grabs the Burger King, pops the greasy bag under one arm, Ava under the other, and they lurch-hop toward the house.

"He didn't mean to do it, you know, " Ava says at the front door while Charlotte fumbles for the keys. "Ralph's a good dog. Not a mean bone in his body. He'd never hurt me on purpose."

"I know," Charlotte says. Ralph lets loose a wretched, hollow wail from the foyer. For a moment, Charlotte regrets that she didn't take Billy's advice and dump the dog in the woods when Ava was in the hospital and she'd had the chance.

"You're a good girl, too," Ava says. Charlotte doubts the truth of the statement.

"How long you been living here?" Billy asks.

"Four weeks," Charlotte says. She's sitting on the front porch, sipping a beer and smoking, watching Billy rake the leaves. Ava passed out after her fifth glass of wine, and Charlotte put her to bed. The sun is barely sinking, but Ava won't wake up until morning. Charlotte considers herself off duty, although the agreement is she's on call 24/7.

"I'm just saying." Billy pokes the pile of leaves with the rake. "I've been working around here for near ten years, and you don't see her offering *me* any sweet deal. You know what she calls me? She calls me boy. Me—almost fifty. Might as well say nigger. Means the same thing."

"She's old. Old people around here are set in their ways." Charlotte thinks Billy might be good-looking if he weren't so skinny, if he weren't so angry.

Billy stops raking, stares at Charlotte. His irises are almost as black as his pupils, and Charlotte finds it difficult to return his gaze.

"Old," Billy says, then snorts. "Are you an idiot, girl? You think that woman just has herself a light, even tan? That she won't leave the house without all that makeup because she's out to catch herself a man? You ever see her kids around here? Any of them? She's got three, and the oldest owns this house. Now, why do you think he'd buy his momma a house in Florida when he lives halfway across the world in California? Not one of them kids ever visits. And you know why?" He pokes his arm out, points with one gloved finger at his dun-colored skin. "That's why. Her kids didn't come out light like her. They can't pass. You see what I'm saying?"

Charlotte isn't sure what Billy's saying, because Billy says a lot. For instance, he says that Zelda, the next-door neighbor, was married to a Nazi, and she's hiding out here in Twilight Pines to keep a low profile. He says that the butcher down at the Piggly Wiggly woos boys into the freezer with Hershey bars and toy gadgets he steals from cereal boxes, that he's seen this with his own eyes. He says that Clinton is a Russian spy who's bent on ruining the country, which might not be such a bad thing, considering that the country has been going straight downhill since they elected the android actor from California.

"She's always been nice to me," Charlotte says, which is not exactly true. She crushes her cigarette against the concrete porch and adds it to the pile beside the potted fern. "I was living in my car when she found me."

Charlotte wasn't so much living in her car as passed out in it with nowhere in particular to go and all her things crammed into plastic crates in her trunk. She was considering going back home to Montgomery, where things were fucked up but at least in a way she understood. She'd stopped for a drink or two at the bar on the corner and woke up in her car in front of Ava's house, Ava rapping on her window. The old woman took Charlotte inside, fed her, let her wash up, and after Charlotte repaid the kindness by listening to some of Ava's life stories, which included the one where the handsome heart specialist with the diamond pinky ring and the uppity secretary told Ava she was going to die sooner rather than later, Ava offered Charlotte a job as a caretaker of sorts. She gets room and board, a weekly allowance, and, when Ava dies, a tidy bonus. Charlotte never considered saying no.

"Mrs. Bean thinks you're weak, that she can own you, that she's on her way out and you're her Hail Mary, her last chance to convince someone she ain't the mean-hearted bitch she is," Billy says. "You being white makes it all the better." He cups his hands together, peers into the little cave he's made, like there's a trapped animal in there.

Charlotte gestures at the crumbling Cape Cod behind her. "Things worked out good. She's got someone to take care of her, I got a place to stay."

"I'm just saying." Billy offers a slow, stretched smile, which makes him look younger than he is. "Mrs. Bean seemed to be doing just fine until you came around, and then *bam*, that little mutt pulls her down the stairs. Mighty convenient for you, don't you think? You almost hit the big payday." He walks toward Charlotte, rips a glove off with his teeth, covers her knee with his bare hand, the rough pad of his thumb moving in tiny circles. This is the first time a man has touched her in a year. "Maybe," he says, "you're smarter than she thought."

"Marlene Dietrich was a man-hungry bitch," Ava says. "I had a good role in *Destry Rides Again*. Three lines. Long ones at that. But she was getting old by then, and she didn't like the competition. They cut me. Not one 'I'm sorry.' "

Ava holds Ralph to her chest with one speckled hand; a cigarette dangles from the other. Charlotte is setting Ava's long, thinning hair, and it's difficult to get the uneven strands to stay wrapped around the rollers. Every time Charlotte's fingers come near Ralph, he gives her a little nip, which makes Ava, who is past drunk, giggle. In front of them, over the kitchen table, hangs a full-length painting of a pale naked woman with three perfect breasts. Her nipples are accented with tinted glass shards. Ava says that it's high art, that it's Charlotte's after she dies, that she'll make sure of it.

"I've got a daughter, you know," Ava says as she fumbles ashes into a giant Chinese vase, which Charlotte knows holds the remains of Ava's third husband, a man she refers to only as The Bastard.

Ava's hair feels silky against Charlotte's hands, not like the wiry hair she expects on a black woman, and she thinks of the soft, yellow lock of hair she keeps in a Bible in her bedroom, the way it feels when she fans it against the sensitive skin of her eyelids.

"So I'm content it turned out that way," Ava is saying. "If Tina had to be one or the other, I'm glad it was smart rather than pretty. I was pretty and it got me nothing but trouble. She was smart and it got her a doctor from Malibu who can make her look like whatever she damn well pleases. If we'd had the same options when I was working Hollywood, there's no telling how far I could have gone." She dumps her cigarette butt into the vase, then peers down into its opening. "Looks like The Bastard is filling up. He always was full of himself."

"I think you still look beautiful," Charlotte says. "How many women your age have hair like this?" She pats Ava's hair, which in spite of being freshly washed, already reeks of cigarette smoke.

"It's funny, being blind," Ava says. "Your senses get really sharp. I could tell what kind of fruit was in a bowl without touching it, only smelling. I could hear someone enter the room just by the breathing." She pauses, scratches Ralph behind his ears. "And I can still smell bullshit from a mile away."

Charlotte's hands stop mid-rolling. Sometimes, not often, Ava gets mean when she drinks. Throws things when Charlotte tells her it's time to eat or go to bed. Shits herself out of spite. When she does these things, Charlotte almost wishes that when Ralph pulled Ava down the stairs, the fall had killed the woman instead of just breaking her leg, wishes she could take the money now and go somewhere new, start over right this time.

Ava leans back in her chair, tilts her face toward Charlotte, stares at her for a long moment, her gray eyes shadowy.

"You ain't pretty neither," she says finally, "but at least you try to be nice to a dying old lady. Nice is better than pretty any day of the week. That's what I told Tina when she was little, but it just made her meaner. She's never visited me here in Florida. Won't even take my calls these days. Can you imagine, knowing your momma's got maybe six months and not taking her calls? What kind of hate is that? The kind that kills you the long, hard way, that's what kind." She kicks the vase with her good foot, and old Ralph releases an irritated bleat. "Just ask The Bastard."

Charlotte understands the complexities of families, and she tells Ava so. Then she begins sharing the story of her father, how he couldn't keep his job at the mill. How he woke her mother up from a dead sleep when he came in after the bar closed, knowing she worked two full-time jobs, and forced her to make him breakfast, eggs and steak and bacon, the whole works. How he kept a lover, a tiny Vietnamese woman who did laundry, for ten years and two babies, not that he took care of them either. How he came to her mother's funeral drunk and had to be dragged out of the cemetery by her uncle. How his hate didn't kill him before he held up a convenience store and shot a widow straight through the eye for less than eighty bucks. How when Charlotte went to visit him that one time in prison to make things right after Lucy was born, after she understood what it meant to be a parent, to bring a child into the world, he refused to come to the visitation room, said he didn't know anyone by the name of Charlotte.

But Ava is snoring before she can finish, her hair only half rolled, the rest already drying in a long frizz.

"She out?"

Charlotte turns to see Billy standing in the doorway, twilight glowing behind him so that he's haloed in russet gold, and for a moment, Charlotte cannot speak. She simply nods.

Billy stomps through the kitchen, his dirty boots leaving tracks on the floor. He stops, stares at Ava.

"I ain't ever touched her before," he says. "Not even to take my pay. She just leaves it on the back porch in an envelope."

"Why do you think she hired you then, kept you around all this time if she can't stand to look at you? Why would she punish herself like that?" Charlotte grabs Ava's half-finished bottle of wine from the table, takes a long drink, trying the whole time not to look at Billy, who's staring at her like he might want to hit her.

"Who knows," he says finally, "why we all hate ourselves so much."

Billy pulls off his baseball cap and sets it on the table with the solemn air of a boy in church, then he plucks Ava up from her chair, her cast swinging, and walks to the back of the house toward the master bedroom. Charlotte follows closely behind, Ralph yipping at her feet. When Billy stops in the doorway of Ava's bedroom, Charlotte almost runs into his narrow back.

"You know, in ten years, I ain't ever been in this room. Not to fix a broken window or a squeaky board or nothing. She always uses a company if something goes wrong in here."

"Like I told you," Charlotte says, "old people are stuck in their ways."

Billy turns toward her sharply. "Can you not say something stupid for five minutes, just long enough to get her in the bed?"

He walks through the doorway, and Charlotte runs to the bed, yanks down the white crocheted comforter, not bothering to pull down the sheets. Billy lowers Ava onto the bed with surprising gentleness, arranges her hands to cover her sagging bosom. Charlotte grabs two pillows from the trunk at the end of the bed to slide under Ava's injured leg.

Ava's eyes flutter open, lock on Billy. "What the hell is he doing here?" she says, quite clearly considering, and then she's asleep again.

"Nice law-abiding old lady, right?" Billy thumbs through a stack of envelopes on Ava's bedside table. "How do you reckon she gets five different Social Security checks? You ever thought about that? About where your money's coming from?"

"It's the same money that pays you," Charlotte says, and immediately she regrets saying it. Billy frowns, slams the envelopes down on the table. Ralph, who is half-blind, barks at the commotion, then bites at Billy's boot. Billy kicks him hard in the ribs, says "That goddamn dog has bit me for the last time." Ralph growls, teeters around dazed for a second, then flops down next to the bed.

"You know how easy it would be?" Billy says, nodding toward the pillows Charlotte is still clamping against her chest. "A minute at most, and it would all be over. Then you'd have your money." Charlotte shoves the pillows under Ava's leg before he can say anything else. He walks up behind her as she fluffs them, cups his hands over her breasts, places his lips against her hair. "I'm just teasing you, girl," he says. "I like teasing you." Then, "Was that true, what you said about your daddy?" He doesn't move his hands.

"True enough," Charlotte says.

"Let's go somewhere else," he whispers against her neck. "I never feel right in this house."

The neighbor, Zelda, has parked her rusting Lincoln behind Charlotte's Chevette, which happens often in the ongoing driveway wars.

Billy works a brick loose from one of the planters lining Ava's porch, shrugs off his T-shirt, wraps it around his hand, then slams the brick through the Lincoln's driver's side window. He pokes his hand carefully through the broken glass, unlocks the door, opens it, then leans into the car, puts it into neutral, and starts pushing it off the gravel strip that runs between their houses and onto Zelda's lawn. The wiry muscles on his dark back shimmy under his skin.

"There," he says, after the Lincoln is soundly on Zelda's front lawn. "Fucking Nazi bitch."

Charlotte thinks that perhaps she shouldn't go off with this man, that perhaps he is indeed as dangerous as he seems. But she can still feel his breath against her neck, his hands cupping her breasts, and it's been a year. She's been real good for a year.

"I'll drive," he says. He shakes the glass out of his shirt, then tugs it back over his head. When he's dressed, he grins at her, a blinding grin, says, "Got to look good for our date."

"This is a date?" Charlotte says.

"Gimme the keys." He shoves his hand toward her, palm out. "I got a place I go."

They drive out of Twilight Pines, past Check Into Cash, past the Piggly Wiggly, past the Keep It Clean Laundromat, and pull into Charley's Fine Liquors, where a group of young black men, their pants slung low, mill about slouched-backed in the parking lot.

"Nervous?" Billy says. He places a finger under a lock of Charlotte's blond hair, flicks it. "You think they'd hurt you if they could?"

"Grey Goose," Charlotte says. "And make sure it's cold." She hands him two twenties. This is the first time she's had any kind of money in months.

Charlotte watches him enter the store, the way he nods gamely at the young men, slapping a few on the back as he passes. Billy says something to one boy, a squat kid with a goatee. The boy looks toward the Chevette and starts laughing. Charlotte slams the lock down on her door, then unlocks it just as quickly, not wanting to give Billy any ammunition to work with.

When Billy gets back to the car, he shoves a bottle of cheap wine toward her, tucks two 40s between his thin thighs.

They drive out of town, toward the suburbs where all the stucco houses come in shades of pink, nice clean-looking houses with a few palm trees growing here and there on carefully manicured lawns. Billy has rolled down the windows. The rush of air when the car's moving fast makes it possible to talk only at stoplights, not that they do.

"Here we go," Billy says finally, turning slowly in to a fancy circle of houses that face a manmade lake strategically lit with dim spot-lights. A fake heron perches on the bank. "I used to work out here when they were building this place. The pond is stocked right. I fished in it some mornings before work until some rich fucker com-plained that he didn't pay dues for any Tom, Dick, or Harry to steal his bass. They usually don't bother you if you just want to stare at the water."

He takes the bottle of wine from Charlotte, screws off the cap, then hands it back to her. "Cheers," he says, knocking his bottle of beer against her wine.

Billy signals that he doesn't want to talk by turning the radio on low, some soft jazz station Charlotte never listens to. They drink qui-etly for a while. The wine, mixed with the pain pills she's been swip-ing from Ava, hits harder than she expects, and Charlotte's head's spinning before half the bottle is gone.

"You ready?" Billy asks. Charlotte nods. He takes her wine and wedges their bottles behind the backseat, then leans toward her, be-gins unbuttoning her blouse, his fingers still cool from the beer.

Charlotte closes her eyes. She's sixteen and lying in a field with Lucy's father, right in the middle of the day. They are naked, their bodies glistening from lovemaking. They wave wildly at cars driving by on the county road. Some of the cars honk as they pass, and it feels like everyone is part of their love story.

"You smell good, girl," Billy's saying, and then his lips are hot against her breastbone, his breath musky and sweet. Charlotte thinks, it's been so long. Charlotte thinks, this feels so good. And his lips are moving, down, down her chest, against the rim of her bra, and her head is spinning. She feels weightless, like air.

When she opens her eyes again, Billy's leaning against the driver's door, smoking.

"What happened?" she asks. Her shirt is completely unbuttoned. Her skirt is pushed up to her waist. There is a new, fist-sized dent on the glove-compartment door.

"Sorry about the car," Billy says, looking at the dent. "You passed out on me."

Charlotte reaches between her thighs, feels for moisture.

"I'm many things," Billy says, "but a rapist ain't one of them." He thumps his cigarette out the window.

"Why are you always so angry?" Charlotte says without knowing she's going to say it. For a second, the time it takes to draw a single breath, his face twitches and softens, and Charlotte can see there's a way in, a way for her to touch all that hurt and want moiling there in the pit of him. And then he's Billy again. This is her weakness. Charlotte knows. This is the kind of man, all of that barely restrained anger, that makes her feel alive. She didn't need the fat-assed condescending social worker to tell her that. She's always known.

"Can you take a break from asking stupid questions?" Billy snaps. "You must be worn out thinking them all up by now." He presses a hand hard against the C-section scar on her belly. "Where's the kid?"

Charlotte pushes his hand away, pulls her shirt over her chest. "They took her."

Charlotte sees Lucy's face in the rear window of the cruiser, her huge, wet eyes. The cops didn't even bother to buckle the girl in, and they'd said she was the one guilty of child endangerment. Charlotte sees herself mouthing *I'll get you soon, baby* at the disappearing cruiser, but even then, in that exact moment she mouthed the words, she knew she wouldn't. That in a way, it would be so much easier not to.

"Where's the father?" Billy asks. "He still around?" His voice drops when he says this, and Charlotte thinks that maybe he is jealous. Just a little bit.

"It's been a long time," she says.

"I got a kid," Billy says. He points at one of the more modest houses surrounded by a moat of light. "He lives there. He asked me not to come around no more. But sometimes I come here and watch. He's done good for himself, you know? That means I've done good. That's how I like to think about, it, anyway."

"You've done better than most," Charlotte says.

"How much is Mrs. Bean paying you?"

Charlotte considers not telling him but figures he probably already knows. He has a way of knowing everything. "A hundred and fifty a week, ten thousand when she passes. The doctor said she's got six months, tops. With the added trauma of the leg, maybe not that long."

"You get it in writing?" He pulls a cigarette from his pack, places it between her lips, curves his hand around the match while he lights it for her.

She nods yes, blows out a stream of smoke. "Not getting things in writing is how I ended up sleeping in my car in the first place."

"It's funny, death," he says. "Even when we know it's coming, it's never expected, not really. Like that boy in the papers on death row in Texas. I mean, he was wormy in the head, but even an animal knows when it's on its way out, and I'm betting he was smarter than most animals. They give him his last meal, and he doesn't finish it. Tells them to wrap it up. That'll he'll finish it when he gets back. You see what I'm saying?"

"Was Ava really in the movies?" Charlotte asks. "Do you think she has the kind of money she promised me?" She has spent weeks staring at the black-and-white framed photos scattered around Ava's house, women in shiny dresses cut on the bias, costume jewelry dripping from necks and ears. Charlotte can't tell if they're real photos or reproductions bought from some souvenir store. She likes to imagine

Ava as young and glamorous, drinking cocktails in long white gloves at Hollywood mansions in the hills, not old and drunk and dying. She wants to believe that this kind of glamour happens for someone. And she wants to believe that Ava will really give her the money she offered, that the agreement she requested Ava to write out and sign is worth more than the paper it's written on.

Billy snorts. "Stupid, sweet girl," he says. "If that woman's got money, you ain't getting it unless you take it." He cups her chin, leans toward her like he's going to kiss her. "It would be so easy," he says. "A few too many pills. An honest mistake. It could take years for her to be dead and done with it. Doctors never get it right. How about Mexico? We could rent ourselves a little hacienda."

His other hand is kneading her belly now, and her blood is warming, her heart quickening.

Then his finger is inside her, pushing hard, the way she likes it. "You want to try again?" he says.

When Charlotte knocks on the neighbor's door, Zelda opens it in mid-rant, the foreign words tumbling out of her mouth, hard as pebbles. She clutches an official-looking document in one hand, and she won't shut up, no matter how politely Charlotte smiles.

"This is America," Charlotte finally interrupts. "I speak English."

"Deed," Zelda says, pointing at the document she's now waving in Charlotte's face. "Do you understand this word? My driveway."

"I'm just looking for Mrs. Bean's dog," Charlotte says. "He's gone missing."

"This is no Germany," Zelda says. The freckled pouches under her eyes quiver, and Charlotte realizes that the woman is on the verge of tears. "You cannot take my things."

"I'm just looking for the dog, ma'am," Charlotte says.

"Maybe the criminals that place my car on my yard took it," Zelda says with a smile. "Maybe they do many bad things around here." Then she slams the door in Charlotte's face.

When Charlotte gets home, she finds Ava sitting at the kitchen table with an empty bottle of wine, her crutches tossed at her feet. A thin line of blood seeps down her forehead, but she doesn't move to wipe it away.

"I fell," she says.

Charlotte walks to the kitchen sink, opens the cupboard, pulls out the large basin she uses to wash Ava's hair, and begins filling it with water. She grabs the shampoo from on top of the refrigerator and sets in on the table.

"It's been a week," Ava says. She's crying now. Makeup clots under her eyes. Her lipstick is smeared across her cheek. "Ralph never leaves my sight. Where could he have gone?"

"We'll find him," Charlotte says, slipping a dish towel around Ava's neck. "He can't have gone far. Somebody found him and they're just holding him safe until we get him. You'll see." She knows that this is not true. Either Ralph crawled off to die, or Billy dumped him in the countryside, or Zelda finally found a way to get back at Ava and the rest of the world for the many injustices she's suffered, but wherever Ralph is, he isn't coming back. But for now, the lie seems kinder.

Charlotte massages Ava's knotted hands until the basin fills. She lugs it to the kitchen table, scoots Ava's stool around until her lower back is pressed against the edge of the basin, then lowers the woman's head into the water. Her hair is matted with blood, and Charlotte is relieved when she sees that the cut looks worse than it is.

"He's the only one that loves me," Ava is saying as Charlotte soaps her hair, so thin that the scalp shows through. Pink-tinged suds cover

Charlotte's hands. "My kids don't give a damn. Not a one of them. Only him. He didn't mean to hurt me. He doesn't have a mean bone in his body."

"I know," Charlotte says. She dips Ava's head into the basin, tries to get out as much shampoo and blood as she can.

Ava sits up sharply. "What did you do with him?" Water splashes on the tile floor, a mess Charlotte will have to clean up. Ava grips Charlotte's hand, the long nails breaking the skin. "Where did you put him?"

"Shhhh," Charlotte whispers, and Ava relaxes, rests her head back against the basin.

"There was a woman in the hospital bed next to me, when I broke my leg," Ava says sleepily. "She'd been in some kind of accident. Her and her husband. Not a scratch on her, but she'd hit her head and couldn't remember nothing you just told her. Her husband was killed, and her kids would tell her and she'd go crazy, and then she'd take a nap, wake up all confused, but happy, you know—happy to be here, but clueless that her husband was gone And then they'd have to tell her all over that her old man had died and she'd lose it again." Ava stares up at Charlotte, heavy-lidded, her eyes unfocused. "What do you think is worse—forgetting or knowing?"

Charlotte is trying not to listen to Ava. She's trying to remember Lucy's father, what he whispered to her when he touched her, how young they were, how they believed the things they promised each other. She's trying to remember Lucy as a baby when she used to bathe her in a basin like this, her chubby baby legs kicking against the water. If Charlotte closes her eyes, she can feel Lucy's fingers curl around her thumb, she can hear her shriek with laughter.

When Charlotte opens her eyes, Billy is standing outside the kitchen window, the sky behind him cornflower blue, his eyes black and vacant. But she knows what they're saying. *It would be so easy.* And then he's gone.

Until Lucy, Charlotte didn't understand anything about how the world works, about how one person can shape the course of another's life as much by absence as anything else, how a stranger's faith might be the closest thing to salvation you're ever offered.

Ava is asleep now, the full weight of her head pressing against Charlotte's hands. She holds her there, suspended over the water. For one forgiving moment, the weight is not unbearable.

Embrace

Roxana Robinson

ONE

They're married, but not to each other.

Nat unlocks the door and then steps back, to let Ella go in first. The hotel room is high-ceilinged and square, and a double bed takes up most of it. On the bed is a cream-colored quilted spread. Pale heavy curtains frame the window; thinner, translucent ones obscure the view. The carpet is thick and cocoa-colored. There is an ornate bureau, imitation French, and a gilt-framed mirror. The room is close and airless. They have no luggage.

Ella moves ahead of him, stopping near the bed. She's in her late twenties, and thin, with long chestnut-colored hair. She turns, so that she won't see herself in the mirror. She stands facing away from him, looking down. She has never done this before. She hardly knows this man, and this is a terrible mistake. She has made a terrible mistake, coming to this airless room with someone who, it turns out, is a stranger. She stands motionless, awaiting perdition.

Nat follows her into the room.

He has never done exactly this before, either, never done anything quite so bold and crude as to rent a hotel room at lunchtime. What he did was always out of town, with women he never intended to see again. It was mostly in Los Angeles, a place full of beautiful, willing girls, happy to be taken out for dinner and then back to his hotel. Those encounters had been brief and distant. But this, now, is in his own city, only blocks from his own apartment, with a woman he does want to see again, and he's afraid he's starting something large and irreversible. What it means is the end of his marriage. He won't be able to go on like this; he's going too far. This is reckless, indefensible, and he's doing it in the name of lust, which is, right now, notably absent. He understands that coming here was a mistake, though he believes he loves this woman.

He wonders if today can be salvaged. Perhaps it's the room— should he have gotten a bigger one? But no: it's the silence, the immobility of the room that's the problem, the implacably fixed furniture, the hushing carpet, the heavy curtains, the whole place awaiting human animation.

He likes looking at her. She's small and slight, with a polished curtain of hair spilling down her back. Her head is bent.

Ella is looking down at the bedspread, waiting for the worst. It is shameful, it is excruciating, that she's become part of this. What if she's seen by someone she knows, in this corridor of bedrooms, with this man who is not her husband? What is she doing here at lunchtime, with a man she hardly knows? She can't look at him. She can feel his presence—large, solid, he's much taller and stronger than she is—as he stands behind her. She's now obligated to go through with this, since she agreed to come. It feels like an execution. She dreads his touch.

She thinks of her husband. He's downtown right now, in his office, in his shirtsleeves and suspenders. He's on the phone, or making a point to someone—he loves making points—or having another cup of coffee. He's doing something completely ordinary. He's not betraying her utterly, betraying her to the bone, though he has. But he's not doing it right now, and she is. She could call him, there's an ivory phone on the table by the bed. He'd answer at his desk, his voice familiar. "Hello?"

It was a mistake, but she has to go through with it. She is obligated: of course she knew what it meant, meeting at the Plaza for lunch. Now she will have to have sex with him in this strange airless room. She will have to offer him her naked body. She would rather die.

Nat steps closer to her.

It was a mistake, that's all.

He turns her body to him and glimpses her grieving face. He puts his arms around her and stands still, holding her close without moving. He can feel her, rigid and fearful. He says nothing, embracing her quietly. It's a mistake, that's all. What he wants is for her not to be miserable. He holds her until he feels her quiet, until she understands that she is safe; that all he wants from her is this close holding, this understanding.

TWO

They're married, and now to each other.

The divorces were tumultuous and unhappy, but Nat and Ella

persevered. They weathered the storms, they made their way deter-
minedly through the torment toward each other.

Now they have been married for nine years, and they love each
other. They're knitted deeply into each other, and they warm themselves at each other's hearts. They long for each other, and their
bodies teach each other pleasure, but they fight terribly. They say un-
forgivable things to each other. Once, Nat took Ella violently by her
shoulders. "You make me so angry," he said. "Someday I'm going to
kill you."

Ella, beside herself with rage, was pleased. "Fine," she told him,
satisfaction in her voice. It seemed a vindication, proof of something.

When they are not fighting they are happy, drunk on each other,
but when they fight, Ella fears they will split apart, and if they split
apart, she fears it will be the end of her. She can't imagine herself, if
this marriage fails. She can't imagine her life if Nat were to leave her.
She can't imagine her existence without him; it would be black and
meaningless, the void. It is terrifying to her, this prospect, like falling
into deep space.

She knows, in one part of her mind, when she is calm, that this is
absurd. She has her own life, with friends and a career—she is a literary publicist, and has founded her own agency. Her life won't really be over if she and Nat split up. Still, there are times, when they
are fighting, when rationality is not available. She has trouble breathing, and she thinks of the blackness of deep space, which seems to be
waiting for her.

Now they are driving from Florence to Siena, along a narrow,
crowded motorway. The cars around them are lunatic: on the left,
Maseratis and Mercedeses pass at a hundred miles an hour; on the
right, huge trucks sway dangerously, taking up one and a half lanes.
Behind them headlights flare constantly, signaling them to move
over. For half an hour they have been driving in hostile silence.

Nat breaks it. "I just don't know why you couldn't have gone on to the market yourself."

"I just don't know why you couldn't have waited for me, with the car. Or given me the car," Ella says. "I don't know why you have to decide what we do and when we do it."

Nat makes an exasperated sound. "I see," he says, " I decide everything. Is that what you think?"

"Do you think I decide *anything*?"

"Do you think you *don't* decide anything?"

They get into these maddening, circular series of questions, each challenging the other, losing the point, going off on tangents, becoming increasingly angry.

Nat is exasperated by Ella's self-centeredness. How can she not know that everything he does is with her in mind? What he wants is for her to be happy. This entire trip—Florence and Siena, the churches, the old hotels, the views—was for her. The impassive faces of the holy martyrs, the mysterious half-smiles of Madonnas. It's early spring, and wildflowers star the long pale grasses in the fields. This was all meant to make her happy, and why does it not?

"I decide *nothing!*" Ella says, furious. "Nothing at all! You decide where we go, where we'll have dinner, what time we'll leave in the morning, what we're going to see, *everything*. You even keep my passport! I don't even carry my own passport!"

"I keep your passport with mine, and with our tickets," says Nat, reprovingly. His face has darkened, his mouth tightened. She has broadened her attack, flailing wildly about, as always. "It's just so I'll know where everything is. If you want your passport, Ella, of course I'll give it to you."

"I don't care if I have my passport or not," Ella says wildly. She feels trapped by him, helpless; he seems both reasonable and unjust.

She knows it's practical for him to keep the passports. Yet why should he have hers?

"Did you not want to come to Italy?" Nat turns his head and looks at her, dangerously, in the midst of the manic speed of the motorway. The car swerves slightly, then swerves back, in and out of the terrifying stream of cars.

Ella hopes they will crash.

"*Of course* I wanted to come to Italy!" She is distraught. "But you don't ask me what I want! You decide everything yourself, and then you tell me what we're going to do, and then you're furious if I have a tiny, remote, minutely differing suggestion! I have to do everything you say, always! It's as though I don't exist!"

What she'd wanted was for him to come with her to the flea market in Florence, wander through the stalls with him. It was a junky market, only odds and ends, but it was Florence. The people offering the broken clocks and plastic dolls were Florentine. Their faces—surprisingly fair, ruddy, blue-eyed, with red-brown hair—echoed those in the old frescoes. Ella loved all of it; she always thought the living scene was as interesting as the museum.

Nat thought it was dreary and trashy. "Why should I want to look at a flea market, full of junk?" he had asked. "I have to move the car. I'll take it back to the hotel, and you come back whenever you want."

But Ella feels crushed by the weight of his disapproval, by the thought that she was someone who wanted to look at junk, someone he disdained. All of it makes her feel panicky and abandoned: she speaks no Italian and has no sense of direction. She knows she'd get lost, trying to find her way back up to the hotel. She is afraid of being lost, and afraid of asking questions of strangers. She loves him. She hates being at odds with him. The flea market was a bad idea; she should never have suggested it. He disapproved of it, and of her. And now she has made him angry again; he may leave her. At any time he may leave her. He is easily angered at her. She starts to weep from despair. She is always doing things wrong. They have been married nine years; she has not managed to give him a child; he may leave her. They are always fighting. She will die if he leaves her. She knows this is irrational; knowing it does not help.

Nat keeps on driving, the corners of his mouth turned down in disapproval. She is so extreme, Ella, so wildly intemperate, and so utterly unfair. Her complaints are wounding: he feels that his life is given over to making her happy, that all their decisions are made on her behalf. He'd thought she'd like the trip to Italy, and she had seemed to. This is the way she acts: at first she says nothing, later she complains bitterly. It's completely unfair. He loves her. He is easily wounded by her, he is outraged by her when they fight. She is irrational, messy, late. She maddens him. He is completely absorbed by her. He cannot wait each night to see her, to see her turn her head, to listen. He waits to hear what she will say; he is endlessly interested by what she will say. His body needs hers. They are joined, which makes all this so excruciating: she levels these wild charges at him, as though she were dismissing their connection. How can she? How can she take such extreme positions over something as trivial as the flea market? These trips seem to be more pain than pleasure. How can she act so brutal and miserable to him? He never thinks of leaving her; she's at the center of his life.

At the end of their fights everything is somehow righted. A great calm happiness floods through them both, like a neap tide rising and moving through the fields, smoothing out the rutted landscape like liquid silk. This is hard for them to remember when they're fighting; it's hard to believe it's a possibility.

Nat swerves more now, across the traffic, into the slower lane, then he swerves again, cutting out of that lane too. He pulls off the highway altogether, onto a tiny semicircular pullout, edged haphaz-ardly by whitewashed stones. A rocky hillside rises steeply above it; just ahead, on the road, is one of the low stone tunnels that perforate Italian mountains. The tunnels are pitch-black inside, narrow and claustrophobic, and the cars race through them at supersonic speeds. Their car was just about to enter this one, and the traffic beside them continues to slide smoothly and hypnotically into the small black mouth, which is like that of a monster. But just before they are sucked into the dark maw, Nat pulls completely off the road and jerks the car to a stop in the turnout, the corners of his own mouth turned down.

Ella sees his disapproving mouth, his lowered brows, his fierce eyes, and she turns away, to the window. A sob swells her chest: what-ever he is about to do will be terrible. She is afraid he will hit her, though he has never done this, or threatened to. She is afraid he will reach across her and open the door, and tell her to get out, to clam-ber onto the steep rocky hillside rising above them. Then he will pull the door shut and drive on, vanishing into the black tunnel and leav-ing her there forever.

Nat puts the car into neutral, jerks on the hand brake, and turns off the engine. He turns to Ella, his brows still dark. He leans awk-wardly across the tiny car, across the gear shift, and puts his arms around her. He pulls her as close as he can, the upright gear shift be-tween them. He holds her against him and strokes her head, her silky hair.

They've gotten themselves into this terrible trough of unhappi-ness, and this is all he can think of to get them back to the other place, where they remember each other. He holds her tightly inside the circle of himself, pressing his cheek against her head. He feels her collarbones against his chest, her shoulder blades beneath his hands. Her hair is shorter now, but still silky.

Ella feels his arms close around her, she breathes in the familiar smell of his skin, and she closes her eyes in relief. She feels her whole body yield, give way. This is more than she had hoped for. It is everything.

THREE

They have been married for nearly a quarter of a century, and they have stopped fighting. Something between them has steadied, and they no longer frighten each other. Instead, they trust each other. She is less intemperate, and when he gets annoyed she finds his exasperation amusing. She waits it out, smiling, and smooths his hair. He finds her exaggerations funny; she no longer infuriates him.

They look different now, of course. She is still small, nearly childlike, but her waist has thickened, and her face bears a mask of fine lines. She is no longer beautiful, but pleasant-looking. Her hair is now short and iron gray, thin and straight, with bangs, like a felt helmet. One knee gives her trouble, and sometimes she limps slightly. This morning, standing in line at the airport, waiting at the ticket counter, Nat saw her lean over to rub it. The sight made him feel tender, and he thought of her moving, with him, toward age, and toward the dark curtain beyond. He takes comfort in knowing that they will approach this, whatever it is, together.

His own body has thickened as well, and his hair has receded. His forehead is rising slowly, like a cliff from the sea. This disappoints him: his father had all his hair until he died, at eighty-one. Nat's hair had once been thick and springy—it was his secret vanity.

Ella doesn't mind his baldness, no longer notices it. She is so used to his face—the deep lines from nose to mouth, the dense eyebrows, the neat pouches beneath his thoughtful eyes—that it might as well be her own. She barely sees herself in the mirror now, her eyes fading, her lips blurring. They have been living together for decades now, and they belong to each other. They have forgiven each other the dreadful acts, and they appreciate the generous ones. They admire and enjoy each other. They have grown together into this marriage, adding year after year to the trunk of it, each line encompassing the one before. The years in which they fought are now enclosed, entirely and forever, by these later ones, in which they do not. These are years in which they simply love each other, years in which trust is dominant.

Today they're on a flight from Boston, where Nat had a business meeting and Ella saw her sister, to San Francisco, where he has another meeting. After that they'll go on to Los Angeles, to see his daughter Beth, who is a screenwriter. As far as they can tell, she is not a really successful one, but who can read the cryptic signs of Hollywood? Beth is funny and bright, always full of optimistic talk about meetings and development. She was angry about the divorce when she was younger, but seems to be over it. All three of them have lived it down, settling into enjoyment of one another's company. Her boyfriend—though is *boyfriend* the right word? It's hard to keep track of the correct word now—anyway, the person who is around more than anyone else, is a psychotherapist/mystic/studio musician named Ralph. He, too, is bright and funny, and if they lived in the East they would have regular salaries and health benefits, instead of this hand-to-mouth existence. Or maybe not. Maybe they are both simply outside the world of regular salaries and health benefits, and so it's a good thing they've found each other in West Hollywood.

Ralph and Beth have promised to take them to their favorite sushi restaurant. Ella doesn't like sushi—why do people still eat raw flesh, five hundred thousand years after the discovery of fire?—but she eats it with Beth. She loves Beth, and in some ways gets along better with her than Nat does. Nat gets frustrated by Beth; he wants her and

Ralph to get married and get jobs with health benefits. Ella finds this funny and touching. She thinks of it now and she reaches out and smooths his shoulder. He is the beloved. She feels grateful for his solicitude, the way he wants to take care of them all, herding them toward shelter like an anxious sheepdog. At her touch, Nat looks up from his book and smiles at her.

They're sitting in business class. Nat works for a large management consulting firm, and he's flown hundreds of thousands of miles. They both benefit from all the times he's been weathered in at O'Hare, fogged out of Portland, delayed at Dallas/Fort Worth. Now, when they fly together, they enjoy these wide comfortable seats, the kindly attentions of the flight attendant, the little compote of warm nuts after takeoff.

They haven't taken off yet; they've taxied out onto the runway and are waiting in line. Not for long, though: the skies are clear, and it's after Labor Day, the summer traveling peak over. Their stewardess has taken away their jackets. She's in her fifties, slightly stocky, with a wide, pleasant, animated face, slightly pockmarked. Her short hair is dense black, maybe dyed.

During the safety video it was she who put on a life jacket and stood in front of the cabin. She made smooth, ritualized gestures, setting the oxygen mask neatly over her nose, pointing out the emergency exits. No one watched her, and Ella wondered if this was because everyone had already heard these instructions, or if it was a subliminal superstition, the fear of naming dangers. The idea that it's bad luck to allow the idea of peril into your mind. By doing so you're calling danger into being, so the less you think about safety measures, the less likely you are to need them.

Maybe to counteract that superstition, Ella pulls out the plastic safety-instruction card from the pocket in front of her. She studies the people, tidily life-jacketed, who are sliding down the chute in an or-

derly line. Their faces seem lively and intent, not frightened or unhappy. It's broad daylight, and the chute rests on flat ground. If this
really happened, Ella thinks, there would be clouds of black smoke
and bursts of orange flame. Or maybe they would be sliding into the
ocean, at night, in blinding rain and huge swells. Disasters take place
in perilous conditions, storms and darkness, not on clear days under
blue skies. In any case, it wouldn't be like this—orderly and pleasant.
Ella, feeling she has somehow triumphed over the card, slides it back
into the pocket.

All the stewardesses have disappeared now, up front, perched
on their tiny provisional foldout seats. The sky is blindingly bright,
cloudless. They are in a line of planes, all huge and motionless. Heat
waves shimmer up from the tarmac, and the planes seem to tremble
slightly. The pilot's voice comes over the intercom.

They're number four, he tells them, and it won't be long now. He
speaks with a slight southern accent, and his voice is reassuring. The
reason that so many pilots are southern is that so many southerners
go into the military, and so many pilots are ex–Vietnam War veter-
ans. This comforts Ella—these men are seasoned by dangerous ex-
ploits, which they have come through unscathed. Their experience
is like a bright shield over their passengers. They have always made
the right decisions.

The plane taxies slowly to the end of the runway, turns ponderously, revs its engines, and then begins to rumble down the long concrete strip. As the plane gains speed, the engine noise mounts and
mounts, and when the cabin falls silent with the universal respect
given to takeoff, Ella is gripped briefly by nerves. She reaches for
Nat's hand, and he clasps hers firmly and reassuringly, without looking at her. He is not a nervous flier; he flies too often.

The rumbling, hurtling plane nears the end of the runway, racing toward the moment of breathless suspension, the moment in

which the arcs of speed and lift and burden all intersect, precisely and miraculously, and the wheels leave the ground, and they suddenly rise up, without pause, smoothly and astonishingly into the clear blue air. The landing gear folds noisily into the belly and the plane banks hard, tipping over the rows of dark buildings of Newark, now so tidy and precise. They have done it; they have made the transition from earthbound to airborne, and there is something great and self-congratulatory about this moment. They have all succeeeded in this death-defying venture.

When the stewardess reappears with the lunch menu, Ella is no longer holding Nat's hand. She used to be a very anxious flier, but that has changed, too. She feels remoter, now, from the danger of flying. Once, without Nat, she flew through a thunderstorm, lightning bolts sizzling off the wings, the fuselage jolting horridly with each shock. Her heart had thudded in her throat, but she had suddenly thought to herself, though she is not religious, "You are in the hand of God." At that her panic ceased.

Since then she no longer becomes so frightened during flight. Fatalism, or some sort of calm, has entered her. She is in her fifties, and she has certainly lived over half her life. She feels less responsible now for the care of the world. If she vanishes, the world will rumble along without her.

Right now she is absorbed in her book, and they are climbing smoothly toward thirty thousand feet, heading slightly northwest, toward San Francisco. The stewardess smiles professionally and offers her a menu. Ella takes it, smiling back. She wonders how long the stewardess will go on working. It's a brutal life, they say, especially if you have a family. You're away so much, and you get bloat, and your cycle is disturbed. Plus you're on your feet all the time: Ella thinks of her knee, which will at some point, her doctor says, need replacement, though she's putting it off. She wouldn't be able do this job, but these women must like it well enough.

Ella's reading Anthony Trollope, Nat a book about Alexander Hamilton. She likes the symmetry they create, likes feeling that, together, they are responsibly covering the field of letters: she, fiction, nineteenth-century, English; he, politics, eighteenth-century, American. What more can you expect of a marriage? She sinks peacefully into her book.

At first she hardly notices the disturbance, since the noise level on airplanes is already so high—the loud drone of the engines, the staccato voices of video earphones, the conversations around them. But finally it becomes intrusive, and she looks up to see a dark-skinned young man in a pale T-shirt, with a red bandanna tied around his head, coming down the aisle from first class. He has something in his raised hand, and he is shouting at them angrily. It's the anger that is most apparent, and confusing. It's directed at them, the passengers, for some reason. What is he shouting? Behind him there seems to be a cloud of black smoke: is something on fire? Is the plane on fire? He is shouting at all of them, though the words are too big, right now, to understand, it's hard to sort through the information—the smoke, the rage, the T-shirt and bandanna, who is he?—but his anger is very clear, and his insistence. He is motioning at them urgently, gesturing at the back of the plane. He's angry at them all, he's beside himself with rage. His rage, the chaotic energy of it, is confusing and frightening. The front of the plane is where the pilots are, and where the stewardesses busy themselves. The front of the plane is the seat of authority, but no one in uniform appears—where is the captain, with his reassuring southern voice, his heroic war record? It seems that this dark-skinned man now represents authority. That's where he's coming from, the cockpit, and the black smoke is billowing behind him. He's shouting.

"Get in the back!"

Some people stand, bewildered. "What's going on?" People are asking him questions, but the man is not answering; instead, the questions turn his face darker, thunderous. He has large liquid black eyes, brilliant.

"Get in the back," he says ferociously. "There's been an accident."

"What kind of accident?" More people stand, alarmed, wanting to know, wanting to help.

Behind the man their stewardess suddenly appears, the stocky black-haired one. Her pockmarked face is contorted with purpose. "Help!" she shouts. Her voice is high-pitched, frantic. "Hijackers!"

The man swivels instantly; his arm shoots out and he seizes her by the throat, his arm snaking around her neck. They are directly in front of Ella, and Ella can see the woman's hand shaking, held helplessly across her chest. The hijacker's elbow is raised high in the air, and he holds her chin up. "*Don't move*," he hisses. The stewardess wears a navy cardigan over a white long-sleeved shirt. There is a gold bangle on her wrist, and her hand is shaking. Ella can hear her breathing: slow and strained.

The hijacker looks around. He looks to be in his thirties, with high cheekbones and a broad, slightly crooked nose. His teeth are very white, and his shiny black hair falls over his forehead. No one moves. Behind him, the first-class cabin is full of smoke. The stewardess swallows convulsively. Her chin is still pulled high by the hijacker's arm. Ella can see the shifting of her throat muscles beneath the skin. The hijacker tightens his grip, and her eyes roll upward, then close. She swallows again, with difficulty, and her hand goes up, reflexively, to his arm. Ella remembers the smooth ritual gestures she made during the safety video. The hijacker hisses at her again, then pulls her chin up, further exposing her throat.

What he has in his other hand is a small straight blade, Ella sees its brightness, and he sweeps the blade across her throat. The pale skin parts easily. The smell of blood is very strong, and the rush of it overwhelming, disorienting. It floods out, dark, and in pulses, down her white blouse, which is now crimson, each wave of fresh blood darkening the blouse, the sweater. The stewardess is trying to scream, though her voice no longer works; she makes shuddering noises, sounds of breath and moist tissue. Her arms are all right, and her legs. She grabs at him, and kicks, but her movements are perfunctory, jerky and spasmodic, and she is not really, now, kicking at the hijacker. She is kicking the way the body prepares itself for death, the way it jerks itself loose of its earthly connections. She kicks and struggles fitfully, and the hijacker, with each jerk, holds her more closely, clasping her to himself like a demon lover, the blood pumping out of the terrible dark place on her neck. He holds her closer and closer to his own breast, which is now covered with streams of her dark blood. The blood is on their arms, it is on the carpet, it is everywhere, and the air reeks. The hijacker's eyes are black and brilliant, and he stares at the passengers without blinking. The stewardess is still plucking with her hands and struggling, and her throat makes terrible attempts at speech. Shudders of air move through places where air was not meant to go. There are moist sounds of tissue smacking and flapping, heaves and gasps, a kind of sob.

"Get in the back," the hijacker says. His eyes are hypnotic with intensity.

It seems that they have no will, now. It seems there is nothing for their weakened bodies to do, now, but stand and move heavily, without a will, down the aisle and back into the tourist section. There they can see rows of faces looking up at them, confused, alarmed. Alarm is spreading, deepening, across the faces. There are cries and questions, some screams. The hijacker is behind them, still holding his dreadful burden, the heavy body of the stewardess. The smell of the blood—thick and ferrous—makes Ella feel faint. It's a smell she did not know she knew, but she does. She knows it. The body knows it.

Nat is ahead of her, and she reaches down low, for his hand. There is nothing now but fear. Just behind them, in first class, there is smoke and chaos. Beyond that, up in the cockpit, is beyond contemplation. The mind dares not go there. It is too dangerous to call it into being.

"Nobody move," the hijacker shouts at them. He is beside himself. "Nobody to move."

The rows of faces stare up, stunned.

The plane is doing something, it seems to be descending. They are nearing another city, rows of buildings are reappearing. The engines seem louder now—are they going faster?

Ella and Nat are standing helplessly in the aisle—there is nowhere for them to go. Behind them is the hijacker, with his mad eyes. Ella is right ahead of him, facing the rear of the plane, and she presses forward, against Nat. She doesn't want to touch the hijacker, or the body of the stewardess, whom he holds in front of himself like a shield. The stewardess seems to have stopped moving. The smell of the blood is rich and sickening. Ella moves her feet to one side; she doesn't want the blood on her shoes.

They can all feel the plane shifting now. The smoke in first class is drifting into this cabin, acrid, dense, alarming. Ella's eyes sting, and she closes them. She leans against Nat's back, pressing herself against his spine. She knows his back intimately, and now she pictures its beautiful slope. She knows where the scar is, on the left side, where he fell in a baseball game as a teenager, long before she knew him. The bluish mark, where a BB went in. She knows exactly the texture of the skin, beneath his gray suit, his blue shirt. She puts her nose against his suit and breathes in: she knows exactly the smell of his skin, rich and comforting. She sets her cheek against his shoulder blade, leaning on her good knee.

The plane is definitely descending now, and they're over another urban landscape, streets and buildings in a bewildering pattern. Don't hijackers want to go somewhere else? Don't they want to be taken to Cuba? Palestine? It's New York, she can see the Triborough Bridge. Why are they headed here? Ella feels her body tighten, she is panting, and her stomach is clenched. The roar of the engines seems deafening—is it really louder, or is it fear that makes it seem so? She thinks of the plastic card, the orderly evacuation down the spotless chute. Behind her, the hijacker is still holding the slack body of the stewardess, and when he moves, Ella can feel something—his elbow, or her lifeless wrist—against her back, and she cringes, trying to move away.

Now the hijacker is shouting again, but not in English. It's in another language, guttural, unknown, and there's another hijacker, she now sees, across the aisle, with a red bandanna around his head, shouting too. What they say is incomprehensible, but it's the force of it, the loudness and intensity of what they say, that cows the passengers, defeats them. They are wild-eyed, they are in some kind of insane, triumphal trance, the hijackers, and one of them holds the dead bleeding body of the stewardess, the woman who was supposed to care for them, to minister to their needs. She has been murdered, and the hijackers are screaming at all of them, and the tourist cabin, too, is now filling up with smoke.

The plane is going insanely fast—they can feel it, dizzying, hurtling low, just above the city buildings. Ella cannot see where they are but it is somewhere in New York, no longer a tidy cityscape seen dreamily from above but a nightmare landscape seen too close and too fast, and her whole body is going too fast, her heart, her

lungs, her pulse, are going as fast as the plane. Nat, in front of her, begins to turn.

It's over, Nat can see that. Everything is over. It's strange how, as
the plane speeds up, his mind slows down. It's oddly calming. Everything is over, everything falls away, now, all the intentions and crises
of life, the small things, his report for the meeting, the conversation
with Beth, getting the car inspected, all of these don't matter, and
the large things—what were the large things? None of them matter,
now. It's all moving faster and faster, and here they are, all of them,
trapped together, their doomed faces staring ahead, stunned, caught
in this thundering, rumbling, accelerating plane, and he thinks, his
mind slow and calm, that this is, really, what they all faced every day,
hurtling through space together on the spinning planet, rushing, un-
aware, toward their final moments. And the spinning planet has been
spinning like this, as it is now, for all time, sweeping through the endless black of space on its long elegant loop. It will go on, though for
him, for them, it's all over, whatever happens. There is time now to
do only one thing, the last thing; he's grateful that there's time and
he's conscious. Gratitude floods him for this.

Nat shifts carefully, keeping his head low, avoiding the wrathful
gaze of the hijacker, who is shouting something over and over at the
top of his lungs, some sort of fanatical chant, and now the other hijacker is shouting it too. They seem, mystifyingly, to be flying through
the buildings of Manhattan, and the engines are whining unbearably, their pitch is rising higher and higher toward some unthinkable
climax, but before this, and just before the plane opens the black
maw of its own tunnel, Nat turns and takes Ella in his arms.

The Epiphany Branch

Mary Gordon

Florence Melnick went to the library every day. Well, not every day: the library was closed on Sundays and legal holidays. Christmas was considered a legal holiday although in her opinion there was nothing legal about it, it was religious, and Florence was Jewish and Christmas was nothing but another day to her. So she resented it that everything was closed up on that day. She thought it violated the principle of separation of church and state, which had been so important to the Founding Fathers.

The branch of the New York Public Library that was, unfortunately in her opinion, closest to where she lived was called the Epiphany Branch. It was on Twenty-third Street between Third and Lexington Avenue, or, as everyone who didn't have something wrong with them said, Third and Lex. That was one thing she took comfort from when she moved there from Brooklyn: it seemed friendly that she'd be living on a street that had a nickname.

But she'd never been happy in the neighborhood, never. She'd never felt that she belonged. In the old days in Flatbush, she'd known everybody, but everybody had moved out when they had the chance. Including her, when her nephew Howard had presented her with the opportunity. Her sister Ethel had had a stroke. Ethel was a widow and Florence never married. Why exactly she never knew. She would have been willing with the right kind of man. But not a fool, not someone with nothing in his head except what was between his legs, not someone with no ideals who only thought about food and money. Florence loved to read, she always hoped to meet someone who loved to read, but it hadn't happened. None of the men she'd met in the forty-five years she'd worked as a saleswoman at Lerner Shops on King's Highway. Of course, you could say, in her line of work, retail clothing for women, it wasn't that likely that you'd meet so many men. Salesmen you'd meet, but rarely of the right type.

So she'd retired after forty-five years. They gave her a lovely party and a silver tray with her name engraved. Everyone said, "Keep in touch, Florence," but when she tried to think who she really wanted to keep in touch with, no one came to mind. Her parents had died; Ethel was in Manhattan, but she had a life of her own, they didn't share too many interests. But when she had the stroke and Howard made the suggestion—tactfully trying to point out that Flatbush wasn't what it had been, and that his mother had a two-bedroom apartment that he was paying the maintenance on, not chicken feed but nothing compared to what a nursing home would be, to say nothing that his mother would rather die first—well, it all seemed to make a great deal of sense.

And really there was nothing she really missed about Brooklyn except the main library at Grand Army Plaza. That was a library: marble and carpets and big ceilings and mahogany. They knew how to use materials in those days. They spared no expense. The library was right on Prospect Park, and the other side was a square with a statue of a soldier. When she walked into the door, the word *cavernous* came to her mind: empty space, dark air; even the air was scholarly. You could take a book off the stacks, walk up the stairs, and read it in the reading room. Real wood paneling. The Epiphany Branch was one big room, materials skimped everywhere. But what could she do? It was where she lived, she was seventy-eight, she wasn't up to much traveling. Not in Manhattan.

Ethel only lived two months after Florence moved in. And there she was, in the middle of Manhattan, but no, not in the middle, it wasn't really midtown. It was the middle in the worst sense. It was in the middle of a lot of things, downtown from the theater district and the museums, uptown from the village, which she'd always wanted to explore. She had come too old to Manhattan; the streets overwhelmed her and she never ventured uptown to the Forty-second Street library or to the Metropolitan Museum, which she'd thought she'd visit quite often when she'd imagined herself a Manhattanite. She didn't move far beyond a five-block radius. Even so, she didn't really know anybody in the neighborhood. Nobody seemed to speak English, or at least no English she understood.

Once she went into one of those coffee places, she thought maybe she'd meet people there. But they were very young and asking for things she'd never heard of—skim lattes, macchiatos. And they charged what she considered an arm and a leg. And the conversations were ridiculous, people talking about horoscopes: "Are you a Capricorn, that means you're a warrior, but there must be something rising, because I not only see aggressiveness, I feel gentleness as well. You're a person in conflict. Like, I see that you're really a people person but sometimes you need to be alone." "I can't believe you see that," the girl said. The man in his fifties with a ponytail and the girl no more than twenty-five, a lovely blond girl. Scandinavian-looking, though she didn't have an accent. She sounded well educated, although Florence didn't understand how a well-educated person could believe in something like astrology. "I see it completely," the guy said. Well, girlie, I hope you see he's not interested in horoscopes, just hanky-panky, Florence wanted to say. She left the place disgusted. She would never go back.

The only good thing she could say about the Epiphany Branch was that it was convenient to her apartment. Other than that, it had nothing to recommend it. Although she thought the name was interesting. She thought it had some kind of other meaning, so she looked it up in the dictionary. It meant "manifestation," a sudden understanding or revelation. She loved dictionaries; she wondered if people would be surprised if they knew she personally owned four different dictionaries: a Webster's Third Edition, a Merriam-Webster's Eleventh Edition, a Random House, and an American Heritage. If she'd had a lot of money she would have bought herself a copy of the *OED*. But that would be ridiculous. She wasn't that kind of person. But she very much liked looking things up in it in the library. Although she sometimes worried who'd touched the magnifying glass before her. There were all kinds in that library, all kinds.

People you wouldn't think belonged in libraries. People who didn't even know how to be quiet. In her day, librarians were strict about enforcing quiet. And people respected them for it. They respected libraries as places of quiet. Now, people seemed to her to be making all kinds of noises left and right. When she complained about it once, the librarian said, "We think of a library as not just a place where people come to read, but a community resource center." What the hell does that have to do with people keeping their voices down, she wanted to say. But she didn't want the librarian to turn against her. She was very good at getting things from interlibrary loan.

But there really were all kinds. The boy who always wore one of those undershirts with the straps, winter and summer, with a kerchief on his head. Very well built, like a lot of black fellows. Studying some kind of mathematics. But he'd say the problems out loud, and not quietly. She supposed he deserved credit for trying to better himself, but he disturbed her, and he frightened her a little, so she didn't want to move, in case he took it the wrong way.

Some of the people in the library didn't seem completely clean to her. A couple of the men never seemed to shave, and some of the older ones gave off that smell of old men who never wash their hair. She hoped she didn't give off some kind of old lady smell, but she showered every day, and also used deodorant and talcum powder, which she was sure these types had never heard of. Or if they'd heard, they'd long ago forgotten. Some of the Chinese people looked very respectable, but she didn't know if they spoke English. Some younger people came in to use the computers, and sometimes they'd curse so loud everyone in the place could hear them. Because of having trouble with the machines. And some people just seemed crazy. They made big fusses about nothing. There was one man, a young man too, he never wore socks, whatever the weather, and he was always calling the librarians morons and idiots and saying, "Do you have to be an imbecile to work here, is it a requirement or does it just help?" She thought the librarians were very patient with him. In their shoes, she would have been tempted to kick him out for good. Forbid him entry forever. She wished they would, for her own sake. And she knew there were other people who agreed with her, but everyone pretended not to notice him, whenever he started up.

Some people, and mostly they were older, came in, went to the bathroom, sat down with a pile of books, and fell asleep on top of them. She was very careful about never falling asleep. At her age, she thought it made a bad impression.

No, it wasn't the best, the Epiphany Branch, but still there was a lot to learn in this world if you applied yourself. She felt she was giving herself the education she'd never had a chance for when she was younger. Now everyone went to college; there was no doubt she'd be considered college material nowadays. But then it was a big deal, especially for a girl. She was determined to make up for what she hadn't been given; sometimes she had a daydream that a very distinguished woman, someone about her age, would engage her in conversation about a book, and, after a few cups of tea, maybe a few lunches in the diner, she'd say, "Florence, even though you have no formal education, you have much more learning than many with a college degree." She could imagine the woman very clearly. She had fine white hair that she clipped to the back of her head with a silver barrette. She had eyeglasses with silver frames that hung around her neck on a silver chain. She always wore gray sweaters or gray silk blouses that had a touch of lavender in them. Very well made.

Florence would assign herself a subject and then read a lot of books on it until she felt she'd really got it under her belt. By which she meant ten books on the subject; she wouldn't quit unless she'd read ten books, cover to cover, even if she was feeling a little bored. She'd make notes; write down words she didn't understand, look them up in the dictionary and copy down all the various meanings. Now it was the Civil War. Before that it was Ancient Greece. The cradle of democracy. She certainly would have rather lived in Athens than Sparta, she had no doubts about that.

She never talked to anyone at the library, but there were people that she recognized, people she thought of a better type. They kept to themselves and she kept to herself; they all seemed to like it that way.

The last thing she wanted was striking up a friendship with someone in the neighborhood who she'd never be able to get off her back. Sometimes someone looked possible at first, but she was always disappointed. Like the woman she thought looked so refined, but not stuck-up, wearing a very nice sweater set, Fair Isle, they called it. She wondered where Fair Isle was. She wondered where she could look that information up. The words *Fair Isle* kept going through her mind; she imagined it was an island somewhere in Scandinavia, but it was always green, in spite of the cold, and the ground was always covered with a light green moss and deer ate berries off the bushes there. Fair Isle. She thought she might get herself a Fair Isle sweater. Although maybe it was too late, she was too old for that. She considered asking the woman where she'd got her sweater set. That would be a good way of striking up a conversation.

But when the woman got up and put her coat on, Florence was glad she'd never spoken up. On her lapel was a very large button that said LOSE WEIGHT NOW, ASK ME HOW. Florence knew that was ridiculous. She'd never had a weight problem, but she knew that if she did she would never just walk up to somebody, some stranger with a button, tap her on the shoulder, and say, "Excuse me, how do I lose weight now?" Any fool would know that wasn't the way to go about it. And if the woman didn't know that, she was a fool. Or money-hungry.

That morning she thought the older man in the plaid shirt and the tweed cap might be worth talking to. She thought he looked like a cultured gentleman; he wore tortoiseshell glasses and his nails were nicely kept. Was coming to the Epiphany Branch lowering her standards? Did she now think anyone who looked like he bathed regularly was a gentleman? Because she was wondering why this man didn't take off his cap. A gentleman wouldn't wear a hat indoors. But maybe it was doctor's orders. Maybe he had to keep his head warm at all times. Or he might have been some kind of intellectual. European. The plaid shirt and the tweed cap, and then that tie in the abstract expressionist pattern. She had recently learned the term *abstract expressionism*. Before she would just have called it modern art. She learned it when she read that book on art by that nun. A very intelligent woman. Florence thought it was a shame she hadn't done anything about her teeth. But maybe it was against her religion. Florence was glad that in Judaism there was nothing against looking your best.

She herself would never have mixed prints and plaids. But then she thought maybe that was the style in Europe and she shouldn't judge. She wondered if he had a college degree from Europe, maybe a Ph.D. She wondered what he had done for a living. Probably not a doctor or a lawyer, not with that kind of mixing of plaids and prints. She thought he probably was some kind of college professor. Maybe some kind of scientist. Maybe he had worn one of those white coats to work every day so he wasn't used to making choices about fashion. Maybe he was a widower, and his wife used to make sure his shirts went with his ties.

She sat across from him when she arrived that morning; she was pretty sure he'd know how to be quiet, that she wouldn't be disturbed. As always, she was curious about what people were reading. Often she'd try to get a look, although sometimes she was sorry she did, like the time the week before when she saw the young blond woman reading the "Alternate Therapies" section of *Dr. Susan Love's Breast Book*. And then she had to think about the girl having breast cancer. A man came up and stood behind her, put his hand on her shoulder, and started reading along with her. Florence wondered if it would ruin their sex life if the woman lost her breast. She kept thinking of what the breast would look like on the operating table after the doctor had cut it off. What did they do with cut-off breasts? Florence had made herself go back to her book on the Battle of

Antietam. It did no good to dwell on unpleasant things. That had always been her motto, and she believed that it had served her well.

The European gentleman was reading a book called *The Nothing That Is: A Natural History of Zero*. So perhaps he had been a mathematician. But after fifteen minutes, he put that book down and walked around the room. She followed him with her eyes, trying not to. She saw that he went to another table, picked up a book that had been left there by someone else and brought it back to the place where his coat and hat were, where he'd settled himself originally. This book was called *Radical Walking Tours of New York*. He sat down with a smile and a satisfied sigh, as if he were about to tuck into a good meal. But in about ten minutes, he got up again, walked around the room as he had before, and picked up another book that someone had left on another table. Again, he brought it back to his original place. This one was called *How I Play Golf* by Tiger Woods.

Florence could not concentrate on her own book, a history of women in the Civil War. She'd been very absorbed in it before she started paying attention to the European gentleman. But maybe he wasn't a gentleman. A gentleman would not put a book down so quickly, having read so little in it, just leaving it aside for something else. She felt the disrespect in it. The way she figured it, an author had worked very hard on a book. Whatever you thought of it, it probably had a lot of information in it that someone had spent a lot of time putting together, and you had no right to put it down until you'd finished it to the very end.

It drove her crazy to see him flitting around like that. Every time someone left a book on one of the tables he picked it up and read it. And there were a lot of books on the tables; the librarians preferred that you leave the books on the table rather than putting them back. Too much misshelving, one of them, a Puerto Rican girl, had told her. There was no rhyme or reason to what he did. Sitting down, picking up one book, putting it down. It drove her crazy.

Florence was trying to read her book on women in the Civil War. And not just nurses, either. Then she felt a call of nature. She never liked using the bathroom in the library; sometimes men didn't put the seat down and she'd have to touch the seat herself when who knows who had been there before her. She didn't know why some men didn't have the consideration. It was beyond her, that kind of mind.

When she came back to the room, he was sitting in the chair next to hers, where her coat was, a place that was obviously still hers. He had taken the book off the top of her pile—underneath it was a dictionary of American history and one of American biography, and a book with maps of the Confederate states. He was reading her book on women in the Civil War. As far as she was concerned, this constituted a bold-faced theft.

She was a lady, though; she had no intention of stooping to his level.

"Excuse me," she said, "you seem to be inadvertently reading my book."

He gave her a very warm smile, she thought, considering the circumstances. "It's not inadvertently, not inadvertently at all. I'm reading it precisely because it is yours. I spent a lifetime as a scholar, devoting myself to one specialty: Romance philology. Now, I'm picking up knowledge in a different way. I like to wander after people, like a kind of gleaner in the fields of knowing: I pick up what someone else has put down. I think of it as a kind of quilt made up in a community of learning. I just pick up a scrap of what someone else has taken in, and with that scrap I connect with that person. It seems much friendlier to me."

Florence didn't know when she had ever been so angry. Romance philology. She didn't even know what it was, but the man must have had to study for a long time to even be involved in something like that. So he had had all the advantages. Languages, probably. All those hours studying, with people who respected him, took him seriously. The greatest gift a person could be given in this world. And what did he do with it? Did he sit down and put his mind to something, his mind that had been trained like a professional's? What did he do? He picked up and put down, as if it were nothing, as if books were toys, as if learning was just a game. He was nothing but a spoiled brat. Learning was sacred, and he was treating it like a game. You didn't treat sacred things like a game, you just didn't do it in this world. Not for her money. Or he could do it if he wanted to, but she wasn't going to get away with it.

She tried to put on her most judgmental face. So he would know she had authority. Where her authority came from she wasn't sure for a minute. Then she figured it out: she had authority because she knew what was important and what wasn't. Because she knew what was what.

"You're nothing but a butterfly," she said. Even though it was a library, she was thinking of the movies. She was trying to sound like Bette Davis, when she talked to a man who wasn't worthy to lick her boots.

But in the movies, the men always seemed to be crushed; they backed out of the room, or hung their heads. That didn't happen with the gentleman from Europe. He did two things. Three things. He took his cap off. You could say he tipped his hat, or cap. And then he laughed. And then he put his cap back on.

"And if I am a butterfly, then pray, dear madame, tell me, what are you?"

He was trying to insult her. She knew what he was implying. Because what was the opposite of a butterfly? She tried to think. A caterpillar, no, that was a stage in the butterfly's development, it would suggest that one day she could become a butterfly, one day she could become him. And that was impossible. No, the opposite of a butterfly was something heavy, slow, and dull. That was what he was trying to suggest. That was always what people tried to suggest when they were lazy and careless and your hard work made them look bad. Well, what about the story about the grasshopper and the ant? But she wasn't buying into that one either. Whatever he had in his storehouse, the ant was still dull, still nobody you wanted to be around. She wasn't going to fall into that. Because what she had stored up wasn't just pieces of grain, it was treasure. Knowledge, learning, wasn't just something you put in your mouth to keep alive, it was gold. Shining, precious, valuable. People like the European gentleman didn't realize how valuable it was. They took it lightly; they felt they could take it or leave it. Or throw it away. Or flit around it.

No, she knew the real value of things. Knowledge was a treasure, and it had to be guarded, fiercely guarded. Thinking about it, she felt fierce. And it came to her then: that was who she was. If he was a butterfly, she was a tiger, standing at the gates, guarding the treasure. Maybe one of those tigers with the turquoise eyes that come from Asia, that she'd studied when she'd studied Asia. She was a fierce tiger with turquoise eyes standing at the gates of knowledge, guarding. Guarding against who, against what? She didn't know exactly. But that wasn't important. What was important was that she was on guard.

The gentleman from Europe had got up from his seat and settled himself at another table. He was reading some book, she wasn't even going to give him the satisfaction of trying to find out what it was. He thought he was smart, but he wasn't going to make a fool out of her. She was the white tiger, standing at the gates of knowledge, keeping guard.

And then it came to her, the words that she would say to him, the answer to his question. It wasn't just ordinary words, it was poetry. A poem she'd learned when she'd studied the poets of the Romantic era. William Blake. That poem about a tiger. She'd wished she'd been able to ask somebody why tiger was spelt with a *y* and if you pronounced the last syllable of symmetry *try* or *tree*. Probably that was something the European gentleman knew. She shot him a look of pure contempt across the room and spat the words of the poem straight at him: "Tyger! tyger! burning bright," she muttered, "In the forests of the night, / What immortal hand or eye / Dare frame thy fearful symmetry?"

But he did not look up, because of course he didn't hear her. It was a library, after all, and she didn't want to disturb anyone, so she had said it low, under her breath.

Joan, Jeanne, La Pucelle, Maid of Orléans

Judy Budnitz

Her neighbors in Domrémy

There she goes.

Who?

That girl.

What girl?

You know. What's-her-name. Old Jean and Isabellette's daughter. Off to fetch the cows, probably.

How you know it's her?

See the red dress? See the long black hair?

Every girl in the village wears a red dress. They all got black hair.

She walks a particular way. Head in the clouds. They say she is devout. She goes off praying by herself. Kneels every time the church bell rings.

Hunh. All girls are like that at her age. Always crazy about something. First it's dolls. Then it's religion. Or maybe horses. And then it's boys.

Her first time

You can hear many things if you open your ears; you can feel many things if you open your skin; if you lie very still among the grasses of the field and wait, you may feel the earth twitch like the hide of a sleeping animal; if you watch the clouds long enough, you can feel the pressure of things unseen, the way an insect pauses, waving its feelers, sensing the shadow of a child's foot poised above it.

I have been waiting for this since I was born. When it comes I am not afraid.

Oh, in truth I am afraid. But I am ready.

In the plainest language: I see a bright light. I hear a voice.

I fall to my knees. I will do whatever it asks. I will go anywhere, do anything.

And what does the voice say?

Be a good girl.

What?

Be a good girl, Jeanne. Go to church.

The Pitch

I've got an idea, Bob.

Okay, Diane, let's hear it. Not another athlete-triumphing-over-adversity profile, is it?

Better than that. I heard about this girl. Lives way out in the sticks, in some French backwater called Domrémy. Named Jeanne.

Joan, you'd say in English. Says she hears voices. Saints and angels talking to her. Messages from God.

Go on.

Now she says they're telling her to drive the English out of France. They're telling her to get Charles VII crowned as king.

And?

She's only seventeen. A little peasant girl from the boondocks talks to God and aims to start a war. Isn't that enough of a story? She calls herself the Virgin. That's her shtick. She's relying on this widely held prophecy that France will be restored by a virgin.

A real virgin? I want that verified. Can you do that?

What? Um, absolutely.

Vow of chastity. I love it. Go out there. Shoot the scenery. Interview her family, friends, everybody. Take a crew. How many people do you need?

As many as you can spare.

Take Burt. Karleen. And the intern, what's his name?

But Burt's from craft services! And Karleen? She's from makeup. So?

This is supposed to be a documentary.

Sometimes the truth needs a little touching up. You can always make the truth a little truer.

What she sees when she sees
what she sees

The first one to come is Saint Michael, he who speaks with the tongue of angels and once led the armies of Heaven in battle against the Devil. Then others join him, Saint Margaret and Saint Catherine. Always accompanied by bright light. They come only when I am alone. I am twelve years old the first time. They come almost every day. They come when I hear the church bells.

They tell me to be a good girl. For five years they tell me this.

Finally one day they come to me and say: God has a mission for you.

I say: I am ready.

The intern

I'm in an editing suite working on this naked-skateboarding video thing I'm doing for a friend when Diane sticks her head in and I think she's going to yell at me because I'm not supposed to be in there but instead of yelling she says, hey, do you still have that friend who makes fake IDs and passports and stuff? and I say yeah and she says see if he can put together some press credentials, something that looks really official, something that'll get us in anywhere, and I mean *anywhere*, anytime, can he do that? and I say sure and she says thanks babe you're the best and I say hey wait did you say us? and she says oh, yeah, didn't I tell you, you're coming too.

First contact with subject

I see a bright light. I hear a voice. I fall to my knees and await instructions.

Figures come near. One holds the light in its hand. Which saints are these? New ones I've never seen before.

A voice says, Good, now get closer, closer, get riiight up in her faaaaace—now cut.

This light is not the usual heavenly light. It scorches my eyes. Then it stops but my eyes are dazzled, I can see only splintered black shapes like shattered crows.

My eyes clear, but the figures are still black. Their clothes are wrong—where are the white robes and crowns? They wear black tight garments and hold in their hands machines, sharp glittery metal machines that look like weapons. I wonder if God has sent them to teach me the ways of war.

Are you Joan? Jeanne? says one. Jeanne d'Arc?

They know my name.

Great to meet you, Joan, says another. It is a woman, in men's clothes. I've never seen such a thing before, though I can see how it could be a good idea in certain circumstances. She says, Before we get started, I wondered if I could get you to sign this little release form . . .

She holds out a page covered in tiny square letters.

I say, I cannot read or write.

They look at each other. It is some kind of test. I close my eyes and pray to God for guidance. I open my eyes and they are still standing there shifting their feet like cows with full udders.

I can sign with an X, I offer.

That's fine then, the woman says. Right here, at the bottom.

I do. All four sigh with relief when I finish.

I am beginning to suspect they are not visions, merely strangers from very far away. Then again, they may be saints or angels in disguise.

What do you want me to do? I say.

Well, Joan, the woman says, we want to record your story. We want to follow you on the journey you're about to take.

Now I understand. They're my first volunteers, the first seeds of my future army. I look them over. Where are the sturdy French soldiers I imagined leading? These people have the unkempt hair and lurching air of madmen.

We must go to Charles VII and win his approval, I say, so that I may fight on his behalf. And then we will reclaim the city of Orléans from the English.

Of course, of course, the woman says, scraping manure off her shoe. But first would you mind showing us around your hometown?

Burt shoots establishing shots

I can see that Diane's practically drooling. This girl Joan/Jeanne is
the documentary subject she's been dreaming of for years. Promi-
nent cheekbones and those big light-catching eyes—she's photo-
genic as hell.

Is that the only dress you have? Diane asks her.

Yes.

Good, Diane says. I know what she's thinking—how striking the
red looks against the grays of the gulchy countryside.

I didn't think we should have snuck up on her like we did. But
she almost seemed to be expecting us.

Hurry up, Burt! Diane yells. Get a shot of this.

They're waiting beside the biggest tree I've ever seen, a tree out of
a storybook, bulbous and twisted, branches the size of ordinary tree
trunks drooping to the ground. I hear the cries of children hidden in
the leaves.

What *is* this? Diane breathes.

People call it the Fairy Tree, Jeanne says. I used to come here as
a little girl. We all did. Once a year we'd come and eat our bread and
sing and dance.

Stand in front of it, Diane says. Right here.

Why?

It'll make an amazing shot. You, the tree, the setting sun, those
kids dancing around singing like maniacs. Come on, Joanie. It's the
magic hour. This light won't last much longer.

But it's a children's game.

Diane says, Go on. Saint Michael said you should.

The girl buys it. She stands in front of the tree. The shot is amazing.
The sun has just barely disappeared, and the hillside is bleeding red up
into the sky. The tree looks like it's on fire. The girl is flaming, aglow.

Just act natural, Diane says. Act like we're invisible.

Karleen the makeup girl, on Jeanne

She has good skin despite all the time she's spent outdoors. Years of sun and wind, killer combination. Tight pores, a nice fresh complexion. I keep telling her she won't age well unless she starts using a product with SPF, but she doesn't seem to care. It's always the ones with perfect skin who don't bother to take care of it. The locals here talk about a clear and unbesmirched brow indicating moral purity, but I still have to prune her eyebrows now and then.

I overhear people talking about her new "radiance," her "glow." They attribute it to her closeness to God or whatever. You know what I attribute it to? Peachy Keen Klean translucent dusting powder judiciously applied, thank you very much.

What J's mother thinks

My Jeanne? Special? Gifted? Of course I think she's special. I've known it since the day she was born. She was the most beautiful baby in the world. And she's grown into a beautiful, intelligent girl, modest and devout. She will accomplish anything she sets her mind to. But of course *I* think this. I'm her mother, after all.

What J's father thinks

Now that she's going off to drive out the English and crown Charles VII, who's going to look after the cows?

Karleen on hair

So we head out, first to her cousin's place, and then she wants to go to the local lord to get him to escort her to this Charles VII guy, who must be some kind of incredible dreamboat the way she keeps talking about him.

Her cousin gives her some men's clothes, a tunic and breeches and boots. She says it's necessary because she will be traveling among men now and must protect herself. But when Diane sees her she freaks out and is all like, Joan, what are you doing, the red dress is so perfect.

I look at the others and I'm like, What's the big whoop about her virginity, anyway?

It's the source of her superpowers, says the intern. Like Samson's hair.

Hey, Karleen, Diane says to me, could you at least pretty her up a bit? If the clothes have to stay, we can at least make her a bit more feminine.

So I sit Jeanne down and work on her face a bit, but she keeps pushing my hands away, saying vanity's a sin.

When I'm done I step back and we all study her.

It's not enough. Diane walks away, frowning.

Maybe if I do something with her hair . . . I'll just trim it to frame her face . . .

I start cutting.

It's not going so well. I cut and cut. Each snip of the scissors is louder than the last. Maybe my mirror's hanging crooked. Now the left side is uneven, now the right. The scissors make a crunching sound as they chew through the thicket.

I'm a makeup person, for God's sake, not a hair person. You can't expect . . .

I tell Burt to quick run get a bowl from the craft table. We stick it on her head.

There's no way I can fuck this up, right? Just cut along the edge of the bowl . . .

I fuck it up.

You try, I tell Burt. Years of peeling grapes and pinching phyllo have put dexterity into his fat fingers. The hair scraps make a black ring around her, like the charred circle left on the ground when you shoot off a bottle rocket.

I didn't realize before, but now that it's gone it's obvious that her hair was her one true beauty. Now her features stick out bare and cold as a statue's.

Jeanne watches the bits of hair fall, the last vestiges of her vanity gone.

Jeanne, distracted

I need the counsel of my voices. But the voices will only come to me when I am alone, and I am seldom alone anymore. There are always men coming to meet me. And then there is this woman, Diane, who follows me everywhere asking strange unceasing questions. More than anything she wants to meet the voices. To film them.

I still don't understand *film*. Anyway, they will never come when she is near.

The intern discovers points and laces

She's getting fans now, groupies who follow her everywhere, and as she speaks to them in her low husky voice they go quiet in order to hear, then repeat her words like they're riddles or prayers. Jean de Metz was the first but now she has a whole entourage, like that duke of Alençon. Man, I can't stand him, with his long curly hair flowing over his beefy shoulders and his big noble chin. You should see the fuss she makes over that horse he gave her, that knock-kneed flea-bitten thing, and besides, he's married.

I go look for Jeanne and find her by the stream, fastening up her clothes, her hair wet; she's been washing herself and I'm about five seconds too late. She smiles at me not like a woman smiles at a man but like a general does at the rawest recruit, and it's all I can do not to salute.

What are those? I say, pointing at the flaps on her clothes.

Points and laces, she says. For my own protection.

The laces are leather thongs threaded through eyelets set in flaps cut into the edges of her clothes; they stitch her tunic to her breeches all the way around the waist. How long would it take to undo them, one by one?

A documentarian must maintain an objective distance, at all costs. I keep telling myself that.

Karleen observes party etiquette

So finally we get to where this Charles VII guy is hanging out, and they take us to this big stone hall crowded with people all dressed in the kind of threads you'd see in a second-rate wardrobe department. You know, gold brocade, embroidery, but dirt on the cuffs and every-body with grimy fingernails. They're all gawking to get a look at this Jeanne they've heard about; some think she's holy and some say she's a witch and they're afraid to meet her eyes, but she marches right in cool as a cucumber. At the far end the people are clustered deferen-tially around this man with copper hair and rings on his fingers, he's wearing the fanciest of outfits, and I'm thinking, well, I guess she *was* right to gush over him, Charles is a pretty good-looking guy.

But Jeanne marches right past him, right over to this little rat-faced man in the corner who's got food caught in his beard.

My king, she says, and goes down on one knee.

You can hear everybody gasp. The intern groans. There's this awkward silence. It's really embarrassing.

I am not your king, the man says, and everybody tries to steer her over to the other guy. She won't budge.

You are my king, Jeanne insists. God has sent me to you.

It's getting very tense in here; I'm looking for the exits, thinking, hey, don't look at me, I'm just the makeup girl, I don't even *know* her.

And then the tension breaks up into astonishment and rejoicing, because the little rat-faced man in the corner *is* Charles VII and the other guy is a decoy. It was all a test, some elaborate party trick.

The intern is glaring at the knights and noblemen gathered admiringly around Jeanne, packed so tight their swords are clanging into each other.

Charles VII looks disappointed. Maybe I'm wrong, but he doesn't seem very excited about the idea of being king. He seems like he's perfectly happy hanging out here with his wife and mistresses and would rather not go through all the fuss and bother of ruling the country.

Private conversation: Charles and advisors

Do you trust her, Charles?

She can read my very thoughts. Is she sent by God, or by the Devil? Saint or witch? Is she a virgin, as she claims? I can't decide.

You're always so indecisive, Charles.

No I'm not! Am I?

We'll send her to Poitiers.

Yes, the scholars there will examine her and give us a definitive answer.

The intern's encounter with Yolande

We're here in Poitiers waiting around. Jeanne's shut up in a room being interrogated day after day about her visions, her intentions, is she good, is she evil, blah blah blah. Then one day Diane yells for me and says, What are all those women doing out there?

I go take a peek, and sure enough, a bunch of noblewomen have assembled in the main hall, sailing around in their trailing dresses, buzzing like bees. It's Yolande and her pals and ladies-in-waiting, Yolande, the mother-in-law of Charles VII, Yolande d'Aragon, the Queen of Four Kingdoms, Yolande with a drop perpetually hanging at the tip of her long nose and a lady-in-waiting perpetually hopping forward to blot it with a hanky, Yolande with her headdress shaped like an enormous mushroom draped in veils. Yolande scares me almost as much as Diane does.

Jeanne walks in, and they gather around and take her somewhere and Diane hisses at me to grab a camera and follow them and I whisper no, they'll notice me, clearly it's some kind of girl thing, why don't you find Karleen, and Diane says there's no time, here, put this on. What is it? Jeanne's red dress. How did you get this? Never mind how; put it on.

I put it on. It smells like her. Two spots at the knees are worn thin from her kneeling.

I follow the women up stone steps, down stone passages, up to a dark room high in a tower bare except for a table, and the women all reach into the folds of their dresses and pull out metal instruments, I don't know what for, they're going to knit, maybe, or cook something. Oh, women. Now they are spreading a cloth on the table, now Jeanne is lying down upon it and they are ringing her body with candles, circling her, bending over her with their utensils in their hands, what are they doing? They're fixing to *eat* her! Without even cooking her first! These people are barbaric!

Stop, stop it! I shout. They all turn and stare. Jeanne sits up.

They kick me out but I can hear their voices through the door.

When they're done I go tell Diane, Yup, she's a virgin all right, she passed the test with flying colors.

Diane grabs my shoulders and screams, But did you get it on film?

Burt says, For God's sake, Diane, what kind of film are we making?

Jeanne's minor miracle

Jeanne finally gets the thumbs-up. They've decided she's one of the good guys. Time to suit up and go seize Orléans. Men are streaming in from all over the country, eager to join her.

Jeanne says, Go to Fierbois, to the Church of Saint Catherine there, and bring me the sword buried behind the altar.

No one knows what she's talking about, but they go to the Church of Saint Catherine at Fierbois and dig behind the altar and lo and behold, they uncover a sword, ancient and covered with rust. At the merest touch, the rust flakes away and the sword shines as if newly forged.

They bring it to her, marveling.

The intern prepares for battle

Wow. That's some armor, Jeanne. Where did you get it?

They made it especially for me. Now please. Just hush.

Jeanne, Jeanne, what's wrong?

I'll tell you something. I'm going to be wounded at Orléans. I know it. Right here, in my shoulder, above my chest. The weapon will strike and penetrate my flesh to a depth of six inches.

Then don't go, Jeanne!

I have to, she says calmly.

I run over to Diane and tell her what Jeanne said and that we have to somehow stop her from going, the thought of Jeanne hurt makes me sick, but Diane's eyes light up and she says, Hmmm, penetrated to a depth of six inches, eh? That sounds like a euphemism if I ever heard one, sounds like Jeanne's planning to finally lose her virtue. I say, What, with her shoulder? And Diane says, Don't be stupid. She says, Hmmm, I wonder who's going to get to pop her cherry. We've got to get it on film.

Waiting outside Orléans

The army is assembled. Jeanne is impatient to attack. She has waited so long.

The captains tell her they must wait. An unfavorable wind is blowing, making the approach difficult.

The wind will change, she says.

It does.

La Hire, a captain, speaks

Yes, my name is La Hire, I am known for my fighting spirit, my fiery temper, and my filthy oaths. Jeanne has made me promise to stop swearing, and I *am* trying, but, f—— it's hard.

If you must swear, say *mon matin*, she tells me.

I say, S——, Jeanne, I try, but then when I see those f—— s—— English, I can't wait to p—— their a——. Please, can't I swear a little? If it's only on the battlefield?

No, Jeanne says sternly, not budging an inch. Now tell me, she says, when did you last go to confession?

She has driven all the loose women out of the encampment. She spurs us on to battle with passionate words, she carries her standard into the fray to give us hope. We know that God is with us.

You should see the men, how they love her.

She keeps her clothes laced up tight and sleeps in her armor. But truly it is unnecessary.

We love her, I love her, but not in the carnal way.

A loose woman speaks

Yes, it's true that Jeanne drove us away. We were having a fine time in the camps till she came chasing after us yelling about sin and God.

I don't see how it's any of her business, really.

She screamed threats but never got close enough to spit. We ran fast and laughing, dresses undone to give the men one last glimpse of what they'll be missing. She was too slow, all weighted down with armor as she was.

People talk about her radiance and purity, but no one seems to mention the plain fact that she possesses not one iota of beauty. She is short and dumpy and homely, with her cropped hair and bulging eyes and her neck always stretched and knotty, like an old plow horse straining against the harness.

The other loose women like to joke that she is not a virgin by choice. She's jealous of us.

That must be the case. Otherwise, why won't she share? I ask you, why does a woman who professes to be a virgin need a thousand men all to herself?

Burt describes her sustenance

I do my best, I try to provide anything anyone could want. Seventeen different kinds of bottled water. Vegetarian, vegan, lactose-free. I've been doing craft services for seventeen years. I keep telling Jeanne, just say the word and I'll whip it up. But no. Eats nothing but her disgusting bits of bread dipped in water. She hardly drinks either. That's probably, you know, to avoid the bother of constantly having to take off her armor. I worry about dehydration, electrolyte imbalances. It's no wonder she's seeing things.

Burt on the battlefield

The way they fight is like nothing I've ever seen before: men bellowing and horses thrashing around and the screech of metal on metal, and the whiz and thud of things flying through the air and landing and embedding themselves. On the ground everything is ponderously slow. The men's armor is so heavy it makes them move like they're underwater. While they're locked in combat they snarl vile insults at each other, trying to ruin the other's concentration. Sometimes in the midst of their straining and heaving and smashing, one will come out with an epithet so flowery and excessive that the other can't help but laugh.

Diane will have a fit when she sees this footage, the intern moans. It's all going to look slo-mo. She'll say we had the camera on the wrong setting.

Of course it's not a game. They inflict hideous damage on each other. The intern keeps puking up the truffle omelet I made him for lunch. I hate to see my work wasted like that.

Where's Jeanne? he keeps saying. I can't see her, where is she?

Diane, on Jeanne's wound

The arrow pierces her right where she said it would. They have to drag her off the battlefield and pry the standard from her fingers. Even as they're cleaning the wound she's still screaming about driving out those rotten goddamns.

Goddamns. That's what she calls the English. She doesn't know what it means, but it's the word she hears them shouting more than any other on the battlefield. She thinks she's throwing the ugly sound of their language back in their faces; she doesn't realize she's breaking her own no-swearing rule.

Victory

Yes, the French are victorious, of course. Didn't she promise they would be? The inhabitants of Orléans claim Jeanne as their own. La Pucelle, the Maid of Orléans, they call her.

Diane says, She never actually fights, you know. She's never struck a single blow. She just charges into the thick of things, yelling and waving her standard, and the men follow her in. They're the ones who do the actual fighting. The captains allow her in their meetings, but they ignore her. She's not a leader, she's a mascot.

The intern says, I was there. I saw her. She was magnificent.

Burt shooting the battle at Jargeau

We're in the thick of battle. The intern excused himself a while ago, pleading nausea. I'm getting a little tired of carrying everybody's weight around here. I've got enough of my own.

I've given up on trying to follow Jeanne. She likes to launch herself practically into the enemy's lap, crying for the men to follow her, clinging to her standard for dear life like it's an umbrella in a hurricane. It's too hard to keep up. Instead I'm trailing the duke of Alençon around. He's pretty impressive. He makes me want to start working out.

All of a sudden Jeanne is right next to us, calmly telling the duke, Move away from that spot, or that piece of ordnance up on the rampart will kill you. The duke jumps like a scared rabbit. A second later something whistles through the air and strikes a man who's standing right where the duke was standing a second ago. The guy goes down without a sound. The duke is goggle-eyed. Jeanne is already gone, sprinting toward the castle walls screaming at the top of her lungs.

I look up above her, up along the stone walls, at the rampart from which the mysterious missile was fired. And who do I see skulking around up there among the English soldiers? The intern! He's the one who tried to drop that deadly piece of rock on the duke. The jealous little sneak. If Jeanne ever finds out, she'll never forgive him.

Karleen at the coronation

Am I the only one who thinks a coronation seems a little premature? I mean, I know I'm not some big-shot God-sent general or anything, so what do I know. But the English and their allies are still occupying a good bit of France. Shouldn't we be dealing with that, first?

But hey, who am I to stand in the way of a good party.

The duke of Alençon knights Charles, and then the bishop crowns him. Jeanne stands right beside him the whole time, holding her standard, which is filthy by now.

You'd think she'd be proud enough to burst, but her face is solemn, thoughtful, almost sad, like she's already thinking about the next task and troubles ahead.

And there's a subtle shift that happens the minute the crown settles on King Charles VII's greasy hair. It's almost like, before, Jeanne was sort of in charge, she had the support of the people and the love of the soldiers and all the forces of Heaven on her side, and he was almost afraid of her and would do what she told him to do. And now, thanks to her, he's the one with the power. She'll bow to the authority of the king. It's sad to see.

J & A on Paris

Alençon, let's go to Paris.

Jeanne, let's not.

Please, I've always wanted to go to Paris.

Jeanne, now is not a good time to go saving Paris.

Please?

Non.

Please?

Non.

Pleeease, *mon beau duc?*

Oh . . . all right.

Jeanne forced from Paris

I have abided by the counsel of my voices at every step.

They have not advised me to make an attempt to take Paris.

But I am impatient. I am running out of time, I feel. King Charles VII is dragging his heels, the army is losing momentum, all will be lost if we do not press on.

We try Paris.

I receive an arrow's wound in the flesh of my thigh. I want to keep fighting, but Alençon and the others beg me to retire. I consent only when they promise to renew the attack in the morning.

The next day King Charles VII insists on a retreat. Why? Doesn't he want me to take back Paris for him? The army is disbanded for lack of funds; King Charles VII is going back to Gien and orders me to accompany him. Why? Why? Why? But I cannot ignore the command of my king.

Alençon will leave us soon to go home to his wife. I will never see him again. I know this.

What has happened to my clarity of purpose? The voices are far and faint.

I take off my armor and leave it lying in the Cathedral of Saint Denis, before the image of Our Lady.

The intern observes Jeanne in private

I'm afraid to talk to her anymore, but I've started following her everywhere. I have this sort of fantasy about her being in terrible danger, and me being the only one who can save her.

She spends a lot of time in churches, praying. She takes long walks through fields and forests. She wades through mud knee-high, never noticing.

One day I see her stop in her tracks far ahead of me, and as I draw closer I see that she is talking to three people, I don't know how to describe them, I can't think of the words.

When they are finished they take themselves away, and again I don't know how to describe it except that it was a sort of dipping a sort of a sweeping a sort of swooping themselves away. Jeanne turns and spots me.

You saw them, my voices, didn't you? she says.

Yes.

What do you *want*? she says shrilly.

Will . . . could you show me how your points and laces work?

Is that all? she says, and her hands go to her waist. She unties one lace and I see the flash of skin. Two postage stamps' worth, at the most. It's as frightening and amazing as if she'd ripped open her belly to show me her secret jeweled organs. Before she can even begin on a second lace my hands are on her, grabbing and groping.

Enough! she cries, pushing at me, kicking feebly, amazing, I can barely feel it. She's only a short, teenaged girl after all—you forget that once you've seen her leading hundreds of men into battle. She knocks me to the ground, but only because I let her. I watch as her skin gets tucked away like a wound being stitched up.

I'm sorry, I say.

It's nothing, she says, abruptly calm, as if her anger got laced up tight along with everything else. I don't know what you are, she says.

I am a man who loves you. That is what I would say if I were a different sort of person. And then I would take her in my arms instead of watching her run down one hill and up the next until she is just a brown spot that flops down on the ground, spent.

Karleen, on Jeanne's drive

I'm packing up my makeup kit because Jeanne's decided it's time to go to war again. It's the same old song as before—drive out the English, France for the French, blah blah blah. If you ask me, we're the ones driving her back to the battlefield, not the English. What with the intern trailing her around like some lovesick puppy, and Burt constantly trying to get her to eat something, and Diane with her relentless interview questions, and me chasing her around with my moisturizer and cover-up, we must be driving her mad.

Jeanne on Jeanne

A new thing happened this morning. I rose early and went to the stream beside the camp. I dipped my face in the water. I opened my eyes underneath and watched the weed and drift and bubbles. And then I heard footsteps, heard someone calling Jeanne, Jeanne, and I quickly sprang up and leaped over the stream and ran toward the trees to hide. I did not want to have to talk to anyone, man or angel, so early in the morning.

When I reached the trees I looked back over my shoulder and saw myself still kneeling by the stream, my face in the water, bubbles rising around my ears and the intern shuffling uncertainly up to the bank, waiting for me to come up for air.

I ran into the trees, abandoning the other Jeanne. Let her answer his inane questions for a while. I walked among the trees, feeling soundless, invisible. Later I returned to the camp and no one mentioned the other Jeanne or seemed to have noticed anything amiss.

It was bliss.

I'll try to summon her again sometime.

I have a feeling the voices will scold me when they find out. We will have to keep it a secret.

At Compiègne

Jeanne says, I will be taken by the enemy at Compiègne.

The intern says, Why won't anybody stop her?

Burt says reluctantly, Objective distance, remember.

At Compiègne the enemy surround her and pull her from her horse.

Diane says, Burt, did you get all of that on film?

Waiting

They pass her from hand to hand, from prison to prison, castle to castle. We follow along. No one seems to notice us; all eyes are on the famous Jeanne, in captivity at last.

At Crotoy she sees the sea for the first time. The little country girl from small-town inland France looks at the heaving gray waves of the English Channel and sighs.

Why are you sighing, Jeanne? Diane shouts over the crashing wind, holding the microphone close.

This is where they imprisoned the duke of Alençon, she says, and sighs again.

The intern sighs loud enough to drown out her sigh, and the wind and the waves as well. Is he still pining?

Later, Jeanne leaps from a seventy-foot tower, without so much as twisting an ankle.

Jeanne, how could you? her captors admonish her as they lead her back inside. You know suicide is a sin, they say.

They don't want her to die before they can put her on trial.

I wasn't trying to kill myself, she says. I was trying to escape.

Burt observes the trial

Her trial is conducted by the Church, to determine whether or not she is a witch (heretic, sorceress, schismatic, or other). The inquiries are carried out in dim, dank, dungeony rooms. Diane loves it.

Mind if we bring some lights in here? says Diane. No one stops her.

Could we raise Jeanne up a bit? I can't get her in the shot . . .

They put Jeanne up on a high stool, alone inside the circle of questioners, swaying and shifting.

The questions must seem nightmarishly familiar for her: Describe the visions, what do they sound like, what do they look like, what do they *taste* like, what are they wearing, do they have faces, do they have wings, do they have crowns? These are all questions she's answered a hundred times for Diane already.

Jeanne answers calmly and firmly. But sometimes she gets confused, or saucy, or clams up inexplicably. It's going badly for her.

Her questioners keep coming back to the Fairy Tree. No, she says over and over, I never went there to practice black magic or convene with witches. It was a place for children to play, that's all; I haven't been there since I was a little girl.

But you were seen, by reliable witnesses, standing by the tree just before you left Domrémy. You were seen standing by the Fairy Tree speaking to five black figures of unnatural appearance.

Jeanne chooses to say nothing. She is unwilling to point us out though we're standing right there in the room with her.

The clothes, that's another point they get stuck on. Why the male clothes, why the cropped hair?

Karleen and I both feel like shit whenever they mention the haircut. But Jeanne never so much as looks our way.

Will you confess to inventing the voices?

No, I will not.

Are you driven by God, or Satan, or your own mortal pride?

I've been through all this already, Jeanne says calmly. My testing at Poitiers. I was found acceptable there. Send for the record of that trial. You'll see. It's all there.

Get the trial records from Poitiers, she says over and over.

But the records have disappeared.

The folks at Poitiers never sent the records, or they got lost on the way. Or else the records have been hidden or deliberately destroyed. If they were here, Jeanne might actually stand a chance.

I'd forgotten about it till she spoke, but now I remember . . . the trial at Poitiers: we filmed it! Not the whole thing; we got bored. But at least half. Surely it's enough. We could bring in a monitor, show the judges.

Burt, we can't do that, Diane says. Objective distance, remember?

I race back to the old stable where we've been storing the earlier stuff. I sift through the reels and videotapes for hours but can't find the Poitiers stuff anywhere. Diane? Did she destroy it? She's certainly capable of it. She'd do it in a minute if she thought that footage might prevent her from getting the dramatic, tragic ending she's hoping for.

It's black night outside. I think of Jeanne lying in her cell, maybe in chains, guarded by five loutish English soldiers of the lowest sort. But what can I do? I sit on the floor, straw pricking through my clothes, feeling fat and old. I try to remember the last time I was home.

Jeannes

I find I can do my trick when I am alone in the cell at night. I'm sitting on the floor and then I go lie on the bed but I'm still sitting on the floor. And then I stand up and go lean against the wall but I'm still sitting on the floor. And then I move again until there are four or five Jeannes in the cell and we can talk to one another.

It only works if we all stay very still. If we started walking around, we might bump into one another and I don't know what would happen then.

There's a Jeanne on the bed and a Jeanne in the corner and a Jeanne crawling around on all fours on the floor panting and begging and wiggling her bottom, from which a small tail protrudes, hairless and curled like a pig's.

Jeanne d'Arc has a *tail*. Who knew?

We must be very quiet. We don't want Saint Michael or Saint Catherine coming in here and overhearing us.

Who's your favorite saint? one Jeanne wants to know.

We all look at one another guiltily. We know we're not supposed to play favorites. The saints are all equal, all messengers of God.

But the truth is that the saints are all quite distinct. Saint Margaret with her spectacles and her knitting, Saint Catherine with her mournful eyes.

It's easier when there are many of us. There's less of a struggle. If one of the Jeannes believes, then another can have her doubts. As long as one of the Jeannes can offer her heart unflinchingly to God, the rest of us are allowed to have our own opinions.

I know that what we're doing is wrong. But I'm so *lonely*, what can it hurt?

Besides, the saints are always saying that I belong to all of France. Now there's just more of me to go around.

The indictment

They find her guilty of being a heretic, a sorceress, a schismatic, an apostate. This means the Church will no longer protect her, they will hand her over to the mercy of secular justice. Which sounds nice until you realize it means handing her over to the English, who are already piling up the wood to burn her.

The intern's rescue mission

I disguise myself in her red dress again. I go to her cell in the middle of the night and stick my arms through the bars to touch her, comfort her, but she presses herself against the opposite wall.

Jeanne, Jeanne, don't do it, I say. Recant, tell them you lied about the voices. You don't really want to die, do you?

She doesn't answer. She doesn't seem to know who I am. Maybe this dress makes her think that somehow I am her, that she is talking to herself.

Don't you want a life of your own? I say. Don't you want to, I don't know, go home, raise cows, get married, have children?

No answer.

I take a deep breath. *I'll* marry you, I say, but she only blinks at me.

I try a different tack. What about France? I say. Think of that. Aren't you being a little selfish? Are your principles more important than the French people? Who's going to lead them in battle against the English if you're dead?

Burt, at the reading of the verdict

They've erected two high stages in the graveyard beside the abbey, and thousands of people have crowded in to watch, both townspeople and foul English soldiers.

Jeanne stands up there looking tiny, hunched, stubborn, filthy as a street urchin in her bunched clothes, chewing her fingernails, muttering to herself, inclining her head to one side and then the other, weighing two invisible options. This, or that?

They read out the verdict— . . . and for these reasons we declare you excommunicate and heretical, abandoned to secular justice as a limb of Satan severed from the Church . . .

A cluster of English soldiers stands waiting to grab her. She is made to turn and behold the ugly surprise of the executioner waiting, the wood already piled up around the stake. This is it. The end of the story.

But then she breaks down. We've seen her weep before—Jeanne was always a big crier—but this is a thousand times worse. She gives in, she recants, she admits to everything. She was wrong, from now on she'll defer to the Church in all things. She renounces the visions she only pretended to have—yes, yes, she made it all up, she is a silly girl and will do whatever her judges and her Church tell her to do.

It's hard to watch.

The English are furious. They won't get to execute her after all.

They make her sign something, and she frowns over it the way she did signing our release form. They take her back to prison.

I ought to feel relieved, but somehow I don't. She seems so miserable, so defeated, so not herself.

They tell her to put on a woman's dress, and she obeys.

The intern versus Diane

Diane's pissed. She really wanted that execution, the spectacular finish.

I don't know if Jeanne did it for me, or for France, or for some other reason entirely. I'd like to think she did it for me. She didn't say yes to my offer, but she didn't say no either. I go to her cell again that night. Diane's already there, murmuring at her through the bars.

Jeanne looks awful. They've shaved her head. Her scalp glows with unearthly light, and her eyes are rolling all around. I have made a mistake, a terrible mistake, she's saying over and over. Then she sees me.

You, she says. You have been sent by Satan. I know it now. I was uncertain at first, but all along you have done nothing but drown out my voices and cloud my judgment. You tempted me and confused me and led me to betray everything I hold dear.

I saved you, I say.

She sticks her chin out at me and says, Tomorrow I'm going to put on men's clothes again. I'm going to reclaim my voices. I'm going to say I was weak before and spoke out of fear but now will speak the truth. I will put myself in God's hands as I have always done.

They'll declare you a relapsed heretic and hand you back to the English, I say.

I would rather die honestly than live with hypocrisy.

Well, Diane says, sounds like she's made up her mind.

Jeanne, Jeanne, I say, but she's already sinking to her knees and beginning to pray, shutting the world out. I look at Diane, who's struggling to hide the smirk of satisfaction on her face. She's going to get her big ending after all.

Burt witnessing the condemnation

Ten thousand citizens are watching when they condemn her. This time as she stands on the platform she looks as she should: steadfast, fervent, fiery, glorious. She gives a half-hour speech that reduces everyone present to tears. She prays to God, she asks everyone to pray for her. There's not a dry eye in the place. It is a most amazing speech, I don't know how to describe it. And unfortunately we won't have it on tape either—there's something wrong with our equipment, we can only get picture.

They lead her over to the stake.

I'm nauseous thinking of what's about to happen. I'll never do barbecue again. I may never cook again. Diane's beckoning. What the hell does she want now?

Diane at the burning

It takes a long time to burn a person. You think it's going to be one quick whoosh of obliterating flame, but no. It's more of a cooking process, a slow toasting starting with the feet. It takes hours.

I made Burt and Karleen leave before it started. I was afraid Burt would do something stupid, like try to stop it, run up there and try to save her or something. And probably Karleen would be upset to see the skin she's tended for over a year charring and blackening and flaking off.

But I've made the intern stay to film the whole thing. We've got hours of footage, except for the small breaks when he's puking. I've got the second camera trained in close on her face. Maybe now, after all that's happened, I'll finally get the shot I need to tie the whole film together, the moment of realization when it dawns on her that maybe she's not the messenger of God, maybe she's just a delusional little farm girl who got in way over her head.

But the moment never comes. She never wavers, never stops believing, steadfast to the last.

A few minutes ago some fireworks exploded in the flames, spelling out JESUS in five-foot-high letters. A white dove flew out of the fire, circled and winged away. The people gasped in wonder. I thought, That damn intern.

He's done it before, planting fireworks as a joke. He's ruined a lot of shots with pranks like this. The last time he did it I nearly tore him a new one. I'm amazed he'd have the balls to do it again.

He comes back from puking for the umpteenth time and sidles up to me. Nice job with the pyrotechnics, I tell him. When did you rig it?

He says, I didn't rig anything.

And the white bird. That was nice. Subtle. I didn't think you were capable of subtlety.

I don't know what you're talking about, he says, looking nervous. I didn't do anything.

Ubiquitous Jeanne

I saw them lead one of the other Jeannes up to the stake. I saw her crying out and didn't feel a thing. Should I feel guilty that she is being burned in my place? When the burning began I saw other Jeannes streaming out of her, leaping down the piles of wood like mountain goats and pushing their way unnoticed through the mesmerized crowd, and I wondered, How will they ever burn us all? They can't even catch us! There is not wood enough in all of France!

What happens now? I had been so sure that I would be flying straight up to Heaven in a blur of bright light. But now I worry that there will not be room in Heaven for all of us Jeannes. I see it all as if from a great distance, countless Jeannes swarming, a thousand sooty specks. It's getting awfully crowded, since each one has her horse and her sword and her standard held aloft. One comes galloping up to stand beside me. Is that really what I look like? Is that Jeanne? Is that *me*?

The executioner

I go to the pub afterward, I don't know what else to do, my hands are shaking. I've done this a hundred times but it's never been like this.

I was ordered to reduce every bit of her to ashes, to prevent those who still believe in her from using her remains as holy relics. But her heart and entrails remained. They would not burn, they would not burn. I tried and tried and then I panicked and threw everything in the Seine.

Now I drink and drink but still I see her heart in my hands.

Out of nowhere this woman comes up to me, a bony woman dressed in black, she pinches my arm and says she's heard about me, heard the stories, heard what happened. It's just a joke, she says. This intern, this guy who works for me, he likes practical jokes . . . Calm down, calm down. Drink your wine, here, drink.

I drink my wine. She's still here. Come on, she says, it's just a prop. Can't you tell the difference between a rubber heart and a real one?

I say, Listen, woman, I am an executioner. I know body parts. This was her heart. It would not burn. It is a sign. I have committed a terrible sin and burned a saint.

The intern: synapses

So I finally got to see Jeanne without her clothes. Without her skin, too. I smelled her burning and it smelled like a red dress. I took her atoms into my lungs and they will travel through my blood and lodge in my brain, making a sooty smudge there, all the signals tangled together but strong as ever. If you were to take off the top of my head and jab an electrode at the spot, I would smell her gray eyes, see her low husky voice like a plume of smoke, taste the texture of her hair.

Gabriella, My Heart

Cristina Henríquez

I

I loved a girl once. Every story starts that way, right? She was from my old neighborhood, in San Miguelito in Panama. Her name was Gabriella.

I saw her on the first day of my last year of high school, on the minibus that lumbered up our street, swallowing students waiting in their starched cotton uniforms and spitting us out again at Luis Martín High School. I had lived on that street my whole life and thought I knew all of our neighbors, but I had never before seen the girl who climbed onto the bus that day with her navy blue knee-highs pulled up past her knees like a tramp, her pleated navy skirt perfectly cinching her waist, her black hair falling over her shoulders in curls so big you could fit your whole hand inside one.

She sat by herself in the front seat, and I remember feeling embarrassed for her because the front seat was where only the nerds, the *come libros*, sat. I was bordering on being a nerd myself, and even I avoided the front seat, but there was no way to communicate with her discreetly. And truthfully, she didn't seem to mind when Alberto Avila got on and sat next to her even though he wore black glasses that were forever falling off his face and he sniffled constantly, wiping his nose with his fingers. She simply looked at him and nodded and then stared out the window.

There was a buzz around Gabriella from the beginning. By our lunch break that day, I found out from Jaime Torres and Ricardo Solís, who were smoking under the coconut palm in the school courtyard, that she and her family had just moved to Panama City from Colombia.

"*Una colombiana,*" Jaime said. "What do you think of that, Nestor?" He dropped his cigarette on the ground.

"It's fine," I said.

"That's it? Have you seen her ass? Fuck, man."

I shrugged.

"Forget it," Ricardo said, pointing at me. "You know his story. He's for the other side. He wouldn't notice her ass if she rubbed it in his face." He and Jaime laughed.

I couldn't remember when the joke that I was a *pato* started. There had been moments when I wondered whether it was true. Once, in physical education class during my eighth year, someone yelled that Claudio Garces's nuts were hanging out of his gym shorts and I turned to look. But everyone had turned—boys and girls alike—so I figured it didn't mean anything. I didn't really think about guys in that way, I told myself. I didn't really even think about girls that way. I was one of those guys who, while everyone else was walk-ing the halls with their arms draped over girls or was having sex in the library, had never had a girlfriend. Then came Gabriella. And I thought, I get it now. That had been the problem all along. I had never met the right girl.

The first few weeks of my senior year went like a flash. I was taking physics, calculus, English V, and world history and was dedicated to my studies because I wanted to go to college. I wanted to be an engi-neer and work on the canal. It was a big dream compared with all the guys in my class who wanted to work at their fathers' body shops or figure out a way to spend all day at the horse track, making money off lucky bets, or better yet, live with their mamis who would feed them and wash their clothes until their mamis kicked them out and they found wives to provide the same services.

It was a Tuesday when my calculus teacher, Profesor Treviño, kept me after class to ask if I had time to tutor another student. I was so serious then, begrudgingly surrendering my time to anything other than schoolwork, but when he told me the student's name— Gabriella Díaz—I said yes in a heartbeat.

That afternoon I spent ten minutes in the boys' bathroom straightening my clip-on uniform tie and spit-shining my shoes and hair alike. Gabriella was settled in a desk when I walked into the classroom. She had her chin on her hand and was staring out the windows that looked out over the tops of the palm trees in the court-yard.

"Hi," I said. "Gabriella?"

"Yes," she said. "And you?"

"Nestor."

"A pleasure," she said.

The desks were arranged in clusters of four, and I lowered myself into a seat across from her, so we were facing each other. I opened my notebook.

She stared at it and said, "So you're here to teach me about function notation?"

"Profesor Treviño asked me to."

"Function notation is just a condensed way of writing out function values. F of *x*, right?"

"Right," I said.

She turned to look out the window again. "I already know it," she said.

"We can work on something else, then."

"I already know it all." She was still gazing out the window.

"Do you know function composition?" I asked.

She took my notebook and wrote:

$$(f \circ g)\,(x) = f\,(g\,(x))$$

"For example," she said.

I stared at her, though she seemed not to notice. Her bangs fell in her eyes a little and quivered when the tips collided with her eyelashes as she blinked.

"It sounds like you're caught up," I said.

She turned to me. "I guess so," she said. Then she shifted in her chair and reached to the floor to grab her canvas bag before standing. "Next week?" she asked. "Same time, same place?"

I nodded, and watched her walk away.

After that, I couldn't stop thinking about her. I thought I had finally— finally!—found love. I went home at night and got in bed, trying to imagine her lying beside me in nothing but her knee-highs, the woolly feel of them against my legs, the warmth of her skin against me everywhere else.

The following Monday, I was the first to arrive at Profesor Treviño's room.

"Hey," Gabriella said when she walked in. She dropped her bag and plopped herself into the desk across from me. "What are we doing today?"

"Secant."

She grinned. "Easy."

"Well," I started, "when we're talking about a curve, it's a line that intersects at two points on that curve."

"At least two points," she interrupted. "Could be more. The word *secant* comes from Latin, you know. *Secare*. To cut."

"Why did Profesor Treviño ask me to tutor you if you already know all this?"

"He doesn't know I know it."

"What do you mean?"

"Nestor," she said, "you live down the street from me, don't you?"

I watched her gold bracelet slide up her arm as she ran her hand through her hair. "I think so," I said. "You ride my bus."

"That's what I thought." She tapped her teeth with her fingernail for a minute and then asked, "What's the name of the boy who sits with me on the bus?"

"Alberto Avila."

"Do we like him?"

I loved how she said "we," like the two of us were in on something—anything—together.

"He's okay."

"He never talks to me."

I smiled. "He probably doesn't know what to say. He's not much in the department of social graces."

She smiled, too. "I like how you put that." Then she glanced out the window again, as she tended to do, before turning to me and saying, "You should sit with me on the bus instead. Tomorrow, will you save me a seat? At least then I'll have someone to talk to."

I nodded, half of me sinking in disbelief, the other half of me floating with joy.

"Good," she said. "So what now?"

"I guess we meet again next week."

In school, news that Gabriella and I were sitting together on the bus got around fast, and reports that I was tutoring her one afternoon a week followed close behind. Guys like Jaime and Ricardo who had always teased me in the past were giving me a second look, wondering what I had that they didn't. But they couldn't figure it out, and truthfully, neither could I.

Gabriella and I fell into a sort of friendship. She didn't seem to mind that I was a bit of an outcast. We met every Monday in Profesor Treviño's room and talked—we had long since stopped studying—until the janitor came with his rolling bucket and dingy mop and told us to get lost. Then Gabriella popped up and bade me good-bye.

I hardly remember now what we talked about for so many afternoons except that once, she told me why she didn't let on that she was as smart as she was: her mother wanted her to get married. I asked what that had to do with it. Gabriella said that her mother had drilled it into her since she was little that finding a good husband was the best thing a woman could do for herself. Forget about schooling. Find a decent man.

"Do you really believe that?" I asked.

"Why not? It doesn't sound so bad."

"But why can't you do both—school and marriage? Why does it have to be one or the other?"

"Guys don't marry smart girls."

"I would marry you," I said. I trembled as the words came out. It felt like my big confession to her.

"You're different."

"What do you mean?"

"You know."

"What?"

"Forget it," she said.

"I really would. I would marry you."

"Thanks," Gabriella said, unfurling a soft laugh.

The next few months were torment. If anyone had asked me then, I would have told them: Gabriella was my every breath. She was my beating heart. I felt as if every moment of my existence was spent trying to figure out how to stand next to her in the hall, deciding whether I should take a chance and hold her hand on the bus. Watching her longingly from afar as she hung out with her girlfriends, I was terrified to make my move.

In April, two months before graduation, I received a letter of acceptance from the Universidad Tecnológica. To celebrate, my mami threw me a small party. Gabriella had told me she would come. I was standing on the patio when I saw her walking down the street, dogs barking at her from behind driveway gates. She had on white linen pants and a tank top, and I realized I had never seen her in anything but her school uniform. Her hair was pinned back on one side with a jeweled barrette, and there was gloss on her lips instead of her usual pink lipstick. She looked spectacular.

"I'm glad you made it," I said as she stepped onto our patio.

"I wouldn't have missed it," she said.

She looked around. Most everyone was inside, dancing to an old Willie Colón album. There were *pasteles* on the TV tray my mami had set on the porch.

"Looks like a nice party," she said.

I nodded, and took a step closer to her.

"So you must be excited," she said. "It's a good university. You'll do well."

"Gabriella," I said, and then found I didn't have the rest of a sentence.

She looked at me and smiled. She put her hand on the side of my face. "You've been a good friend to me, Nestor. I thank you for that."

"It was no problem," I said, my voice teetering on a whisper.

Gabriella dropped her hand and gazed at the floor. She turned her gold bracelet in a half-circle. I was desperate to tilt her face back up to mine, to kiss her finally, when she said, "I have a lead on a guy from Guatemala. Larissa, from my circle, knows him and hooked me up. We've written to each other a few times and talked on the phone once. He seems like a good guy. I'm going to Guatemala tomorrow to meet him. I'm not sure when I'll be back. It depends on how things go."

"What?"

"I haven't told my mami yet. I don't want her getting all excited in case it turns out to be nothing."

"You never said anything."

She shrugged. "I have to see how it turns out. It might not be a big deal."

She fixed her eyes on mine and we stared at each other for what felt like a long time. I wanted nothing more in life right then than to hold her, but she had other plans.

Finally, she broke her gaze and said, "Okay, Nestor. This is it, then." She gave me a hug. I was acutely aware of the warmth of her body against my chest and the soft brush of her hair against my chin.

When she pulled away, she offered a half-smile and then a wave as she retreated down the steps of our house and back up the street to her own. Everything emptied out of me. My mami came out while I stood watching Gabriella's white linen pants swish down the street.

"What are you doing, *hijo,* just standing there?" She flicked my shoulder. "Bring the rest of these plates to the sink. I'll wash them."

When I didn't move at first, she asked, "Are you okay?"

I nodded and started collecting the stray plates and the glasses with melting ice, fighting through my stinging sadness as I worked.

II

I started college in March. The university was in the city, so I was able to live at home. I walked a kilometer to the edge of our neighborhood and then took two buses to get to classes every day, but it was worth it. College felt like what I had been waiting for my whole life—getting deeper into my studies; no one goofing off, running around, throwing vegetables like hand grenades over lunch tables. I'm sure there was some of that, but overall the atmosphere was earnest.

I majored in physics. Academically, I was steady. I kept my nose in my books, went to lectures on magnetics and energy, and even got a job in the library, checking people's bags as they left. It was an easy gig, and since things were slow a lot of the time, it gave me time just to study and do homework.

At home, I kept my mami company and made dinner on Sundays, my specialty of *arroz con guandu* and *plátanos en tentación.* I sat on the patio in the evenings, watching the geckos dart along the stucco exterior of the house and listening to dogs howl while I paged through textbooks in my lap. The air was full and sweet and always I hoped that Gabriella would show up, that she would stroll down the street to say hello, returned from Guatemala at last. Always I was let down.

In between classes, when I had an hour or two to spare, I went to the library to read. I found a table on the third floor, in a corner behind the stacks, where I liked to go. I sat with my back toward everyone and, when I got tired of doing physics problems, I worked on the day's crossword, which I would bring along. One day I was studying for midterms when someone came up behind me and put their arms around my shoulders and kissed my cheek. I turned quickly to see a guy, whose mouth dropped open at the sight of me.

"Hey!" I said loudly.

The guy covered my mouth with his hand. "Quiet," he said. He uncovered it just as quickly. "Sorry, *hombre*," he said. "I thought you were someone else, you know." He held up his hands in defense as if he thought I was going to punch him. "I'm really sorry," he said again.

I was breathing fast. Adrenaline, I guess, and something about him. "It's okay."

"Thanks," he said, and hurried away.

I sat there for a long time, stunned. I had never been kissed anywhere by anyone other than my mother. It was incredible, by the time I stood up, how much I wished I *had* been the right person.

The next week in my thermal-physics class, I saw the guy again. It was a big lecture class, and that day he sat in front of me. I could smell his hair gel, a minty scent. It sounds like the stupidest thing — being turned on by the smell of a man's hair gel — but it got me. The whole period I kept thinking I would tap his shoulder and say, "Remember me?" but I couldn't bring myself to do it. I kept thinking about how it had felt when he put his arms around me the week before, and I got pissed off that I kept thinking about it.

When class was over, I stayed in my seat. He started packing his things and looked back at me. He nodded. When I still didn't leave, he said, "You have a bunch of friends waiting for you after this class? You guys all gonna jump me as soon as I walk into the hall?"

"No," I said.

He eyed me skeptically.

"I swear."

"What's your story?" he asked.

I didn't know what to say.

After a second, a smile lit up on his face. "I got you, man," he said. "You don't have to say anything."

"My name's Nestor," I said.

"Wise one, no?"

"What?"

" 'A lie will Nestor not utter, for he is wise indeed.' Homer's *Odyssey*, man."

I nodded, though I didn't know the quote. I was impressed anyone would.

"You *panameño*?" he asked.

"Yes."

"*Cubano*. My name's Reynaldo." He adjusted his bag. "So I'll see you tomorrow, Nestor." I watched him walk out of the lecture hall.

When I stepped into the light of day, I was shaking. I skipped my next class, hurried home, and cured myself with a cold shower. In the shower, I kept asking myself: How could I be thinking about another *hombre* like this? My mind sped back to Claudio Garces in his gym shorts and I started crying. Right there in the stall. My mother's shampoo bottles toppled when I crouched in the corner. I covered my face with my hands, leaned my back against the slick tile, and sobbed.

Every day after that Reynaldo sat in front of me, close enough that I could breathe him in. We talked briefly—he turned around once and asked for a sheet of paper, smiling at me for longer than seemed normal before facing front again—but I wasn't sure what any of it meant. To him or to me.

Then one night Rey came to the library during my shift and asked me to a movie. I said no. I said it quick and looked around to make sure no one else had heard. Rey was leaning against the tall checkout desk. He asked if he could walk me to the bus at least when my shift was over. I said no again. Pointing to a chair he said, "I'm going to wait for you here until your shift's through. Then I'm going to ask you one more time. If you tell me no again, I won't bother you anymore." He sat. At the end of my shift I said yes.

On the way to the bus stop, Rey tried to hold my hand. He said, "You're into this, aren't you?" and I didn't know what to say. Because there was no doubt I loved the feeling of our hands touching, that the nearness of him thrilled right through me, but if he was asking was I gay, I didn't know the answer to that. I stopped walking.

"Look," he said. "I thought you knew I wasn't just looking for a friend."

"I knew," I said. The city was still wide awake—dim car headlights cut through the darkness, tinny horns honked, buses churned their engines, sending exhaust into the air like dirty bombs.

"So then what?" Reynaldo asked, his tone patient.

"I don't know what's going on. I never felt like this about a guy before."

"Consider yourself lucky. Where I come from you'd get a fist in your face for even saying that. At least Panama is easy. A hell of a lot easier."

I was quiet.

He smiled. "Have you ever felt like this about *anyone* before?"

It took me a few seconds to say it. "A girl. In high school. Her name was Gabriella." I shoved my hands in my pockets. "I don't know what that means. I've been trying to sort it out, but I think I'm just fucked up."

Reynaldo laughed. "Nah," he said. "I've seen this before. You only *think* you loved her. At the time you knew her, subconsciously you knew you liked guys. You knew it. Only you didn't want to admit it. You weren't ready to *be* it, you know. So you talked yourself into loving this girl, to make yourself seem more normal, to make yourself *feel* more normal. It's a classic reaction. Happens to a lot of people."

"No, I really did love her," I said.

Reynaldo shrugged. "Well, then, you really did love her. If you say so. But ask yourself whether you can imagine ever loving another woman again."

"No."

"Even being turned on by another woman?"

I shook my head.

"And how about a man? Any number of men? Me, for example?"

I nodded.

"So forget about it. You are what you are. She was just one woman. She must have been a damn special woman, but she was probably the only one in your life. One person doesn't change who you are."

I decided to get my own apartment. I told my mami I was tired of the commute, but in truth I wanted to get away from my old life.

"You can't leave me," she said. "Children are supposed to stay with their parents."

"I have to, Mami. I just have to."

She pursed her lips and shook her head at me. "I know there's something going on with you," she said.

"No, Mami. I just want to be closer to the school."

She took my hand in hers. "You still come for Sunday dinners, though."

"Of course."

My apartment was small—one cutout in the middle of a high-rise—and the toilet tended to overflow, but it was mine and I loved it. I took more shifts at the library to help pay the rent. I told Rey I had moved and he brought me a small *mola* in a wooden frame as a housewarming gift. "Isn't this what Panamanians hang in their houses?" he asked. He told me he had taken a bus to Panamá la Vieja, the old city, and watched a Kuna woman layer the fabrics over one another and cut them out into a pattern that looked like a fish with colorful scales. He went and had it framed, too. I hung it above my desk.

I invited Rey over to watch movies (I insisted we not go to the theater together because I was afraid of being ridiculed), and we watched them on my secondhand couch, Rey's hand on my stomach under my shirt. We kissed in the flickering darkness—they were the first kisses I had shared with anyone—and his lips were soft and warm. He always tasted like a mixture of beer and popcorn.

After a while, Rey started spending the night. The first few times, I got in bed fully clothed while he stripped to an undershirt and boxers. He had played *fútbol* in his youth and his legs were strong. The sight of him sent my heart racing. He said, "Those are your pajamas?" and raised his eyebrows in amusement. But when I nodded, he let it go. Usually, he talked until I fell asleep. We were two grown people crushed into a twin bed, which often meant one of us woke up with a sore neck or a numb arm, but we didn't mind.

Once, in the dark, after we'd been kissing, he asked me, "Was it like this with the girl?"

"No," I said. I was trembling a little with joy. "That was something else. That was not this at all."

During the day, both of us went to classes as usual. I was light with the feeling of having found someone. And, I guess, of having found myself.

On the weekends we mostly stayed in, saving our affection for private moments and private spaces, although once Rey talked me into going to a *fútbol* game, saying that we would be safe from scorn because we would look like any two friends together. It was Panama versus Cuba and I could tell it meant a lot to him, so I said I would go. Panama lost, as usual, but there was something exhilarating about being there with him, about knowing we were more to each other than met the eye.

Another time, Rey invited me to take a weekend trip to San Blas.

"Before I came to Panama," he explained, "everyone told me it was one place I had to go. What do you think?"

"I've never been."

"I already made us a reservation on the plane. It's small. Just a thirty-minute flight. Do you have a bathing suit?"

I smiled and put my arm around his waist. "Why?"

"Good one," he said.

When we got there, we dropped our things in our room and walked barefoot until we found an uninhabited stretch of pale sand and crystalline water. We didn't have to walk far. We stripped off our clothes, leaving them in one pile on the shore, and dove in naked, grabbing at each other's ankles and laughing as we spiked our wet hair into short Mohawks. We swam out until we could barely touch the bottom with our feet and held each other in an embrace under the water, both of us balancing on our toes, every gentle wave making it feel as though we might float away. When we were exhausted, we climbed back onshore to find our pile of clothes inhabited by sand crabs. They scattered like feathers tickling over the sand when we shook them out. Rey and I spent the next two days lying on towels on the beach, drinking beer, eating chicken at an outdoor restaurant, and swaying in the hammock in our bungalow, which hovered over the water on stilts. The evening air was humid, and I had my head in the crook of Rey's shoulder as the hammock rocked slightly. I felt a tugging at my scalp. I raised my head to see Rey sucking on a piece of my hair.

"It tastes like salt," he said, grinning.

I tightened my arms around him.

III

Only a few months after I would've said to anyone that I was over Gabriella Díaz, she came back into my life. Out of nowhere, she called me on the phone the first week of my sophomore year. I hadn't heard anything from her or about her in over a year, and the only people who called me were my mami and Rey, so when I heard Gabriella's voice, it jolted through me like lightning.

"Nestor?" she said. "It's me."

"Gabriella," I said.

"What are you doing?" she asked.

"I'm studying. Where are you?"

"Are you busy?"

"I can't believe I'm talking to you. It's been so long. How are things going?"

"Nestor, I'm in your apartment building."

"What do you mean you're in my apartment building?"

"I mean I'm in your apartment building. By the elevator. I followed someone else in."

"What?"

"I went to your house first. Your mami told me you moved.

Nestor, she almost started crying when she told me. I can't believe you abandoned your mami like that."

"What?"

"Do you want to let me up? Or can you come down and get me?"

The phone felt light in my hand. I was having trouble processing what was going on. "I'll be down," I said, breathing fast.

If I had happened to walk by her, there's a good chance I wouldn't have recognized her. She looked so different. Her hair was a light caramel color now and shoulder-length, tucked behind her ears. She wore torn jeans and an oversized purple T-shirt. An enormous red duffel bag rested at her feet. She smiled when she saw me. That's what gave her away. And then she practically jumped on me and buried her chin in my neck and said, "Oh my God," over my shoulder. When she pulled away, she said, "I knew it would be like this, seeing you again. It's so great." She grinned fiercely.

I drew her back to me and hugged her again, something I never would have attempted before. But I felt different now, like I knew who I was, and because of knowing I could handle her, could control her effect on me.

In my apartment, she left the bag just inside the door and glanced around. She went to the window and gazed out. "All Latin American countries look exactly the same," she said. "And they also look completely different. Don't you think?"

"I don't know."

She turned around.

"Did you just get here?" I asked.

"I came for you," she said.

I smiled blandly, not knowing what she meant and not wanting to ask. I picked a shirt off my desk chair and motioned for her to sit. I sat on the bed.

"How's your mamá?" I asked.

"The last I heard, she's fine."

"You don't talk to her?"

"Not lately. She thinks I'm still in Guatemala. I want to let her believe I'm happy. Happily married."

"Gabriella, what's going on?"

Gabriella smoothed her hair behind her ears. "Nestor, do you remember the time you said you would marry me?"

It seemed funny to think about now, but I did remember. "Of course."

"Would you still?"

"You didn't already get married?"

"He kicked me out." I watched her work her jaw a bit.

"What happened?" I asked.

"It hardly matters. How are things going for you here?"

"Actually, they're going well. Really well. But wait—"

Her eyes widened. "Really? That's good. We could stay around here, then. This apartment is nice."

"Wait a second. I still don't understand—"

"I married that guy. Larissa's friend in Guatemala. The one I went there for, you know. It was fine for a while. He had a good job. Good enough that I had ten pairs of pajamas. Can you believe that? Pajama *sets*. Who do you know that has ten pajama *sets*?" She swallowed. "He kicked me out about a week ago. We're getting a divorce."

"He kicked you out?"

She nodded.

"Why?"

"He had another woman on the side. He told me I was finished, that he loved her and that he wanted to marry her. She started moving in the day I left." She sighed and slid her hands under her thighs.

"So I was thinking," she continued, "now you and I could get married. I don't know. Back when we knew each other, I wondered whether you were a *pato*—I'm sorry, but everyone used to say that—but then a few weeks ago I remembered that time you said you would marry me, so I started thinking maybe we were all wrong about you. And I wanted to come and see."

I stared at her, not knowing what to say. *This* was why she had come to me? To see whether I was gay? To see whether I would marry her? Because she was desperate? I wasn't mad at her exactly—even after not seeing her for more than a year, even with this being why she had come, I still looked at her and simply couldn't muster anger—but I felt like she had walked in and socked me one right in the gut.

Gabriella got up and strode toward me. "Nestor," she said softly. She put both her warm hands on my face and leaned down—I could feel her breath against my skin—and kissed me. It startled me so much that I didn't stop her at first. I could smell the scent of baby powder lifting off her. When I pulled back a second later, she kept her hands on my face and held me close enough so that our noses were almost touching. Her eyes were shut.

"You weren't wrong about me," I whispered.

She was the first person from my old life I had told.

Her eyelids popped up and she straightened. She tucked her hair behind her ears and darted her eyes around the room. "Bathroom?" she asked. "Where's the bathroom?"

I pointed. "Over there."

I slumped on the bed. I felt lightheaded. Through the window, the day was growing dark and the sky was a deep, shimmering violet color.

When Gabriella came out of the bathroom, she said quickly and without looking at me, "Do you mind if I stay here tonight? I don't have anywhere else to go."

"Gabriella, I'm sorry."

She shrugged.

"Of course you can stay. You can take my bed." I stood and pushed the textbooks off my bed, laid the bedspread on the floor. She got in right away, even though it was still early in the evening.

"Don't you even want to change into your pajamas?" I asked.

"I hate pajamas now," she said, her hair spread over the pillow-case. "Ten pairs of pajamas! It's ridiculous." She forced a laugh.

Since I didn't know what else to do, I turned off the light and lay down, too, folding myself in the bedspread. After a few minutes of listening to her breathe, I said, "Gabriella—" but she cut me off.

"I don't really want to talk anymore tonight," she said.

There was such weariness in her voice, and I didn't want to push her. "Good night," I said.

Later, I woke to the sound of her weeping. My clock read 2:30.

"Gabriella," I whispered. My mouth was dry. She didn't answer.

"Are you okay?" I asked.

She was absolutely quiet, and I thought maybe she was holding her breath to make me think she was sleeping.

"Please," I said.

"It's too bad," she murmured. "I always thought about you."

I felt my stomach tighten. "I loved you once, Gabriella. I know it doesn't make sense, but it's true." I don't know why, but I felt tears tickle down the side of my face as I said it.

"But you don't now?" she said.

"It's just different. I'm different."

Silence swelled in the room. After a few minutes, she said, "I loved you once too, Nestor. I bet you never knew that. I would have told you back then, but I thought it wouldn't matter. I mean, I thought you knew you were gay, but you just weren't open about it."

My voice was weak. "No, I didn't know until later," I said.

"So I missed my chance."

I didn't say anything.

"I guess it all ended up the same anyway. A broken heart back when I *thought* you knew. A broken heart now when you *do* know." She sniffled. "It's all the same."

In the morning, she was gone. There was a note on the floor where her duffel bag had been.

Don't worry about me, N. I'll be fine. Thanks for the bed.
—G.

My first thought was to call Rey, but I hung up before he answered. I went to the window, foolishly thinking I would glimpse her, then took the elevator to street level and stood in front of my building, looking around in desperation. The air was humid and the sky was threatening rain. I had no idea what to do. I didn't know whether I would ever see her again.

After a time, I went back to my apartment and crawled into bed. I smelled her—baby powder—in my sheets. I lay there all day. In the afternoon, Rey called. He left a message on the machine.

"Ne*stor*!" he shouted. "The movie place finally had *Pi*. I rented it. Call me if you want to watch it tonight."

I smiled with my face pressed against the pillow. I knew that in a little while, I would call him. I would go on. My heart would reassemble itself with a part for Gabriella that I would keep but that would stay closed, and a part for Rey that would burn and stay strong. And no matter what configuration my heart ever took, this was the truth: even though I never would again, I had a loved a girl once. But every story starts that way, right?

The Red Coat

Caitlin Macy

In the afternoons before the holidays Trish had started frequenting a restaurant a few blocks west of the apartment. It was an expensive place inside, with hard, cushionless chairs that seemed to suggest that if you found them uncomfortable, you didn't belong. Trish had actually dined there only once, to celebrate Tim's promotion. But a cappuccino could set you back only so far, even on Madison Avenue. Trish fancied the idea of becoming a regular, and it worried her to think that the progress she had made had been wiped out by the recent two-week Christmas vacation. She hurried a little as she walked the crosstown blocks, leaning forward into the wind, her chin stuck out, as if she were trying to catch up with someone.

The restaurant was empty and quiet, with the conspicuous exception of a noisy party at the bar—two long-haired, angular women—models, probably—getting messily drunk and practically pouring themselves, too, all over the bartender. The man did not detach himself to wait on Trish, as he should have, and after several long minutes, she looked around peevishly, a summoning hand raised in the air. One of the women had a cigarette between her teeth and was leaning forward across the bar to solicit a light. "Oldest trick in the book," Trish thought disgustedly, wondering what kind of woman would stoop to such an obvious, clichéd come-on to get a man's attention. "Excuse me!" she called peremptorily. Then she snapped her head back around and hunched down in her chair, hiding herself. For it was Evgenia.

It was four months since she'd met the girl—four months since Beth and John had been transferred to London. "We're moving!" the invitations said, and the apartment on East Ninety-third was mostly packed up and people stood around drinking Dom Pérignon out of plastic cups amid stacks of boxes, and making bids on the DeSilvas' IKEA couch and console. Early on in the evening, Beth had come out of the kitchen with a tray of bacon-wrapped shrimp and said, "Hey, does anyone need a great cleaning lady?"

At first everyone seemed to have a cleaning woman she was satisfied with. Perched on the arm of an L-shaped sofa, Trish had listened, smiling from time to time, as Karen and Kelly and Meg and Christine griped happily about their inadequate help—Lupe, who shrank a $250 cashmere sweater; Nadia, who refused to clean the oven; Sancha, who called from São Paulo one day to say she wouldn't be back; Liubov, who eschewed the organic cleaning products purchased by her employer and instead seemed to clean the whole apartment with industrial-strength bleach that made even the cat's eyes water. Trish laughed in unison with the others, clutching her champagne, but said nothing—for what could she add? She didn't have a cleaning lady; she never had—she cleaned their apartment herself. It wasn't until the end of the party, when only the stragglers remained, that Trish caught Beth alone in the kitchen, tying up the garbage, and asked for the woman's number.

"You're gonna love her," Beth had said. "Real self-starter. I've had her over a year and I don't have a single complaint."

"Just 'Evgenia,' huh?" Trish asked, eyeing the Post-it.

"I don't know her last name," Beth said, taking obvious pleasure in the fact. "I just put 'Cash' on the check."

Trish née Moore had come to New York in the late eighties with a degree in communications from her state university. The industrial town she'd grown up in, in southern New Hampshire, was a former mill city, with all that the phrase implies: the rows of abandoned factory buildings lining a polluted river; the deserted downtown with the barely subsisting, family-owned department store displaying corsets and fedoras in its windows, and other dusty anachronistic goods. For several years after moving to New York Trish's emotional sustenance had derived almost entirely from that achievement alone.

There were days, well into the mid-nineties even, when she could hardly believe she had done it. She had announced to her family and friends that she was moving to New York, and she had moved to New York. She had squeezed some money out of her mother and gone back once for some more, but by the end of the summer she had found a job crunching numbers at a midtown consulting firm. She had rented herself a studio apartment on York Avenue; later on she put up a wall and advertised for a roommate so she could afford the rent hike. When she took the Greyhound bus up to New Hampshire at the holidays, she would tell people she lived in Manhattan, and she vowed never to leave, no matter how poor she was, for an outer borough. Though her own apartment building was a former tenement, a site of peeling linoleum, bare bulbs in porcelain sockets, and knotted plastic grocery bags of trash left on landings, at least it was well away from the outer boroughs, which Trish associated with dinginess.

The city was different when Trish arrived. The gaunt, unshaven men who wore undershirts in the middle of the day had not been driven out of the Village. There were no Starbucks franchises to kill time in without arousing suspicion, and in certain neighborhoods, where trash cans were chained outside of buildings, the doorframes and stoops of which were painted over in mud brown, you could still catch the grotty scent of the 1970s as it fought its way up from the subway grates—a stimulating aroma for some, suggestive of funkier, more authentic times; alarming, merely, for someone like Trish, who had, from those first few years in the city, before she knew better, half a dozen unsavory memories.

One involved answering a roommate ad in *The Village Voice* and realizing, when the man offered her a glass of sweet wine before showing her around the apartment, that she was complicit in something sleazy. Another time she had taken a cab home from a bar in the Village when she knew she didn't have the fare. She went through the motions of having the driver stop at a cash machine, knowing her card would be rejected, but figuring that, as a pretty girl, she could charm her way out of it this once. She emerged from the bank with a goofy smile, saying, "I cannot believe this . . ." and was about to launch into a highly nuanced apology for just why she could not, at that particular moment, access her checking account, when the cabbie demanded, "How much you got?" And when Trish said, "A dollar fifty?" he said, "Ah, fuck you!" It was the tone of his voice that bothered Trish—the disgust, yes, but what made her feel painfully humiliated, months later, when she lay awake reviewing the moment, was the man's utter lack of surprise; it was as if, the cabbie seemed to imply, she did that kind of thing all the time.

Trish had been raised Catholic, and for years, when she woke up hungover and full of recriminations, she would revisit a laundry list of these moments of mortal shame in an attempt to marshal the evidence outstanding against her. Once in a while, when she was at her lowest, Trish would go to church on Sundays and pray, the way she had as a girl, with her eyes squeezed tight. But most Sundays she lay in bed till noon and then rose and cleaned the apartment from top to bottom, scouring the ringed bathtub, scrubbing the patch of kitchen floor on her hands and knees, washing all of her lingerie by hand and hanging it out to dry, and finally taking a shower and combing out her hair to let it dry naturally.

All those first years, too, Trish believed that until she changed her ways and stopped waking up hungover she would be punished. She assumed the punishment would manifest itself in the thwarting of her most obvious goal: marriage.

But life did not seem to play the retributive role Trish had cast it in. Life was altogether more charitable—it was almost Christian in its forgiveness. At the midtown firm where she'd worked her way up to research manager, she met Tim, fresh from business school in the Midwest. Trish got drunk and slept with him on the first date—he married her anyway. She floated the subject of matrimony two weeks into their relationship—he was not deterred. She had not changed her ways, and yet she had been rewarded.

After she got the ring, Trish gave up her own apartment and moved into Tim's bachelor studio. It was an upgrade for her, in that, though the studio was small, it was in a luxury building, with a health club in the basement. The cooking and cleaning were the least she could do, said Trish, who had given notice at her job at once. And she honestly didn't mind housework. In fact, reaching down to scour the bathtub or feeling her muscles begin to tire from running the German vacuum over the bedroom carpet were among the times that Trish felt most robustly connected to the promise of her and Tim's union.

"It's not like we were rolling in dough," Tim liked to say of his childhood in Detroit, "and yet my mother never worked."

"Of course not!" Trish would agree, a scornful edge to her voice. "It's so much better for the family," she would say, as if she, too, could remember family dinners of roast beef and mashed potatoes rather than the broiler fish sticks or macaroni and cheese out of a box she and her older sister, Jan, had made the nights neither her mother—an ICU nurse at the hospital—nor her father—a tax advisor—could be home to prepare a meal. In public and in private, too, Trish and Tim would agree on this one issue with that avid, defensive posturing that is characteristic of all kinds of traditionalists in Manhattan. Tim's latent desire for a stay-at-home wife, teased out by Trish on their second date, had become their sustaining vanity as a couple.

Then had come the DeSilvas' going-away party. Perching there on the arm of the sofa, faux-commiserating with one of the women for her inability to fire a particularly careless cleaner on account of the known exigencies of her personal life (single mom, etc.), Trish felt duped. She was ill at ease, and the feeling of anxiety stayed with her for some weeks as it slowly occurred to her that perhaps there was a whole host of other things she was ignorant of, standards no one had told her about, and that she would discover belatedly and by accident, in some unsympathetic public forum.

The week before the cleaning lady was to start, Trish noticed that she was more attentive to the mess in the apartment rather than less. When she collected the dirty dishes from the bedroom and living room and stacked them in the sink, she couldn't just leave them there for a night as she usually did—she rinsed them right away and loaded them into the dishwasher. When she put several days' worth of old newspapers into the recycling box, she thought, "I'm being really nice not to leave these for the cleaning lady," and yet she wondered whether, in the future, Evgenia would take over that task. On the morning itself, Trish stripped the weeks-old sheets from the bed and organized the things on Tim's bureau, and before she could stop herself, she had wet a sponge with Comet and run it over the bathroom sink. Polishing the mirror, she caught sight of her face, angry red from exertion.

Trish had pictured someone middle-aged. She didn't know what to say when she opened the door to find somebody she might have hung out with, in her single days, on a Friday night. The cleaning lady didn't look like a cleaning lady at all. She had blond hair, pulled back from dark roots into a devil-may-care ponytail. Her face was made up dramatically, with heavy eyeliner and long streaks of blush on both cheeks. Her outfit, when she took off her coat, made Trish look away, embarrassed: Evgenia was wearing a ruffled blouse and a miniskirt over tights and sling-back sandals.

"You sure you want to wear that?" Trish said, after showing her in.

"I have apron." The young woman removed one from the large zippered black bag she was carrying and put it on.

The Meehans' apartment was new since the honeymoon, and Trish liked to show it off: the custom L in the living room, which backed up to the wall of windows onto—if not a park—at least Eighty-sixth Street; the kitchen decked out with gifts from their registry—the standing mixer and cappuccino maker, the cedar knife block filled with German steel. On top of the television stood the silver-framed picture of Tim and her cutting the cake at the wedding—black-tie, it had been, and they'd had seven attendants apiece. She rather expected a compliment, but the girl was silent, offering only nods, and unsmiling ones at that, that forced Trish to keep up the conversation.

"So, how do you spell your name, Evgenia?" she asked politely. "I hope I'm pronouncing it right."

Evgenia was squatting down to peer into the cabinet under the kitchen sink where the cleaning products were kept. "It is complicated—Russian name," she said.

"Oh, I know," Trish said. "Where are you from, Moscow?"

"No, no." Evgenia's voice was muffled. She withdrew her head from the cabinet and turned up to Trish a face that was sardonic in the extreme. "Every American say that! Every American think I from Russia. I am from Ukraine," she said. "Former Soviet Union."

"Oh, okay," Trish said.

"Look on map! You find." Evgenia held up a box of Brillo pads and shook it in Trish's direction. "Empty."

"No problem," Trish said. "I'll buy more." She asked Evgenia how long she had been in America. When Evgenia said three years, Trish asked if she had come by herself, and Evgenia, closing the cabinet door and standing up, laughed loudly and said, "Oh, my God, no! I come with my mother, my father, my two brothers, and my husband."

"You're married?"

"Everyone marry young in Ukraine," Evgenia explained. "Not like here." She was leaning back against the sink, a manicured hand on either side of her waist. She looked very much at home there, Trish noticed, as if she were leaning against her own sink. "I was married at eighteen," said Evgenia, and it was clear from her intonation that she expected Trish to react with awe or at least surprise; that she had developed, as Trish had noticed the savvier immigrants did, a sense of what went down big in the States, had perhaps herself learned to be impressed with the fact, where once she had not been.

"God, I just got married last year and I'm thirty-one," Trish said, as she led Evgenia through the bedroom and into the renovated bath. "I still beat all of my friends, though," she added quickly. "Half of them don't even have boyfriends. They'll be lucky to find someone by the time they're forty. It's different in New York. Women have careers, you know? Other priorities."

"You work?" asked Evgenia.

"No," said Trish. "I mean, not now. Not anymore. We're trying to get pregnant." The truth, though, was that Tim wanted to pay down their wedding debt before thinking about a baby. When she stopped to think about it Trish felt her days were sort of aimless, that she was always very busy but never accomplished anything. It seemed to take all day to pick up the dry cleaning, and then when Tim got home he would say, "Why don't you just have it delivered?"

"What about you?" Trish asked quickly. "Do you have any kids?"

Evgenia shook her head.

"Well, maybe you will soon."

She felt like dropping the subject and was about to explain how the shower worked when Evgenia said, "No, not soon." Trish looked at her, and Evgenia said, "I cannot."

"You can't—not?" Trish faltered.

"No."

"My God." Trish hid the hand-shower nozzle under her arm as she tried to summon some appropriate words. "I'm so sorry," she said finally. "I'm sorry I even brought it up."

Evgenia wiped a finger along the inside of the tub, holding it up to show the grime. "You have Soft Scrub?"

Trish stared at her. "I think we ran out."

"No Soft Scrub? Okay, next time," Evgenia said, shaking a finger at Trish. "And Brillo. Don't forget."

"Look, why don't you just make a list, okay?" Trish told her. They came out into the bedroom, and then into the living/dining area. Then she said, "Well, I guess I'll take off." She lingered a moment for the girl to ask her where she was going.

"See you later," Evgenia said.

"I think I'll head over to the Met," Trish said. "There's supposed to be a good exhibit right now."

But when she got outside it was gray and threatening rain. All of her energy seemed to dissipate. It seemed odd to go to a museum on a weekday morning, like a punishment for bad behavior. After hesitating a minute, she walked two blocks to the Starbucks, sat down with a latte, and made a list of errands that needed taking care of: buy stamps, exchange wedding gift, drop off Tim's shoes at the cobbler, replace lost lipstick.

Trish herself had never cleaned for money, but all through her teens she'd held tedious after-school jobs, babysitting mainly, some office work (stuffing envelopes for a state rep; typing and filing for a father/son dental practice), and she knew how irksome and debilitating it was to have the mother, or the boss, lurking around, checking up on you, so you couldn't even use the phone to call a friend and joke around or make the kids watch TV for five minutes just to alleviate the boredom and drag the minute hand back around to 12 again, chalk up another dollar fifty. She considered those endless afternoons the most hateful, wasted hours of her life. Even now, she would feel her face get hot when some acquaintance of theirs mentioned, as if it were onerous, having had to go to "practice" every afternoon after school, and yet at the same time it could cheer her, twenty years out, to remind herself that she would never have to take another babysitting or filing job again.

Having whiled away four full hours and having dawdled all the way home, Trish was taken aback when she finally returned, exhausted in the exasperated way that only killing time can make one, to hear the television on in her apartment. As she stood outside the door listening, she became more and more irked by the noise—whether it was that Evgenia had carelessly forgotten to turn it off when she left, or that she was still working and worked with the television on. In the case of the latter, Trish decided, her key in the lock, to say something. But when she came in Evgenia was sitting on the couch with the remote control in her hand. Seeing her there confused Trish, and the apartment itself, which was fantastically clean and smelled of Murphy's Oil Soap, confused her and touched her somewhere also. She felt at once that she was being hasty, and so she swallowed what she was going to say.

"I go now," Evgenia announced. She clicked the TV off, crossed the room, and took her coat from the rack. Put it on and buckled the belt snugly around her waist. It was a red coat, cut long and gathered in the back, with a stand-up collar and two rows of gold buttons down the front that gave it a smart, military appearance. A hammered-silver mirror hung to the right of the door as you went out—another of Trish and Tim's wedding presents—at which Evgenia paused to redo her lipstick.

Trish said uncertainly, but with a touch of impatience, "Were you waiting for me?"

Evgenia rubbed her lips together to blend the color. "No," she said, making a pout for the mirror. "Just waiting." She turned and smiled at Trish. "It's okay. I am student. I go to class now."

Again Trish sensed that she ought to assert her authority, but she couldn't think fast enough how to do it. "The apartment looks great," she said. When Evgenia merely nodded, continuing out, Trish called after her, down the hall, "So, what is it that you study?"

Fashion design, Evgenia told her. "I want to be next Donna Karan!"

There were bound to be growing pains in any relationship; Trish understood that. But she wasn't prepared for the television incident to repeat itself just two weeks later—the very next time Evgenia came—but again she heard the noise from the hallway, and again when she entered, she found Evgenia sitting on the couch, remote control in hand.

"What are you watching?" Trish asked, detaching several plastic grocery bags from her arm. She was unable to keep the irritation out of her voice.

"Oprah," said Evgenia, standing up. She was not tall—Trish was taller—but the girl's posture was so erect that when she came toward Trish she seemed to lead with her collarbone. "She is so great. You know, your cable remote is totally screwed up," she added. "You should get universal." She handed the device to Trish, who turned it over in her hands several times, frowning, and followed Evgenia to the door. As Evgenia was buckling the belt of her coat, Trish told her not to wait in the apartment in the future, but to leave when she had finished cleaning. "My husband and I just don't feel it's professional," she said. She shut the door and bolted it and went to the fridge to see if there was an open bottle of wine. Standing at the counter, she poured herself a glass of Chardonnay and drank it down.

After that, Evgenia was always gone when Trish got back.

The holidays neared, and there was a lot to do: presents and cards— Trish was meticulous about keeping in touch—booking flights, decorating the apartment, and her annual bake-a-thon with Jan. Trish's sister would come in for the weekend from Hoboken, where she was an assistant kindergarten teacher, and they would make sugar cookies all day Saturday and all day Sunday, rolling out the dough, cutting them and frosting them, and finally packing them up in tissue-papered tins for a long list of unsuspecting recipients. It was a habit from high school. Even then, it had been their private project; their mother didn't bake, and they had taught themselves from a column in *Gourmet*, to which Trish had a subscription. Once they started they never missed a year. Jan's list was always half as long as Trish's, but Trish knew she didn't mind, she liked to come into Manhattan and crash on the foldout and be taken out to dinner Saturday night.

This year Trish had forgotten to make a reservation, and after striking out at a number of places, finally she and Jan walked up Third Avenue to the local Chinese. It was more a weeknight place and a lot of the tables were empty, but Trish tried to make the most of things. She ordered fancy cocktails while Jan was in the bathroom, so she couldn't protest, and drank half of hers before her sister reappeared, sucking in her cheeks and pursing her lips at herself in the mirror above the banquette. When Tim came through the door of the restaurant, freshly showered from the gym and with his hair slicked back, his eyes found their table and he came right over. Trish felt such a rush of pride she had to look away. "Ladies," Tim said. He kissed Jan and Jan looked pleased. Trish was glad as she always was that Jan was there to share the bounty. She made up her mind on the spot to take Jan shopping in the morning and get her an extravagant Christmas gift, something she would never be able to afford herself and, in any case, would never buy for herself—the "in" designer clutch bag of the season or a day of beauty at a Madison Avenue spa—something decadent like that.

"Come on, Tim!" Trish said when the food arrived. "Think— there must be someone! It's ridiculous with the ratio at that firm that you haven't found anyone for Jan yet." In referring to her sister's single state, despite the fact that Jan, who wore no makeup and didn't believe in spending money on her clothes or her hair, had never had a boyfriend, Trish always adopted the can-do, breezy tone that she felt had been so disastrously lacking in their mother's attitude when they were growing up. Then she bugged Jan about moving into Manhattan—"Or you'll never meet someone!"

But Jan, struggling unattractively with her moo shu pancake, put down her chopsticks and looked at Trish with disgust. "How am I supposed to do that?" she said. "I'm not going to bleed Mom and Dad like you did!"

Trish's eyes smarted. She felt her jaw harden. She took a big sip of her cocktail, and she said, "Well, maybe you'll meet somebody in Hoboken."

"Yes, Trish," said Jan. "I'm sure it's surprising to you, but it actually does happen."

The morning they were to leave for Christmas was a Tuesday; when Trish realized she hadn't bought anything for Evgenia, she felt bad until she remembered a final tin of cookies, as yet undistributed. It was one of the big ones and had been sitting on the dining table for days, earmarked for an ex-colleague. As she showered and made coffee, Trish decided conclusively against delivering them to the bitch. In two years Avery had never invited them to a thing, though Trish happened to know she threw dinner parties all the time. Her decision made, Trish ripped off the "Avery" half of the gift tag and on the half that remained wrote "Evgenia" next to the "Merry Christmas!" Then all at once she stopped and held the pen aloft. It had occurred to her that there might be some expectation of an actual bonus. But as a bi-weekly employee, Evgenia just didn't seem to fall into the category of people you tipped. As she was debating what to do, Trish walked to the wall of windows and looked out onto the street as if seeking an answer from the pedestrians below. And there she was—Evgenia—walking up the block in her red coat. She looked rather jaunty, carrying her lunch, stepping around a dog. It was not a beautiful coat, but Evgenia seemed to take a huge amount of pride in it. There was an unbecoming arrogance in her carriage, Trish had noticed, when she was wearing the coat. Watching her make her way up the block, Trish suddenly recalled something that had happened in the first few weeks Evgenia had worked for her. Trish had made some muffins the night before Evgenia was to come—more than she and Tim could eat. She left a note for the girl, beside her check— "Muffins in the kitchen—help yourself!" But when she returned, the six muffins were sitting on the counter where she had left them, only now they were covered in plastic wrap.

"So I guess I'll see you after the New Year," Trish said when the girl arrived. She had left the cookies on the dining table so she wouldn't have to give them directly to Evgenia, a gesture she instinctively avoided. "We're going to see my husband's parents in Michigan, and then we're going to some black-tie event in Chicago for New Year's—probably totally ridiculous. My husband's always saying, 'Why should we pay a hundred and fifty dollars to stand around with people we don't know and drink cheap champagne?' But I think it's important to get out, you know? Get dressed up and go out on the town?"

Evgenia seemed distracted, frowned, and said, "Okay," and turned back to removing the mop, broom, and bucket from the utility closet by the door.

Trish immediately felt it had been callous to mention her own expensive plans for New Year's when Evgenia probably couldn't afford to go out at all. She wished their parting would have more of a Christmas flavor to it. Impulsively she added, "You do such a good job here, Evgenia. Tim and I are always talking about it.

"It must be really tiring," she went on when Evgenia didn't answer. "I'm sure if I were in your place—"

She only meant to get started, but Evgenia cut her off with a laugh and said, "Are you kidding? This apartment is nothing! Wednesday, I have classic six! Classic six have two bedrooms, two and half bath—"

"I know what a classic six is!" Trish said furiously. "You don't have to tell me."

Later that day when she and Tim were locking up the apartment, the phone rang. It was Evgenia. A half-smile on her lips, Trish steeled herself for gratitude, but Evgenia did not mention the cookies. "You forget my check," she said. "I look in drawer but you never put." In her distraction, Trish had forgotten to leave it. She took down the address and promised to send it right away.

For nearly an hour, Trish sat at her table nursing her cappuccino and planning what she would say when Evgenia, inevitably, saw *her*— whether, for instance, she would be civil, or cold, or, in fact, rather blatantly condescending. "Oh—*hi*," she could say, sounding puzzled and faintly put out. "How are *you*?" But her back was to the bar, Evgenia didn't notice her, and in the end Trish shied away from such an encounter, waiting to leave the restaurant—staying much longer than she would have, in fact—until Evgenia had slid off her stool and staggered to the ladies' room.

Among the menial jobs Trish had held to eke her way through her very first summer in New York, one of the less disagreeable was that of coat-check girl. In the last few years she had developed a habit of smiling at whoever was manning the closet as if to wish her luck or pass on some shred of optimism about the future. And she was tediously exacting about making Tim tip the girl generously. At this hour, of course, the tiny room was deserted; Trish glanced into it on her way out. There was no one minding it, the door was ajar, and the circular rack was empty except for a few forgotten items in the overhead bins—umbrellas, scarves, the odd briefcase or backpack, and one coat. The red coat. *The* red coat: ludicrously, solitary on the rack. Almost unwillingly Trish noticed it hanging there. Or not hanging so much as clinging precariously to one of the numbered hangers, one sleeve on, one sleeve already fallen off, as if it had been carelessly tossed there and left to its own wits to hang on or be trampled underfoot when the traffic increased. For a moment Trish actually believed she was going into the room to set something aright—to hang up the coat properly by buttoning the top couple of buttons. But instead she slipped the coat from the hanger and tucked it over her arm.

"I'm sorry?" she was going to say, if anyone caught her. "Oh, my God—how stupid of me! Of course it's not! Jeez"—she would shake her head for emphasis—"I don't know where my head is today."

A block away, she stopped to replace her khaki trench coat with the coat she had stolen. Slipping her arms into the sleeves, she saw the coat's lining: cheap red satin, rent in several places beyond repair. But as she gathered the belt around her waist and buckled it tight, Trish felt her head rise a few inches. She threw her shoulders back. It was getting dark out, and she wanted to be home.

The next week she met Evgenia coming out of the apartment, as she had suspected she might. Each of them smiled, and they said an awkward hello in the threshold. "Did you get the check I sent?" Trish asked her. "I'm sorry about forgetting that. I was so busy before the holidays." Evgenia seemed to give her a strange look when she replied, and Trish was so preoccupied with reconstructing the whereabouts of the red coat (in the last few days she had moved it from the coatrack to her bedroom closet to a box under her bed, and finally, one evening when Tim was working late, to the storage locker in the basement) that Evgenia was nearly gone before it occurred to

Trish to turn around to see its replacement. It wasn't a proper coat but a jacket, an unflattering man's football jacket in kelly green and black, with what looked to be a new zipper sewn in.

"What happened to your red coat?" Trish asked.

Evgenia made a disgusted noise in the back of her throat as she rang for the elevator. "I lose it—in a bar somewhere."

"You're kidding me," Trish said. The recounting of the fact dismayed her. "You mean someone took it?"

Evgenia shrugged. "Is my fault—too much party." She made a gesture of raising a glass to her mouth.

"But—that's awful!"

"Yeah, and I really like that one, too," Evgenia said, shaking her head.

"Did you go back and look?" Trish inquired. Still carrying her shopping bags, she came back toward Evgenia. "I mean—you asked at the bar and everything? Because sometimes—you'd be surprised— things turn up. People say New York is such a tough town, but people are actually really nice when you get to know them. People are honest—more than you'd expect. If somebody found it I'm sure they'd turn it in."

"Jeez, what's taking so long today?" Evgenia jammed her thumb against the lit-up call button several times. "I'm gonna be so fucking late!"

"Is this a bad time for you?" Trish said. "Or a bad day? Tuesday?" She moved closer to Evgenia. "Because you know, you just have to let me know—I mean, if you ever want to change. My schedule's pretty flexible at the moment. I'm thinking of going back to work in the spring, but if that happens, I'll be sure to give you plenty of advance notice—"

"God—finally!" The elevator had arrived, and the doors, which made a preemptive attempt to close, were stopped by Evgenia, who gave a little shriek and stepped between them.

"Oh, sorry!" said Trish. "You go ahead! Don't let me keep you." And, continuing on as if the cleaning lady had protested: "No, really—we can talk another time. I'll see you in two weeks, Evgenia!"

Awkwardly, because of the bags, Trish pushed through the door of her apartment. She let it slam shut behind her as she looked around greedily, fascinated by the cleanliness of her home.

The Matthew Effect

Binnie Kirshenbaum

Squinting against the late-afternoon sun as it cut through the birch trees, the sugar maples, the oaks, and the elms, the tips of the leaves yellow and red, Bee Elyot—Elyot from the Hebrew, a persuasion of which Bee decidedly was not, meaning *God is salvation*—parked her forest-green Saab or Volvo, whichever, behind her husband's beat-up van. It irritated her, Jonathan's van in the driveway, but hardly enough to disturb a marriage.

Middle-aged, forty-six to be exact, on good days Bee could pass for forty-one. Not that she ever lied about her age. In matters of small importance, Bee Elyot was excruciatingly honest. She prided herself on telling the truth, and she prided herself on other things too, such as her house. A Cape Cod with a fieldstone foundation and chimney to match, built in 1883, it was painted an eloquent shade of powder blue, which might sound atrocious but wasn't. Jonathan had a stellar eye for color; it was his business. Painting houses. Not your everyday housepainter, Jonathan had trained as an artist. After four years at the Pear School of Art and Design, he came to specialize in Mediterranean glazes, Venetian plaster, decorative painting. He was an artisan; not exactly an artist but often people assumed they were one and the same, which was what Bee wanted them to assume. Like the owl and the pussycat or the fork running off with the spoon, there was something smartly unconventional to the marriage of an artist and a professor of biological sciences, as Bee was. A professor at Middle River College, which was not Princeton, but she had tenure, which was one half of that dream come true, which *is* one half more than most dreams are realized.

If only the interior of the house were as charming at the exterior, then Bee would've really accomplished something. Bee was desperate for, among other things, a new dining room table. Not a *new* new one. An *old* new one. The table she had was a reproduction. Bee wanted authentic antiques from the Spinning Wheel Shoppe in town. A solid-oak rolltop desk and a pair of captain's chairs. There was a pellet-sized hole in her heart that only a maple tilt table with cherrywood inlay could fill.

Bee could not afford these antiques because she spent too much money on clothes. Her closet was not unlike a spinster's trousseau. So many pretty things—silk, velvet, taffeta, even—pristine and waiting to be worn, with hope that grew slimmer with each minute for a day less and less likely to come. Bee had no occasion to wear such things until, along with the phone bill and *The Penny Saver*, came an invitation to the annual blowout hosted by the president of Middle River College. Faculty were rarely, if ever, invited, and Bee had been carrying on as if this invitation were an invitation to something amazing, like a trial by water or the Oscars, which is why Bee, not always the easiest person to like, was capable of inspiring love.

In the kitchen, Chelsea, mother's helper and Middle River College sophomore, was at the butcher-block counter skinning cucumbers for the salad. Middle River had no immigrant population, but the college supplied a steady stream of exploitable help for a crappy six bucks an hour. Opal sat at the table, drifting off into space. That Opal was a healthy child was reason to feel blessed, particularly since Bee gave birth, for the first and only time, at age forty. Still, Bee clung to the chestnut: geniuses are often late bloomers.

An hour later, over dinner, as if the thought had just occurred to her, Bee said, "I'll bet you Liv Barrett is going to be at the party. You know she has a daughter Opal's age."

"Bee." Jonathan stabbed a cucumber with his fork. "Don't get your hopes up."

Liv Barrett was Deliverance Barrett because this was New England and you still came across the occasional Patience Smith or Preserved Hutchinson. The Puritan mark, like that of Cain, although not always apparent, was by no means worn away. It was as if the flesh and bone of Abiah Frost and Fear Whipple, gone unto dust, had fertilized the soil and seeped into the drinking water.

"I don't see why not," Bee said. "We're lovely people, and we have a lovely child."

Another indelibility of the Puritan ethic was the adherence to the embodiment of the Matthew effect: *For unto everyone who hath shall be given, and he shall have abundance.* For those not favored by God, well, *from him that* shall *hath not, shall be taken away.* So it was written. Which didn't mean it wasn't still something of a piss-off.

If this story were "Cinderella," now would be the time for the talented pair of white pigeons to show up, to help out with the shoes.

Bee had big feet, size ten and a half—transvestite size. Because she didn't much pay attention to her feet, and therefore assumed no one else did either, she blithely stepped into a pair of black, square-toed, chunky-heeled shoes best suited for nubby wool tweeds and all wrong for a red silk dress with a sweetheart neckline. Social suicide in some parts of the world, but this was Middle River, where the women routinely wore mukluks and Tod's slip-ons, so, really, would anyone notice?

Bee came down the stairs. Jonathan got up from the couch and said, "You'll be the envy of every woman there." This was the best compliment; somehow Bee had the idea that to be envied was to be loved. Chelsea concurred. "You look way beautiful," and in full agreement, Opal bobbed her head, keeping time with her hand picking at a scab on her elbow, which was maybe an indication that the child had excellent coordination skills, which would be nice, the possibility that the child had an ability.

Bee adjusted her husband's tie. Now they could go. Bee closed the door behind her, as if closing a chapter in her life.

And indeed another door opened. Justin Langly, president of rinky-dink Middle River College, was wearing, for real, a blue blazer with a Harvard insignia on the breast pocket, which would've been sad enough if he were an alumnus of Harvard College, although to be fair he did get his doctorate from the School of Education. "Mrs. Elyot, welcome." Mrs. Elyot? Surely Professor would've been more to Bee's liking. "And Jonathan," Justin Langly said. "Come, come. I have people waiting to meet you."

Even since last summer when Jonathan did Justin Langly's walls—the living room in yellow ochre threaded with genuine impure iron ore and the library a dusky rose, a color Jonathan mixed himself because the shade he was after demanded a twilight blue under base—Justin Langly had been bragging about Jonathan Elyot the way we brag about a little bistro we'd stumbled upon, and who ever dreamed we'd find braised rabbit, truffle emulsion, and foie gras with macerated figs in *Connecticut*? Although it's not a word common to Middle River diction, all the same, Justin Langly was a spectacular schmuck.

Bee tagged along as Justin Langly led her husband to a coterie of five women and said, "Ladies, didn't I promise you I'd invite him?" He ushered Jonathan into the group. "This is the artiste who did my walls." All along, all these weeks, Bee had assumed they were invited to the party because of her, because of her position at the college. To learn otherwise made Bee's face burn, as faces do burn with comeuppance.

A woman who looked a lot like the Quaker Oats guy gushed, "Mr. Elyot. Tell me, please. If the house is white, must the trim be Adirondack green?"

"Not at all." Jonathan titillated them with possibilities of reds and mauve and sea green. With her husband occupied, Bee was free to circulate, although for the moment, unsure of her footing now, she stood still. The other guests—mostly significant donors to the college, which is analogous to a big fish in a cup of water—were decked out in their flashiest beiges, grays, and herringbones. Bee—her red dress, in these circumstances not unlike a negligee or a clown suit—took a moment to fake pleasure in the entertainment. A Celtic folk harper, in medieval garb, accompanied herself on a floor harp as she warbled aires and ballads, best appreciated when shitfaced.

"Professor Elyot?"

Smile ready, Bee turned.

"Shrimp with Creole dipping sauce?" A girl, a student, wearing the requisite black skirt and white blouse, held out a tray. Not quite jumbo shrimp, but not puny ones either, speared with toothpicks. Bee dipped one into the bowl of brown goo and held it over a paper napkin. With no trash can in sight, Bee surreptitiously put the tooth-pick and the soiled napkin in her purse, and edging near to a trio, two men and a woman, so tight as to be a huddle, Bee overheard the woman say, "The vet bills alone for those horses . . . " At that, Bee shifted direction. On her way to the bar, she caught a snippet of con-versation about matching patterns for, Bee guessed, silverware or china. She stopped to join in the fun, and, the way a snapping turtle clamps its jaws tight, the two women abruptly quit talking and gave Bee a beady eye. As if matching patterns were a private affair.

The bar was manned by three college boys. One of them, Kirby White, was in her Bio II class the previous spring. Kirby White got a C in Bio II. Midway through that semester, Bee had spoken to him. "If you put in just a little effort, you are capable of a B," she said, but B or C, he didn't give a flying fuck either way.

"White wine," Bee said, and Kirby made a face like he was going to barf, which detracted not at all from his overall honey-bunness, his sleepy green eyes and towhead.

"White wine? Forget that," he said. "I'm gonna make you a cos-mopolitan." Cosmopolitans had been the drink of the minute the year before, but even light takes time to travel to Middle River.

After taking a sip of the frothy pink drink, Bee said, "Very nice. Really," and Kirby's smile warmed the room considerably.

Never the most beguiling of women—Bee did not always make a lasting impression—she had a nice figure and her dress showed some bosom, so you'd think the three men at the end of the bar would've welcomed her, if only to get a peek. One of them, a portly and bald guy, said to the others, "He's applied for early acceptance," and Bee, a tenured professor, on cue, stepped up—the fourth leaf to the clover—and asked, "Oh? To where?" At once, the cluster of men broke apart like the splat of a drop of water.

Bee sipped at her drink and studied the bookshelves as if she were at the library instead of at a party.

"Professor Elyot?" It was the same girl who'd before offered her a shrimp. "Salmon on toast points?"

"No," Bee said. "No, thank you," because there, all of two steps away, was Liv Barrett, alone, taking note of an object on a shelf, art for sure, and carved from stone, a shape of a woman, Botero-style, round, and headless. Set before it was a place card: PLEASE DO NOT TOUCH.

Barely moving her lips, which were so severe as to be almost sexy, and without looking over at Bee, Liv Barrett said, "Have you ever seen anything like this before?" Was she referring to the place card? To the implied threat of a YOU BREAK IT, YOU BOUGHT IT sign in someone's house? Or to the art itself? And if so, praise or damnation?

To buy herself time, Bee brought her empty glass to her lips, like a child with a toy tea set, before coming out with it. "You know, our daughters are the same age. Opal, my daughter, is six. We should arrange a playdate for some afternoon."

"A playdate?" Liv Barrett echoed, just as that putz of a college president stepped in. "I see you were admiring my . . ." Justin Langly steered Liv Barrett away, and Bee never did learn what that thing was, which was not a real loss.

Bee wafted through the party as if she were a faint and distant sound, not a seductive sound like a train whistle in the night or a foghorn, but rather, like the sound an old house makes when it settles, a sound not worth investigating. Even her own husband did not take note of her as she stood by while Jonathan detailed the secrets of a shabby-chic finish to the adoring women whose husbands did not work with their hands. "The trick is the thin layer of gray undercoat," he explained.

Having looked out each window as if there were a view to admire beyond the darkness and her own vague reflection, Bee returned to the bar for another cosmopolitan. That smile of Kirby White's, and you had to wonder how many Middle River coeds dropped their drawers for him. "I hope this isn't gonna get me kicked out of school or nothing," he said as he handed Bee a fresh drink, "but I gotta tell you, you look mad hot in that dress."

An impropriety to be sure, and forget the double negatives. Faculty, deans, and presidents of Middle River College employed students to babysit, walk dogs, clean out garages, serve at parties, but fraternization? Due to a mutual lack of interest and respect, they took not so much as a cup of coffee together at the Roasted Bean on Maple Street. But what woman would not go soft at *mad hot*? Bee arched her back and idled around the bar *mad hot* while Kirby went on about last year's baseball season as if she were interested. "Third in the division," he said.

"Is that good?"

"Fuckin' A it's good," and he laughed. "Oops. Sorry."

"I've heard the word before," Bee told him.

"Last season I pitched five shutouts." Half boasting, half shy, the cock-of-the-walk could still trip over his own feet.

"How about a deal?" Bee proposed. "I'll pay more attention to the baseball team if you pay more attention to your studies."

"Sure thing. As soon as Hell Week is over." And off he went riding some story, the long version, of fraternity shenanigans. Unable to listen to one word more of this blather, Bee turned to see Deliverance Barrett, coat over her arm. Bee's heart jump-started as if defibrillated. Leaving her drink on the bar, Bee slid into place as if stealing home plate. She could not let Liv Barrett leave, taking her hope away, the way some guests have been known to leave with a small object of worth—a Battersea box or silver sugar tongs—snug in their coat pockets—we all know there's a klepto at every party. "Our playdate," Bee said. "For the children."

Liv Barrett patted herself down. "I'm sorry," she said. "I don't have a card with me." She stopped there, but Bee blocked all incoming signals. Opening her purse, she took out the Creole shrimp-soiled napkin along with a pen. Writing her name, her phone number, and *Playdate*, she pressed the greasy napkin into Liv Barrett's hand, which was not unlike giving her a used tissue.

Outside, Liv Barrett let the napkin fall away, and the autumn wind picked it up and rushed it along until it stopped, caught in a drainpipe.

Deliverance Barrett did not call, and Bee grew despondent. Whatever Jonathan suggested to lift her spirits—Take in a movie? Go for a pizza? Scrabble?—had no effect, except to make matters worse. When, on the following Saturday night, he said, "Come on, sit and watch some television with me," she stomped off and slammed the bedroom door behind her, but remember: when *the Lord taketh away*, He also delivers. Come the next Tuesday, Kirby White stopped by her office, just to say hi, and there was something of a kick to that, to a cute boy taking a shine to her. Not that there wasn't a tediousness too, interacting with a boy that age. In the chair beside her desk, unable to contain his enthusiasm, as if who wouldn't be thrilled to shake a can of beer, puncture it, and swallow it all in the jet spray, he said, clearly beside himself, "It gets you so wasted."

"That's because you are getting more alcohol per unit time," Bee explained.

Who knew knowledge contained valuable information? "Awesome," Kirby said.

Awesome. Now there's a word we could easily do without; yet Bee was as charmed as if he'd said something thoughtful. His eyes saved him from vacuity, the eyes hinted at something, like maybe his father died when he was a kid or maybe his mother was a drunk.

Two days later he was back again, and Bee asked, "So what's on the agenda for the weekend? Another party?"

"No. I'm going home. I go home lots of weekends." Home was in New Hampshire, in a town of chain-link fences, boarded-up store-fronts, vacant lots, shotgun houses, an abandoned mill, and a girl-friend who worked the front desk at an auto-parts store. Kirby's mother worked in a nursing home. Nine years ago his parents divorced, but they still lived together because his father was unemployed and had nowhere else to go. He slept on the couch in the living room. "My girlfriend wants me to quit school," Kirby said. "Move home and get married."

Bee was appalled. "What kind of future could you have without your degree?"

"Baseball," Kirby reminded her. "Last year, a scout from the Houston Astros said he was gonna come back and look at me again this season. For real."

"Just promise me you won't quit school," Bee said, but that's not a promise he'd keep given the opportunity to go pro, and why would he? The only reason he came to Middle River College, on a baseball scholarship, was for this, this chance, which for him wasn't as slim as it might've been for another boy. Since Little League, he'd been told he could make it to the big league. Kirby White, he could throw a baseball.

On the Tuesday following Kirby's weekend home, he took his seat in Bee's office and said, "So, we broke up. Me and my girlfriend."

"Oh, I'm sorry to hear that," Bee said, in that way we do when really we couldn't care less. "Are you okay?"

"I dunno. We were together for six years."

Bee leaned in toward him, to tell him that there would be plenty of other girls, that he was very young, that it was better this way. She took his hand in hers, to console him, but like the way a car is hot-wired, as the ignition wires touch and it starts up, Bee purred. The distance from her lips to his was that of an instant, which was not enough time to talk herself out of it.

A kiss. What could one kiss matter?

Together they stood up, face-to-face, arms at their sides, not touching but for their mouths, their mouths touched, the tips of their tongues touched, and who can think straight when need and want and a vital life force funnel like a tornado?

Oh yeah, a kiss could ruin a life but good. Bee sank to her knees on the carpet the color of liverwurst, unzipped his jeans, yanked them, along with his boxer shorts, down to his ankles. The tails of his oxford shirt rested on her head like a veil.

During her office hours on Thursday, Bee graded quiz papers while waiting for Kirby. She waited until well after dark, when she gave up and went home. Another week went by, and, a shade off her rocker, Bee went to the cafeteria looking for him. He sat at a table with six or seven boys, and coming up from behind, Bee tapped him on the shoulder. "I need to speak with you," she said.

Kirby pushed away from the table and walked off with Bee, but not far before he said, "What do you want?"

He had a good five inches on her, so she had to stand on her tip-toes in order to cup her hand around her mouth to whisper in his ear. She whispered no words, but her tongue flicked out and around in a way that mere days before caused paroxysms of pleasure. Now he did not groan but pulled away as if stung. "Cut that out," he said.

"What's going on?" Bee asked, and he told her, "Nothing." Then

he walked off as if Bee were nothing too, and in that moment, something ruptured. Not her heart—she did not love him—but perhaps
her pride, which might be located next to loathing, in the spleen.

The Middle River College library had fewer books on the shelves
than empty space. The laboratory facilities were not equipped for
anything more complicated than the rudimentary dissection of a
fetal pig. The teaching load was heavy. The pay was chicken feed.
What the college did have, aside from a winning Division II baseball
team, was a façade. Sturdy elm and maple trees flanked red brick
pathways that wound around lawns and gardens. Stone buildings that
were a century or more old. The white Congregationalist chapel was
officially baptized nondenominational during the brouhaha of the
1960s, but no one was fooled. The chaplain was, as the chaplain always was, a Separatist at heart. Middle River College appeared to be
a fine institution of higher learning, the way plywood and paint on a
Hollywood set can appear to be San Francisco.

On a February afternoon when a barometrical fluke sent the mer-
cury soaring to a balmy fifty-eight degrees, as if spring were just
around the corner, a group of boys were having themselves a game of
touch football out on the lawn alongside Barrett Hall. On that same
afternoon, at the start of her two o'clock section of Anatomy and Phys-
iology II, Bee went to open the window, to let in a breath of air on this
false-spring day—almost cruel it was, juxtaposed against the certainty
that the next day would be cold and bleak—when her gaze fixed on
Kirby White. It might or might not have been his golden hair that
made it seem as if he were under the high beam of a spotlight as he
took a few steps backward to toss the football, which spun as it went,
as if rotating on an axis. Another boy leapt to make the catch.

Inspired, Bee turned to her class and said, "Let's do fieldwork
today."

Like ducklings, they followed their professor down the stairs and out the door to the far corner of the lawn, where Bee instructed them to scour the wet ground for specimens that they could later examine under the microscope: dead leaves, bits of tree bark, a bug, all of which had jack shit to do with A&P II.

It took a couple of minutes, but Kirby did see her there, at the sideline. Bee was sure of it because as the other boys zipped left and tacked right, ran forward and around, Kirby was as fixed as a pillar of salt looking straight at her when two boys collided like a pair of hands clapping with Kirby in the middle. Down they all went, and right away the two boys got up, but Kirby was writhing on the ground, screaming, "My shoulder! My fucking shoulder!"

As with all accidents, there was that moment when time froze before it started up again, before one boy sprinted to his backpack for his cell phone and called for an ambulance. Another rushed off to get the school nurse. The girls who were watching the game surrounded Kirby like a clutch of Florence Nightingales, carrying on as if his neck had been broken instead of his clavicle.

And Bee, she slipped away, as if she'd never been there, as if she'd played no part in this accident, which was hardly life-threatening, although it did mess up a fine pitching arm, and all that went along with it. She went to the parking lot and got behind the wheel of her forest-green Saab or Volvo, whichever, where she sat and wept from the shame of longing for this boy. The shame of the truth as she believed it to be, but—get real—we all, with unrelenting frequency and vehemence, lie to ourselves like braided rugs. Mostly about big-ticket items: love, happiness, desire unfulfilled.

The Recipe

Lynne Tillman

—Sadness, that's normal, it goes with the territory, but becoming bitter, bitterness is to be avoided, he said.

—Be a saint instead, she said.

Instead, he'd live from the largesse of a common madness, not just his own, not just from his sadness, he'd lament and move on, lament and move on.

My lament, can't do it, my way.

Clay wouldn't ever want to relinquish internal rhyme, rhyming was a mnemonic device, too, and venerable for a reason, and, along

with that, he relied on the beautiful histories meshed inside the roots
of words.

—We don't determine what words mean, they determine what
we mean, Clay said, later. We don't determine much.

. Cornelia was a film editor and also translated documents and ti-
tles for a movie company, she also plied her insightful eye as a photo
researcher and archivist for a wealthy eccentric, who never left his
house and liked to know what was going on, but only in pictures. The
eccentric hated to read.

—It would be great if pictures told a story, Cornelia said, but they
don't. They tell too many, or they don't tell any.

—Words, also, he said.

—Images are easier to misread, she said.

—I don't know.

Subtitles crowded the image, she explained more than once, they
changed the picture, even dominated it, and besides, reading words
on a screen disrupted the cinematic flow. He wasn't sure that was all
bad, but then he was suspicious of images, which he didn't make. He
was wary of words, too, which he used and tried to remake, so he had
reason for anxiety. In her business, they talked about "getting a read
on" a script, on meaning, sort of instantaneously.

A place for words , orphaned, wayward, no words,
no images, what then.

The lovers argued about the small things, about cleaning up after
themselves in their apartment, as responsible adults do, supposedly,
and petty problems, at work and with relative strangers, and also the
large things, love, politics, history, friendship, art, poetry, which he
wrote, when inevitably inconsiderate matter that had earlier settled

in words and sentences extruded layers of their pasts, lived together
and separately.

Code, just for now, when you mean its opposite,
bright lust of sullen night.

He'd been stunned by an obituary: "To my dear friends and
chums, It has been wonderful and at times it had been grand and for
me, now, it has been enough." The man—it was signed "Michael"—
had had the presence of mind to write and place his own death notice, it resonated a unique thoughtfulness, sad and mad, was he a
suicide? And, on TV, a Fuji commercial declaimed a new longing
for the fast-escaping present: "Because life won't stay still while you
go home and·get your camera."

Writing death, perpetual, language like a
house, an asylum, an orphanage. In a dream I
wasn't, argued with someone or myself, so lost.
Perpetual death of words, writing.

He wasn't his dream's hero, but there are no heroes, just cops.
Clay stopped to watch two beat cops, surreptitiously he hoped, while
they canvassed the street for errant civilians, ordinary or unusual, and
the cops, they're ordinary and they're not, and out of uniform they're
nothing, or they're nothing just like him, dumb mortals compelled by
ignorant, invisible forces, which happened to be, in their case, part of
the job. A police car sped by, like a siren, in time or too late to stop it,
the robbery, murder, the robber, murderer. He asked the butcher for
stew meat but studied another butcher at the bloodstained chopping
block who expertly sliced off a layer of fat, thick and marbled, from a

porterhouse. Fat enriches the meat's taste, his mother taught him, and also she warned, it's better to be dead and buried than frank and honest. She said she knew things he didn't that she hoped he'd never know, it was the part of her past she wouldn't tell him.

—At the end of the day, everyone wants someone to cook for them, a woman, who was probably waiting for the porterhouse, announced to a man by her side.

The man appeared to understand and nodded his head, a gesture that presumed a semblance of understanding. Clay wondered if giving the appearance of understanding was actually understanding, in some sense, and if duplicity of this sort was necessary for a society's existence, maybe even at its basis or center, and not the ancient totem Émile Durkheim theorized. People regularly don't understand each other, but if that were constantly apparent, rather than gestures of tacit agreement and recognition, a stasis, punctuated by violent acts everywhere, would stall everyone for eternity.

"Security has now been doubled at the stadium, but people's enjoyment won't be hampered, officials say." The radio announcer's voice sounded out of place in the warm, yeasty bakery, where he now was, doing errands like a responsible mate. The baker tuned the radio to a station that gave bulletins every few minutes, which some people listened to all day long, so they knew the news word by word, and Clay imagined they could recite it like a poem.

An epic, way to remember. A gesture, song, war,
a homecoming. Fighting writing my death,
persistent oxymoron. Perpetrator. Victim.
Terror to fight terror. Fire or an argument with
fire. Firefight. Spitfire. Lawless, Eliot Ness,
childhood. Fighting against or for terror, lies

in mouth. Can't leave home without it. Get a
horse instead.

People expected the unexpected, unnatural and natural disasters,
a jet crashing in the ocean, all lost, hurricanes beating down towns,
all lost, bombs doing their dirty work, lives lost and shattered, houses
destroyed, and attentive listeners needed to know, instantly, for a
sense of control or protection, and for the inevitable shock of recognition: I'm still alive.

The baker's son Joey, dressed in white like a surgeon, the skin on
his florid cheeks dusted with flour, asked him what he wanted, then
bantered with him as he always did.

—Sun, Clay, ever see it? You're pasty-faced.

—You're flour-faced. I want a sourdough loaf, and the recipe.

—Forget about it, Joey the baker's son said. Family secret for five
generations.

—I'll get it.

—You're just like your mother, Joey said.

His mother had played the violin, and when he couldn't sleep at
night, to quiet him after a bad dream, she'd stand in the doorway to
his bedroom and pluck each string with adoring concentration. A
lullaby, maybe, some song that consoled him for having to leave consciousness at all. He was attached to her concentration, like the
strings to her instrument, and this specific image of her, mother vio-
linist bent and absorbed, resisted passing time's arbitrariness, its uneven dissipations. Her face, for a long time now, rested only against
walls or stood upright on tables in framed photographs, and he
scarcely remembered a conversation they had, just a sentence or two.

Here, waiting. Can't leave home, without a
horse. Get a read on. Long ago, here, a drama

with teeth, reneging, nagging. Cracked plates,
baseball bats, stains on home room floor, same
as before, stains like Shroud of Turin.
Jesus bled, writing death, fighting terror.

He hadn't moved away from the old neighborhood, waiting for
something, teaching English and American literature at the high
school he attended, while he grew older in the same place, without
stopping time, though he found his illusions encouraged and indem-
nified by traces of the past, like the indentations in the gym's floor,
and, more than traces, bodies, like the baker's and the butcher's, and
their children, who would replace them, and stand in their places, in
a continuity Clay wouldn't keep up, even by staying in the neighborhood.

Cornelia believed the cult around the Shroud of Turin demon-
strated that people do appreciate abstraction, an image instead of a
body, though it wasn't exactly an abstraction but close enough. Even
if the cloth had once rested on a body, theirs was a reverence for an
impression, drawn from but not the same as the body—even if the
body wasn't Christ's, since scientists carbon-dated the cloth much
later than his death. The cloth was just matter, material separate
from and attached to history.

Not the thing, the stain, palimpsest of pain.
Life served with death a sanction.

Sometimes Joey the baker's son let him go into the back of the
store to watch other white-coated men knead dough, their faces also
dusted in white, their concentration, like his mother's on her violin,
complete, and he viewed them as content, absorbed in good work.
Their hands knew exactly how much to slap and pound, when to

stop—every movement was essential. Then Clay ruminated, the way he always did in the bakery, about being a baker; in the butcher shop, he thought about being a butcher. He wanted to be like Joey, they'd gone to school together. If he were, he'd know simple limits, why an action was right or wrong, because the consequences would be immediate, and as usual he rebuked himself for romanticizing their labor and imagining an idyllic life for, say, the old baker and the baker's son he'd known since he was a child, with a life better than his, because, he told Cornelia that night, their work was what it was, nothing else, its routine might be comforting, his wasn't. In the moment, as he watched their hands and smelled baking bread's inimitable aroma, he also felt that the bakers dwelled, as he did, in fantasy, that it enveloped them daily, and that what they did might be something else for them, too. Joey thought he was funny, but Clay loved the way Joey treated him, he felt Joey appreciated him in ways no one else did.

—The butcher, the baker, the candlestick maker, Cornelia teased.

—Cut it out, Clay said.

—Your heroes might surprise you someday, she said.

—I'd like that, Clay said.

—I bet you wouldn't, Cornelia said.

He told her about a distressed woman in the news who had found out she'd been adopted when she was twenty-one, which made sense to her, she was even glad, because she had never felt close to her parents, who were like aliens to her, and then the woman spent years searching for her birth parents. When she was fifty, she found her mother, who'd given her up for adoption because she'd been unmarried and only fifteen. But the mother she unearthed wasn't the mother she expected or wanted, so the woman was very disappointed. Also, her birth father was disreputable and long dead.

—Do you think people have the right to know? Clay asked.

—A constitutional right, Cornelia said.

—Okay.

—What about the right to privacy?

—Maybe some rights kill others.

If Clay turned violent, deranged, on the street, the cops would sub-
due and cuff him, take him in, interrogate him, or they might just
shoot him on the spot, if he charged them menacingly, resisted
them, or appeared to be carrying. The cops waited to arrest him and
others from doing things they didn't know they could do or felt they
had to do or did because inside them lurked instinctual monsters. He
didn't know what he had in him, but he knew restraint, and he recognized, as Max Weber wrote early in the twentieth century, that
only the state had the right to kill, no one else, and that fact alone de-
fined the state. But where he lived everyone had the right to bear
arms, to answer and resist the state's monopoly on power. That was
the original idea, anyway, but if Clay carried a gun, he might use it,
because he didn't know what he had in him.

Better to be dead and buried than frank and honest, his mother
had said. His father ghosted their dining room table, his tales gone to
the grave with him and now to his wife's grave also. One night his father hadn't come home from work the way he always did, Clay was
seven, and his mother's face never regained its usual smile. She
smiled, but not the way she once had. When little Clay walked into
the butcher shop or the bakery, he felt the white-clothed men looking sympathetically at him, prying into him for feelings he hadn't yet
experienced. The fatherly baker gave him an extra cookie or two, and
in school, even on the baseball field, Joey the baker's son didn't call
him names anymore, even when he struck out. But his mother
clutched his little hand more tightly on the streets, and he learned

there was something to fear about just being alive. He learned his father was dead, but it didn't mean much to him, death didn't then, and soon it became everything.

—It's why you're a depressive, Cornelia said. Losing a parent at that age.

—I guess, he said.

—It's why you hold on to everything.

Clay didn't throw out much, like matchbooks and coasters from old restaurants and bars that had closed, outdated business cards, and with this ephemera he first kept his father with him. There was dust at the back of his father's big desk that he let stay there. There was hair in his father's comb, which had been pushed to the back of the bathroom cabinet, so Clay collected the evidence in an envelope, and wondered later if he should have the DNA tested. What if his father wasn't his father? Maybe there was someone alive out there for him, a father, but his mother disabused him of the possibility, and played the violin so consolingly that Morpheus himself bothered to carry him off to a better life. Now, scratches on a mahogany table that once nestled close to his father's side of the bed and his mother's yellowing music books, her sewing cushion with its needles tidily stuck where she'd pushed them last, marked matter-of-fact episodes and incidents in their lives, when accidents occurred or things happened haphazardly, causing nicks and dents, before death recast them as shrines.

How long has this scrap been in the corner of a bureau drawer, he might ask himself, did it have a history. He could read clues incorrectly, though it didn't matter to him if his interpretations were wrong, because there was no way to know, and it wasn't a crime, he wasn't killing anyone. Cornelia's habits were different, heuristically trained and developed in the editing room, where she let go of dialogue and images, thousands of words and pictures every day, where she abandoned, shaped, or controlled objects more than he felt he could, ever.

> At last. To last. Last remains. What lasts
> remains. What, last. Shroud of Turin, Torino
> mio, home to Primo, Levi knew the shroud.

In Clay's sophomore English classes, in which the students read George Eliot's *Mill on the Floss* and Edith Wharton's *Ethan Frome*, his charges contested the rules for punctuation and grammar and argued for spellings and neologisms they used on the Internet and in text messaging. They preferred shorthand, acronyms, to regular English, they wanted speed. He argued for communication, commonality, and clarity, the three C's, for knowing rules and then breaking them consciously, even conscientiously. He attempted to engage them, as he was engaged, in the beauties and mysteries of the history that lives in all languages. It's present, it's still available, he'd say. And, by tracing the root of a word and finding its origin in Latin, Greek, or Sanskrit, and then by delving into its etymology, they could find how meanings had shifted over the years through usage. A few students caught his fervor, he thought, and who knew what would happen to them as they grew up, maybe they'd discover that love, that attachment. Curiously, there were many more new words each year, an explosion added to recent editions of dictionaries, more proportionately than had previously entered editions of the tomes he revered, and yet he remembered, always, what the words once meant, their first meanings. Cornelia told him it was another way he hung on to the past, and grammar countered his internal mess.

The problem is proportion, Clay thought, how to live proportionately. He passed the bakery on his way home, maybe he'd buy cinnamon buns for him and Cornelia for breakfast, and with an image of the pastries and her at the table, so that he could already taste morning in his mouth, he entered the store. It was busy as usual, and Clay waited on line, listening for the casual banter of the bakers, and when he drew nearer to the long counter, he overheard Joey the baker's son.

—I'd kill all of them, nuke 'em, torture's too good for them.

Clay continued to wait, suspended in place, breathing in the bakery's perfume, when finally he reached the front of the line, where the baker's son smiled warmly, the way he always did.

—I got you the recipe, you pasty-faced poet, Joey said.

He always teased him, ever since they were kids. Clay thanked him, smiled, and asked for two cinnamon buns, and then Joey handed him the famous recipe for sourdough bread, which in their family's version was littered with salty olive pieces. The cinnamon buns were still hot, fragrant. Fresh, Clay thought, fresh is a hard word to use, fresh or refreshed. There were suggestions, associations, and connotations always to words, he should stress this more to his students, because the connotations of a word often meant as much as its denotation, sometimes more, and there was ambiguity, ambiguity thrives, because words were the same as life.

Traces, stains, call it noir, in the shadows,
torture for us. And the child, the hooded
childhood. Fresh ambiguity to contradict
contradictions, refresh
what remains somewhere else.

The beat cops stationed themselves on the same corner, at the same time, so in a way they made themselves targets or spectacles, Clay thought, or even, by their presence, drew enraged, desperate civilians to them, like a recipe for disaster.

Walking home, mostly oblivious to the familiar streets, Clay looked over the ingredients. A teaspoon of balsamic vinegar, that may have been the secret the baker's family treasured for generations. Or the molasses and tablespoon of rum, that might have been their innovation. Cornelia wasn't in the apartment when he arrived home, she was the one who wanted the recipe, and the rooms felt emptier than usual.

He boiled water, brewed tea, opened the newspaper, couldn't look at the pictures or read the words, stared at the cabinets, they needed fresh paint. He'd cook tonight, a beef stew, because at the end of the day, he remembered the woman saying, everyone wants someone to cook for them. He stood up and, without really thinking, opened a kitchen drawer and tossed the recipe in the back.

Meaning of Ends

Martha Witt

This version of the story is in English. In Milan. Standing tiptoe on the edge of a king-sized bed. She is shutting a window cut into the slant of the ceiling. She is naked. It is the largest bed she has ever seen. Since she arrived, the nights have been good. Good summer nights, dark and bold as a shape. This night, a friendly night she can shut a window on. Later, open the window to the same good night. For seven weeks, she has been teaching the verb *to be*, the verb *to lie*, the verb *to want*, the verb *to go*. Some verbs more active than others. All verbs conjugate. All verbs useful. Some more useful than others. Not the confusion she studied in college, people asking, "But what does the verb *to be* really mean? What is Being?" Maybe there was "Having" too. She dropped the course and took Italian, where she asked the professor, "You mean to say that the past participle of a verb conjugated with the verb *to be* has a *masculine* end even if the subject of the sentence is hundreds of women and only one man?"

"Ending," the professor corrected. "Yes. That is true of any Romance language. As long as a man is part of the group, the past participle of a verb conjugated with the verb *to be* will have a masculine ending."

"An old-fashioned idea of romance," she joked. No one laughed.

Someone else said, "The notion of romance is more old-fashioned in English. In English there is never any discussion of sex between verb and subject."

This story includes him. He is here, too. His English is basic, so words should be chosen with care. He is lying on the king-sized bed. To create the Italian version of this story, possibly all the words of the English version must be tossed into the air, allowed to fragment and fall back down onto new pages. Or perhaps the English version is created from Italian words thrown this way. But why talk about possibilities? There is little enough room for fact. In the Italian, all the verbs of this story are in the present perfect and therefore require past participles. This is not true in the English version. For him, the English version tries very hard to stay in the present and the present progressive. There are a few past tenses, one or two conditionals.

He is lying in bed. He is thinking about the sleek front of the new refrigerator door his company is marketing. His girlfriend is in Rome. She is marketing the new refrigerator door in Rome. She would call him a cheater. A liar. An ass. Obvious, stupid names. Names for millions of men, not meant only for him. He has been taking English classes for seven weeks. He never imagined lying naked in bed waiting for his teacher to shut the window in the slant of his ceiling. She is naked. On tiptoe. That is it. Enough. *Sleek* is a hard word. *Slant* is a hard word. The story slows down. Explains more. Now. He lies in bed. The window. A large rectangle. She, naked. Summer. Milan. Night. Words American and other English-speaking people use. Useful words. *Useful* is *use* in its adjectival form.

She is standing tiptoe on the edge of the board at the end of the bed. *Edge* is a hard word. Here. This. *Edge*. The edge of the footboard or baseboard? She is not sure. Not important, really. The word. Not all beds have them. Naked. She. Footboard/baseboard. Window. Night. Milan. Oh—Summer. Bed. *King-sized* bed. The footboard/baseboard runs from the edge of the bed under the window to the edge of the bed near the closet. Complicated use of *run*. The footboard/baseboard goes from the right edge to the left edge of the bed. It lies flat. Complicated again for both *goes* and *lies*. (Runs. Goes. Lies.) Boards have an active life we know nothing about. He does not laugh. No. Sorry. Sorry. No. Nothing. A joke. Complicated. Nonsense. She stands on the footboard/baseboard. No longer tiptoe. The flat board. The moon is round. Flat is the opposite of round.

Remember shapes? The window is a rectangle. The moon is a circle in the center of the rectangle. The circle is at the center of the window. The moon is central to the rectangle. The light lies in a square on her naked back. Prepositions are not easy. *Lies* has different meanings depending on context. He can lie. He is lying. He waits for her to lie. She steps on the footboard/baseboard. Foot over foot, like a tightrope walker. As in the circus. The circus with clowns and horses.

Naked in the circle moon and square light. She understands now. Now she sees. A complicated see. Not with the eyes. A seeing of the flat in the round of the moon. She does not want to lie on the king-sized bed. Not now. Not naked. Not with him. Her walk has to end at the closet edge. A complicated form of *have*. Different from the ownership *have*. *Must* has the same meaning as *has to*, in this case. The first *has* in this last sentence showing ownership. The meaning belongs to the *must*. Now. Like a tightrope walker. *Must* owning meaning and *has to* meaning must. Ownership central to the rectangular window. She sees. Her back flat in the round moon. Naked. Walking. Milan. Night. Summer. Teacher. Footboard/baseboard. Tightrope. Flat. Foot over foot. Lie. Her walk must end at the edge near the closet.

Maybe there is a better way to explain the verbs? Let us see. The same complicated *see* as before. Not with the eyes. (Flat. Naked. Round.) Does *see* make sense now? (Summer. Milan. Night.) Does *slant* make sense now? (Light. Naked. Moon.) Does *lie* make sense now? (Round. Naked. Eyes.) Does *run* make sense now? Adjectives are harder to explain.

The story ends with her at the edge of the footboard/baseboard. The story's end in English is different from the story's end in Italian. In English, this story ends with her running. Remember, run? (Round. Naked. Eyes.) In Italian, this story ends in the king-sized bed with a verb in the past participle conjugated with the verb *to be*. It is that gender agreement between verb and subject that makes the ending of this story in Italian different from the prudish English ending. Let us point out that he sees and she sees (Flat. Naked. Round.) that the meaning of the different ends is the same.

She does not love him, and he does not love her.

Acknowledgments

Every book is a group effort, anthologies exponentially so. I am very grateful to each of the contributing authors, whose imagination, prowess, and generosity are an extraordinary example for all writers. Special thanks to Julia Cheiffetz, whose prodigious editorial skill and belief in the cause are an inspiration, and to all the folks at Random House who have been so excited by this collection, especially to Jynne Martin, publicity genius, and to Beth Pearson, production editor. Many thanks to Quinn Heraty, a patient and brilliant protector; to the talented and generous Joan Beard and Wendy Kenigsberg; to Tess Strand Alipour, who always comes through; to Angela Heckler; to Jessica Crispin; to the remarkable beings keeping all things Grace bubbling along, especially Emberly Nesbitt, Anne Ishii, Eryn Loeb, Jen Kirwin, Jessica DuLong, Sara Zuiderveen, and design god Kevin McElroy. Deepest gratitude to my students and to my friends, who showed such support, in New York and from remote perches, and to Carol and Jack Merrick.

Contributors

CHIMAMANDA NGOZI ADICHIE was born in Nigeria. Her first novel, *Purple Hibiscus*, won the Commonwealth Writers Prize and the Hurston/Wright Legacy Award, was shortlisted for the Orange Prize and the John Llewellyn Rhys Prize, and longlisted for the Booker. Her short fiction has won the 2003 O. Henry Prize and has appeared in various literary publications, including *Granta* and the *Iowa Review*. She is a 2005/2006 Hodder Fellow at Princeton University and divides her time between the United States and Nigeria. Her second novel, *Half of a Yellow Sun*, will be published in September 2006.

AIMEE BENDER is the author of three books, most recently the story collection *Willful Creatures*. Her short fiction has been published in *Granta*, *GQ*, *Harper's*, *The Paris Review*, *Tin House*, and other publications and has been heard on Public Radio International's *This American Life*. She lives in Los Angeles.

JUDY BUDNITZ'S stories have appeared in *The New Yorker, Harper's, Story, The Paris Review*, the *Oxford American, Glimmer Train, Fence*, and *McSweeney's*. She is the recipient of an O. Henry Prize, and her debut collection, *Flying Leap*, was a *New York Times* Notable Book in 1998. Budnitz is also the author of the novel *If I Told You Once*, which won the Edward Lewis Wallant Award, and was shortlisted for the Orange Prize in Britain. Her most recent book is the collection *Nice Big American Baby*. She lives in San Francisco.

JENNIFER S. DAVIS is the author of *Her Kind of Want*, winner of the 2002 Iowa Award for Short Fiction. Her fiction has appeared in such magazines as the *Oxford American, The Paris Review, Grand Street*, and *One Story*. Her new collection of short stories, *Our Former Lives in Art*, is forthcoming from Random House in spring 2007.

JENNIFER EGAN is the author of the novels *The Invisible Circus* and *Look at Me*, which was a finalist for the National Book Award in 2001, and a short-story collection, *Emerald City*. Her short stories have appeared in *The New Yorker, Harper's*, and *McSweeney's*, among other publications. Also a journalist, she writes frequently for *The New York Times Magazine*. Her new novel, *The Keep*, will be published in August 2006.

CAROLYN FERRELL is the author of the short-story collection *Don't Erase Me*, which won the Art Seidenbaum Award for First Fiction, the John C. Zacharis First Book Award, given by *Ploughshares*, and the New Voices Award from Quality Paperback Book Club. Her stories have been published in several anthologies, including *The Best American Short Stories of the Century*, edited by John Updike, and *Children of the Night: The Best Short Stories by Black Writers, 1967 to the Present*, edited by Gloria Naylor. A recipient of a National Endowment for the Arts fellowship, Ferrell teaches at Sarah Lawrence College. She lives in the Bronx with her husband and two children.

MARY GORDON'S novels include *Pearl, Spending, The Company of Women, The Rest of Life,* and *The Other Side.* She is also the author of the memoir *The Shadow Man,* among other works of nonfiction. She has received a Lila Wallace-Reader's Digest Award, a Guggenheim Fellowship, and the 1997 O. Henry Award for best story. She teaches at Barnard College and lives in New York City.

CRISTINA HENRÍQUEZ is the author of the short-story collection *Come Together, Fall Apart.* She is a graduate of the Iowa Writers' Workshop, and her fiction has appeared in *The New Yorker, Ploughshares, Glimmer Train, TriQuarterly,* and *AGNI.* She was featured in *Virginia Quarterly Review* as one of "Fiction's New Luminaries." She lives in Dallas with her husband.

SAMANTHA HUNT is a writer and artist from New York. She is the author of *The Seas* and the forthcoming novel *The Invention of Everything Else.* Her stories have appeared in *The New Yorker, McSweeney's, Cabinet,* and *Seed Magazine* and have been heard on Public Radio International's *This American Life.* Hunt teaches writing at the Pratt Institute in Brooklyn.

BINNIE KIRSHENBAUM is the author of two story collections, *Married Life* and *History on a Personal Note,* and five novels, *On Mermaid Avenue, Pure Poetry, A Disturbance in One Place, Hester Among the Ruins,* and *An Almost Perfect Moment.* She is a professor at Columbia University, Graduate School of the Arts.

DIKA LAM was born in Canada and lives in Brooklyn. She was a New York Times Fellow in the MFA program at New York University, and her work has appeared in *Scribner's Best of the Fiction Workshops 1999, Story, One Story,* Failbetter.com, and elsewhere. The first chapter of her novel-in-progress won the 2005 Bronx Writers' Center Chapter One contest.

CAITLIN MACY is the author of the novel *The Fundamentals of Play* and is at work on a collection of short stories. Her short fiction has appeared in *The New Yorker* and she is the recipient of a 2005 O. Henry Prize. She lives with her family in London.

FRANCINE PROSE is the author of fourteen books of fiction, including, most recently, *A Changed Man* and *Blue Angel*, which was a finalist for the National Book Award. Her nonfiction includes the national best-seller *The Lives of the Muses: Nine Women and the Artists They Inspired* and *Caravaggio: Painter of Miracles*. Her next book, *Reading Like a Writer*, will be out in summer 2006 from HarperCollins. A recipient of numerous grants and awards, among them Guggenheim and Fulbright fellowships, Prose was a Director's Fellow at the Center for Scholars and Writers at the New York Public Library. She lives in New York City.

HOLIDAY REINHORN lives in Los Angeles. Her debut collection of short stories, *Big Cats*, was named one of the best books of 2005 by the *San Francisco Chronicle*. She is a recipient of the Tobias Wolff Award for Fiction and a Carl Djerassi Fiction Fellowship from the Creative Writing Institute at the University of Wisconsin/Madison. Reinhorn's stories have appeared in *Zoetrope*, *Tin House*, *Ploughshares*, and *Columbia*, among other publications. She is currently at work on a novel.

ROXANA ROBINSON is the author of seven books: three novels, three short-story collections, and a biography of Georgia O'Keeffe. Her most recent book is the collection *A Perfect Stranger*. Robinson was named a Literary Lion by the New York Public Library and has received fellowships from the National Endowment for the Arts and the Guggenheim Foundation. Four of her books were named Notable Books of the Year by *The New York Times*. Her work has appeared in *The New Yorker*, *The Atlantic*, *Harper's*, *One Story*, *Daedalus*, *Best American Short Stories*, *The New York Times*, and elsewhere. She lives in New York City and teaches at the New School.

CURTIS SITTENFELD'S first novel, *Prep*, was a national bestseller. Chosen as one of the Ten Best Books of 2005 by *The New York Times*, it will be published in twenty-three foreign countries, and its film rights have been optioned by Paramount Pictures. Her second novel, *The Man of My Dreams*, was published by Random House in May 2006. Sittenfeld's nonfiction has appeared in *The New York Times*, *The Atlantic*, *Salon*, *Allure*, *Glamour*, and on Public Radio International's *This American Life*.

LYNNE TILLMAN'S last novel, *No Lease on Life*, was a finalist for the National Book Critics Circle Award for fiction and a *New York Times* Notable Book of the Year. Her most recent book is *This Is Not It*, a collection of stories and novellas. Her new novel *American Genius: A Comedy* will be published by Soft Skull Press in October 2006. Tillman is a fellow of the New York Institute of the Humanities and a recent recipient of a Guggenheim Fellowship.

MARTHA WITT is the author of the novel *Broken as Things Are*. Her short fiction and translations are included in the anthologies *Post-War Italian Women Writers* and *The Literature of Tomorrow*. She is a recipient of a Thomas J. Watson Traveling Fellowship, a Spencer Fellowship, a Walter E. Dakin Fellowship, and a New York Times Fellowship, as well as residencies at the Yaddo and Ragdale artist colonies. Originally from Hillsborough, North Carolina, she now lives in New York City with her husband and two children.

About the Editor

ELIZABETH MERRICK is the author of the novel *Girly* and the founder and director of the Grace Reading Series. She received a BA from Yale University, an MFA from Cornell University, and an MA in creativity and art education from San Francisco State. Recent honors include fellowships from the Saltonstall Foundation, the Ragdale Foundation, and the Virginia Center for the Creative Arts. She has taught at New York University and Cornell, and lives in New York, where she directs a writing school. Visit her at www.elizabethmerrick.com.

About the Type

This book was set in Electra, a typeface designed for Linotype by W. A. Dwiggins, the renowned type designer (1880–1956). Electra is a fluid typeface, avoiding the contrasts of thick and thin strokes that are prevalent in most modern typefaces.